MW00587813

RECKONING

**DAW BOOKS PROUDLY PRESENTS
THE SCIENCE FICTION NOVELS
OF W. MICHAEL GEAR:**

The Donovan Series

Outpost

Abandoned

Pariah

Unreconciled

Adrift

Reckoning

The Team Psi Series

The Alpha Enigma

Implacable Alpha

The Spider Trilogy

The Warriors of Spider

The Way of Spider

The Web of Spider

The Forbidden Borders Trilogy

Requiem for the Conqueror

Relic of Empire

Countermeasures

★★★

Starstrike

The Artifact

RECKONING

DONOVAN: BOOK SIX

W. MICHAEL GEAR

DAW BOOKS
New York

Copyright © 2022 W. Michael Gear.

All Rights Reserved.

Jacket design by Adam Auerbach.

Jacket illustration by Steve Stone.

Edited by Sheila E. Gilbert.

DAW Book Collectors No. 1928.

Published by DAW Books
An imprint of Astra Publishing House
www.dawbooks.com
DAW Books and its logo are registered trademarks of Astra Publishing House.

All characters and events in this book are fictitious.
Any resemblance to persons living or dead is strictly coincidental.

The scanning, uploading, and distribution of this book via the Internet or any other means
without the permission of the publisher is illegal, and punishable by law. Please purchase only
authorized electronic editions, and do not participate in or encourage the electronic piracy of
copyrighted materials. Your support of the author's rights is appreciated.

ISBN 978-0-7564-1773-4 (hardcover) | ISBN 978-0-7564-1774-1 (ebook)

First Printing, November 2022
1st Printing

DAW TRADEMARK REGISTERED
U.S. PAT. AND TM. OFF. AND FOREIGN COUNTRIES
—MARCA REGISTRADA
HECHO EN U.S.A.

PRINTED IN THE U.S.A.

TO
SHEILA GILBERT
THANK YOU

All Taglionis were engineered to be perfect. Falise could see it in the image reflected from the transparency's smooth glass: a tall woman, athletic and slender, dressed in a shimmering wrap that brought to mind a rainbow-effect sari. Her hair had been perfectly coiffed, ash blond, auburn, and black streaks layered to create a striking and artistic pattern. She elevated her chin, staring thoughtfully at the perfectly proportioned face—though against the glass, her emerald-green eyes weren't shown to their best effect. She had been designed to be beautiful, right down to her long fingers with their immaculately manicured nails.

She stood in *Turalon*'s observation dome and stared out at the galaxy. For the last year and seven months, she had missed seeing stars. After *Turalon* inverted symmetry, the only thing to see had been a weird gray haze that seemed to suck at the eyes. Thirty seconds of staring at it brought on vertigo. Captain Margo Abibi had informed her that it had to do with how photons were absorbed by the fields that surrounded the ship while in the state of inverted symmetry that popped it "outside" of the regular universe. Physics wasn't one of Falise's interests, though through her implants, she could call up anything she needed to know.

In her eyes, it was sufficient that fusion reactors generated electromagnetic and gravitational fields powerful enough to press the ship outside of regular space. And once "outside," a dauntingly sophisticated statistical program calculated the probability that *Turalon* would be at the right location when it cut power to the fields and "popped" back into normal four-dimensional spacetime. Sort of like a bubble of air being forced underwater, *Turalon* could only remain outside the universe as long as the generators kept it there.

The trick, however, lay in the statistical probabilities calculated by the quantum cubit computers deep in the ship's guts. Probability.

That was the key. For a year and seven months now, *Turalon* had been in whatever dimension of the multiverse a ship entered when symmetry was inverted. And then—according to the computers—less than an hour ago, probability suggested that if the fields were shut down—*Turalon* would pop back into the universe to which it belonged. It would find itself in the Capella system, thirty light years from Solar System.

Probability. Not certainty. Nothing was guaranteed.

While she lingered in the observation dome, the ship's crew and passengers were sweating it out in the mess hall. Waiting as the astrogation officer—or AO—made observations, comparing star charts, spectra, and navigational information to determine the ship's position.

Probability.

Space travel wasn't for the faint of heart. *Turalon* could be anywhere, tens, hundreds, or thousands of light years from the nearest star. Lost. Condemned to a lingering death in the cramped warrens contained within *Turalon*'s hull.

Falise stared anxiously out at the billions of stars, the unfamiliar swirls of nebulae, the inky black voids created by dark matter. None of the constellations were familiar. This was a whole new view of the Milky Way, one that alternately filled her with wonder and dread.

What if we're lost?

The thought pierced her like a thrust dagger. The thing that each and every one of *Turalon*'s crew and passengers had been fearing from the moment the ship had inverted symmetry back in Solar System.

She didn't realize that she'd lifted her hand, was chewing at the joint of her thumb. Forced herself to lower her arm, to raise her chin, and glare out at the galaxy. But that didn't stop the thumping of her heart, or the worry that slipped around her guts like a liquid serpent.

She heard his arrival, could see who it was in the observation blister's reflection: Cinque Suharto. Her family rival stepped into the room, stopping at sight of her. Said, "Oh, it's you."

"Thought I would take a look for myself. Where are the others?"

"Still crowded into the Crew's Mess, waiting for word from the captain. Same for the riffraff down on the Transportee Deck." Cinque stepped in, stopping beside her to contemplate the view. He wore a midnight-black outfit tailored to his massive frame; an inky cape added to the effect. Like her, he had been engineered to be his family's perfect progeny. At nearly two meters, he was a striking man. The perfect image of a male, well-muscled, every curve in proportion, his dark brown skin almost radiant with health.

She shot him a sidelong glance. Yes, he'd chosen the expensive suit. The one made of fibers that shunted light down and out at the heels so that the fabric seemed to have depth, as if it sucked light from the room. When he wore it, it added to the air of menace Cinque liked to project. But why he had chosen . . . ? Ah, yes. If it turned out that they were lost, he was positioning himself for the inevitable struggle to be the last one standing.

Falise fought a shiver. She never liked being close to Cinque. Not that she held any Suharto in high regard, but, like her, Cinque had been chosen for this mission for a very specific reason: he had been sent to win. No matter the cost.

They all had.

"What will it be?" she asked. "Have we arrived at the Capella system? Or are we staring out from our tomb? Destined to be a floating mausoleum among the stars?"

He crossed slab-thick arms over his muscular chest. In the reflection, she could see his lips pinch into a thin line, his completely black eyes fixed on the swirling patterns of stars. A faint shrug barely lifted his shoulders. "It will be what it will be. They chose *Turalon* because she made it to Capella and back. The other ships, all of the ones that were lost? Who knows? Must have had some flaw. Maybe a fatal error in the statistical programming."

"*Nemesis* made two successful trips before she vanished," Falise reminded. "And then . . . poof. Gone."

She waited, once again studying him for any tell, any reaction that would give her an edge.

He shifted, slid a black-booted toe across the sialon deck in a dancer's move. He did that as a way of reminding people of his speed and balance. He was, after all, his family's most formidable weapon. Smart, deadly, and focused. The perfect choice when it came to sparring for Suharto interests on Capella III.

"Let us assume that we're lost," he said in a mild voice. "Assume that the fail-safes don't work. That we're so far from a star that we can't recover enough fuel to refill the tanks. That we're marooned out in the black. Forever. Your aforesaid mausoleum."

He was speaking to her deepest fears. Not that she'd give him the slightest hint by word or expression. Voice flat, she said, "We promptly eliminate the nonessentials, as they did with *Freelander*. Find and plot a course to the nearest system that looks like it might have resources. Split the living quarters between the families. After that, we hold on as long as we can until we make it to someplace where humans can survive."

"Was that your briefing from your family?" Cinque asked mildly.

"Was it yours?" she shot back.

When he said nothing, she told him, "We all know why we were chosen: Donovan has turned out to be worth more than even sordid old Radcek himself might have hoped. With *Turalon*'s and then *Ashanti*'s sudden arrival in Solar System, The Corporation is now shaken to its core. Hidden away in his quarters just down the hall is a Board Appointed Inspector General—the renowned Suto Soukup, no less—granted unlimited authority to investigate the situation on Capella III. After a century and a half of stability, the precarious balance between the families is now threatened. And by what? A handful of human rabble who appear to be sitting on the greatest wealth in the galaxy."

His sidelong glance was measuring. "I met Dan Wirth at a reception. He's your brother Derek's tool, isn't he? A poison-coated sliver aimed right at your dear Uncle Miko's heart. I thought the good Mister Wirth, despite all his exotic wealth, was little more than a loathsome creature escaped from the sewer."

"A cogent assessment," she agreed, remembering her own reaction to the man. Loathsome? A creature? She couldn't have said it better. "To our dismay, he's also the richest bit of toilet-sucking slime in Solar System. Whatever Derek's goals, Dan Wirth hasn't just upset the Taglionis. All of the families have been stunned by his sudden explosion on the scene."

"Explosion?" Cinque asked.

She tilted her head to see him better. "Seems like every action he takes sends tremors and shock waves through the highest tiers of society."

He gave her a studied nod; it served as the barest acknowledgment in the dangerous game they played. "A narcissistic and antisocial criminal personality, one without empathy or the capability of remorse, is suddenly catapulted into the highest realms of power and culture." His eyes narrowed. "Uncle should have let me break his neck." His hard eyes met hers. "But Wirth has Taglioni protection."

"Not mine," she told him, weighing the implication of her words. "Doesn't matter to me that he is Derek's protégé."

Cinque laughed, the sound of it harsh. "Ah, but that's why you were chosen, wasn't it, dear Falise? Because you're Derek's sister. The one who could always wheedle her way around her pouting and sullen big brother." He raised a hand. "Don't deny it. The posturing would be a demeaning farce. The other houses know why you were dispatched on this fool's errand. Miko and your other cousins are as worried about what Derek's doing on Donovan as the rest of us."

"I'm not sure that worried is the right—"

"Of course it is." Cinque reached up to run a finger along his smooth jaw as he stared out at the stars. "It's common knowledge that surly and spoiled Derek ran off in a snit. A figurative 'fuck you' to his father and Uncle Miko. Everyone, including you, little sister, considered it good riddance. Even found no little relief when *Turalon* returned to Solar System to report that *Ashanti* was lost in space. I can hear it now, the voices whispering among the Taglionis, 'Too bad, the little Cretan got what he deserved. Problem solved.'" Cinque paused, smile mocking. "Right up until *Ashanti* shows up, loaded past the hatches with enough wealth to buy half of Solar System. And worse, it arrives with news that Derek's not only alive, he's laying claim to vast amounts of Donovan's riches."

Falise kept her expression blank, irritated that Cinque had such a complete understanding of her family. But then, it wasn't like she didn't have the same insight into his, or Chad Grunnel's, or Bartolome Radcek's. Her other companions on this benighted gamble. They, too, had been delegated to make the dangerous transition on *Turalon*. Like Falise and Cinque, they were sent to scout, assess, and establish their family's interests. That the Montanos, Xian Chans, and Terblanchs didn't have representatives on board was only due to their inability to scramble fast enough to get a warm body to Neptune in time for *Turalon*'s departure. As it was, the ship was detained for three days pending the arrival of Inspector General Soukup and his "Four." The genetically engineered and cyber-designed humans who recorded and analyzed his evidence.

But representatives from the other families would be coming. Just as soon as the Board could turn *Ashanti* around and space her back to Donovan.

As she studied Cinque's reflection in the transparency, she had to admire Derek's cunning. By sending Dan Wirth—a criminal psychopath afloat in wealth—back to Solar System under Taglioni sponsorship, Derek had ensured that the families would employ every resource they controlled in The Corporation to ensure that Capella III would be developed. As to how? That would depend on which family gained the upper hand. Not to mention the wild card of having a Board Appointed Inspector General of Soukup's reputation given free rein in the middle of the scramble.

She'd had a year and seven months to consider just how brilliant Derek had been. And knowing that, she hated him for it. Right down to the depths of her soul. Hated him like she'd never hated another human being. Because, had he not, she wouldn't have just wasted a year and seven months of her life on this suffocating bucket of air. Instead of suffering Cinque, Chad, and Bartolome and eating reprocessed yeast in the Crew Mess, she'd be enjoying the finest of companions on Transluna, and dining on the culinary creations at Tiborrone.

Until Derek shocked the family, she'd been thriving in the

company of Boardmembers, enjoying the fruits of wealth, prestige, and the power that came of being a rising star among the Taglionis. She'd been the cherished daughter—the one her father, Claudio, had fawned over. Falise had proven her worth to her Uncle Miko, the current Board Chairman and the most powerful man in Solar System. She'd been the clever arbitrator of the Board's clandestine and Machiavellian politics. By her own calculations, she had a straight shot at a Board seat. Her talent as unrivaled as Kalico Aguila's had been before the woman made the fatal mistake of shipping off to Capella III, as Donovan's world was officially known.

Things couldn't have been better. Right up to the moment that Dan Wirth stepped off *Ashanti* as a supposed Taglioni prize.

If I live to see Derek, I'll rip him into little pieces and ship his remains home in a jar, she promised herself.

Instead of anticipating a marvelous supper at Three Spires with a gorgeous male from the Hetaira guild hanging off each arm, she was standing here—next to one of the most odious and dangerous human beings to have ever lived—after nineteen months of incarceration in the cramped warrens that *Turalon* called "executive cabins." Waiting. Terrified that at any moment, Captain Abibi's voice would inform them all, "Our apologies, ladies and gentlemen, but it appears that we are far off course. We will inform you of the details as soon as we establish our location vis-à-vis the galactic core."

At which instant, she would turn, reach into her sash, and pull the small dagger from its hidden sheath. If she were fast enough, she would punch it into Cinque's side. Dance away. And hope that the poison would immobilize the big man before he could grab hold of her. If he got to her before the poison put him down, he'd snap her neck like it was a glass rod.

Then—assuming she survived long enough to escape the observation blister—she only had Chad and Bartolome to deal with. Each was just as intimidating in his own way. But then, none of the families that controlled The Corporation demonstrated scruples when it came to power.

The worst part for Falise was having to share the blister with the

Suharto agent. She would rather have had the observation blister to herself. Endured the wait without an audience, let alone one as formidable as Cinque.

He kept glancing at her; his marble-black eyes almost creep-freaked her. Genetically engineered—just like hers—they had no visible pupil or iris, and even the sclera was black. They came off as inhuman, alien, and unnerving. Which was the whole point.

Goaded to say something, Falise noted, "Having been to the Capella system, you would think that Abibi's people could verify our location instantaneously."

The longer they waited, the more desperate she was becoming. Not only over whether she was doomed, but if she should kill Cinque. With each passing minute, the terror increased. They were lost. Adrift in space. With no chance of rescue.

I will die here. In this ship. Alone. Abandoned.

As that reality sank in, she shifted, crossed her arms so that she could place her right hand beside the hidden sheath.

If we had arrived in the Capella system, Abibi's people would have already announced it.

She clamped her teeth, fought the urge to close her eyes, to gasp for breath. Since shipping out from Neptune, this had been her worst nightmare. Not being lost "outside," not being trapped in some unfathomable alternate universe, but popping back into real space . . . only to realize that they were doomed to slow starvation and to live out what was left of their lives in the prison that was *Turalon.*

She carefully took a breath, charging her lungs as she slipped fingers between the layers of fabric that hid the small knife.

She didn't dare telegraph her moves, had to keep Cinque from anticipating her strike. In her mind, she ran through the steps. First, rip the knife out, balancing with her left arm. Whirl on her feet, pivoting off of her right heel as she stepped out with her left. Right arm back as she shifted her weight. Drive the arm forward in a fast thrust. Slam the blade through Cinque's side so that the quillions triggered the charge that would jet the poison down the tube inside the blade.

In that instant, she had to recover and leap back. If she caught him by surprise, she'd have enough time to twist out of his reach. Dash full-bore for the hatch. Once through, she'd sprint down the hall as fast as her legs could carry her.

Not that she'd ever outrun Cinque. She just needed to buy enough time to let the poison work.

"Magnificent stars, don't you think?" she asked, dropping into the trained nonchalance her mentors over the years had cultivated for moments like this. "So very different than we knew at home."

"They are indeed," Cinque told her, his shoulders slouching, as if he were starting to relax.

She eased her hand deeper into the fabric, slipped them around the knife's handle. The knife was designed specifically for her, and her fingers and thumb conformed to the short grip.

The beat of her heart was now like a hammer against her sternum. She'd killed before. But never like this. Never when the ramifications had been so great, the stakes so high.

The worst part was not knowing.

What if she struck? Killed Cinque, only for Abibi to announce that they had arrived safely? That Capella was in the ship's scope, and Donovan lay but a few days' transit away?

If she did, the repercussions would be overwhelming. Chad Grunnel and Bartolome Radcek would know it was an assassination and that she'd acted from fear. Abibi would have her arrested, tried for murder under ship's law. Being in Capella III's orbit, there would be no reason to fight for control of the ship's resources. No survival of the fittest in the vain hope that somehow, in the coming decades, some miracle would allow them to escape.

Falise had read the logs from *Freelander* as well as the testimony given by Captain Miguel Galluzzi. Uncle Miko had ensured that they were in her briefing materials for the trip. That was one side of the nightmare. If she assassinated Cinque too soon, there would be another.

Wait? Or kill now?

"Who will we eat first?" Cinque asked reasonably, as if he, too, were following that path of logic. "I think we should toss the marines into the hydroponic vat to start with. For one thing, I don't want them wandering around in full armor down on D Deck, thinking up mischief. Not to mention that they're all pictures of health. Lot of vitamins, proteins, and fats in those bodies. Perfect to charge the hydroponics, don't you think?"

Her grip on the knife secure, she half turned—all the better to rip the blade free—and glanced up at him. "A bit premature, aren't you? Abibi hasn't even announced that we're lost, and you're murdering the marines?"

His gleaming black eyes, even more inscrutable in the observation blister's half-light, fixed on her. "I assume you're familiar with the history. I know the kind of captain Abibi is. She'll act immediately to save her crew. Just like Gem Orten did on *Freelander*." He paused. "Do you think that's why she hasn't made the announcement yet? Even as we stand here, she's locked the hatches to the Transportee Deck? Evacuating the air? Suffocating them before they can organize and try and storm the ship?"

"Everything that happened to *Freelander* was classified. How would the transportees know?"

Cinque's thin lips betrayed amusement. "That's four hundred people. Marines, technicians, engineers, scientists of various stripes. A lot of fodder for the hydroponics."

"Then you think we're lost?"

"It's more likely with each passing second." The smile mocked her. "As you have come to conclude, yourself. Otherwise, you wouldn't have your fingers on that knife you carry hidden away under your sash."

And so saying, he backed a step, posture still slightly slouched, as if daring her to strike.

A dry chuckle formed in her throat. "Impasse."

"So it would seem." Again he crossed his arms, studying her. "I know that you're well-trained in the use of that deadly little knife. I suspect, however, that I will kill you before the poison can take effect. Seems a shame to leave the ship to Grunnel and Radcek to fight over."

"What do you have in mind?"

He gave that slight shrug that hinted at diminished interest. "I intend to be the last one standing. When it comes down to absolutes, leaving you alive won't diminish my chances for long-term survival. Nor will my continued existence hinder yours. Rather, working together, we can definitely eliminate Grunnel and Radcek. And, of course, Soukup and his Four. Then take the ship as ours, keeping only those of your staff and mine that might be of continued service, as well as essential personnel from the crew."

"What expectation do I have that, once the ship is ours, you won't take the first opportunity to shoot me in the back when I'm not looking?" She arched an eyebrow, hating the sinking feeling in her gut.

Cinque gestured out at the stars. "That's our future. We both know that *Turalon* doesn't have enough fuel to reinvert symmetry and run the math backwards. If we're lost out in the black, it's for a minimum of decades, if not eternity." His thick black brow lifted. "I've given this a lot of consideration. Since with every passing second it looks like we're stranded out here, I thought I'd see if you would work with me. Quite frankly, Falise, if I'm to spend the rest of my life floating in the trackless black between the stars, you are the only person on this doomed ship who might make those endless years bearable."

"Is that a joke? I don't even like you."

His opaque black eyes didn't convey the same humor his bent lips did. "Like has nothing to do with it. I don't expect us to be lovers, not even friends. But if I'm locked in this bucket of air for the rest of my life, I want someone around who's interesting. Get it?"

Interesting? Well, there was an amusing compliment if she'd ever heard one.

She gave him a slight nod, feeling sick to her stomach. The worst nightmare was unfolding before her. "That being the case, we should probably find our way to the AC. If Abibi's taking action to secure the ship, euthanize the transportees, and prepare for disaster, that will be the safest place for us. Assuming that Abibi doesn't do our work for us, we'll need to take down good old Chad and Bartolome after she's secured the rest of the ship."

"You take Chad, I'll deal with Bartolome. Never liked the Radceks. Arrogant pricks, all of them."

She considered the extent of the disaster. Shit. It was real. With a feeling of desolation, she took a deep breath. "Deal." Then a humorless chuckle. "Knowing what we're in for? I should feel a lot worse than I do."

"Yeah," he agreed. "Sucks toilet water, doesn't it? Come on. There's nothing like mass murder to keep your mind from dwelling on how fucked you are."

She took one last look at the swirls of stars, the endless new constellations, and the white glow of the Milky Way. Where the hell were they?

She followed him out into the hall, watching his opaque-midnight cape swirl around his photon-sucking black suit. The way he walked, she knew he was keeping track of her position, ready at a moment's notice to turn and kill her.

They made it to the companionway that would deposit them at Astrogation Control when the intercom announced, *"Attention all hands. This is the captain speaking. Apologies for the delay, but we had a little trouble with an electrical fault in the equipment. Once we managed to track down the glitch, we made our initial observations."* A pause. *"Let me be the first to tell you: Welcome to the Capella system. We made it."*

Falise didn't realize when she'd stopped. Let alone sank back to brace herself against the sialon wall. Her heart felt like it was about to explode from her chest. She took a deep breath, realized she was smiling.

She looked over at Cinque; he, too, was grinning, the lights shining in his stone-black eyes. "Those are the finest words I've ever heard," he told her through an exhale.

Falise let loose the hilt and pulled her hand free of the knife. Apparently the IG, Chad, and Bartolome would live to set foot on Donovan after all.

2

Talina Perez flew warily above the mixed chabacho and aquajade. She was headed across the bush lands northwest of Port Authority. The low profile of the Blood Mountains lay just ahead. Beyond them, against the far horizon, the high and jagged peaks of the Wind Mountains rose like a serrated quetzal's jaw.

As the aircar passed, the branches on the trees below twisted so that the leaves could follow her movement. That was one of the eerie things about the scrub aquajade that grew in the broken country around Port Authority. Hunting in the bush was always a mixed bag. The trees fixed on movement. The hunter's as well as the prey's. Made detecting movement a tricky game for both parties.

The country here was mixed, with short trees, brush, scrubby thorncactus, sucking scrub, low-growing gotcha vine, and bite ya bush interspersed with patches of ferngrass and claw shrub. The names were descriptive and might have offended a botanist, not that Donovanian plants were really plants in the terrestrial sense. But, hey, what else would you call them? The colorful names got the point across: Bite ya bush, with its peppery odor, would extend a branch in the direction of an unwary passerby, and the clamshell-shaped pod on the end would snap closed on flesh or fabric. About the only way to get loose was to cut the pod free.

Taxonomy wasn't Talina's concern as she piloted her way west-northwest from Port Authority. Rather, it was Liz Baranski, a wizened and salty forty-year-old miner who'd made a strike at the foot of the Blood Hills. Liz was one of the few Wild Ones—as the free-roaming prospectors were called—who was female. For whatever reason, Liz wanted little to do with people. She preferred the bush with all of its dangers and seemed to revel in the solitude of Donovan's wild country. A little over six months ago, Liz had barged into Yvette Dushane's office in the admin dome, slammed a fifteen-hundred-carat uncut diamond onto Yvette's desk, and declared, "That's one of the little ones. I'm staking my claim."

The last anyone had heard from her, Liz had caged a ride into town from Stepan Allenovich, dropped a twenty-kilo canvas sack full of uncut stones for safe keeping with Shig Mosadek, traded for ammunition, tools, and two months' worth of dried vegetables, and headed back to her claim. That had been three months ago.

Not a word had been heard since.

That morning, Shig had collared Talina over breakfast, asking, "Could you run out to Liz's claim? Two Spot tried to raise her on the radio and has heard nothing. She's overdue."

So here Talina was, cruising along under a partly cloudy sky, wary eyes on the lookout for mobbers, headed for the low headlands where the Blood Mountains thrust up from the crater bottom. The range got its name from ocher-colored mantle rock and ruddy magma released from deep within Donovan. A big metal-rich rock had hit the planet more than a million years ago. The force of the impact had squirted magma and buried strata from the depths; the rich olivine deposits that resulted were rife with diamonds. It was in one of these kimberlite concentrations that Liz had found her jackpot. The wealth was exposed where a drainage had eroded down through uplifted strata.

A herd of chamois broke from beneath Talina's aircar, the fleet creatures bolting in all directions, racing ahead of her, dodging, leaping, and darting between the trees. In their flight, they spooked a flock of scarlet fliers that rose around her aircar, flitting and whizzing on their agile crimson wings. Talina enjoyed the whistling shrieks as the flying creatures vanished back into the trees as rapidly as they'd appeared. The quetzal part of her went into hunt mode, raising her heart level, pulsing in her blood.

"Easy," she said. "No hunting today."

Her phantom, the one called Rocket that rode on her shoulder, whispered, *"Yes"* just behind her ear. Demon, down behind her stomach, hissed his disappointment. She was surprised to hear from either one. Both were being abnormally quiet. Flying bothered her quetzals. Made them nervous. And, for the most part, left her in peace.

Talina grinned as she turned the wheel, heading for the broken uplift where Liz had her claim. This was epic country, great blocks of quartzite, slate, and schist that reminded Talina that she was seeing the very bones of the planet. These formed the resistant core of the Blood Mountains along with younger sandstones, shales, and mudstones higher back in the range.

As Talina approached, Capella's light caught the red and black quartzite ridge above Liz's camp, giving it an almost vitreous gleam.

Talina slowed, scanning the low forest at the mouth of the draw where an alluvial fan spilled out of the deep drainage. She saw no sign of a camp. But according to Step's information and the claim location, this had to be it.

"*Careful.*" Rocket's voice came from her left shoulder.

"Waking up now that we're this close to the ground, huh?"

She could feel Demon stir down behind her stomach. Spectral. Imaginary. Knew it was all in her head. As if her brain had to give them a physical location and identity when in reality they were just molecules floating around in her blood: TriNA. The Donovanian version of terrestrial DNA. It was a three-stranded deoxyribonucleic acid that carried three times as much information as DNA. An intelligent molecule, the stuff thought. Used RNAs and recombination to exchange and process information. That she was so infected made Talina a hybrid, a mixture of human and quetzal.

I just want this shit out of my body. Didn't matter that it had been years. That her features and anatomy had been forever altered. She was and would remain a freak, though Shig and the rest never referred to her as such.

"Careful?" she replied. "This is the bush, guys. Out here, I'm never anything but careful."

As she drifted closer to the canyon mouth, she saw it. Liz had made her camp on a rocky prominence at the base of a stony slope leading up to the exposed quartzite on the heights. Here, layers of kimberlite lay interbedded with the country rock. And given the rocky soil, it was a smart location. Not the sort of place where slugs would be found. Additionally, the more noxious of the vegetation had been cleared away and piled in a semicircle around the camp to create a kind of protective barrier, like the traditional African *boma*. Outside of that, twine had been strung, to which tins, bits of foil, a couple of bells, and tinklers had been attached. It might have been low-tech, but quetzals had never been known to figure out how trip wires worked. Anything approaching the camp would run afoul of the strings, send the whole thing crashing down in a noisy alarm. That it was still up was an encouraging sign.

Talina let her aircar drift closer and rose high in her seat, studying what she could see of the camp. A couple of cabinets stood atop skinny stainless-steel legs. The kind that couldn't be climbed by invertebrates. That the doors hung open—the contents scattered on the ground—didn't bode well. An elevated bed in a plastic cocoon— the kind commonly used by Wild Ones—looked to be undisturbed, and through the transparency, Talina could see the bedding. No Liz was inside.

The firepit looked long-cold; what had been a stack of chabacho branches to one side was now scattered. No smoke rose from the hearth, and from the looks of the ash, it didn't appear to have been used since before the last rains.

Talina reached under the dash, retrieved the megaphone, and called, "Liz? You around? Hello?"

That's when she saw the clothing. What might have been tattered rags were strewn across the rocky ground, sort of like they'd be if the wind had blown them. And there, to one side, she could see a boot. Lying on its side.

Not good. Wild Ones left boots upright so that creatures couldn't crawl inside. And if the boots were being left for any length of time, Wild Ones put them—and anything else leather—into a sealed container to keep the invertebrates from turning the edible portions into a meal.

"Well, that sucks toilet water," Talina said softly, her heart dropping.

She accessed her com, saying, "Two Spot? You copy?"

"Roger that, Tal." His voice came clear through her earpiece.

"I'm at Liz's camp. It looks abandoned. Worse, it looks like something got her. I'm going to set down and take a closer look."

"Roger that. Watch your ass, Tal. You need anything, holler."

"You've got it, old friend."

Talina gave the terrain a look, shook her head. There was no good place to land away from the more deadly plants or the questing roots that would trap an aircar. Instead, she turned toward the dry streambed fifty meters to the west. There, she could set down on the sand and gravel, knowing that the vegetation wouldn't send roots or branches to tangle themselves in the aircar's fans.

As the fans spun down and the sand and dust settled, Talina reached over and pulled her rifle free of the rack on the dash. Habit made her do a chamber check as she carefully surveyed her surroundings. The chime rose in a familiar melody, a sort of off-tune symphony. A slight breeze blew down the canyon, carrying the scents of water and damp soil on the perfumed air. The odors of anise and cardamom came from the plants. She caught no vinegary hints that would indicate a bem or spike anywhere close. Nor did her quetzal-augmented senses detect so much as a trace of quetzal.

"Well, boys, what do you think?" she asked.

"Careful," Rocket reminded.

That Demon said nothing, just seemed to shift next to her spine, put her on alert. What was the little shit thinking?

"Yeah," she told him as she took in the bank on either side. "I'll bet you're wishing I'd finally get mine."

Slipping over the aircar's side, she walked warily to where the bank had been broken down and climbed. At the top, she skirted wide of a sucking scrub and started into the trees. These were aquajade and stunted chabacho. None of them reaching more than three or four meters in height given the poor soil and shallow bedrock.

The chime changed as she passed, the invertebrates reacting to her presence. The branches on the gotcha vine seemed to track her as she stepped wide around it.

Winding her way up through the trees, she could see where

wood had been collected, branches lopped off, and prospect holes had been dug here and there. Nothing looked recent.

At the camp, she circumvented the trip wires and other early warning devices Liz had laid out to alert herself to the presence of a lurking quetzal. Stepping into the camp, Talina stopped, and yes, there, old and barely detectable, she caught it. That faint tang, almost a memory of scent.

Demon shifted, flipping around inside her with excitement.

Talina nodded to herself, asking, "You know that smell?"

"Whitey,'" Rocket replied.

No wonder Demon was bouncing with joy. Her first infection with quetzal TriNA had been from Whitey's lineage. Nor had it been the last. She'd been dosed with strains from the same tainted TriNA several times over the years. They'd all tried to kill her in one way or another. The hatred went all the way back to Donovan himself. He'd been eaten by one of Whitey's ancestors, and the lineage had been at war with humans ever since.

Talina—catching no recent trace of Whitey's presence—stepped over, took another look around, and then inspected the tattered clothing that lay on the ground. She could see the long-dried bloodstains where the invertebrates hadn't eaten them. The rips had that characteristic look: quetzal claws shredded rather than cut through fabric. Left it looking frayed. Same with the boot, though it had been partially eaten and still swarmed with some variety of red-shelled invertebrates.

"Two Spot?" she accessed her com.

"Here, Tal. What have you got?"

"Bloody and torn clothes. And the place still has Whitey's scent. It's old. Maybe a month."

"Roger that, Tal. Stay frosty out there. Anything goes wrong, I'll have the cavalry sent your way ASAP."

"Roger that."

Talina made a careful circle of the camp, seeing that invertebrates had cleaned out the vegetables. A solar refrigerator had been opened, the contents spilled. She picked up most of the tools, the pick, shovel, chisel, and hammer. Then she boxed Liz's radio, seeing that the battery still held a feeble charge. Batteries and radios were too damned precious.

The rest of the gear, including the bed, would require an additional trip. The best way to handle it would be to list it as salvage. Some Wild One would be by to pick it up.

On the last trip to the aircar, Tal took a different trail down through the trees. One that took her close to the base of the slope along what had obviously been Liz's main route to the canyon. Tal walked with her rifle hung from her left hand, the pick and shovel handles over her right shoulder.

Here and there she found evidence that the claim had been worked, the olivine in the kimberlite marred by metal tools. And at the side of the dry drainage, a large hole had been dug, the waste pile partially washed away by one of the periodic rains. In a quartzite boulder above the hole, an arrow scratched into the rock pointed up the canyon.

Talina laid the tools down, hefted her rifle, and followed the faint trail worn into the alluvial soils at the base of the bedrock. A metal hook had been driven into a cleft in the quartzite; from it dangled a canvas sack. It hung maybe a meter and a half above what looked like a pile of . . .

Talina chewed on her lip, glanced warily up and down the canyon, her nose sniffing for the faintest scent of quetzal. And caught Whitey's distinct odor.

Yeah, she knew what that off-colored pile was. Could recognize the splintered bone sticking out of the dried matrix. What made it particularly gruesome was the human skull perched atop the desiccated pile. Whitey had defecated here and placed Liz's skull atop the pile in some sort of macabre quetzal statement.

Down in her gut, Demon was chortling in delight.

"Eat shit and die, you little maggot," Talina growled as she stepped closer. Invertebrates had riddled the dried fecal material, their holes everywhere; Some were shuttling around as Talina inspected the pile.

She carefully lifted the skull, shaking it to dislodge colorful shelled creatures that chittered and glistened in the shadowed light.

They'd pretty much cleaned the skull of meat and brain. Looking closely, Talina could see the characteristic grooves left by quetzal teeth. Whitey had chewed off the face and scalp. Maybe he'd used his ropelike tongue to slurp out most of the woman's brain, too. No way of telling that.

And then he'd deposited the skull atop the pile.

Who said quetzals didn't have a twisted sense of humor?

Talina sighed, studied the pile, and decided that digging out the splintered bones would be too much trouble. Just trying to pick the fragments from the hardened pile, she'd get the crap bit out of her by the angry invertebrates. The skull would be enough. Something to put in the cemetery beneath a marker. Liz deserved that, and as for what was left behind? Well, everyone on Donovan understood they could end up as quetzal shit.

Reaching up, Talina unhooked the heavy canvas sack. Looking in, she could see a collection of rough-looking almost frosted stones. A small fortune of diamonds, most of them the size of walnuts. One as big as a peach.

"Hell of a strike you had, Liz," Talina thoughtfully told the skull. Then she placed it and the mandible in the sack with the diamonds.

Retracing her way back to the aircar, she laid the bag on the seat in the back, loaded the last of the tools, and stepped into the vehicle. Taking one last look around, she spun up the fans and lifted off, blowing sand and gravel in all directions.

"On my way back, Two Spot," she called into com.

"Roger that, Tal."

As she flew south toward Port Authority, she considered. For more than a year now, they'd had no sight nor trace of Whitey or his kin. Some had even started to think the fearsome quetzal was dead. Maybe killed by younger members of his lineage. Quetzals did that. That's how they passed information from generation to generation. By ingesting their elders' TriNA.

"But the way you killed Liz?" she mused. "You made a show of this."

In her stomach, Demon snickered. Piece of shit that he was.

"You wanted us to know that you're back."

"*Warning,*" Rocket insisted from her shoulder.

"Why warn us?" Talina wondered. "We'll be ready. And this time, forewarned. Whitey's going to end up as steaks and leather."

"*You'll see,*" came Demon's cryptic comment from down inside her.

3

The airplane curved off to the southeast as it banked tightly over the deep forest. Where she sat at the controls, sixteen-year-old Kylee Simonov kept an eye on the screen set in the dash. The readings kept climbing, dropping, and then climbing again; different signatures for organic compounds appeared and then vanished. The data came from the sensor they towed on a two-hundred-meter cable behind and below the VTOL aircraft.

For the most part, her quetzal sense, that part of her personality that had grown up and merged with Rocket's TriNA, was still. The human part of her had come to accept flying. Actually enjoyed it while the quetzal engrams in her brain went mostly silent.

"Get anything?" Dek Taglioni asked from where he sat in the passenger seat.

"Not sure," Kylee told him. She pointed at the screen. "Got a weird spike on the organics. Something big, animal, but the signature is like nothing we've seen so far."

Dek tapped the screen, pulling up comparative data. "Doesn't have the same signature for proteins or gases that the treetop terror did."

Returning her attention to the controls, she told him, "Keep in mind, that one was wounded. It had been shot, a lot. Was bleeding. And it had snapped off the spike it used to spear people. Not to mention that it had eaten. We don't know what kind of chemicals it would have given off after digesting otherworldly proteins."

She didn't add, ". . . after eating my parents." But then, Dek had been there. He'd seen Kylee's grief and rage, knew how deeply personal this hunt was for her.

She checked the instruments and heading. She enjoyed flying. The sense of freedom that Dek's airplane gave her; that he'd taught her how to fly was one of the greatest miracles in her life. Not to mention that the quetzal part of her brain shut off and left her in peace for those golden hours when she was in the air. Flying terrified quetzals.

She was in love with Dek Taglioni. He had long sandy-blond hair, wore a quetzal-hide coat, chamois pants, and a claw shrub-fiber shirt. His wide-brimmed hat hung from the seat behind. Dek's skin was tanned into a lovely bronze by Capella's hot rays. The guy had curiously enlarged yellow-green eyes. The color, Dek said, had been designed that way. The rest of the modifications had been compliments of the quetzal TriNA in his body. Same with the man's face; TriNA had played with his handsome features, elongating the chin, squaring the cheekbones, and adding angular planes to his face. It hadn't messed with Dek's perfect white teeth. The glaring scar on his left cheek added to the image, gave him a threatening presence.

Kylee thought he was really good to look at. Would have liked to have done more than look. But Dek was out of reach. Even for her mixed-up adolescent brain. Nor had he ever hinted that he was anything but lineage, and nothing more than her best friend. Besides, trained as she'd been by her mother, she fully understood the hormone rush her sixteen-year-old body was entertaining. And then there were the quetzal molecules. The memories she'd inherited from Talina Perez's brain. Fact was, Kylee spent a lot of time wondering who and what she was.

She adjusted the trim, checked the monitor again, and banked to send them back north on another transect a couple of kilometers to the west. "You're probably getting sick of hearing it, but I really appreciate you taking the time. I know it's been three years. A lot of people would have said, 'Give it a break, kid. The thing's gone.'"

Dek made a dismissive gesture with his head. "I was there that day. Down in that black forest. Could have just as easily been me. Or any of us. And I figure that whatever that thing was, it deserves a payback. Your mother was one of the most outstanding women on the planet."

He paused, grunted. "And a Taglioni doesn't forget his obligations. You could have treated me like shit on your shoe. Didn't matter that I was soft meat, Kylee. You took the time to train me. Taught me things that have kept me alive."

"So did Tal. And your quetzals. And Flute." She couldn't stop the smile as she shifted her grip on the wheel. "And you were fun. It was all so important to you. Like every day was an adventure, and you were doing stuff for the first time. Reminded me of being a kid. One I could teach."

"So, maybe you'll have your own one day." Dek had his eyes fixed on the forest ahead of them. "You're sixteen now. I keep wondering what happened to that cool girl I met at Briggs. Not that you ever acted your age."

"Too much of Talina in my head," she said. "We shared too much TriNA. Every time the adolescent girl in my brain wants to do something stupid, there's the Talina memory lurking right beside it. Wants me to respond like a mature woman would. What a fucked-up way to grow up." She paused. "Not to mention that there's a bunch of quetzals in my head. The part of me that's Rocket views the world with a sense of inevitability. I don't think like a human, Dek."

"But you're still hunting the creature that killed your folks." He lifted a cautionary finger. "That's intimately human."

"It's fundamentally quetzal, too." She eased the wheel back as they approached a low hill. "Both species are alike that way. The human part of me wants to find and kill the terror like a sort of payback. It's primate emotional rage: You hurt me. I'm hurting you back. The quetzal part of me? It's like a drive. We're enemies, and I will destroy you because I have to. It's preordained. Not like the primate emotion, but a gnawing need."

"Yeah, I get it." Dek frowned. "I've got too much of Whitey's lineage in me. And too much of Talina, too."

"How's that work?" Kylee asked. "You two seem to just click into place, like matching pieces of a puzzle. Me and Tip? It's weird."

"You're only . . ." Dek chuckled. "Sorry. You still fool me with that body of yours." A beat. "So, what's up with you and Tip?"

She shook her head, felt the frown line her forehead as she watched the data scroll across the dash screen. "He's not growing up, Dek. He's becoming someone . . . um, something I don't know anymore. Like the TriNA is making him into a new kind of organism that's . . . well . . ."

"Can't put words to it?"

Kylee took a deep breath. "No. And I was trained as a biologist. I haven't even seen Tip. Like for three months. It was after we started having sex. Changed everything. He's just . . . gone."

My fault, she thought. But then, it usually was.

"Broke his parents' hearts. Madison thinks that somehow she failed him. Chaco? He's more philosophical about it. You know Tip best, Kylee. What do you think's going to happen to him?"

"Nothing good," she told him. "Even Flute's given up on him. In Flute's own words, he says that Tip's 'spoiled meat.'"

"Yeah, that's quetzal for wasted and fit only for invertebrates." Dek slapped his knee as if in disappointment.

"Got to reel the probe in," she told him, one eye on the charge level. "We're at the safety limit to get back to the claim and recharge the powerpack."

Dek nodded, reached down and flipped the switch that would reel the probe in.

Kylee made a one-hundred-and sixty-degree turn, taking a heading back toward Dek's claim. Through the side window, she watched the forest pass below. From the sky, it looked almost like a soft carpet: bunched canopies, greens, blues, turquoise, teal, all thickly packed and soft-looking.

Call that an illusion or what? That peaceful carpet of trees was anything but soft and peaceful. Looking closely, she could see the holes where forest giants had uprooted and toppled a rival. And here and there, a lollipop tree stood alone in a clearing it made by whacking and beating its neighbors. The very idea that a tree could be a mobile predator just wasn't in a terrestrial human's cognitive framework.

"So, when are you and Talina having kids?" Kylee wondered.

Dek shrugged. "Don't know that we are. Hell, we don't even know if we can. We're both hybrids. Even if we conceived, there's no telling if a fetus would be viable, or what it would come out to be if it was. Would the kid even look human? Or would it be some weird chimera that was a mish mash of human and quetzal? You don't realize, but there are huge moral implications. We're off the map, Kylee."

She nodded. The same thoughts had kicked off in her own head the first time she'd ovulated. At the time, the only eligible male had been Tip. Having "inherited" a lot of Talina Perez's memories when they exchanged TriNA years back, Kylee had grown up with the memory of Talina's relationships—good, bad, and worse—as if she'd lived them. It was like having access to an entire life's experience. But none of Talina's lovers had ever reacted as sullenly or defensively as Tip had.

When she'd tried to tell him how a man should behave with a woman he was copulating with, he'd just gotten mad and stomped off. Gone.

"What's that look?" he asked.

"Trying to figure out what I'm going to do with my life." Kylee set her airspeed, relaxing in the seat. "Where do I fit in the world? If Rocket hadn't been killed when I was a kid, it would have been him and me. Like a sort of symbiont, I guess. With Flute, I never bonded that completely. We're sort of best friends who live in each other's heads. Hard to put the intimacy of that link into words. But Dek, I was raised human, surrounded by people until Mundo Base was abandoned. And yes, I bear the guilt and shame for what I did to Rebecca and Shantaya."

"You were a wounded nine-year-old girl." Dek squinted through the windshield. "Looks like a flight of mobbers."

Kylee followed his gaze to the column of multicolored fliers that rose, swirled, and dived down into the top of a towering stonewood tree. "Mobbers all right. Looks like they've got some poor creature trapped down there."

"God help it." Dek had had his own close shaves with mobbers. The winged death came within a whisker of killing him twice.

Kylee said, "Grief and rage lead people into some pretty bad mistakes. When Spiro shot Rocket, his death ripped a gaping hole, one that took years to come to terms with. I might never have, but for

Flute and Talina. At least I can understand the pain, even if it will never go away."

She hooked a thumb toward the forest they were flying over. "That's part of what drives me to find and kill that treetop monster that killed Mom and Mark. I was just starting to atone for what I'd done at Mundo, and that thing killed them. It just made the guilt and grief worse, you know?"

"Yeah, I know. I have my own burdens to bear. I told you about some of the things I did and regret." Dek shared a conspiratorial wink. "Living is all about making up for past mistakes. What you and I know is that we can make decisions about who we want to be and then dedicate ourselves to living that kind of life."

"Can I?" she asked. "I don't look human anymore. My legs are too long, my musculature is different, my eyes are too large, and my cheekbones are too sharp. With my pointed chin, I don't look anything like Madison and Chaco's kids. I'm alien. A whole new phenotype."

"I think you look exotic," Dek told her.

"Yeah, but you're just as infected with TriNA as Talina and me. Can you imagine the impact I'd have walking down the main avenue in Port Authority? Me and Flute? We'd be shot down within seconds." And that really grated deep down inside. They'd hated Rocket. And he still lived inside her.

"It's not the same town it was back when you were there. We know a lot more about quetzals now, and Talina and I, we've had an impact. Actually, there's a lot of speculation about you. People know that you and Flute saved Kalico and Private Muldare, and that you took down Batuhan. Not to mention the times you've worked as a scout for rescue parties."

"I still don't trust them." But, at the same time, she felt a bit of excitement. Hard as it was to admit it to herself, since Tip had wandered off, she'd been at a loss. Sure, hanging around at Briggs' place, teaching the little kids, filled some of the need, but a new sense of longing had been growing inside of her.

"What do you hear about Damien?" she asked as they sailed over a deep canyon in the basalt. He was her older brother and Rebecca

Smart's oldest son, now a geologist working with Lea Shimodi and employed by Kalico Aguila. He was doing minerals and mapping survey.

"He's fine." Dek shot her a knowing glance. "Kalico has him down at Southern Diggings logging core samples with Flip. Su asks about you. Kylee, your family understands. They don't blame you for what happened to Rebecca and Shantaya."

"Some sins can't be erased, Dek."

"No," he agreed, "but they can be understood. And, once understood, they can be forgiven."

If only it were that easy, she thought as the airplane arrowed its way east.

4

C aptain Margo Abibi was seated comfortably in the command chair in *Turalon*'s astrogation center, or AC. What once would have been called "the bridge" was the center of the ship's navigation and operation. For hours now, *Turalon* had been taking readings, trying to refine her position relative to Capella III and to chart the most efficient course that would take *Turalon* to a satisfactory orbit.

In the chairs around the AC, her command crew sat at their stations, attention on the monitors that provided navigational data. The swelling feeling of relief at having made the transition, not only from Solar System, but to the exact place and time they'd hoped, was like instantaneously being given new life. Especially when, according to the ship's clocks, they'd only spent nineteen months in what should have been a twenty-three-month transition.

When the reactors had reestablished symmetry so many months ahead of schedule, Margo Abibi had been terrified. Especially given the amount of fuel *Turalon* had consumed. The tanks had been down to sixteen percent. So where had it all gone? Why was this trip so different from the first voyage to Donovan? With the missing ships—not to mention *Freelander* and *Ashanti* lurking like the specter of the *Lost Dutchman* in her mind—Margo had almost broken out in tears of joy when her navigation officer, Sunyap Tamiki, had announced, "From the spectral reading, that star to our right is Capella, Captain. We're right where we're supposed to be."

So, she wondered, what explained the missing months? Why the rapid transition?

God, traveling outside the universe using inverted symmetry is crazy!

Yeah, whatever. They'd made it. She was alive, her crew was safe, and her passengers were spared a gruesome fate.

Margo thought she could walk on air.

"Got a plot on Donovan," Sunyap called. "Inputting the course now. Estimate establishment of planetary orbit in, let's see. Yes, that will be eighteen days, ten hours ship's time, ma'am."

"Input course and initiate, Mr. Chin," she ordered.

"Yes, ma'am," First Officer Tadeo Chin acknowledged in a voice that almost sounded musical with delight. He bent to his controls, ensuring that *Turalon*'s computers were sending the proper instructions to the massive thrusters where they were mounted on pods below the giant spherical reactor.

Abibi felt the familiar shift as *Turalon* began to change attitude and accelerate.

"All systems are go and reading in the green," *Turalon*'s voice assured as the AI monitored the initial burn.

"Couldn't be more perfect," Second Officer Madra Arapava said as she straightened from her console. The forty-year-old gave Abibi a smile. "Think we'll get home as quickly?"

"Hope so," Abibi told her. "I don't think I could take another couple of hours like these last ones. I'm getting too old for this."

"Go right ahead, Captain," Chin quipped from the first officer's chair. "Retire. With reluctance, I'll have to move from my wonderfully comfortable chair to yours. Took me months to adjust this one perfectly. Settling into yours, I'll have to start over from scratch."

"Dream on," Abibi told him. The joke came from the fact that Chin stood a little over two meters tall and Abibi barely cleared a meter and half.

"Captain?" Com Officer Cissi Butooro's voice came through the speakers. *"We've got a hail on the hyperlink."*

Abibi frowned. "Last time we were here, all communications were by radio. Put it through."

"Attention, this is the Corporate explorer ship Vixen. *Identification IS-SE-17. We're reading your hyperlink beacon. Please identify. This is Captain Torgussen of the* Vixen. *If you are receiving, please reply."*

"Hello, *Vixen*. And greetings! This is Captain Margo Abibi, IS-C-26 *Turalon*. We're receiving, Captain Torgussen. Our compliments to *Vixen*. We have just arrived in-system and are boosting for Capella III. What can we do for you?"

"Welcome to Donovan, Captain. Congratulations to Turalon *on a*

successful transition. Let us be the first to tell you, your arrival is not only welcomed, but will be received with relief in a lot of quarters. Query: Do you have news regarding Ashanti? *She shipped more than three years ago for Solar System with* Vixen *personnel aboard. We'd appreciate any word."*

"Roger that, *Vixen.* We are delighted to inform you that *Ashanti* arrived off Neptune orbit with all hands safe and sound. We've been advised of your history, and your people made quite a splash upon their arrival."

Splash was an understatement. Hell, *Ashanti's* arrival had been more like a detonation. Abibi was cognizant only of the initial impact. *Turalon* had upset enough people with the containers of minerals, metals, gemstones, and clays, let alone the stunning news of so many lost ships, tales of renegade colonists, and derring-do. Then the horror and tragedy that had befallen *Freelander* had sent shock waves through The Corporation's uppermost management. That Board Supervisor Aguila had stayed behind after signing over ownership of Port Authority had caused its own consternation. Abibi had been debriefed in a closed session of the Board. And debriefed. And debriefed some more. All of *Turalon's* records had been downloaded, studied, and promptly restricted.

Given the brouhaha that was consuming the Board, Abibi immediately requested reassignment to *Turalon.* She'd occupied herself with the turnaround, only mildly distracted by *Ashanti's* arrival. Pus in a pocket, but better the uncertainties of space compared to the shenanigans of Corporate politics. And she'd *hated* being under the spotlight, not to mention having her decisions second-guessed by a bunch of soft-assed Boardmembers.

Torgussen asked, *"Was our data downloaded?* Vixen, *since her arrival, has conducted a comprehensive initial mapping of the Capella system. A copy of our research, mapping, and survey was included in* Ashanti's *manifest."*

"Oh, we can assure you," Abibi said with a smile. "Every qubit of data, the ship's records, even the daily logs have been downloaded from *Ashanti.* Honestly, Captain, we inverted symmetry before the proverbial shit hit the thrusters, but there was no way The Corporation could have kept the lid on. A cult of cannibals? Lost in space for seven years? And then the wealth? You ask me, nothing's going to be the same from here on out. We had applications in the tens of thousands seeking a berth on *Turalon*. As the *Ashanti* news broke, Corporate Interstellar Operations were inundated with requests for transit. Whatever data and discoveries you sent back, Captain, I can guarantee you that it's being scoured for information, right down to the placement of decimal points."

Abibi could hear cheers in the background.

"Thank you, Captain." Torgussen's voice was laced with emotion. *"You just made a lot of people on* Vixen *very happy. Back slaps and high fives are the order of the day here. When opportunity presents,* Vixen *would like to do you and your officers the honor of a fine supper in our galley. And we'll have our latest survey data to send back with you."*

She grinned. "Invitation accepted, Captain. It will be our pleasure."

"We've just had radio confirmation. Two Spot, down in Port Authority, has received your beacon. They know you're here."

Abibi settled back in her chair. Well, the die was cast. She crossed her legs and considered. The last time she'd arrived in Donovan's orbit, it had almost ended in a bloodbath. To stem it, Kalico Aguila had granted deeds and titles to the Donovanians. News of that had set off a firestorm among the Boardmembers. In the end, it might have burned out. Might not have meant a thing to The Corporation if *Ashanti* hadn't arrived in *Turalon*'s wake dripping with even more unimaginable wealth. The Board had been so unsettled it had appointed Inspector General Suto Soukup. Given him Board authority and even delayed *Turalon*'s departure in the rush to get him aboard. Not to mention the few families who had scrambled the fastest to ensure their agents made the trip.

Agents? More like venomous reptiles.

And then there were thirty marines under the command of Colonel Stanley Creamer. All with tech.

And Abibi had no idea whose orders they were to follow.

She'd ensured that throughout the transit, she and her crew kept their distance.

And when they'd popped back into the universe, in those few

moments of uncertainty, Margo Abibi had had one finger poised over the button that would have locked and sealed the Transportee Deck and vented its atmosphere into space.

Not only had she learned the lessons taught by *Freelander* and her old friend Miguel Galluzzi aboard the *Ashanti*, but never in her life had she transported people like her current high-ranking family members. These people scared her right down to the marrow. She would have rather shared the company of quetzals, bems, spiders, scorpions, and sidewinders.

And then there was the Board Appointed Inspector General Soukup and his mysterious Four: three men and one woman who accompanied him everywhere.

"God help you, Kalico," she whispered under her breath. "You're going to need it."

Then aloud, she said, "Captain, since you're in radio communication, could you get a message to Board Supervisor Aguila?"

"Yes, ma'am. She's not more than an eighteen-minute delay by radio. What message would you like delivered?"

"Tell her Margo Abibi sends her compliments. We need to talk."

5

The simple slab of engraved duraplast read: HERE LIES LIZ BA-RANSKI, KILLED BY WHITEY. It wasn't much of a marker or much of a grave. Just big enough to hold the box that enclosed Liz's skull. Talina watched as old Fred Han Chow shoveled the rich red dirt back into the half-meter-deep hole.

Shig Mosadek stood to the side, arms crossed on his narrow chest; his worn quetzal cape draped from his shoulders, protection against the misty rain that fell from the thick overcast. Shig's thatch of unruly hair—black sided by gray—now sported beads of water. Round and brown, his Indian face had a serene look that not even his mashed mushroom of a nose could disrupt.

Talina let her gaze rove over the familiar headstones, the occasional fake floral display, and the larger and more ornate stone monument to Donovan himself. He'd been the first human buried atop this small hill back when *Tempest*—the initial survey ship to reach Donovan—had landed here to sample the clay deposits. Donovan had stepped out to take a leak and was grabbed by a quetzal. After his crewmates had killed the beast and pried what was left of Donovan out of the predator's gullet, they'd buried his remains here on the heights.

Upon the founding of Port Authority, it only made sense to put the cemetery here. Give old Donovan some company. Somewhat depressed, Talina took in the graves; she was surprised by the number of them she'd stood over as they were filled. Yonder was Mitch, the first man she'd ever really loved. And next to him lay Cap. And over there, Trish. Just across the way was Felicity's grave. Down at the bottom there, they'd interred the remains of Deb Spiro after Tal had shot her. Tens of others were friends, acquaintances, people she'd known. Some, like Paolo and Pak, that she'd murdered.

Demon stirred at the thought. The piece of shit always enjoyed it when she experienced a pang of guilt and regret.

"Lot of history here." Shig seemed to read her mind.

"Yeah. Thanks for coming. Liz would have appreciated the gesture." Tal pulled her hat up as the misty drops began to turn into a more spirited rain. "Buy you a drink?"

Shig gave Liz's grave a last look and donned his wide-brimmed hat. Thumbs stuck in his belt, he matched pace with Talina as she wound her way through the graves. "With *Turalon* coming in, we'll send Liz's diamonds back. As I recall, she had family back on Earth. The Corporation should have some record of their whereabouts."

"Think the pus-licking Corporation's actually going to deliver a wealth of uncut diamonds to Liz's family? Be more like those puffed and perfumed Boardmembers to confiscate the lot of them as some sort of compensation or according to some farfetched technicality."

"They might. Who knows? But something tells me that *Turalon*'s arrival is going to give us a whole new perspective on The Corporation. Two Spot has been in communication with Captain Abibi. While she hasn't mentioned that The Corporation has sent a replacement Supervisor, she has hinted that she has bigwigs aboard."

"Kalico know this?"

"I sent word. She's down on the southern continent, taking a look at the big terbium and palladium deposit that Lea Shimodi has been mapping. I guess they've also got a vein of almost pure copper mixed with aluminum that she wanted to check out. She's got a hyperlink on the shuttle. She can talk directly with *Vixen*. Torgussen can patch through on the photonic com to *Turalon*."

"She hasn't been around nearly as much since they finished that adit on the Number Three," Talina reminded him as they slogged past the high stack of shipping containers that formed a seven-high fortress-like wall around the landing field. Talina kept a wary eye on the nooks and crannies, the places where a quetzal might be waiting in ambush. All of Port Authority had been on alert since she'd determined that Whitey was back in the area. Not that anyone ever got lazy when it came to keeping the town safe, but knowing that Whitey was around had galvanized the locals to double vigilance.

They slogged past the PA shuttle where water dripped from its sleek lines and passed the loaders and forklifts where Pamlico Jones—who oversaw the shuttle landing field—had parked them.

The perimeter fence that surrounded Port Authority was an ugly thing, patched together with mismatched sections of woven and welded wire that rose some fifty feet into the air. While the big cargo gate was closed, the smaller "man gate" that allowed people to pass stood open. Wejee Tolland—the outline of a rifle visible beneath his slicker—gave her a big grin where he stood guard. Atop his bushy red-blond hair, the hat brim was pulled low and dripped rain.

"You get Liz taken care of?" he asked.

"We did." She glanced back, seeing old Chow, shovel over his shoulder, as he came plodding across the landing field. "Once Chow's in, you can lock up for the night."

"Got it." Wejee narrowed an evaluative eye as he glanced up at the darkening clouds. "Gonna be a quetzal night, if you ask me. The air's got that feel to it."

"You keep everyone sharp," Shig reminded, mimicking Wejee's suspicious glance at the sullen sky. "Last time Whitey was around, they tried a mass attack, remember?"

Wejee shifted his hat, rubbed at his thick brow. "We don't take any chances. Everybody's on alert. Most of us are a bit nervous that he's been in the area for a month now. Wish we'd been running scouts, searching for him. Better to kill that son of a bitch before he has a chance to hit us at a time of his own choosing."

"Yeah." Talina gave him a knowing squint. "Whitey and I have some unfinished business." She'd been the one to maim his left front leg, and the bullet scars she'd left him with still marred the big quetzal's side and had given him a limp.

She and Shig followed the graveled avenue into town. This was a wide passage used by haulers carrying clay from the big mine five kilometers to the north. This late, the two remaining operable haulers were parked.

Stepping into the biggest—and only—town on Donovan wasn't

inspiring. The original settlement had been laid out in a Cartesian grid, with inflatable—and then hardened—domes lining the streets. As the town grew, any empty lots were filled with stone-and-chabacho-timber buildings. As equipment wore out or became inoperable for lack of spare parts, it had been abandoned, set on blocks, or scavenged to keep other equipment working. As a result, the place was half maze and partial junkyard.

Talina remembered that Tamarland Benteen had referred to it as an "inhabited trash heap."

They turned on to the main avenue. Lined with businesses, the school, warehouses, and workshops, this was Port Authority's manufacturing, administrative, and financial center. As the rain increased, lightning flashed across the heavens. Moments later, the bang and crash of thunder followed.

"Tal? Shig?" Yvette's voice queried in Talina's earbud. *"We need to talk."*

"Heading to Inga's," Tal told her. "If it's anything shitty, you can tell us over a drink."

"Be right there."

Talina glanced sidelong at Shig, but the short Indian just shrugged.

Inga's was officially known as The Bloody Drink. It was named during a more sanguine period in Port Authority's history, and most people had forgotten the moniker. These days, folks just called it Inga's, or maybe the tavern. As Donovan's one-and-sole restaurant and bar, it served as the social center for the planet. Originally, it had been established inside a dome, but as business boomed—and with space inside the fence in PA being at a premium—Inga had excavated a large room beneath the dome. It was a mining planet after all.

Talina led the way through the tavern's double doors and across the foyer, its duraplast floor already wet and muddy from previous customers. At the head of the steps, from old habit, she took a moment to scan the room below.

About two thirds full, the place was roaring. Word had passed that *Turalon* was heading for orbit. Everyone in PA who wasn't on duty would be coming, anxious to hear the latest gossip, speculation, and news about the ship's arrival.

Last time *Turalon* showed up, it had almost started a war. Who knew what this arrival might bring? A topic that preoccupied Talina's mind from the moment Two Spot first announced it. Somewhere along the line, there had to be a reckoning for all the things Donovanians had done in their bid for survival. It wasn't like The Corporation was just going to let bygones be bygones.

Her people, dressed in occasional coveralls but mostly wearing chamois-hide shirts or pants, or some of the locally produced claw shrub fabrics, were packed around the long chabacho-wood tables. Floppy hats hung down their backs and multicolor prism-bright quetzal-hide cloaks for protection against the rain draped their shoulders.

"Looks like it will be a lively night," Shig noted. "Hope that Inga has that newest keg of ale ready to decant."

As Talina started down the stairs, she called over her shoulder. "You tap a keg, Shig. It's wine that you decant."

"I've never fully understood the art and vocabulary that gives nuance to the whole world of alcohol."

Call that an understatement.

At the bottom of the stairs, they were met by a fusillade of called questions: "What do you hear?" "When's the ship getting here?" "We going to have to fight again?" "Who's aboard?" And so forth.

Shig raised his hands, crying, "Hey, we don't know yet. All Two Spot has overheard on the radio so far is that Captain Abibi has 'Corporate bigwigs' aboard."

As people started to crowd around, Tal bellowed, "Sit your asses back down! We'll give you the news when we get it. Got it? So the next asshole who gets between me and a beer, I'm whacking him up alongside the head."

The closest of the crowd, Terry Mishka, Lee Halston, and Pavel Tomashev, backed away, as did Mac Hanson and Frank Freund, the gunsmith. All were grinning, calling things like, "Yeah, we're with you." "Sure thing, Tal." "Whatever." And "We know the drill."

Talina led the way to her stool on the bar's far right. There, she hoisted herself up into the worn seat and propped her rifle in its usual place, butt on the floor, barrel resting within reach. As Shig climbed onto the stool next to hers, Talina placed her hands on the battered and dented chabacho-wood bar.

Inga Lock was a big woman, late forties, with silver-blond hair, a big bust, and thick arms. Most people called her *formidable*. She ran her tavern like a well-oiled machine, dispensing drinks and keeping accounts on the large chalkboard on the bar's far end. In the two-story stone-and-timber building behind the tavern, she brewed, distilled, and fermented the finest spirits, wines, and beer on the planet. Which—given that the only other drink was fermented in bathtubs or jugs—made Inga's product outstanding.

Now she looked Tal's way, calling, "You and Shig? The usual?"

Tal gave her the high sign, shouting back, "And two plates of whatever the special is tonight."

"Crest chili," Inga answered before turning toward the kitchen and bellowing, "Two specials!"

"On it!" came the answer.

Shig lifted a shaggy eyebrow. "We take this for granted. Wonder how these bigwigs that Captain Abibi refers to are going to adapt to our little world?"

Talina tipped her hat back and let it hang from the strings. She stared at her reflection in the backbar mirror: The too-triangular face, her dark eyes larger than normal for a human and alien-looking. The point of her chin was too pronounced, as were the diamond-shaped cheekbones. Her nose had a sharper look to it as well. Dek had been the one to place it. He said she looked like an exotic cartoon princess, with her too-large eyes and angular features. All of it genetic remodeling of her body orchestrated by the quetzal TriNA in her blood. And that was just her facial features.

Over at the hospital, Dr. Raya Turnienko was still cataloging the augmented senses, musculature, immune response, and brain remodeling.

When *Turalon* arrived, she'd have to endure that awkward staring as the soft meat and Skulls gaped.

"Bigwigs?" she wondered. "What do you think that means?"

Shig slid his forearms onto the bar, fingers laced. "First, *Turalon* reached Solar System. And then *Ashanti*. Nothing like the wealth they carried has been seen since the treasure fleets in the sixteenth century as they pillaged the New World. And with them comes news of the Supervisor giving us title to Port Authority. Additionally, The Corporation hears about the missing ships, not to mention the tragedy of *Freelander*. When *Ashanti* arrives, they learn about *Vixen's* unexpected arrival after it's been missing for fifty years. A series of shock waves running through a system that was built specifically to function without surprises."

"The Board must have been stunned to its roots."

"And the families that have dominated the Board for the last century would have been the most stunned and threatened of all. They control The Corporation, all of its assets, mining, manufacturing, distribution of resources, information, and management. The algorithms might run The Corporation, but the families oversee them. Nothing, not even old Calypso Radcek's attempted coup, has been as potentially destabilizing."

"So, you think it's a bunch of Boardmembers?" Talina shook her head. "No, those candy-assed bastards would never take the risk."

Talina gave Inga a nod as the woman came hustling down the bar to place Talina's mug of stout on the chabacho wood. Then she set Shig's customary glass of wine—only half full—in front of him. She took a swipe at the bar with the damp towel she had slung over her shoulder before hurrying back down to where Fenn Bogarten and Rude Marsdome had bellied up with empty glasses.

"They'd send someone," she told Shig. "Someone with power. My bet? It might be another operator like Tam Benteen."

"Hope not," Shig told her. "We'd have to cut the door off the AC up in *Freelander* before we could toss the new guy in with Benteen. It might be getting crowded in there with all the ghosts."

He frowned and added, "From my experience on *Freelander,* a great number of ghosts can fill a very limited volume. I suspect it's an existentialist argument without a solution. Are the number of ghosts limited to the number of dimensions intersecting at a given point in Hilbert space?"

"Until *Freelander,* that was a question without any bearing on reality." Talina lifted her glass of stout and sucked a mouthful of foam off the top. Squinting, she said, "My bet? Given my security training? The Corporation will respond with caution this time. Surely Kalico had filed reports aboard *Turalon.* And they'll have Abibi's records and commentary and everything from the crew debriefing. And, of course, they've got the returning contractees: Marston, Shankrah, Mollie, and the rest. They'll know that Kalico gave us title to Port Authority, and after *Ashanti* popped back inside, they'll have an update that the colony is surviving."

"Think there's an army on *Turalon?* Some overwhelming force that will descend from on high, arrest us all, and take over?" Shig's eyebrows lifted. "Tell me they wouldn't, would they?"

Talina ran fingers down the side of her glass as thunder boomed in the night and lightning flickered on the dome overhead. "No, my call is that this will be a sort of reconnaissance. I mean, why send in the marines? That didn't work the first time. And as long as we're sending ships back brimming with every valuable metal, mineral, and gemstone in existence, it's not in their interest to screw it up." A beat. "Yet."

"Ah." Shig cast a look over his shoulder. "I suspect that at least a few of our questions will be answered. Here comes Yvette."

Talina watched as Yvette Dushane stalked her way across the room, passing the same gauntlet of questions. She did so with grace, waving them down, telling them with a smile that they'd have to wait for further news.

Yvette—in her mid-fifties—wore a fine lace dress, one she'd crocheted and overlaid on a claw-shrub fabric one-piece shift. A water-speckled quetzal-hide cape dripped onto the flagstone floor as Yvette removed her rainhat to expose the high-piled silver-blond hair beneath. Talina wondered what it said about Yvette, that being one of the tallest women on Donovan, she always wore her hair in an elaborate pile that made her appear even taller?

She climbed up on the stool next to Shig and removed a folded piece of paper from one of her cape's internal pockets. This she placed on the bar, and with long fingers, smoothed it out flat. She shared a conspiratorial glance, her green eyes thoughtful. "Okay, here it is. Tallia O'Hanley, who runs the radio down at Corporate Mine, got this from Margo Abibi, who'd sent it along as a sort of heads-up to Kalico. It's a list of the Corporate assets aboard *Turalon*."

Talina took the paper, scanned it. "Screw me with a skewer. Abibi's bringing us a Board Appointed Inspector General?"

"What does that mean?" Shig asked.

"For us?" Talina shrugged. "Nothing. We're not Corporate, but it could mean everything for Kalico."

Yvette cautioned, "I wouldn't get too cocky, Tal. The next thing to notice is that thirty marines are aboard under the command of Colonel Stanley Creamer. Thirty marines could take PA in an afternoon and arrest us all."

"Son of a bitch," Talina almost spit the words. "Creamer's the guy responsible for getting Cap busted. A real piece of work."

"No big gig. We'll feed him to a quetzal," Yvette said dismissively. "But check these names. Bartolome Radcek, investment management director, whatever that is. Next comes Cinque Suharto, cargo and logistics security operations."

Talina said, "That's the sort of agent The Corporation would dispatch if they thought someone was skimming or if they suspected blatant theft somewhere in the transportation or distribution."

"That doesn't sound so bad." Shig rocked his wine glass on the dented wood.

"Chad Grunnel," Yvette noted. "He's supposed to be a 'resources procurement specialist.' And it says he's with Asteroidal Assessments. That mean anything?"

"Yeah," Talina told her. "That's the company that exploits mining in the Belt. They funnel raw materials to the manufacturing stations. My guess? Good old Chad makes sure the production quotas are met. One way or another."

"And, finally, we have Falise Taglioni." Yvette spared Talina a knowing glance. "Dek ever talk about her?"

Talina leaned back, ran fingers down the sweating side of her mug. "Oh, yeah. That's his younger sister. Claudio and Malissa's first daughter. What's her supposed occupation listed as?"

Yvette pointed at the paper. "Says here that she's a 'business effi-ciency consultant.' Dek ever say what that was?"

"Yeah, Falise does the Taglionis' dirty work." Talina narrowed her eyes. "She gets information on rivals. Conducts industrial espi-onage. Destroys threats to the family. Eliminates what you'd call 'problem' people. You know, the ones who might get in the way. Call her the family's enforcer, spy, and assassin."

Shig lifted his wine, studied the red liquid. "Remember that Dek sent Dan Wirth to Solar System with a Taglioni family seal. We don't know what Dan would have told them. However, dropping a sleazy psychopath who's swimming in wealth on their doorstep? I assume that Fabio, Miko, and the rest of the family are fully capable of understanding exactly what message their long-lost errant son might be sending."

Talina said thoughtfully, "They don't have the first fricking clue what kind of man Dek's turned into. Last they knew, he was that pompous and spoiled little prig they all detested."

"Agreed," Yvette noted. "But whatever Dan Wirth might have told the Taglionis, they've sent little sister to check up on her brother."

Talina took a deep breath, the Demon quetzal in her stomach shifting, unsettling her guts. She accessed com. "Two Spot? Any word on Dek's location?"

"Last I heard, he and Kylee were out at the claim hunting the treetop terror. Want me to fire up the big radio and send him a message?"

"Yeah, tell him his sister, Falise, is coming to town."

"His sister Falise . . . ? Uh, you mean like the one on the Turalon *passenger list?"*

"That's her. And tell him I send my love. Oh, and let him know Falise has thirty marines at her disposal."

And that, she speculated, was really going to make Dek's day.

6

The core drill was a cumbersome thing; its derrick—made of a white triangular lattice—extended thirty meters into the blue-green Donovanian sky. Not to mention that the big machine was deafening. The whine from the electric motor was one thing, the way the drill stem and running gears clattered was another. A pump was blatting as it sucked mud from the pit before forcing it down-hole to lubricate the bit where it chewed through metal-rich rock. It was loud enough to blot out even the raucous local chime, which was different from anything Kalico Aguila had heard in the north.

Kalico's team from Corporate Mine was drilling the first explor-atory hole in the Southern Continent, half a world away from Cor-porate Mine and its smelter. Lea Shimodi, Corporate Mine's head geologist, had been intrigued by this particular formation for years.

This was all a metamorphic deposit—hard and dense stone that had been cooked under incredible pressure then fractured, faulted, and compressed so that liquid metals had been squeezed up through cracks in the rock.

Kalico Aguila—wearing a chamois-hide coverall—watched the tubular drill stem where it rotated in the deck, mud and cuttings oozing up around it to run off into the pit. Since she'd first learned that a Board Appointed Inspector General was aboard *Turalon*, her nerves had been on end. Her gut dyspeptic.

She'd known Suto Soukup a decade ago when she'd been Board Supervisor at Transluna. His reputation had been as an uncompro-mising ferret when it came to corruption, malfeasance, and graft. Now he was arriving on Donovan with a Board Appointment. Carte blanche to stick his nose into anything he wished, ask any question he desired, interrogate any person, with the power to ar-rest and charge anyone he found culpable.

At that moment, Lea Shimodi hurried forward with a sample cup and scooped up some of the goo. Retreating, she skipped her way across the deck and down the ladder. Staring fixedly at her sample, the geologist hurried across the scorched bedrock to where the shuttle ramp was down. Two marines, Abu Sassi and Sean Finnegan, in full armor, helmets on and weapons at the ready, stood to either side. Lea barely gave them a glance as she trotted up the ramp and into the shuttle bay, now a makeshift laboratory.

Kalico took another look around.

The well pad had been built atop a low promontory formed by up-thrust bedrock. First the vegetation had been scorched, then peeled away. The topsoil and dirt had been scraped off and piled down below as a makeshift dam to hold back the curious trees and brush. Stuff Kalico had never seen. The dominant variety was a spiral tree. For every one-hundred-and-twenty degrees that it twisted, a branch sprouted from each edge of the triangular cross section. The branch ended in huge three-sided blue-green leaves that would have covered a king-sized bed. Anything that touched them would die from contact with the little hairs that coated the leaf's surface. Each of those little hairs secreted a microscopic drop of dew-like poison.

And of course, there was the wildlife. Kalico had recognized the scimitar monster, a variation similar to the ones she'd seen in the sea. Then there was something new that they'd offhandedly called a "land tank" for its flat hull-down shape and the spike that extended like a cannon barrel from its front. Despite the name, explosive rounds from the rifles would take the things out. A southern variation of mobbers—just as vicious as their northern kin—lived here, as did a smaller species of treetop terror that Kalico had barely spotted before it vanished into the high canopy surrounding the drill site. Local takes on sidewinders, slugs, skewers, and pin cushions were present. But a lot of the creatures she'd barely glimpsed were going to need a slew of new and equally descriptive names. Like the flying bat creature with all the claws and the proboscis-shaped snout.

Kalico took a moment to scan the forest; it looked so different here, lumpier, with tall bluish spikes of trees that extended above the high canopy. They kept getting glimpses of giant flying creatures, four-winged things that rode the air currents and seemed to find sustenance in the treetops. From her high vantage point, and looking to the west, Kalico could see the sea, shining silver in the afternoon light. To the north, the curve of beach six kilometers distant was hidden by the rumpled forest.

Resting her hand on her pistol's grip, she turned and strode across the folded layers of gray-and-black gneiss, studded as it was with endless sparkles of muscovite. Veins of exposed metals, silver, copper, and gold shimmered in the sunlight where they interspersed with white swirls of quartz. She nodded to Abu Sassi, the marine who stood guard at the corner of the ramp, and climbed up into the shuttle.

Here the deafening chatter and banging from the drill was almost bearable.

Kalico stepped over to Shimodi's table where the woman was studying the latest cuttings under her microscope. On the table behind, Damien Smart was bent over the scanner. As the young man ran the machine, it slowly pulled the latest section of core sample past the scanners. The machine was analyzing the chemistry, minerals, metals, and stratigraphy millimeter by millimeter. So far, when it came to rare Earth elements, this was some of the most productive rock discovered on this world or any other. To Kalico's ears, the list of elements was a litany of "iums" starting with cerium, all the way down to the list to yttrium.

She bent over Shimodi's shoulder, asking, "What do you think?"

Still staring at the cuttings, Shimodi called back, "Tell the driller to shut down. I know why we're stopped."

Kalico accessed her com, ordering, "Shut it down! Lea's found something."

"Roger that," came through her earbud, and moments later the whine, clatter, and banging dropped to a low hum as the drill ceased turning.

Lea straightened. "Want to see?"

Bending to the scope, Kalico tried to make sense of the bits of spalled metal, each looking like clippings with ragged edges. "What am I seeing?"

"An alloy of titanium, scandium, chromium, and ruthenium mixed with fragments of drill bit. That's why we stopped making the hole about five minutes ago. The stuff is harder than our drill bit."

Kalico lifted her head from the scope. Arched a questioning eyebrow Shimodi's way. "Which means?"

Lea grinned. "You looking for a new place to put a mine? This might be the richest hill in the universe." She shrugged thoughtfully. "Might be a bastard to dig, though. Some of these veins are almost a meter thick. You'll have to excavate the softer rock around them, lift out the almost pure metal in chunks. The biggest drawback? Transportation to the smelter at Corporate Mine."

"Or is it rich enough that we should move the smelter here?"

Shimodi ran dirty fingers through her blond hair, her narrow nose pinched. "Your call, Supervisor. It's a win either way." She made a balancing gesture with her hands. "If you wanted, you could export this stuff as is. Let them process it on the other end."

"What should we do about the drill?" Kalico asked. "If the rotary bit won't cut through the alloy we've hit, should we switch to the laser bit? Melt our way through?"

"Again, your call." Shimodi frowned. "But I guess my advice at this point is: What for? We're at two hundred and seventy-seven meters. All of it through the richest metal-bearing rock formations ever recorded. We can mine this open pit with a strip ratio of zero to one. The only limitation is how far this formation extends laterally. From surface sampling I've done in the forest and the seismic imaging, I'm thinking you've got at least a couple of kilometers in every direction. And that's not counting the dip. No telling how far it might extend underground. The other unknown is how thick the strata is. Given that we're already at two-seventy-seven, anything deeper is gravy. We can determine that by additional drilling and mapping the formation."

"How long would that take?"

Lea chuckled. "That's the bottleneck. You've got this one rig, which we're going to have to overhaul before you start the next hole. Soon as we tear this rig down, it's got to be packed back to Port Authority for a rebuild." She shrugged. "The good news is that the geology is not going anywhere."

"Lawson and Montoya will be so delighted." Kalico told her. "So, that's what? A couple of weeks?"

"Probably." Shimodi frowned. "Once we get off the hilltop and out onto colluvial soils, you'll have to fight forest after you build a pad. And there's a nasty species of invertebrates down in the deep forest. They bite. And it's poisonous. Won't kill you, but it will make you really sick while your system fights it off. And then there's the bigger stuff." She made a face. "I've only worked in the forest around here when I'm wearing armor. Still scares the geewhilies right out of me, and the roots are really vicious and aggressive."

Kalico considered, heard Damien mutter, "Holy shit," where he was working on the section of core. "That's some of the strangest stuff I've seen yet."

"What have you got?" Lea asked.

"A fricking fortune," the boy replied. "Must have been the way the metal was forced through the rock, but it's all interwoven strands of gold, platinum, copper, and rhodium with streaks of chromium."

Kalico ran fingers down the thin scar on her jaw as she considered. "Then, my call is that we shut it down. Pack the rig back to PA and let Lawson and Montoya work their magic on the machinery." She smiled. "Like you said, it's not going anywhere."

Kalico narrowed her laser-blue eyes. *Besides, God alone knows what kind of trouble is coming in on* Turalon.

Inspector General Suto Soukup? For all Kalico knew, there might be some order from the Board stripping her of position and authority. Maybe even an order for her arrest.

In her latest communication, Margo Abibi had been circumspect. Offering the bare minimum of detail. Just a note that she had Soukup, a Taglioni, a Radcek, a Grunnel, and a Suharto, along with thirty marines aboard. And that they needed to talk. Face-to-face.

To do that, Kalico would have to shuttle up to *Vixen* to use the photonic com.

Which meant what? That the family members were to function as a sort of mini-Board to run The Corporation's operation? That they would use the thirty marines to bring Port Authority back under The Corporation's boot? Good luck with that!

She smacked a fist against her coveralls, feeling frustrated. She needed more information.

Now that she had hit a bonanza at what they'd come to call "The Southern Diggings," she could concentrate on getting ready for *Turalon*'s arrival.

Because, after all, she had a few surprises of her own. And no one aboard *Turalon*—not even Margo Abibi—knew what kind of woman Kalico Aguila was these days.

7

D erek Taglioni flew a wide circle over Port Authority, staring down at the town. Surrounded by its high fence and ditch, the place reminded him of pictures he'd seen of Iron Age forts. And the green fields surrounding to the west and south added to the effect. They stopped abruptly at the bush. There, the aquajade and chabacho made a speckled pattern on the light-green background of ferngrass and shrub. The bush was lined with the lighter red of trails lefty by chamois, crest, fastbreaks, and hoppers.

To the east, and abutting the fence, the landing field stuck out like a swollen thumb. The setting sun cast a shadow from the wall of cargo containers. Three layers thick and stacked seven high, they gave the field the appearance of a fortress surrounding the flat where Port Authority's shuttle was parked. From this altitude, the forklifts and loaders parked along the fence looked like toys.

On the west, the aircar and airtrucks were parked in rows that radiated out from the gate. The outer row of vehicles—being stripped carcasses and scavenged frames—had been left on blocks to molder and decay. Not that duraplast decayed that much. Solar panels on the fence fed cables that kept the still-operative vehicles charged.

On Port Authority's north, the bush ran right to the big gate that sat astraddle the mine haul road. A twenty-meter-wide strip of graveled dirt that ran a couple of klicks due north to the open pit mine with its shops, buildings, and gaping depths.

Home. The center of Dek's world.

He banked again, taking in the weathered domes, the hodgepodge of building styles, some with stone walls, others just flatroofed shops. And interspersed among the structures were lean-tos, sheds, and derelict equipment.

He could imagine what Falise and her bloodsucking companions were going to make of it.

That brought a sliver of a smile to his lips. The first he'd entertained since learning that his sister was in-system and headed for Donovan.

Dek dropped his flaps, lowered the landing gear, made his approach to the landing field. Having the only operative airplane on the planet, he pretty much had the skies to himself, and the aircraft's VTOL abilities allowed him to come in low over the shipping containers and settle next to the fence just down from the gate. The familiar sensation of the quetzal part of him came aware, as though the alien presence in his mind suddenly stirred and shifted within him. That the quetzal presence went dormant and hid while he was in the air still amused him. But then, fear was what let him thwart Demon's attempt to kill him in the first place.

The location beside the gate put his precious airplane well out of the blast radius of either the PA or Corporate shuttles, as well as close enough to the fence that he could run a charging cable and check the craft without having to leave the security of the compound after dark. No one wanted to be outside the fence after the sun went down.

Dek followed the shutdown procedure, retrieved his bag, rifle, and other gear, and locked the cabin behind him. After plugging his bird in, he made his way through the growing shadows to the gate.

"*Home safe,*" Rocket's voice whispered in his head.

"*Should have crashed into the forest and died,*" the Demon voice rasped in return.

"Oh, go suck toilet water, you little beast," Dek muttered under his breath. Talina had given him the Demon TriNA. Hadn't meant to, but he'd been dead. Tal gave him mouth-to-mouth, got his heart started again. He found a certain irony in the knowledge that after that, the Demon TriNA had done everything it could to kill him.

"*Came close.*"

"Yeah, you did, you little shit." But Dek had won, figured out how to dominate the new personalities in his head.

Ko Lang was on duty at the man gate and gave Dek a smile. "How's life in the wild these days?"

"Never a dull moment. Found a great new prospect. Have to get an assay on it, then I'll register the claim. After that, went hunting again with Kylee Simonov."

"Still looking for that thing that killed her folks?"

"Call it a reckoning, Ko."

"Been years, now." Ko shifted, his dark eyes looking past Dek to the landing field.

"Yeah? And I heard that Tal has found sign that Whitey's back. That's been years, too."

"Point made." Ko cracked a sort of smile. "We're all on double alert. That son of a bitch cost us too much."

"Yeah, same with the treetop terror."

Dek passed through, giving the landing field a last look. Whitey had tried this gate more than once, killed people right out there, within meters of where he stood.

He made his way to the dome he shared with Talina, calling greetings to friends and acquaintances as he walked through the afternoon's lengthening shadows. At the dome, he unloaded his gear, took a shower, and dressed in chamois-leather pants, a claw-shrub fabric shirt that Yvette had embroidered with colorful tooth flowers, and pulled his good quetzal-hide town boots on.

So Falise was aboard *Turalon?* Would she even recognize him after all these years and effects of quetzal TriNA? Dek studied his image in the bathroom mirror. First were his eyes, the irises still yellow ringed with green, but larger than they'd been. Alien with their expanded pupils. His face had a more triangular look, the cheekbones wider, not to mention the sharper chin. The dimple was still there, but the glaring white scar under his left eye distracted from it. His hair was longer now, sun-bleached. Fourteen years. A lot of changes since he had seen her last at the residence on Transluna.

Slinging his equipment belt with its pouches, pistol, and knife, around his waist, he clamped his wide-brimmed hat on his head, and checked in with com.

"Two Spot? You got a location on Talina?"

"Roger that. She's in Admin with Shig and Yvette."

Dek shouldered his rifle, stepped out, and locked the door behind him. Walking down the main avenue, he passed The Jewel, hearing music inside along with a whoop of pleasure. Allison was raking in plunder tonight. The casino, saloon, and brothel sounded as if it were on full boil. Walking south, he passed the assay office, Inga's, the gunsmith's, glassblower's, and metal shop, then the bootmaker's. Just past the cafeteria, he pushed the double doors open to the admin dome. The building was old, its outside stained and dusty, the duraplast starting to weather under Capella's brutal rays.

Heading down the hall, he passed the weapons locker, various offices, including Yvette's, where she kept the colony records. At the conference room, he pushed the door open and stepped inside.

Shig, Yvette, and Talina sat at the close end of the table, Stepan Allenovich and Raya Turnienko across from them. Allison Chomko, in a gleaming silver suit, sat at the far end.

"Dek!" Talina cried, rising and stepping close to hug him.

He closed his eyes, savoring the feel of her taut body against his. Then he pushed back and took a moment to just revel at the sight of her. Didn't matter that her eyes had an alien look, deeper and darker, and too large, or that her face was all sharp angles. God, she was exotic and beautiful.

Falise was going to be shocked to her core.

"Kill her and eat her," Demon suggested from deep in Dek's head. But then, that pretty much summed up Demon's solution for every problem.

"So, what did I miss?" he asked.

"Lots of talk about what to do when *Turalon* arrives," Yvette told him. "It's a conversation we've had before. What do we do when The Corporation finally takes us seriously? But for a couple of bumps in the road, the last time didn't turn out so badly."

Dek took a seat next to Talina, lacing his fingers into hers. "The last I heard, *Turalon*'s captain had sent a list of passengers—including my blood-sucking sister—and that she was carrying marines and a Board Appointed IG. Anything else new since then?"

Shig leaned forward, a benign look on his round face. "Captain

Abibi expects to be in orbit ten days from now. She's forwarded a cargo manifest that we've been going over. Much to our surprise, her bays are full of material we can actually use for once. Like new powerpacks for the airtrucks and aircars! A full pharmacopeia. Parts for scientific equipment and even techs to install them. It would seem that The Corporation actually paid attention to our needs."

"Thank God," Raya growled, the flat planes of her Siberian face emotionless. "Real medical equipment? And a couple of techs to run it? If the passenger manifest is correct, I might faint." Glancing at Dek, she said, "I could repair that scar on your cheek."

"I'll keep the scar," he told her. "Kylee says it makes me look like a pirate."

"What would Kylee know about how a pirate looks?" Talina asked. "She was raised on a research base in the forest."

"They had books, vids, and holos," Dek reminded.

"Getting back to the subject," Allison interrupted. "Before Dek got here, we were discussing Suharto, Grunnel, Radcek, and this Falise Taglioni." She turned her hard blue gaze on Dek. "You called her a blood-sucking sister? Want to elaborate on that?"

Dek nodded, shifted his attention to Allison. Though she was only in her mid-twenties, the woman was one of the most powerful on the planet. She ran The Jewel, Betty Able's brothel, and had controlling interest in real estate, numerous mining ventures, investments, and was forty-nine percent of the Port Authority bank. Despite being orphaned, widowed, having her child eaten by a quetzal, and then having been seduced and prostituted by Dan Wirth, she'd emerged as a tough, capable, smart, and ruthless force in Port Authority politics. To Dek's delight, she was the perfect mix of beauty and brains, and she pulled no punches.

"Yeah," he said through an exhale. "Just because Falise is my sister, don't expect any teary-eyed swelling of love and affection upon our reunion." He glanced around the table. "You all know that I sent Dan Wirth back to Solar System with a Taglioni safe conduct. Sort of used him like a human time bomb." He turned his attention back to Allison. "My honest estimation? I figured he had about a ten percent survival chance when he was thrown into the middle of Board politics. That, most likely, Dan wouldn't be up to the game, that they'd eat him alive."

Allison gave him a deadly smile. "I like those odds. But how does some Boardmember killing Dan lead us to your sister?"

Oh, yes. Always smart. That was Allison. "I expected Fabio and Miko—they wield the power in the family—to send a courier. One of the trusted family retainers. Or maybe an expendable cousin from somewhere down the line. Said courier would arrive with instructions, platitudes, and reassurances, and all the while, he or she would be assembling all the information he or she could on my activities."

Dek chuckled in appreciation. "My compliments to Miko and my father. That they chose Falise? Worse, that they *ordered* her to Donovan? They just upped the game."

"How?" Step Allenovich asked. The big botanist, hunter, and security second to Talina had leaned back, a chamois-clad leather knee keeping his chair balanced on the back two legs. Step might have been a drinker, gambler, and womanizer, but he was bush-wise and as hard-bitten as any Wild One.

"Given what Dek's told me, she's the Taglioni master of dirty tricks, duplicity, and double-dealing," Talina said, then glanced at Dek. "But it's been almost what? Fourteen years since you've seen her? That's a long time. Maybe she's not the woman you remember."

Dek looked around the table, meeting their eyes, one by one. "Quetzals can change their colors, my sister cannot. She's what they made her to be: a deadly instrument meant to infiltrate, evaluate, and either seduce, coerce, or destroy. She took to it with glee."

"What about the others?" Yvette asked, tapping a paper on the table that had the list. "Like this Cinque Suharto. You know him?"

"Met him a time or two in passing. He was younger. What does he call himself on the manifest?"

Shig told him, "It says he's a cargo logistics security specialist."

Dek fingered his scar and nodded. "Okay, means he specializes in making supply chains work. Things like ensuring the flow of raw materials from the miners on the ground up through refinery, man-ufacturing, warehousing, and ensuring the distribution of end product. He's the guy they send to ensure things operate smoothly. He'll be an intimidator. But just as smart as he is dangerous."

"And Chad Grunnel?" Yvette asked. "They call him a 'Resources Procurement Specialist.'"

"Him, I knew," Dek said. "He's one of the guys who ran the Grunnel interests in the Asteroid Belt. Enforcer. He broke up strikes, capped off malcontents, ensured that dissenters—or more effectively, their loved ones—inexplicably vanished. Kept the stations and workers in line. Squashed any unrest." Dek glanced around the table. "Everyone here understands, don't they? Mining out in the Belt, that's about as brutal, nasty, and inhuman as it gets. It's our modern gulag. Where you send people who are embarrassing or expendable. And the Grunnels aren't known for their empathy or enlightened humanity."

"And this Inspector General?" Talina asked.

Dek shrugged. "While technically, he has no authority in PA, given that he's Board Appointed, he's a real threat to Kalico if he decides she's acted inappropriately. And, people, that's something we need to be preparing for as a worst-case scenario."

"So far, it appears that all the forces of *dukkha* are descending upon us." Shig had a curiously amiable smile on his wide lips. "What of this Bartolome Radcek? Investment Management? That's a rather innocuous title, don't you think?"

Dek sighed. "In many ways, he might be the most dangerous of the lot. He's been around for a while. Descended from the old Radceks. Think Calypso and his ilk. Remember, too, that once upon a time, back in Solar System, they called Donovan 'Radcek's World.' Donovan is like a festering wound, something that grates deep down in the Radcek family psyche. Bartolome, or Bad Bart, as he's known, works from the shadows. Doesn't tip his hand. Isn't as blunt as the others."

"How so?" Allison asked as she shifted her long legs.

"Falise or Chad? And I suppose Cinque. They'll smile disarmingly and pat you on the back with one hand at the same time they're slipping a knife between your ribs with the other, or maybe slit your throat after beating you half unconscious. They want you to look them in the eyes while you're dying. So that you know just who brought you down. Bad Bart? He'll slip a drop of plutonium into your scotch, nod politely, and ease out the door, never to be seen again. He's not into notching his gun; only results matter."

"And they are coming here?" Shig mused. "With thirty marines under the command of a rather distasteful and fawning commander? I wonder how many are going to die before this is over?"

"Expect things to get bloody," Dek agreed. "But given the arrival of this Suto Soukup, our biggest worry is Kalico and her people. We at least have the fiction of being independent. Kalico is still a Board Supervisor. Still technically 'one of them' and subject to Corporate law. And most of her people are still under contract."

Allison had steepled her fingers. "I think we need a plan for just that contingency. I have options available. A network we can use if we need to relocate some of her people from harm's way."

"No indenturing." Yvette pointed a stern finger. "Not this time."

Allison arched a pale blond eyebrow. "I'd like to think I'm smarter than Dan when it comes to things like that. Meanwhile, we might want to check out some of the other abandoned research bases. Places like Jade, Wide Ridge, and Ytterbium Base."

"And we can always filter people out to some of the Wild Ones." Shig's eyes had gone thoughtful. "Poor time for Whitey to show up again. You know he'll try something."

Talina glanced at Dek. "But, as I understand it, the real danger is this IG. The rest of these people, they're just family representatives. Not sanctioned by the Board. So, it's not like Falise outranks you, is it?"

"Not ipso facto," Dek glanced around the table. "But you all need to be aware, we're about to engage in a most dangerous game. And you are about to play it with some of the most amoral human beings alive."

8

Just down from the AC, on Command Deck, the captain's lounge was little more than a cramped closet stuffed back against the curve of *Turalon*'s hull. It consisted of a central table, com projectors, and six chairs. In the back was a small galley with a stove, hot and cold drinks, and a limited selection of food packets. It was designed as a refuge for the ship's captain and his/her ranking officers. A place where they could retreat from the more public areas and duty stations.

When Bartolome Radcek had first expressed a desire to use the room, Captain Abibi had graciously and wisely acquiesced. Falise suspected that the good captain—even if she didn't know Bart's reputation—had sensed somewhere down deep that she was dealing with a human tarantula, no matter how sweet his smile or amiable his expression. And, no sooner had Bart taken to relaxation in the lounge than Falise, Chad, and Cinque had claimed similar privileges.

While they had divided the personal quarters into separate territories during the transition, the lounge had become neutral ground. The place where the four could meet for candid discussions without entourages, posturing, or staff.

After all, a year and seven months was a long time to play each other. Feel out each other's weaknesses. Score points, wins, and losses. Like Falise's successful seduction of Kramer, Bartolome's valet. It had taken Bart almost three months to figure out that she had compromised his personal servant and bodyguard. Kramer's sudden death from "cardiac arrest" had shocked everyone. But the good thing about servants? They provided as many nutrients to the hydroponics system as anyone else.

Cinque had scored his biggest triumph by brokering an alliance between Chad and Bart that, for almost six months, froze Falise out.

Came within a whisker of weakening her to the point that she might have been politically neutered. Fortunately, she had anticipated just such a move given that her uncle, Chairman of the Board Miko, had pushed *Turalon*'s rapid turnover. His authority had been behind getting the ship spaced before the other families could fully understand the implications.

While Kramer's revelations had been instrumental in breaking that alliance, it helped that Falise had betrayed Chad's artful intent to cut Cinque out of any share of Donovanian profits should they actually reach the planet.

For that, Falise had needed to compromise Colonel Creamer, who'd been a Grunnel sympathizer from the start. She'd compelled Lieutenant Malanda Tomolo to violate regulations and use tech to spy on a meeting between Chad and Creamer. All of which she'd spilled to the others in this very room.

Since *Turalon* reverted symmetry and popped back into regular space, that alliance between Chad, Cinque, and Bart had begun to reassert itself. She, after all, was a Taglioni. Miko's niece, and sister to Derek, who was already doing who knew what on the planet. That implied that she suddenly had the inside track on Donovan, which necessitated that they align against her.

Fine. Let them. They didn't know about Charlotte, Chad's valet. About how much she hated space travel, or what she would do to escape her present situation.

Falise leaned back in the captain's chair and pulled up a long leg, grasping it by the ankle as she studied the holo projection of Donovan. So much was different now that they knew they were going to live. The stakes in the game had changed: They no longer played for survival in case of the worst, but for wealth, power, and control when they reached the planet. And the key to that might be Derek, though God forbid how that might work out. How her spoiled, drugged-up, and womanizing brother might be a player stretched the imagination. He'd always been a groveling fuckup given to tantrums.

So what exactly is your game, Brother?

Falise chafed. Every communication she'd sent Derek's way had been—after the piss-sucking radio delay—replied to with *"Unavailable at the moment."*

She held that against this mysterious Two Spot, who obviously didn't understand that upon receipt of a Taglioni message, every priority in his life must change until said message was delivered.

She glanced up when the hatch to the Command Deck opened and Chad and Cinque stepped in. That she'd already claimed the captain's chair granted her a small amount of clout. Chad settled for the astrogation officer's seat, reaching for the coffee pot that steamed on the galley stove immediately to his left, which was a smooth move on his part. Gave him control of the refreshments. Cinque took the chair by the door, the ghost of a smile hinting that he was above such petty concerns as who sat where. As always, he wore form-fitting light-absorbing black. What was the point of being physically intimidating if you didn't dress the part?

Chad, as usual, wore the finest of Silurian silks and photofabric that played light patterns in geometric shapes and colors over his finely tailored suit. The man's amber designer eyes sparkled with challenge as he locked them with Falise's and poured his coffee. For today, he'd had his long blond hair coiffed into a flowing wave that curled up and out above his left ear. Made his head look off balance. He'd oiled his walnut-brown skin so that it shone in the light.

And yes—unlike the crew and transportees—they and their staffs all had hair. They were, after all, the privileged scions of Board families. Regulations didn't apply to them like it did to the menials who flew the ship or the transportees down in the warren on C Deck.

"Good of you to come," Falise opened, giving Chad a winning smile. "So much to do now that the planet's close."

"Bart's on the way," Cinque said in an offhand manner. "Detained, you know. It's so hard to break in a new valet. Takes so long to train them. Oh, it's not so hard to get them to bend over and spread on command, but those pesky nuances of clothing? That takes a lifetime of training and study. After all, who could stand being given a red scarf to go with an orange jacket?"

"Black does make it so much easier," Chad agreed. "When it

comes to your own valet, they don't need to know anything about fashion, taste, or design. While I can see why it's forced you to wear the darkest of the dark, should you ever care to explore a more worldly wardrobe, I'd be delighted to loan you Charlotte for a week or so. I think she could do wonders when it comes to building a new you. And, my friend, you are in desperate need of a new you. Dressed in stygian darkness as you are, you'll vanish into the shadows when surrounded by Donovanians in their rainbow colors."

Cinque fixed his obsidian eyes on Chad. "I've never found that 'fitting in' suited my cause. And, though the offer is appreciated, after the pitiful and almost ascetic use to which you've accustomed your poor Charlotte, why, sending her back after even a modicum of lusty fulfillment would just be frustrating and cruel, don't you think?"

Chad mocked him with a solemn nod. "You're right, of course. After that kind of bestiality, it might take weeks to get her back to an understanding that art and technique always triumph over aggressive penetration, even though it might be over almost before it began."

The hatch opened before Cinque could riposte. Bartolome Radcek—dressed in a casual gray business suit with an imperial collar—stepped into the room. His quick gaze, as always, cataloged the situation and seating. Then he stepped past Cinque, finding the First Officer's chair next to Falise.

Sharp as ever, he'd read the tension between Chad and Cinque, smiled as he took in Falise's posture, her knee still pulled up. "Miss anything?"

"An enlightening conversation about sharing valets and how they may not return to service with quite the same dedication to duty," she told him, well aware that she was twisting a thorn in an already festering wound, given what she'd gotten out of Kramer. But then, for the time being, until the new equilibrium was achieved, it was all about keeping one's adversaries off balance.

Ignoring the barb, Bart smiled amiably, fixed his yellow eyes on hers, and said, "I do hope you are offering Ednund. I would so love to discover his secrets when it comes to your sartorial perfection. I expect he'd a be a font of information. So much so that I'd be loath to send him back after I'd drained him dry."

The disarming look he was giving Falise might have fooled someone who hadn't been trained as well as she. "I'm honored that Ednund is so coveted. It reminds me to keep him close and cherished."

"Actually," Chad said through feigned weary reluctance, "Cinque was wishing for Charlotte."

Ah! Perfect. Falise let no hint of satisfaction betray itself.

"She does dress Chad nicely," Cinque agreed, "but despite fashion and fine dress—as enchanting as they are—we really need to get on to this Donovan business."

He leaned on his forearms, glancing from face to face. "So, now that the waiting and wonder is over, we're alive. Headed to Donovan orbit. The game is changed. As much as I've enjoyed the sparring and repartee for the last nineteen months, my review of the situation on the ground is that we need to formulate a plan of action. The Corporation's success has depended upon the unity of the Board. The families might have their differences, but ultimately, those concerns must be set aside in order to ensure more pragmatic concerns when it comes to neutering threats and maintaining control of Corporate assets."

Chad said, "We checked with com. Still no reply from Board Supervisor Aguila. After waiting out this damnable radio lag, her com officer, O'Hanley, says the Supervisor has been appraised of our communication and will be in touch upon her return from the south."

"What does that mean?" Bart wondered, leaning back in a pose similar to Falise's and stroking his chin. "The south?"

Chad shifted his amber eyes in Falise's direction. "Is that some sort of code? Something you've been privy to?"

Falise shook her head. "As nice as it would be to have an inside track, and as much as you'd like to believe that Taglionis are way ahead of you in the game, I'm as much in the dark as you are." She pointed at the holo of the planet spinning above the table. "I've read the same reports that you have. I'm privy to the same information, right down to Dan Wirth and what he means to the family."

Bart's gaze bored into her hers. "Let's just say that he's a major source of interest to all of us. You've met him. Looked him in the eyes. Taken his measure. What's his role in all of this? What does he give the Taglionis?"

She let loose of her ankle and extended her leg, pointed at the coffee pot and sat forward. As Chad poured a cup for her, she said, "What does he give us? A headache. I'll tell you what I know. And *all* I know, because I think it might be critical to our success here. The man I met is a sleazy piece of work that comes across as a common a street thug. I'd call him a psychopath, but that's without having a professional diagnosis."

"Why did your brother send him back? And with all that claptrapping wealth? Word is that just the rhodium in his possession, alone, could bankrupt one of the noble houses. And that's before calculating the value of the gems and other precious metals." Cinque wondered, "A street thug? Really?"

She glanced from face to face as she took her coffee from Chad. "I think Derek expected that the moment Dan Wirth stepped off *Ashanti,* the Board would panic. That no matter what, *Turalon* or *Ashanti* would be immediately turned around, re-provisioned, and spaced for Donovan. Very perceptive on his part, because to our dismay, here we sit. It's all according to Derek's plan."

Bart said, "Then maybe you'd better tell us what your brother is up to. What are we walking into down there?"

"I haven't a clue. He still won't answer my requests." She thumped a fist onto the tabletop. "This damnable *radio*! Who communicates at speed of light anymore? There's a pus-dripping photonic com on *Vixen.* Why don't they use it?"

Cinque had been chewing his lip; now he said, "Maybe because they don't want to. Especially with Soukup aboard. Maybe they want us thinking that they can't communicate. That they're buying time."

Chad pointed a hard finger. "It's your brother I'm worried about.

Derek was always an arrogant snot. Too damned full of himself for his own good. What was his competency score? Low eighties?"

"Something like that." Falise sipped her coffee. "But Kalico Aguila is an entirely different matter. I knew her well. Admired her." She glanced around the table. "That woman was on a fast track for the Board. Miko speculated that she'd be Chairman in ten years. Do you know what kind of talent that takes?"

Bart tapped at the implant behind his right ear. "I've read the reports. The woman is running a mine. She *signed over* ownership of the entire Port Authority colony, for God's sake. She's surrendered herself to a bunch of halfwit contractees and rogues. On Transluna, these people would be little more than gutter trash. The kind we send to the Belt. Living on subsistence at best, eliminated as non-essential or criminal at worst."

"Which is why the Board appointed Soukup," Chad reminded. "He's the random element here. One we might be able to direct and channel once we get a feel for what's on the ground. We all know that the Board sent him to discover the truth behind all the stories about Capella III, and especially about Kalico Aguila. Once he ferrets out what's really going on down there, he could change the entire game for better or worse. Expect him to remove Aguila just out of prudence."

And that means he will appoint one of us as interim Supervisor on Donovan.

Cinque raised a skeptical eyebrow. "Let's not forget the value of the cargo she shipped on *Turalon*. And, impressive as that was, the wealth that poured out of *Ashanti*'s holds was ten times as stunning. All of it the product of Corporate Mine, whatever that is. So, while Supervisor Aguila may have signed over Port Authority to a bunch of colonists, with one shipment, she matched the entire output of *three years* of Solar System's extractive production."

"More stunning," Chad said, "that one cargo contained more beryllium, rhodium, and ruthenium than the Belt could produce in ten years. And at a fragment of the cost per ton."

Bartolome added dryly, "Not to mention the gemstones. No one will forget Dan Wirth strolling into Tiboronne wearing his rhodium and gold chains in addition to that garish ruby at his throat. So striking was it that no one noticed that he had Sharascena, the most sought-after courtesan in Transluna, on his arm. All they saw was that giant red gem as big as a goose egg."

"So, here we sit." Again, Falise took their measure. "None of us wanted to be here. We've lived for a year and seven months in limbo, wondering if we were going to live or vanish in space. But we made it." She gestured at the holo of Donovan, spinning in the air before them. "The other families couldn't react in time, so it's the four of us." A beat. "Now, what are we going to do about it?"

"Take it all," Cinque met each of their eyes in turn. "What can a bunch of rustic colonists, or Kalico Aguila, no matter how capable, do to stop us? We have a ship full of supplies and thirty marines."

Chad nodded. "And Creamer will do as we ask. He knows exactly where his best interests lie."

Falise shrugged. Sounded like a plan, but something down deep bothered her. Like she was missing some elemental piece of the puzzle.

9

"Kylee?" The word sounded frail. Barely penetrated the night chime. Brought Kylee Simonov upright out of a sound sleep. She blinked, senses clearing as Flute shifted beside her. Had she heard the call or dreamed it?

"Wake up!" Rocket's voice insisted, the part of him that remained inside her bringing her upright where she was propped on Flute's warm belly. Alert, she opened her senses to the night.

She was in her cabin on the outskirts of the Briggs homestead where the agricultural fields gave way to the bush. It wasn't much of a house, just four plastered walls, a roof, and a cistern-fed sink with a small kitchen. She shared it with Flute and Tip—or had before Tip vanished into the bush to "find himself." Whatever that meant.

Flute's deep chittering and the expulsion of breath through his tail vents was followed by the sound of wind in the aquajade and chabacho trees that surrounded the Briggs' farmstead and claim. Behind that, the night chime shifted, harmony building, only to reset, rise, and crest again.

Glancing around the cabin, Kylee's quetzal-augmented night vision penetrated the gloom. No moon or stars tonight. The sky had been overcast when she and Flute had retired for the night. Sniffing, she could smell rain on the air. A flicker of white light from distant lightning illuminated the window on the east. Meant the storm was coming.

Kylee shifted where she was curled against Flute's soft tummy; her head had been pillowed on one of the quetzal's forelegs. A slight gurgle came from somewhere in the beast's gut as it digested a roo. They slept together, having created a "nest" of the blankets and padding. She, Tip, and Flute. A bonded trio. Lineage. Or they had been until Tip had stalked off into the forest.

"Something's wrong," the part of her that was Rocket warned. Though he was dead all these years, she still cherished and nurtured the part of him that survived inside her.

Kylee made a face, irritated. Easing out from Flute's belly, she climbed to her feet and crossed to the window; she stared out at the night, seeing ever more flickers of white as they strobed in the clouds off to the north and east. The wind had changed, coming from the north. Typical spring storm. Wet cool air blowing down, hitting the curve of the Wind Mountains where they circled northeast to the coast. As the air was compressed and forced westward along the orographic barrier, it brought heavy rain to the forests around the Briggs holdings. This had the makings of being just such a storm.

"I'm so tired of being your little boy!" Tip's angry words rang in Kylee's memory. *"You're no older than I am!"*

But she was. She'd absorbed too many of Talina's memories back when they'd shared TriNA during those trying days at Mundo Base. Was it a blessing or a curse to have a mature woman's perspective constantly popping into her head?

More of a blessing, Kylee decided. She crossed her arms, staring out at the fields where lines of barley, wheat, onions, garlic, peppers, cabbage, corn, broccoli, and the rest of the crops grew. And there, at the edge of the forest, was the big suspended bench swing where she and Tip used to sway. Cocking her head, Kylee could just hear the squeak of the chains as the strengthening breeze played with the hanging seat.

That left her with a feeling of longing. Too many memories were tied to that swing. Times she and Tip had sat side by side, telling each other stories, plotting hunts . . . just being. And maybe that was part of the problem. The two of them had been thrust together. Condemned to association by virtue of their solitude and exile. Hers imposed and Tip's chosen.

And then there was the bonding with Flute. Always more hers than Tip's, predisposed as she had been by Rocket, and then by her desperate need to fill the void left by Rocket's death. In the beginning, Tip had been the leader. It was his country after all. He knew the trails, the wildlife, the best places to trap chamois, fastbreaks, and roos. Where the dangers were most likely to hide.

And he'd taken to Flute and the bonding, though not as well as Kylee. Or maybe even Talina. As if a part of Tip's body and soul resisted. Sometimes Kylee wondered if it might have been immunological. Tip had never cared, happy to be himself.

That had always been a problem. The boy had no ambitions beyond the next hunt. Wanted nothing more out of life than the next meal.

Whereas Kylee had been raised from day one with the understanding that she would accomplish great things. Follow in her three mothers' footsteps as a scientist. That expectation might have taken some hard knocks along the way, and seemed impossible at times, but it had been hardwired into her worldview. Cemented by her biological mother Dya's death the day the treetop terror had speared her and hauled her up into the canopy. Looking back at a life that had more than its share of seminal moments, the day Mark Talbot and her mother died, had been yet another pivotal event.

"Nothing was quite the same with Tip and me after that," she told herself as she watched the storm intensifying in the night. Maybe that was why, in the last three years, she had taken the lead in their relationship. Like it or not, she had Talina's memories—all those experiences to draw from. She wasn't just an adolescent girl feeling her way.

No, more like sixteen mixed with thirty. Not to mention the quetzal instincts. Hard to put them in perspective given that quetzals killed and ate their elders. Figured that she was a fucked-up mess.

"God, Tip," she told the night. "I'm sorry."

She'd always expected too much of him. They had shared everything. Looking back, sex had been a mistake. She'd viewed the event through a mature woman's perspective, having Talina's experience as a rule and guide. Yes, it was supposed to change their relationship. Make them closer, more like intimate partners, and less like childhood friends. Maybe she thought it would make their relationship more like what she'd known with Rocket. That total intimacy.

Something that Tip, despite shared TriNA, couldn't comprehend.

"My fault, Tip," she told the night. "I was expecting you to turn into someone you've never had to be."

"*I'm not your child! I'm done. Finished. You're not giving me orders anymore.*"

That declaration preceded his stalking over to his pack, slipping it on, and charging out into the night. "*Gonna find myself on my own!*" were the last words he'd hollered over his shoulder before vanishing into the forest.

Wind gusted out of the night, rustling the leaves, stirring the aquajade. The chime changed as the invertebrates began singing to the storm, or about the storm. One never really knew with invertebrates. Kylee suspected the little creatures were a lot more intelligent than humans had ever given them credit for.

She heard Flute shift, the quetzal rising, stretching, before crossing the room on mincing steps. Kylee made room so that Flute could look out at the night. As good as her augmented vision was, Flute's was even better. The quetzal's big head filled the window, his inhalation audible, only to be followed by the jet of air from his vents. It made a slight whistling tremolo, hence her name for him. To his lineage, he was known as Third Orange. Third was his birth rank, and orange referred to his willingness to bond with a human.

Thinking of Tip? Flute's hide reflected in infrared as he formed the question.

"Yeah." She cocked her head. "Missing him. Hope he's okay. Thought I heard him call my name. But it's probably my imagination."

Time of rogue. The images formed on Flute's collar as he expanded it.

Rogue, the period when young quetzals left their home territories, went scouting for new lands. A rite of passage.

"I guess. There are human cultures who made their young men go out. Tip said he was going to go find himself." She scuffed the floor with her bare foot, arms still crossed defensively. "Guess I never knew how lost he was."

Flute's lateral eye turned her direction. *He should kill and eat Chaco.*

At the symbols running down Flute's side, Kylee laughed. "Yeah, well, don't let me rain on your chamois hunt, but you damned well know humans don't kill and eat their fathers. We can't synthesize someone else's knowledge by digesting them. Our DNA doesn't work like your TriNA. I've explained all of this before."

Still trying to learn.

"Hey, we all are." She slipped in beside Flute's big head, peering out at the night. "Funny thing. I should really be missing him. Should be worried sick."

Chaco and Madison are. They make different sounds and smells.

Kylee leaned her cheek against Flute's jaw, feeling the warmth and hardness of the polymer bone beneath. "Human parents do that. Remember how frightened you were when we bonded? Quetzals don't feel emotions like we do. Quetzal emotions are . . . different. More pragmatic."

She rapped at the side of his serrated teeth, adding, "Probably because you kill and eat your parents so you can synthesize their knowledge."

Efficient.

"Wasteful," she shot back.

It was an old argument between them.

So is letting a human die of old age without saving the knowledge he has learned.

"Yeah," she agreed. "I hear you. Next you're going to tell me about the way terrestrial life is born 'empty,' as you call it. And yes, we have to learn everything over from the beginning with each birth. So, don't tell me it's inefficient. We build starships. Quetzals don't."

Don't have to tell. You know. He made mocking chirps through his tail vents. *Quetzals are better.*

She jabbed him with an elbow, her body pressed against his as he wrapped a foreleg around her and held her close. Her side fit perfectly into the curve of his claws. "Where are we going, Flute? What comes next? Lately, especially after Tip left, I've started to wonder."

What?

If it had been light, she'd have seen his hide turn yellow, green, and pink with interrogative.

"Like Tip, I guess, I've been wondering if this is a dead end. What comes next? What are we doing with our lives? There's more to living than just the next meal."

Flute uttered a deep guttural clicking, his sound for incredulousness. His way of asking: *Like what?*

"Making a contribution," she told him. "Accomplishing something. Achievement. Purpose. Being able to look back and say, 'I did that.'"

Flute huffed from his vents.

She gave him a playful shove. "Don't scoff. You know just what I mean. Why did they call you Third Orange? It was because you agreed to bond with Yellow Girl and Brown Boy, as your lineage called Tip and me. You said yes. To make a difference. To learn something new. Achievement. Purpose."

He was signing something she couldn't see when she heard it: "Kylee?"

Weak. Strained. Barely audible over the increasing wind.

"Dear God," Kylee peeled free of Flute's hold.

Then she was out the door, the quetzal close behind her.

"Tip!" she cried, lightning lancing across the sky overhead.

"Here!" he answered an instant before the crack of thunder deafened. It came from the direction of the swing.

Flute, with his better trinocular vision, veered right, shooting across the field. Quetzals could hit one hundred and forty kilometers per hour in a sprint. Kylee, despite her longer-than-normal legs and augmented muscles, was left behind.

When she pulled up at the edge of the trees, Flute lifted Tip's limp body with his forelegs, signing *Injured* in the infrared.

Tip looked sick, his sharp face lined, the long brown hair unkept. The glint was gone from his brown eyes, leaving them sunken and dull. Normally laughing and wry, Tip's lips now looked white and thin. Even Tip's once-healthy tan-brown skin had gone pale, slicked with sweat despite the cool night. His shirt was stained, and the left pantleg . . . God, what was wrong with his left leg? It looked huge.

"Tip! You all right?" she demanded, taking one of his limp hands. It felt fevered. Something smelled really bad. Like fermenting pus.

"Kylee?" Tip craned his head around where he hung in Flute's clawed forefeet. "Leg. Really . . ." He made a face. "Hurt."

"To the house," Kylee ordered Flute. "Let's get some light on it."

But she could see. Tip had slit the left leg of his trousers to free the swollen and blackened skin beneath.

Her heart dropped at the sight. This looked about as bad as it could get.

"Got you, Tip. You made it. We'll get you fixed."

But how were she and Madison going to fix that mess?

10

The way Kalico Aguila figured it, she was probably due for a reckoning, one way or another. She considered that as she watched
Donovan fall away below her shuttle. The A-7 had been the Corporate Mine's workhorse, hauling cargo up to L5 in orbit, transporting her personnel back and forth to PA, not to mention around
the planet where her prospects were being evaluated for further
development.

But the hours had piled up. Depending on how this coming
meeting worked out, she was hoping to swap *Turalon* for an A-7
with fewer hours.

She glanced out the shuttle's side window as they passed into the
exosphere, and she could see *Freelander,* like an eerie white dot,
where it followed its orbit around Donovan. She could have switched
for another of *Freelander's* mothballed shuttles, but as the PA bird—
taken from there years ago—proved, there were constant problems.
Kalico wasn't sure if it was due to the fact that, like *Freelander,* the
shuttle still had the taint of that other universe, or whether it was
just that *Freelander* birds were almost a century and a half old. Things
deteriorated. Even if they hadn't been used.

In the pilot's seat, Ensign Juri Makarov glanced at his instruments
and turned her way. "Fifteen minutes to match with *Vixen,* ma'am.
First Officer Vacquillas offers her compliments and wants you to
know that you are expected."

"Send my regards, Juri."

Kalico stared out at Donovan's subtle curve, at the glow that
Capella's rays gave to the atmosphere. They were coming up on the
terminator where it cast the eastern ocean in shadow. The line had
to be close to where the Maritime Unit lay submerged on its reef.

Night would be falling, leaving the sunken research station in
darkness. Not that the intelligent slime that had taken the place

really slept. She wondered if the mutated children down there did. They'd been human once, after all. How much of that humanity was left? How much taken over by the slime's TriNA?

Wonder if we'll ever know?

She pondered the ramifications of the disaster that had doomed the first maritime expedition to study Donovan's oceans. Donovan wasn't Earth. That had to be understood. There were places where humans might never dare to venture. The oceans might be just such a place.

The Maritime Unit also served as a reminder that humans might be full of hubris, but Donovan had its own agenda. She need look no farther than the nearest mirror—and the sight of her scars—to be reminded of that.

In the forward window, the dot that was *Vixen* grew larger, the survey ship's navigational lights blinking. *Vixen* always amazed her. Originally listed as missing, it had popped back into Donovanian space after a fifty-year transition from Solar System. The kicker was that to *Vixen's* crew, the trip had seemed instantaneous. Faced with the prospect of making a return trip, the crew had opted to conduct a survey of the Capella star system, mapping and exploring all of the planets. To date they had finished mapping and reporting on most of the inner planets.

Some of the crew had spaced back to Solar System on *Ashanti*, but for most—with everyone they had loved back home dead of old age—the Capella System had given them new lives and purpose.

As her shuttle pulled even, Kalico could see the pristine hull, the crew torus, the giant reactor pod, and the fuel tanks gleaming. Call it ironic. Built over one hundred and twenty years ago, *Vixen* looked new. *Freelander,* built a decade ago, was a decrepit derelict. Traveling through inverted symmetry didn't come without risk, not to mention a great deal of uncertainty.

"Docking," Makarov called, as he maneuvered the A-7 into the unoccupied shuttle bay on *Vixen's* starboard side.

"*Shifting ballast to accommodate your mass,*" came the reply from *Vixen's* ship's AI. "*Proceed with docking. Matching rotation to your approach.*"

Kalico marveled at the skill with which Makarov eased the shuttle into the bay. The illusion was that *Vixen* was lowering itself down onto the shuttle. She watched the bay slip around them. Then the slight bump as Makarov eased them against the grapples. A clank and shudder.

"We have lock," Makarov announced. "Hard dock."

"Hard dock. We have lock," Vixen replied. *"Extending airlock. Seal. We have hard seal. Umbilical attached."*

"Roger that, *Vixen*. Thank you for your help."

"Welcome aboard," the ship told them. *"Captain Torgussen is waiting at the hatch."*

Makarov powered down and lifted his hands from the controls; it was the kind of move a master concert pianist would have made as he finished at the keyboard.

Kalico took a moment to adapt to the angular acceleration seeking to pull her slightly sideways after all these months in standard Donovanian gravity. Then she unbuckled and climbed carefully to her feet.

"Need me at my station?" Makarov asked.

She shook her head. "I don't think so. Can't think of any reason we'd have to dust off in a hurry. We're only here so I can make a call and have a social visit with Torgussen and his officers."

Makarov gave her a saucy wink. "Good. I've got a duffel in the back filled with special orders. A couple of bottles from Inga's, fresh peppers and veggies, dried crest meat, some clothing that needed shipping up from the Dushkus."

Kalico led the way to the lock, double-checked that it was green on the other side, and then cycled the hatch. Atmosphere balanced with a hiss, and she swung the outer door open.

On the other side stood Tayrell Torgussen, resplendent in his dress uniform with the braid and piping. He pulled himself to full attention, saluting, as he announced, "Board Supervisor Aguila, *Vixen* bids you welcome."

"My pleasure, Captain." She stepped through the pressure doors and into the corridor. *Vixen* was always immaculate, everything gleaming, polished, and fit. But then, Tayrell Torgussen originally had been chosen for the Donovan mission because he was one of the best.

"Photonic com is ready," Torgussen told her as he took the lead and started up the companionway to Crew Deck. "Captain Abibi is expecting your communication."

"Excellent." Kalico gave the man a measuring glance. "How are things going with *Vixen*? It's been a while since we've talked."

"Ship's fit. Crew's doing well. We keep busy, Supervisor. And as long as we're busy discovering new things, being the first to record phenomena no human has ever seen, morale is good. But even then, having made the trip back to Donovan, we're ready for some R & R. Captain Abibi assures me that *Turalon*'s engineers could give our reactors a refit and refresh while they're here."

"Take whatever time you need." She lifted an eyebrow. "With *Turalon,* your people have some decisions to make. Think they'll stay or go back?"

The captain squinted as he considered. "We're going to start a massive data dump to *Turalon*'s computers as soon as they're in orbit. Everything we've recorded since *Ashanti* spaced. After that, I've got about a third of my people saying they'll opt to go home. Even knowing that the Solar System they knew is gone, they're ready for people, excitement, and the rush and buzz of Transluna, Earth, or Mars. A few are thinking about calling it quits for a while, want to go dirtside at PA and warm the benches at Inga's. Others want to prospect. And then I've got a core few who figure to make *Vixen* their home for the foreseeable future."

He paused, started to say something, and winced.

"Go ahead, Captain. We're long past any need to mince words."

Torgussen nodded, took a breath. "I want your permission to ship Dortmund Weisbacher back to Solar System on a medical discharge. I don't know the psychiatric term, but he's creep-freaking batshit crazy. Just hides in his room for the most part. I want him off my ship, but he's under your supervision."

"Done." Kalico nodded. "What else?"

He fixed her with serious eyes. "Supervisor, I'm going to need more crew to replace the losses. What are my chances of recruiting them from Abibi?"

Kalico ran a finger along the scar on her jaw. "We'll have a better idea of that after this call. For all I know, *Turalon* is carrying orders that relieve me of my authority and demand my arrest. With thirty marines on board to back it up, I could be apprehended and locked away in an instant. The game of Corporate Board politics is not played by those of faint heart and timid spirit."

"Seems to me that would be cutting their own throats. Not even those cherry-assed Boardmembers would be stupid enough to recall you after first *Turalon* and then *Ashanti* arrived with their holds bursting with rhodium, beryllium, platinum, and all those freaking big gem stones."

"Captain, you're a good man. Smart. Competent. And you probably think everyone is just like you. Well, you're wrong. Never bet against either human or Corporate stupidity. These VIPs *Turalon* is carrying could be a new governing body for Donovan."

Torgussen grunted. "How's that going to go down? Even with thirty marines?"

"About as well as last time," Kalico told him dryly as they walked out on Crew Deck and headed down the hall. "Even with thirty marines."

Torgussen hit the hatch, and Kalico strode into *Vixen*'s Astrogation Control. The room wasn't all that big, mostly consisting of the command staff's workstations, the walls covered with monitors and holo projectors. This was the ship's central nervous system, where *Vixen*'s AI interfaced with humans, decisions were made, and commands implemented.

Kalico stopped just past the hatch as First Officer Seesil Vacquillas jumped to her feet a half second before the rest of the command officers and banged off a crisp salute. For the occasion she and the rest wore their dress uniforms. A fact that brought a wry twist of amusement to Kalico's lips. She was dressed in quetzal-hide cloak and boots, wearing a chamois shirt, though it was a finely tailored one, and, for Donovanian standards, intricately embroidered with quetzals interspersed with squash blossoms.

"As you were," she called, striding over to the com chair. "Good to see you all, and my congratulations on your latest survey of Cap VII. Even for a gas giant, it's a stunning planet. I've only skimmed your report so far; I'll have to wait until my schedule settles down a bit before I attempt an in-depth read of the entire six thousand pages."

That brought laughter from around the room.

"Seesil?" Torgussen asked, "are we ready for transmission to *Turalon?*"

"Aye, Cap." Vacquillas turned back to her station, hands, eye movements, and slight nods cuing the system. "Supervisor? If you'll focus on the dot, we'll have photonic com linked to *Turalon* in just a couple of . . . Yes. Here we go."

Kalico watched as Captain Margo Abibi's image formed in the air before her. The captain's familiar features, head shaved bald, knowing tan eyes, and thin-pressed mouth. That old, slightly amused lift of the left eyebrow actually brought a smile to Kalico's lips.

"Hello, Margo. I see that you made it."

Even as she spoke, Abibi's expression went from professional to shocked. "Dear God, Supervisor! What happened to your face? I mean, how . . . ?"

"That's Donovan for you, Captain. From here on out, I'm going to look like a jigsaw puzzle. Despite how it looks, in the end, the mobbers got the worst of it."

Abibi shook her head. "Sorry, ma'am. My apologies for the outburst. I was out of place and shouldn't have said—"

Kalico raised a soothing hand. "Margo, forget it. No offense taken. I have to say, it's good to see you. Really good. I had every confidence that you would make the transition back to Solar System without incident. Not that I didn't have some sleepless nights despite that. That you signed on for another trip? You're one hell of a fine spacer, Captain."

She could see Abibi's tension drain away, that old wry smile bending the woman's lips. "Glad to hear that, ma'am." A pause. "I had some sleepless nights myself. Especially since I didn't hear from you prior to *Turalon* inverting symmetry. I hoped it wasn't just equipment failure."

Ah, of course. "Margo, you made the right call. No regrets. I'll fill you in on all the gory details over a chamois steak and a beer at Inga's once you're dirtside. It's the stuff of novels. But, in the meantime, I'd appreciate it if you could drop a privacy field. I'd like to talk candidly and off the record."

Abibi nodded, leaned forward, and said, "Already done, Supervisor."

Kalico got the nod from Vacquillas, could see the slight shimmer that formed in the air around her. "So, Margo," she began, "what's the full story? A Board Appointed Inspector General is aboard. Is there something I should know? Like to prepare to be arrested, relieved of duty, or replaced?"

Abibi's slight surprise was reassuring. "No, ma'am. Not yet. At least not to my knowledge. Though—den of vipers that the Board is—I'll not rule it out sometime in the future." She hesitated, expression straining. "But given that I'm carrying Suto Soukup? I don't know what his actual authority is. Mostly he sticks to his cabin with his Four."

"Given that he's a Board Appointed IG, he can do just about anything. OTR, Margo. Just between you and me. Any gossip?"

"Supervisor, his mission is officially listed as a fact-finding expedition. That the Board sent him is a measure of how seriously they take the situation on Donovan. But, to my knowledge, he has no Board directive. As to the rest of my bigwigs? The families are worried."

"Yeah. I got your list." Kalico frowned. "I know who they are, especially Falise. I've had dealings with her before. The others I had limited exposure to while I was Supervisor at Transluna. Are they traveling with a Board mandate? What's their official capacity?"

Abibi chuckled at some private amusement. "Supervisor, you've got to understand the situation back home. *Turalon*'s arrival was like kicking an anthill. Not just the wealth, but the revelations concerning the missing ships? The unsettling data from *Freelander*? That you had sold Port Authority? I was called into one board of inquiry after another to give testimony. Every data bank on the ship was down-loaded and scrutinized. Talk about security? My entire crew was bundled off to top secret locations, their every communication to friends and family monitored and censored. We were grilled up and down and back and forth. The Corporation tried to control the narrative, and they did a pretty good job at first. Lost colony found, and all that. But questions were being asked. The names of the re-turning transportees who had fulfilled contract had been released in the beginning, but family members hadn't seen or heard from them. Rumors started to circulate. Then the leaks started: 'Disaster at Capella III' and 'Rebellion at the lost colony.' Stuff like that."

"What about my selling Port Authority and its assets to the Don-ovanians? How did they react to that?"

"At first? Howls of outrage. At least until the plunder started to mount up and they really got to thinking about your log entries. Your justification that it would be easier to just establish another base rather than deal with a crazed bunch of libertarians. Some-where in there, you'd made a note that leaving them cut off to starve and be eaten by quetzals was a fitting end to their lunacy. I think your words went something to the effect of 'Sometimes it's more efficient to allow a cancerous lesion to die of its own stupidity rather than waste the blood, effort, and pain necessary to cut it out of the Corporate body.' And they had more than your word on it. They also had the returnees. Marston, Shankrah, Myers, and their hard-headed companions."

"How did they fare?"

"Just about as well as you'd expect a bunch of leather-clad, quetzal-killing Donovanians to integrate into calm, hyper-regulated, and boring Corporate life. They were all involved in contract litigation when we left. Most applied to ship back as soon as they heard *Turalon* was spacing for Donovan again."

"And?"

"They were turned down as being, and I quote, 'Too political.' Not my problem. The Corporation can figure out how to keep a lid on them. I was happy enough to watch the last of them pack up and walk off my ship." Abibi paused. "They backed your actions at Port Authority. About the titles and all."

"And I'll bet as the questions started to pile up, the families behind the Board started twisting their underwear into knots. Especially since I was a Taglioni tool who'd gone AWOL."

"Oh, yes." Abibi raised a finger. "You want to know why Falise Taglioni is waiting two decks down from where I'm sitting? And the others are watching her every move? They're the advance agents for their respective families. The movers and shakers in The Corporation were just starting to get a handle on how clap-trapping valuable our cargo was. Not to mention that our logs documented that we left plenty of containers behind. They had just started to evaluate the value of the gemstones, let alone how to get them into the economy, when *Ashanti*, deemed lost in space, pops in with even more wealth and a more electrifying story of terrifying years in space, cannibals, and it even has lost crewmen aboard from the missing *Vixen*. Not to mention news of Tamarland Benteen to boot!"

"Must have helped to get you and your crew off the hot seat."

"Damn straight!" Abibi grinned. "I love that term. Learned it here, you know? Anyhow, getting back to the story, that anthill *Turalon*'s arrival kicked? Compared to that, *Ashanti*'s popping back into Neptune's orbit was like a stick of high explosive that blew everything open. Your old pal, Miko Taglioni, backed by Fabio, and with the support of the Grunnels, Suhartos, and the sudden interest of the Radceks, got us fast-tracked for a turnaround for Donovan." Abibi's eyebrow lifted suggestively. "After being locked down in virtual house arrest, we jumped at the chance to get the hell away from Solar System."

"And the thirty marines?" Kalico asked. "What's their mission?"

"To protect and support the colony," Abibi said dryly. "To ensure the peace, orderly conduct, prosperity, and the common good. All the usual claptrap. I'll send you the file for your records, but I think they're supposed to be more for show. A reminder that The

Corporation is still a serious player on Donovan. The problem is, this was thrown together so fast, not to mention that no one knew what to expect when they arrived, so they didn't get a specific set of orders."

"Whose command are they under?"

"Colonel Stanley Creamer. He's cozied up with Chad Grunnel. Figures that when the music stops, the Grunnels are going to be his ticket to a happy and prosperous retirement. Personally, I think the guy is a marionette."

"Stanley Creamer?" Kalico asked. "As in the major who blew Cap Taggart's cover during that raid on rogue miners out in the Belt? They made him a colonel?"

"That's him."

"Doesn't make sense," Kalico mulled to herself. "Thirty marines, a mixture of high-ranking family members, but no Board mandate. I was afraid that you were bringing a new Supervisor to replace me and orders for my arrest."

Abibi's smile was wistful, her gaze going distant. "For the time being, The Corporation—and especially the Board—is scrambling to figure out what it all means. They've got a problem. One typified by *Freelander, Vixen,* and the other missing ships. They've seen the recordings of *Freelander*'s temple of bones and Jem Orten's shattered skull where he blew a hole in it with his own pistol."

"Yeah, well, *Freelander* has gotten even spookier in the years since you were here. No wonder they're scared." She chuckled. "Hell, I was, if you'll recall."

"Supervisor, you weren't on this ship when we just popped out four months ahead of schedule. You didn't feel that building terror, let alone see the expressions as my people waited until the astrogation officer verified our position." Abibi had never looked as grim as she did when she said, "If we hadn't been in Capella system? If we'd been somewhere out in the black? These decks would have run red with blood. *Freelander* would have seemed a cakewalk compared to the carnage on *Turalon*."

"We do what we have to, Margo." Kalico told her.

Abibi was giving her a sober appraisal. "You're not the same woman I watched step on that long-ago shuttle to head dirtside before we spaced home."

Kalico gave the woman a dry smile. "No. I'm not. Donovan has made me into something different."

"Well, God help you, Kalico, because I'm bringing you a ship-load of trouble."

11

Kylee Simonov stood in the back of the room, out of the way, and leaned against the wall, arms crossed. A single lantern hung from a hook in the ceiling; its flame wavered as it cast light over the white-plastered room. Tip lay supine atop the heavy wooden table in the center. His eyes kept flickering and darting, his dirt-smudged face working in pain. Sweat—despite the cool night—popped from Tip's sun-bronzed skin, and he kept gasping, panting for breath. Then he'd swallow hard.

The thought that Tip was dying opened the floodgates. The room faded, replaced by a vision of Mundo, of Capella's hot light burning down on the dark soil. Of Talina crouched over Rocket's bloody body. Of the pain, the impossibility, of the hole that tore a gaping hollow in Kyle's gut.

Everyone I love dies.

In that instant, she was back, crawling into Rocket's grave, wrapping herself around his body. Letting herself fall ever deeper inside. Remembering how she'd melded herself with Rocket, become quetzal somewhere deep in her mind, to the point that nothing human had remained. Not even when she was standing in the forest, watching Flash and Leaper kill Rebecca and Shantaya.

"I brought you back," Rocket told her.

And now Kylee was losing Tip. Grief sucked toilet water. Quetzals were so lucky they didn't feel it. Or hadn't. Rocket did. Flute now did. Maybe sharing human-tainted TriNA wasn't such a good thing for quetzals.

At the table, Madison Briggs bent over her son, scissors cutting away the last of Tip's trousers, leaving him naked below the waist. As the cloth fell away, the extent of the injury could be seen. Madison sucked a hard breath, body tensing.

Kylee's stomach flipped. No wonder it smelled so bad. She clamped her teeth, taking in the swollen and blackened mess that had been Tip's leg. In the meat of the calf, a scabbed-over wound could be seen; it was leaking pus around the edges. The knee and thigh were so enlarged the leg looked more like an over-inflated sausage than a limb.

"Dear God," Madison whispered, bracing one arm on the table. She clamped her slanted eyes closed, her tall body tense as a stressed spring.

Flute's big head stuck nearly a meter into the room where he filled the doorway. There just wasn't enough space for him inside. His three eyes gleamed in the lantern light, his frill of a collar expanded; spots of teal interspersed with bruised purple, communicating his concern. From down inside, a clicking could be heard. The sound he made when he was worried.

"Tip?" Madison demanded, leaning down. "What did this? Was it a skewer? A bem?"

"Don't know," Tip managed through clenched jaws. "I was climbing. On a rocky slope. Steep. Like a cliff. Thing bit me. Through the pants. Ate into my leg."

"What did it look like?" Kylee asked. "A sort of sidewinder or—"

"No." Tip's too-thin face worked against the pain. "Like a tube. Eating into my calf. Pulled my knife. Stabbed it. Cut it in two. But it just kept eating its way inside."

He grunted at the pain as Madison started pressing on his swollen skin. As she did she said, "I'm feeling for it, Tip. Hang in there."

To Kylee's disgust, she could see coagulated blood pooling and slipping around under the too-thin skin. And the smell—as the wound really began to drain—almost overpowered Kylee's stomach. Given the room's confines, how Madison kept from reeling and throwing up was beyond her. But then, Madison was one of the toughest women she'd ever known.

As Madison's fingers pressed down around the knee, Tip threw his head back and screamed, bloodcurdling, his body bucking on the table.

"Something's in there," Madison managed through gritted teeth.

"Guess we got to take it out, huh?" Kylee endured a sensation, like an itch in the roots of her teeth. Her stomach continued to tickle with nausea. This was Tip, damn it. Didn't matter that they'd been fighting; she wanted to do a little screaming herself.

"Hey," Chaco's voice came from outside. "Let me in, beast."

Flute backed out far enough that Chaco could duck past the hulking jaws and into the light. Chaco Briggs was a muscular man in his mid-forties. Sharp dark eyes, a mane of sandy hair that hung down just past his collar, and a dark and thick beard gave him what Talina had once confided to Kylee as "lady killer" good looks.

The story was that tall, dark, statuesque Madison was considered to be the most beautiful woman on Donovan. That once upon a time, a too-ardent suitor—a good friend of Supervisor Clemenceau's—had been determined to possess her, that he'd ignored any warning to leave her alone. According to legend, Chaco had used the man's own knife to kill him, and he and Madison had fled Port Authority before Clemenceau could have them arrested. As Wild Ones, they'd built their marvelous farm and mine, bore and raised a passel of children, some of whom they'd buried along the way, and flourished in the aftermath.

Chaco made a face as he took in the ruination of Tip's leg. Looked like he wanted to puke. "We know what happened?"

"Some creature," Madison told him wearily. "From the way Tip was talking, it wasn't anything he recognized. Something in the cliffs. Part of it's still in his leg. Probably rotting."

Kylee fought back tears. If Tip died. . . . Fuck! Why was it always someone she loved?

Madison choked back a sob, added, "This is more than we can do. Not here."

"I just got off the radio with Two Spot. He raised Dek. He's flying out as soon as he can get the plane off the ground. He should be here by daybreak."

"It's storming out there, not to mention the middle of the night," Madison said woodenly, her almond-dark eyes on the point of tears.

"This is Dek we're talking about." Chaco placed a comforting hand on his wife's arm. "And you know how he feels about the kids."

"So, what's Dek going to do?" Kylee asked. "He bringing Dr. Turnienko with him?"

Chaco gave her a sober look, then glanced again at Tip's leg. "Seeing this?" He shook his head. "I figured it was bad. Kylee, I know how you feel about PA, but Tip's only chance is in the hospital. Just like it was yours once."

"Sure. Right. In more ways than one, it was the end of my world."

"But you walked again," Madison reminded. "That was then. And we're not Mundo, not to mention that it's a different time and world."

Rocket's memory flashed in her mind. The sight of his bullet-shattered body lying on the dirt at Mundo. How he looked when Talbot and Talina laid his corpse in the grave. How it felt to crawl into that gaping hole and press her body against Rocket's cold corpse.

Kylee bit her lip, thought she saw Tip's swollen leg pulsate as if something inside it was writhing. "Those people wanted to kill Rocket. One of them finally did. I *hate* them all."

Flute made a gurgling where he filled the door. His colors had turned to teal mixed with yellow and black: worry and fear.

Madison spun around, bent down to pin Kylee with her piercing glare. "My son is *dying*. Now, I don't know what went down between the two of you, but you and he . . ." She gestured futility. "God, I thought you were inseparable."

Kylee pursed her lips, nodded. "Yeah. My fault. That he left, I mean. He wasn't ready."

"Ready for what?" Chaco asked, shifting, looking sick and on the point of tears.

"To become a man," Kylee whispered.

"What the hell does *that* mean?" Madison's expression had gone volcanic in a way Kylee had never seen.

"Means . . ." Tip whispered from the table, "that part of me still wanted to be a child."

"You're sixteen!" Chaco thundered. "You got a right to be a child."

Madison kept giving Kylee that penetrating look, as if seeing down into Kylee's soul. "No, Chaco," she said. "He doesn't."

"You don't know . . . how hard . . ." Tip paused to wince and stifle a cry.

"What's hard?" Chaco stepped over to take his son's hand.

Tip's throat worked. "How hard it is to be worthy. Kylee's perfect. Remarkable."

"Am not," Kylee cried, knotting her hands.

"Yeah," Tip rasped, a flicker of smile fading on his quivering lips. He fixed her with pain-laced eyes. What she called quetzal eyes, enlarged, like hers. "You know so much. Been so many places. Smart. So fucking competent. It's like . . . I'm just . . . never . . ."

Kylee felt herself reel. So much falling into place.

Madison was still giving her that look.

Kylee forced herself off the wall, walked over, and took Tip's free hand. Chaco still clung to the other. She was aware of Chaco's hot and questioning eyes as she looked down into Tip's face and asked, "If I'm so goddamned smart, how'd I end up hurting you so badly? You're my . . . What? *Friend* doesn't cover it. *Companion* sounds formal. *Lover* isn't comprehensive enough. I'm trying to say that you're the only person I can ever be comfortable and safe with. We're two parts of a whole, Tip. I'm just . . ." She shook her head as she stared down into his eyes. Felt the tears slip past to trace down her cheeks. "Don't die on me."

Tip tried to give her that familiar lopsided grin that made things all right. Lost it as his leg trembled. Pain made a mask of his face. Then he caught enough of a breath to say, "Be here when I get back, huh? We'll try it again."

"Nope." She took a deep breath, fought against the smell from his draining leg, and told him, "I'm not letting you down again. I'll be with you the whole way." She felt her heart skip. "Even in Port Authority."

Flute made a tittering sound, his head cocking slightly.

"Not you," Kylee told him. "They'd kill you. And I'd have to kill them. Means Tip would have to kill what's left of them after they killed me for killing them. See how complicated things would get if you came along?"

alise was in her quarters, reclining in the pathetic excuse that spacers on *Turalon* called a bed. These had been her quarters for the last nineteen months: a featureless sialon cubicle little bigger than a Hong Kong prison cell. Her staff resided in stacked berths in the adjoining cabin. The room was furnished with a fold-out desk and chair—meant to maximize space—a closet, and a small bathroom with a shower, sink, and toilet. She had added her wardrobe, several duraplast crates containing essentials, and a holovid that covered one wall. The rest of her belongings were locked away in a container down in the cargo hold.

Falise shifted on the hard mattress, made a face. She scanned the reports on the projected holo where it hung in the air barely an arm's length before her. She wore a comfortable shift made of luminous soffiber, a fabric that caressed her skin. She had her hair fixed in shimmering golden-streaked coils that contrasted to her brown skin. The scrolling information she was reading might have been the stuff of lunacy, all of it forwarded by the woman named Yvette Dushane. Dushane was listed in the *Turalon* records as one of the leaders, or "triumvirate" of Port Authority. She signed her messages only as "Yvette." No title was attached, no formal term of address or office.

Falise froze the display, glanced at where Clarice sat cross-legged in the chair beside the rudimentary foldout desk. The woman's blue-black African skin had a sheen from the saffron oil that she'd rubbed on her body. Clarice's facial features had been sculpted to exactly match those of the ancient Egyptian queen Nefertiti. A living reproduction of the famous bust. Her true value, however, was in her implants, training, and information-processing skills. Clarice had been raised from birth to serve at Falise's side.

Her menial servants, Fig and Phredo, huddled by one of the du-raplast crates in the corner, trying to be small as they added light-thread adornment to the side panels in her transparent shoes. The ones she wore on formal occasions.

Falise indicated the holo. "According to this, we are to land at Port Authority. We will be given an orientation and provided with quarters." She paused. "You have files on Yvette?"

Clarice nodded. Her dark eyes barely flickered as she accessed the information. "Yvette Dushane, female. Occupation: data tech. Was implicated in organizing resistance during Clemenceau's supervision. She is in her fifties, arrived what they call Third Ship. Husband: Hansen Dushane, killed by skewer. Yvette had not remarried as of *Turalon's* last spacing. Her last proficiency score, taken twenty-nine years ago, was sixty-two. No children of record. Last known activity included administration of titles and deeds after Board Supervisor Aguila granted the transfer in exchange for financial compensation."

Falise looked up as Ednund entered the room—a covered plate and freefall cup on a towel-covered tray. She called him her "blond Adonis" for his two-meter-tall, perfectly formed body. With his alabaster-white skin, his golden curly hair, chiseled jaw, and sparkling eyes, he made a striking valet. She'd designed him as the perfect complement to Clarice. His light to Clarice's dark, his violence and action in contrast to her intelligence and evaluation. Given their duties, both had been trained in social skills, etiquette, dancing, sexual excellence, athletics, the arts, and of course, espionage.

Ednund was dressed professionally, wearing synthalac trousers that shimmered with each step and a white V-cut blouse with black piping and creamy white panels that rose high over each shoulder. Silk slippers clad his feet. He greeted her with a smile that displayed perfect teeth. "I brought you the evening fare, my lady. Each serving taken by myself from the common mess to ensure its safety."

"More green goo?" Falise asked as Ednund folded out the stand and set the tray within reach of her bed.

"Afraid so." Ednund waved around at the featureless sialon room. "No less dreary than this. Now, with escape coming in but days, we can once again talk about what a prison this is."

Falise pointed to the scar in the ceiling. "They took out a wall, you'll recall. This supposedly spacious eighteen-square-meter opulence was originally *two* living quarters. Down on the Transportee Deck, they 'hot bunk.' Rotate bed space. Sleep in shifts." She made a dismissive gesture. "I can't imagine what *that* kind of existence is all about."

"Nor can we, Lady," Clarice told her. "However, from my study, and from the reports made by the returnees from *Turalon*'s last transit from Capella III, we had best not be raising our hopes for lodging in Port Authority."

Falise tapped at her chin, gaze on the holo frozen before her. "Why land us at Port Authority? What is Kalico trying to prove? She has Corporate Mine, Southern Diggings, and the Maritime Unit must have a community somewhere. Why put us down in the midst of a bunch of lunatic barbarians? This reeks of some subtle political slight that I can't fathom."

Ednund set the tray beside her and indicated the foot of the bed. "May I?"

Falise gave him a nod. "We're being kept in the dark. Derek hasn't returned a single communication. That's to be expected. News of my arrival undoubtedly has my brother pouting and petulant. It's his way of punishing me. I can hear him now, 'Oh, so Father is sending *little sister* out to check on me? Well, I don't have to give her so much as the time of day.' Making me go to him is just Derek's childish way of trying to put me in my place."

Ednund—who'd always been spurned by Derek as her "boy toy"—barely granted a shrug.

Clarice, however, said, "Derek's silence might be forgiven. The Board Supervisor's however, is a different thing."

Falise pursed her lips, nodded. "That Kalico hasn't extended so much as a courtesy call? To a Taglioni, no less? And given Miko's sponsorship and patronage in the past? I call that the equivalent of a slap in the face."

Ednund said, "I am told it's the same with the others. This will be counted against her as a major affront."

Clarice, hands clasped behind her, tilted her chin back, eyes half-lidded in thought. "I can compute various permutations on the data. The highest probability is that Kalico knows that IG Soukup is aboard and expects to be dismissed from her position and is scrambling to destroy evidence, establish a defense, remove conspirators, and hide malfeasance before receiving the official notification of her removal."

Ednund added, "The only reason she'd expect that would be if she were truly involved in something remarkably corrupt."

"Like signing over all the Corporate assets on the planet?" Falise reminded. "Her original Board mandate was to investigate Capella III, determine what happened to the missing ships, to reestablish order or otherwise secure the colony. While she couldn't know what the Board reaction would be in response to her selling off Port Authority, she has to know that sending first *Turalon* and second, *Ashanti* back, each ship literally dripping with wealth, was going to buy her a certain amount of good will."

Ednund, a faint smile on his face, said, "Then why hasn't she sent so much as a message welcoming us to Capella III? The cunning and calculating woman you had me bed should be welcoming us with an almost arrogant pride."

Falise shifted her gaze to him. "Yes, I remember detailing that assignment to you. Wanted to know what threat she posed for the rest of us after Miko took her under his wing."

"At the time she was still Board Supervisor of Transluna," Ednund told her, "my assessment was that she would most likely be seated on the Board within a few years. She was that capable."

"Her proficiency score?" Falise asked.

"Ninety-eight," Clarice said. "Remarkable."

"Then, despite the IG, let us assume that Kalico isn't scrambling around covering her ass and destroying evidence. That sounds too clumsy for someone of her competence." Falise tapped at her chin again as she stared at the holo. "What are our alternate hypotheses?"

Clarice said, "A viable alternative would be that she's playing a strategic game with someone on Capella III, perhaps the triumvirate. That we're being used as pawns in some power struggle on the planet. Which might also explain why we're to be housed at Port Authority."

Ednund told her, "From Miguel Galluzzi's report, I got the impression that it's the only place on the planet that has the infrastructure to put us up. Although he also said it was more like a junkyard than a town. And Corporate Advisor Benj Begay called it something even worse."

Clarice—obviously accessing the report—filled in. "He called it, 'a dilapidated series of hovels, abandoned equipment, and squalor unequaled in the galaxy. Not to mention a den of iniquity, sloth, and slovenly-dressed pretenders to the human species.'"

Falise frowned. "So, where does that leave us? If we accept that Kalico Aguila is still the clever and cunning political creature we once knew, what does she gain by putting us in this so-called trash heap of a town? Why not at her Corporate Mine, or better yet, at the Maritime Unit with its modern facilities?"

"Sometimes people change," Ednund reminded. "Who knows what calamity or trauma might have befallen her in the years since *Turalon* spaced?"

Clarice, again accessing her data, nodded. "In the records there is mention of her barely surviving an attack by flying predators, executing deserters, almost dying in the forest. Perhaps she suffered a head injury? Some infection that has affected her abilities?" A beat. "Or another possibility: She might just be exhausted and depressed after this long absence from civilization. She might not even care."

"Also possible." Falise reached for the tray, taking the cup of tea. Rations had been lifted, *Turalon* having shaved four months off the transit. She could now drink all the oolong tea she wanted. "But, forewarned as we are, I want us to be fast on our feet. To expect anything." She glanced at Ednund. "Kalico may or may not be a problem. If we're right that she's mentally impaired, can you slip back into her good graces?"

"If my Lady wills."

"We'll see," Falise thinned her eyes. "After all these years of 'slovenly pretenders to the human species' she might welcome a talented and charming male such as yourself into her confidence and good graces."

"And if she's sworn off males," Clarice told her, "I can supply female company. As I recall, she was never particular to any single brand."

"Always an option," Falise agreed.

"Be nice if Derek could give us some guidance in the matter." Ednund pulled up a knee. "But Kalico so loathed him, I doubt they are on speaking terms."

"Everyone loathed my brother," Falise told him. "Mostly because he was one of the most despicable human beings to ever live." A fact that had more than once served her well. Falise had been able to play the tortured martyr raised in her vile brother's shadow.

She looked at her two servants and gestured in the direction of the holo. "Here's what we have to remember: Once we're on the planet, the gloves come off. Cinque, Chad, and Bart will be setting the ground game for their families. If we have *any* advantage, it's the understanding that for the first time in our lives, there will be no Corporate oversight."

"What about IG Soukup?" Ednund asked.

Falise gave him a dismissive wave. "What's between the families has never been of Corporate concern. We do nothing that might violate the rules when it comes to Corporate assets."

Clarice said, "From my evaluation, Chad will be the most formidable given his influence over Colonel Creamer."

"I concur," Falise agreed. "We remove any threat Chad may pose first thing." She glanced up at Clarice. "You have been maintaining your ties with Charlotte?"

"She is on board, Lady." A quiver of Clarice's lips was her only hint of satisfaction. "She understands her role as well as the opportunities." A beat. "Especially after what happened to Kramer."

"Second?" Ednund asked.

"Bart." She nodded at the rightness of it. "He'll be holding a grudge. One doesn't forgive the compromising of a valet. Not the way I took him. And right under Bart's nose."

"That leaves Cinque," Ednund said.

"He already aligned himself with me once this trip. Depending upon what we find dirtside, he might again." She smiled. "And he desires Charlotte. We will soon know if he's vulnerable."

"No rules." Ednund thoughtfully stared at the featureless sialon overhead. "I think I'm going to like Port Authority."

13

A light rain was falling as Talina made her way down Port Authority's main avenue. Rattled and upset as she was, the last thing she craved was going home to an empty dome with no one but the quetzals in her mind for company. She needed a distraction, anything but thinking about Dek, flying across all those kilometers in the rainy dark. She was going to be jumpy as a tree clinger until Two Spot called in with confirmation that Dek had arrived safely.

And then there was Best Pass. Dangerous even in the light of day. No, don't even think it.

"Hope he dies," Demon spat the words.

"Eat shit and die, you little creep," Talina growled under her breath. "At least while he's flying, Dek doesn't have to put up with your trash, you freaky slug sucker."

She could feel Rocket's presence on her shoulder, as if the imaginary quetzal was nodding in agreement.

The few streetlights that were still working cast a yellow glow, the misty rain slanting through cones of illumination. This was what qualified as the business district: the assay office, the gunsmith's, the glass works, the boot shop, and foundry being the most prominent. Just past them, she could see the circle of light at Inga's door. Even across the distance she could recognize Hofer and Cian Gatlin as they stomped the water off their boots; their slickers and rain hats were shining in the light. But for the fact that Hofer was the best construction boss on the planet, he would have been a complete waste of skin. Gatlin, a nice guy, was the local pipefitter.

She watched them enter, wondered for a moment if this was another night that Hofer would start trouble that she'd have to finish. For the last couple of months, he'd had been unusually mild-mannered. That was the thing about Hofer. He'd gone through phases like that in the past, and just about the time that everyone started to consider him to be a normal human being, he'd blow a gasket, and someone—usually Talina—would have to knock him half silly to make him behave again.

Never a dull moment.

Down in her belly, Demon shifted, hissing as if in anticipation. He'd been affecting her digestion ever since she'd found evidence of Whitey out at Liz's claim. Like he knew Whitey was about to try something. But what?

"Want to spill it, you piece of shit? Tell me what he's up to?"

But silence was her only answer.

She stamped her way up to the door, tilted her hat so the water drained off the brim, and shook her quetzal-hide cape to shed the moisture. Stepping into the foyer, she found the floor muddy and wet, the raucous sounds of conversation, too-loud laughter, and the musical clink of plates and glassware rising from below.

She took her usual moment at the top of the stairs, cataloging faces and attitudes. Hofer and Gatlin had already made it to the bar, gesturing for Inga's attention. All of the usual suspects were present—most sitting in their accustomed places at the long chabacho-wood tables.

When Talina turned her attention to the far right of the bar, she arched an eyebrow. Her chair, of course, remained empty, but Shig Mosadek was bent in earnest conversation with Kalico Aguila. And, to Talina's surprise, huddled with them was Allison Chomko, un-mistakable with her platinum blond locks piled high and the form-fitting dress that emphasized every curve. Even from above, Talina could see that the entire clientele was wondering what that meeting might be about.

Talina trotted down the wooden steps, quetzal-hide boots shoot-ing prismatic rainbows of color as they hammered on the treads. People glanced her way, then back at Shig, Allison, and Kalico. Figuring—wrongly—that this was some momentous occasion.

Talina answered the greeting calls, waved, and nodded to those who dipped a head her direction. In some ways, it was almost like the old days before she'd become a freak infected by quetzal TriNA. She'd made it down the central aisle, was headed down the bar when Hofer turned, drink in hand, and met her eyes. She gave him her "we-going-to-have-trouble-tonight" look, to which he replied with a slight shake of the head and a guilty grin.

Talina gestured with a thumbs up, made her way to her chair, and unslung her rifle from beneath her cape. Placing it butt-first on the floor, barrel leaned in its usual position against the bar, she climbed into her chair.

Shig, Kalico, and Allison watched, the question in their eyes.

"Yeah, Dek's off," she told them. "Took Wejee, Cal, and Ko for security while they escorted him to his airplane. Knowing that Whitey's in the area? That's guaranteed to stand your short hairs on end."

Kalico arched her eyebrow, the one with the mobber scar running through it. "I figured you'd be riding shotgun. Flying alone? Not to mention in the dead of night?"

Talina took a deep breath, gestured to Inga for a whiskey and a stout, and turned to look at the others. "This is Tip Briggs we're talking about. Now, if it was Kylee?"

"We'd be taking the A-7 and marines in armor," Kalico replied.

Talina shrugged. "Dek's got a weak spot for both of those kids. Something more than a bonding with Flute, shared TriNA. This is lineage. It goes back to some event that happened out in the bush a couple of years back." She slapped the bar. "As for me? There wasn't room. Dek figured that with Tip in that bad a shape, he'd have the boy, Chaco or Madison, and Kylee aboard."

"His airplane is only built for four," Shig reminded them as he fingered his half a glass of wine.

"So, here I am," Talina told them. "Waiting for Two Spot to either tell me Dek's safe, or making sure I'm in a place where I can wheel around and call 'Who's up for a rescue mission in the middle of the night?'"

"You'd have plenty of takers," Allison agreed, where she leaned forward over her glass of whiskey.

"That's my hope," Talina told them as Inga brought Talina's mug full of stout and a glass with two fingers of amber spirits.

"My tab," Allison called.

"Thanks," Talina told her. "Didn't mean to interrupt your little confab here."

"Ad hoc update," Kalico told her. "I'm just back from *Vixen*. Had Torgussen patch me through to *Turalon* on the photonic com. I wanted to have a chat with Margo Abibi."

"What does the good captain say?" Talina lifted the whiskey and sipped. This was one of Inga's better batches; she'd let it set in charred aquajade casks for a couple of years.

"The good news is that these thirty marines aren't accompanied by a replacement supervisor, nor is Margo aware of any orders regarding changes in administration for Donovan. The bad news is that Board Appointed Inspector General Suto Soukup is arriving on a fact-finding mission. The salient part is that he's Board Appointed. Means they want him to find out just what exactly is going on. How everything works. Who is responsible for what. And if Corporate laws are being broken. And if, in his opinion, anything is amiss, the Board has granted him the authority to arrest and detain anyone for a violation."

"We're going to have to think about that," Talina said, glancing down the bar to where Iji and Mgumbe broke out in hysterical laughter. "What else did I miss?"

"I was just finishing with Abibi's report on The Corporation." Kalico glanced Talina's way. "You've heard Dek and me talk about it? Well, it worked out just like we thought it would. *Turalon*'s arrival sent a tremor through The Corporation, and *Ashanti*'s unheralded appearance was like a 9.5 quake through the Board itself."

Kalico glanced at Allison. "Dan Wirth stepped off *Ashanti* wearing his rhodium-chain vest, and in his own charming way, has chucked the status quo on its head. They're trying to keep a lid on it, but the story's too big. There will be a reckoning."

"At least Dan isn't on *Turalon*." Allison looked up, her crystal-blue eyes half-lidded. "But he will be back. Someday. I wonder if it will be as a Boardmember or a fugitive traveling under an assumed name?"

"Wish he'd stay. I was always afraid I'd have to kill him," Talina said thoughtfully.

"You weren't the only one," Allison agreed, lifting her whiskey glass and tilting it in Talina's direction in mock toast.

Shig, eyes thoughtful, rolled his wineglass on its base, watching the red fluid swirl. "So there's chaos back in Solar System. Nevertheless, we have an Inspector General with a reputation for taking down bad guys. Not to mention a Grunnel—who Kalico informs us is tight with the marines—a Radcek, a Suharto, and finally Dek's sister. All most important personages."

"And each one is going to be a pain in the ass." Kalico took a sip of her whiskey.

"Radcek I've heard of," Allison said thoughtfully. "Tam Benteen hated old man Calypso. What's this latest one like?"

"Name's Bartolome. A cousin three generations removed," Kalico told her. "Even when I knew him, he was called 'Bad Bart' by both admirers and detractors." The scarred eyebrow went up again. "Ali, I know you like playing with dangerous men, but keep Bart, Cinque Suharto, and sweet and slippery Chad at arm's length. I know you did what you had to with Benteen, but he was a lone fugitive. Didn't come with powerful family backing like these guys."

Allison nodded, expression pinched. "Each of us has done distasteful things. Has sacrificed, risked, and barely survived." She jerked a thumb at the room behind her. "So have they. I'm not going looking for trouble, Kalico, but like you, I'm not going to let any candy-butt Corporate family sweep in and confiscate what I've given so much to achieve." She glanced from face to face. "I assume we're agreed on that?"

"Quite so," Shig said mildly. "Which for the moment, leaves thirty marines."

"Who—and compliments of Abibi, I've seen their orders—are under Corporate command. Not to mention that their commanding officer is Colonel Stanley Creamer." Kalico was watching Talina, saw her start. "Yeah, that Creamer. The one behind the fuckup at Beemer Station."

Talina grunted her disgust.

"You know him?" Shig asked.

Talina said, "He was Cap Taggart's CO. The one who got Cap busted and sent here on *Turalon*. I got the impression the guy was a Corporate ass-kisser."

"Abibi thinks the same of him," Kalico added. "Gives me an angle to play."

Shig had barely tasted his wine; now he set the glass back on the bar. "You know, don't you, that we've reached a turning point."

"How's that?" Allison turned her sharp blue gaze Shig's way.

"Dek may not have known it, but by arranging Dan Wirth's passage back to Solar System, he forced the Board's hand, especially the Chairman's." Shig glanced at Kalico. "Your old patron understood exactly what Dan Wirth represented and the kind of danger he, and others like him, pose for The Corporation. A danger that, to a lesser extent, Lee Marston and the rest of the returnees also pose. But they could be kept under control. Wirth is a whole different problem for the Taglionis. He's under their protection, and they're not only getting a share of Dan's wealth, but full exposure to the extent of it. Better yet, too many people are in the loop. Dan's not the sort of guy you can keep under wraps. He'd come off like a shooting flare, burning too brightly and obnoxiously, and giving off too much smoke and sparks. Within a week of his stepping off *Ashanti*, every family and Boardmember knew that some psychopathic tavern keeper, freshly returned from Donovan and under Taglioni protection, was the richest man in Solar System."

"Why is that a turning point?" Talina asked, her mind half on Dek. He should be approaching the Wind Mountains about now.

Down in her belly, Demon was raptly enjoying her anxiety.

Kalico ran a finger down the scar on her jaw. "Because wealth is power. Miko's the Board Chairman, Dan's his ward. I got the appointment as the Board Supervisor on Donovan through Taglioni influence, and everyone is still reeling at the wealth Corporate Mine just sent back on the last two ships. Not since the days of Calypso Radcek has so much power been invested in one family. It's been a year and seven months since Margo Abibi was so embroiled in the political mess on Transluna that she moved heaven and earth to get back on *Turalon* and chance death in space to get away from it all."

"A lot can happen in a year and seven months," Talina agreed.

Kalico shrugged, gaze distant. "For all we know, they're tearing themselves apart back there. But one thing's for certain: All of the families will have aligned against the Taglionis. Even if it meant civil war."

"That is exactly why I said that Dek bought us time," Shig agreed. "As bad as it is to have IG Soukup landing in our midst, just think what it would have been like if a new Board-appointed Supervisor with control of those marines, and a Board mandate to take control of the planet, had just popped in."

"The end of everything," Allison said softly.

"Or a fast evacuation to the bush," Shig replied.

"Maybe," Talina told them with a shrug. "Let's not forget: We always have an ally. One that, no matter what they might have heard, they still can't conceive of?"

"Oh?" Allison asked.

"Donovan," Talina and Kalico replied in unison.

14

The forest below looked like piled billows of green. Kylee sat in the airplane's back seat beside Madison and tried not to worry about Tip, hard as that was. He kept groaning where he hunched in the seat up front. And there was the smell given off by that oozing wound. She pressed her head to the glass as she watched the plane's shadow race across the forest below. It seemed to alternately leap, squirt, and dart across the high canopy as it crossed higher treetops and dropped into the depths.

Forest. Endless. Foreboding. And snaking through it all was the winding Best River that ran westward from the uplift of the Wind Mountains. The quetzal part of her brain remained mute, huddled around itself, eyes closed, and walled off in panic.

Up front, Tip stiffened and gave off a groan. But he'd definitely been better since Dek brought some of Dya's blue nasty-based anesthetic. A fingertip's worth placed on Tip's tongue had brought him a modicum of relief from the pain. She ground her teeth, aching for him. Wishing she could do something, anything, to ease his suffering.

Kylee blinked against the deep-seated anticipation of disaster; the quetzal instinct down in her bones being to cut her losses—let Tip die. The quetzal instinct was to kill him herself in order to end the suffering. In contrast, her human reaction was to do everything in her power to urge him to fight, to beat this thing.

Quetzals didn't think of death in the same way humans did. To them, it was a termination of one existence—but one through which their memories and knowledge would be preserved by means of the TriNA molecules ingested and passed down the generations. To a human, death was forever. A cataclysmic event, after which a person—and all that they had learned and experienced—vanished. Gone. Death tore a hole in the soul that could never be filled.

So, what will I do if Tip dies?

Kylee was sick of death. Rocket, Rebecca, Shantaya, Flash, Mark Talbot, her mother, all people she'd loved that had been ripped out of her life with finality. It was the abruptness of the loss that always left her staggering. Aching. Howling at the injustice of it.

On impulse, she leaned forward between the seats, took Tip's hand, and called, "You hang in there for me. I *need* you. Understand? I love you."

Funny it had taken her so long to tell him that.

Madison, in the seat beside her, was giving her a knowing look from behind that mask-like expression she'd adopted. She did that to hide her worry and fear. It might work when it came to others, but with her augmented senses, Kylee could smell it: a subtle shift in Madison's normal scent.

Kylee tried to will strength into Tip's cold hand.

Tip had always just been there. Never flashy like the men Talina had loved. Just . . . solid. Reliable. Like a human kind of pillar. There was a lot to be said for that. Made her wonder if there was something wrong with her that she needed to have people die before she could figure out that she loved them?

She bit her lips, squeezed his hand one last time, and sat back in the seat.

"How's he doing?" Madison asked, the pinch behind her slanted dark eyes. "You can tell, can't you?"

Kylee leaned close, whispered, "He's dying. System's poisoned by that thing in his leg."

The simple declarative act, the saying of it, brought tears to her eyes. She blinked, turned her head away to stare through the window as Dek flew them over the angled lines of hogsbacks and climbed to gain enough altitude to fly through Best Pass.

So, the only hope was that Dr. Raya Turnienko might be able to save him.

In Port Authority.

A place Kylee had sworn never to go. Among a people she hated with all of her heart and soul. The people who'd have killed Rocket. One of whom *had* killed him in the end.

She wanted them all dead.

Locked in hollow numbness, Kylee barely registered the jutting walls of rock, or the jagged-edged canyon they flew through. This was Best Pass. She should have been awed by the soaring walls of stone with their twisted strata and exposed veins of metals. Instead, she watched dully as the airplane pitched and bucked in the high winds that curled and eddied in the narrow cleft. The turbulence scared the quetzal part of her into catatonia.

Then they were through, jetting over into the forested and jumbled geology that gave way to the Blood Mountains. Not that Kylee had seen them until now, but Donovan's geography had been beaten into her head from a young age.

"It's the quetzal TriNA, isn't it?" Madison asked softly. "That's what's keeping him alive, right?"

Kylee nodded. "But he's losing. That thing is rotting inside his leg."

"Does he have a chance if Raya Turnienko can take it out?"

Kylee shrugged. "I don't know. She fixed my broken hip and leg. Made it so that I could walk again." But it had come at such a terrible price. What was it going to cost them this time?

Dek's plane sailed out over the rumpled-looking crater bottom, the forest here scrubbier, dotted with trees and mixed with brush. As they encountered patchy clouds, the land was stippled with shadow, the topography threaded by small streams.

"Two Spot?" Dek called into his com. "We're headed in. We need the cart at the landing field. Be down in about fifteen minutes."

Whatever the reply was in Dek's earbud, he said, "Roger that. See you dirtside."

An instant later, Kylee's stomach jumped when the plane began its descent. The quetzal part of her cringed. The only thing quetzals hated more than flying was water.

Kylee clamped her jaw, heart beginning to thump harder as Dek dropped lower, and she got a good look at Port Authority.

The town itself was an oval, a cluster of domes laid out in a north-south grid that had been filled in and clogged by square structures and larger warehouses. She took in the high fence, then the moat-like ditch. Agricultural land ran in a swath from the aircar field on the west, curving around south, green and flat where they butted up against the bush lands and extended almost to the shuttle landing on the east. On the town's north side, the bush ran right up to the fence, the trees transected by a strip of road that ran die-straight a couple of kilometers to the deep-pit clay mine with its few buildings. Transparent greenhouses had been erected on the town's northeast edge; their roofs reflected a glare of sunlight as the air-plane caught just the right angle on its descent.

"The home of my enemies," Kylee muttered under her breath.

Madison gave her a sharp look. "We just want Tip taken care of. We're not looking for trouble."

"Neither were Dya and Mark when they brought me here the first time. Ended up with Mark shot, Kalico Aguila hunting us down, and Rocket murdered."

"Hey ease up," Dek called over the pilot's seat. "Mother Su, Damien, Shine, Tuska, and the rest of your brothers and sisters live here. So, it's not the same town it was then. They're going to want to see you."

Kylee closed her eyes, the stab of guilt cutting through her. "Come on, Dek. What can I say? I'm so sorry I stood there and watched Rebecca and Shantaya get eaten by quetzals? Sorry I destroyed your world? Sorry I ran off to the forest? Sorry I wasn't fast enough to keep Dya and Mark alive outside Tyson Station? Or that I still haven't hunted down the creature that killed them?"

To her surprise, it was Tip, who rasped out, "Stop being so hard on yourself." He swallowed hard. "You always think"—he stifled a groan—"you have to be perfect."

Do I? Through her window, she watched the ground seem to rise; the airplane pressed her into the seat as Dek dropped the flaps and rode the glide down toward the landing field. The airbrakes roared, and the plane passed over the stacked shipping containers with a mere meter to spare; then Dek rotated the thrust, setting them down with barely a jolt. Through her window, Kylee could see two A-7 shuttles parked side-by-side off to the right. Machines with forks were moving crates around at the far end of the field. The reddish clay looked as if it were fired and reflected a slight glaze in Capella's morning light.

"Welcome to PA," Dek called, shutting down the jets and killing the avionics.

Yeah, Kylee thought, *Home of my nightmares.*

She unbuckled, then helped Madison with her seatbelt. As the dust settled outside, Kylee caught a glimpse of people pushing a high-wheeled cart toward them. At the front came Talina. A fact that filled Kylee with no little relief.

The quetzals inside her began to stir, colors changing in her imagination. She caught elements of Rocket's memories, of crouching on the floor in the operating room, of armored marines staring hatefully down at him from behind deadly rifles, and fear.

Kylee sat and waited as Talina opened the door, and with the help of a big man, carefully extracted Tip from the passenger seat.

"How's he doing?" the big man asked in the process.

"Fevered. In pain. Got him drugged with Dya's blue-nasty painkiller," Dek told him. "Bad news is that, as you can smell, that leg's really infected. From Kylee's assessment, it's about as serious as it could get."

"When did this happen?" the big man asked, taking Tip's wrist, feeling for a pulse as he glanced at the chronometer on his wrist. The guy had a block-like head, close-cropped hair, and bloodshot blue eyes. Kylee caught his odor, thought he smelled of sweat and alcohol. He was dressed in quetzal leather, chamois, and wore an embroidered fabric shirt.

"Don't know, Step," Madison called from the back. "Couple of days maybe? He was out in the bush."

Step? Had to be Stepan Allenovich. Kylee gave the big man a curious inspection. He was a known womanizer, gambler, part-time biologist, hunter, and sometimes security second when Talina needed backup. Looked tough enough, and Kylee approved of the way he was being so careful of Tip as he and Talina carefully shifted him to the cart.

"Go," Tal called.

"On it." Step was already wheeling the cart around, headed for the tall gate at a fast trot.

Tal helped Madison out, and Kylee hopped out on her own, taking in the surroundings. So, this was Port Authority. Up there on the hill was the graveyard with its tall stone monument to Donovan himself. Kylee knew the place. Had Talina's memories of lowering Mitch's dead body into the dark red ground. The containers surrounding the landing field were set up seven-tall like a sheer wall. She'd heard it was arranged this way so that it was easier to spot quetzals when they raided the town.

The place smelled of burned fuel. The quetzal inside her hissed, tense, ready to spring to the attack.

Madison was already stalking after Stepan Allenovich and the cart. Kylee reached in for their travel bags and weapons, slinging the straps for each over her shoulders.

"You all right?" Talina asked, eyes on Kylee as Dek rounded the airplane and plugged in the charger for the powerpack.

Kylee spared her a sidelong glance. "Why should I be? Tip's dying. I'm in fucking Port Authority with its quetzal-hating creep-freaked people. What's not to love?"

Dek chuckled at that, laying a hand on Kylee's back. "Come on. You can go to war with PA later. Right now, keeping Tip alive has to top the list of concerns."

Talina matched step beside her. "Kid, just for a moment, I need you to dust that chip off your shoulder. Promise me that whatever happens, you'll let Dek and me handle it, all right?"

Kylee watched the forklifts from the corner of her eye. She'd never seen the like. Last time she'd been here, she'd been drugged, it had been dark, and she'd only seen the inside of the hospital. "Yeah. Fine. Whatever."

"Not your most enthusiastic of promises," Dek told her.

"Do you have any idea how much I *hate* this place?" Kylee stretched out her long legs, striding to catch up to Madison and the cart. She made the gate just as the cart went through. Glancing up, she got a real feel for the soaring perimeter fence, wondered if it wasn't the most astounding and ugly thing she'd ever seen. True,

Mundo, atop its tower, might have been taller before it fell, but this was huge! The composite of woven and welded wire and soaring posts went as far as the eye could see. All the way around the town.

She got her next jolt when the guard at the gate—a complete stranger—gave her a respectful nod. "You've got to be Kylee Simonov. Heard a lot about you. Name's Wejee. You need anything? You call on me."

"I . . . Uh, okay." She returned his slight nod. "Wejee. Got it."

The guy didn't look like a crazed quetzal-killing maniac. Rather, he had kindly dark eyes and a really warm smile.

Stepping through the gate, she might have entered a whole different world. She'd never seen so many buildings. So many people. The grandeur of it set every nerve on end. Hers and every quetzal molecule in her body. Sure, she'd shared Talina's memories, but they'd been impossible phantoms of places like Transluna, Earth, even here at PA. Fantasy dream images. Now she was seeing for real.

Her quetzal nature was awed, curious, wary.

All the bravado evaporated. She swallowed hard, let Talina and Dek take the lead as she gaped this way and that. Her quetzal self was glowing in radiant yellow, black, and infrared. Fear-charged. Anticipating attack from any quarter. Never—not even at Mundo or Corporate Mine—had she seen this many people in one place. Had to be thirty just since she'd climbed out of the airplane. And more were coming. Not to mention the buildings on either side of the gravel road. Hard to believe there were this many buildings on the whole planet.

Everyone they passed greeted Talina and Dek, calling, "How you doing?" "Good to see you." "Heard you made a medical run to the bush?" "How's it going?"

More amazing, Tal and Dek seemed to know them all. Answered them by name.

The worst part was that they all stared at her. Seemed to pick her out, wondering, peering, like she was some freak. Curiosity and judgment in those probing gazes.

It wasn't the first time Kylee wished that, like her quetzals, she could make herself invisible. Nothing had ever made her this vulnerable and insecure. More than anything, she wanted to turn around, run full bore back to Chaco Briggs and her little house, and away from these prying eyes.

At the same time, everywhere she looked, she saw something amazing. Equipment she couldn't name. Buildings of all sizes and shapes. Some of them imposing things of three stories. Who knew what might be inside? Incomprehensibly dressed people carrying tools whose purpose she couldn't fathom. Children. Exotic vehicles.

And the sounds and smells! Her quetzal nose was quivering with the odors of chemicals, cooking food, composting excrement and urine, dust, and sweaty humans, while the high-pitched moan of electric motors, voices from behind walls, clattering and banging, and the rattle of machinery seemed endless.

If they'd just stop staring at me!

By the time they rounded a corner and took an even bigger street south, Dek was giving her a knowing smile, reading her expression of terror and excitement.

"More than you figured it would be, huh?" he asked.

"There's what? A thousand people that live here? I mean, damn, Dek. It's one thing to see the pictures. It's a whole different thing to walk the streets and realize it's all real." She shook her head. "And places like Transluna? Okay, so I know it's huge compared to Port Authority. And complex, but how do I get my mind around that?" She made a face, adding, "And the way people are staring at me? I feel like I'm naked."

"You're new," Dek reminded. "Don't let it get under your skin."

"Yeah? Well, it is."

Talina told her, "You're out of your element. You've always been on your home turf where you knew the environment. What the rules were, the things to watch out for. Now it's your turn to be the newbie. Like when Dek first came to the Briggs' claim. Keep that in that knot-thick head of yours and remember that you're the one who needs to learn now. Do that and maybe you'll survive this with a little less drama."

"How do you know what I will and won't do?"

"'Cause I got too much of you in here." Talina tapped the side of her head, eyes hardening. "I know what PA means to you. What you think of the people. But that angry and hurting little girl should have matured into a smarter and more balanced woman. That, or you never learned a damn thing from my memories."

"Yeah, that's sinking in, Tal." Kylee jumped when a loud bang came from the building on her right. She read GUNSMITH on the sign, and it hit her: that had to be Frank Freund's place. Where her rifle and pistol had been made. She reached back, touching the butt stock where it hung over her shoulder between the packs. For the first time, she felt a connection to this place that didn't make it so alien.

Ahead of them, Step Allenovich had pulled the cart up at the double doors of what had to be the hospital. Not that Kylee had ever really seen it from the outside. The last time she went through those doors, she'd been pain-dazed and drugged.

A woman rushed out. Tall, black hair. That—and the way she was dressed—placed her in Kylee's mind: Raya Turnienko. She immediately bent over Tip's body, shooting questions at Madison.

The doctor, Step Allenovich, and Madison had Tip's litter up and went charging through the door. Kylee hurried ahead, pushing through the double doors, past the waiting room and offices, and down the familiar hall. God, it was almost a relief. Here was a place she knew. The only difference was that more of the lights were working in the ceiling.

At the surgery door, Stepan Allenovich stopped her cold as he exited the room, the litter in his hands. "Whoa, there," he called, fixing her with curious eyes.

"I need to be in there with Tip."

"Kylee, right?" Allenovich continued to block the door, looking up as Talina came hurrying down the hall. "Raya and Vik Lawrence are prepping the kid. Even Madison's going to be kicked out before they start cutting."

"But, I—"

"No visitors," Step said, beetling his brow to emphasize his point. "Not even the famous Kylee Simonov."

Famous?

"Kylee?" Talina laid a hand on her quivering shoulder. "There's nothing you can do in there." To Allenovich, she asked, "How long?"

"No telling. Raya and Vik have their heads together muttering about tissues and immune responses. Cheng's standing by in the lab along with Shanteel Jones. Everyone's waiting to see what's in the kid's leg. My bet? If they've got the boy stabilized by supper, it'll be a miracle."

Kylee figured she'd just push her way past, started to when Talina's hard hand clamped on her shoulder and pulled her back. Kylee's quetzal response was to wheel and hammer Talina in the pit of the stomach; it short-circuited when the woman ordered, "Back down and cool off. Now."

Kylee swallowed, heart thumping against her breastbone as she stared into Talina's implacable dark eyes. "That's Tip in there."

"Uh-huh," Talina told her. "And Raya's going to have a tough enough time saving his life without you driving her berserk in the process. Kylee, you've got to trust Raya. If Tip's got any chance, she'll keep him alive. Now. Stand. Down."

Grinding her teeth, Kylee nodded, prickling at the way Step Allenovich had watched the whole exchange. She gave him her deadliest slit-eyed glare. "You got a problem?"

Step—to her dismay—grinned, exposing a couple of broken teeth. "Nope. I think I like you. You've got spunk."

"What's spunk?" Kylee's quetzal coiled inside, ready to attack. She'd hit him in the trachea, follow up with a knee to the testicles, and break his nose with an elbow, then . . .

"Spunk's good," Talina yanked her back before she could strike. "Step doesn't take a shine to just anyone. Spunk is a compliment, so don't make an ass of yourself, and tell him thank you."

Kylee fixed Talina with a suspicious eye, then turned to Step. "Thank you. Didn't mean to be rude."

"No problem, kid." The grin had widened. "You need anything, you just call."

"I need to eat," Dek said reasonably. "Step? If anything breaks, call Tal through com. Tell Madison we're at Inga's. She's welcome to join us."

Talina leaned close, gaze intensifying. "Kylee, Tip's got the best care on the planet. Step will call me when he comes out of surgery. Remember who's the newcomer here."

Kylee rocked her jaw back and forth, fuming. Panicked. Scared sick that Tip would die.

Reluctantly she nodded. "Yeah. I'm coming."

Dek gave her a reassuring wink. "It's okay, kid. Raya's the best. She fixed you, after all."

And if Tip dies? The thought rolled around in her head.

But then, there really wasn't anyone to hold responsible if he did. It really sucked toilet water when she wanted to kill someone, and there was no one to kill.

15

Falise couldn't sleep. If Clarice had read Charlotte's signals, this should be the night. Not that ship's time was anything like planetary schedules, but at this hour, on this watch, most of *Turalon* was running on skeleton crew. Easing out of her bed as carefully as she could, she made sure that she didn't awaken Ednund. He was sleeping soundly, an arm draped over his eyes, a sheet draped around his waist. Falise pulled on a sheath, wrapped her sash with its out-of-sight poisoned blade around her waist, and slipped on comfortable shoes.

Like a ghost, she exited the room, carefully latching the cabin door behind her. Half-light illuminated the corridor, every third light panel glowing. It cast the overhead pipes, conduit, and wiring in shadows. The same with the doorways, access panels, and recesses in the sialon walls.

God, she was tired of sialon. Would have given anything to walk under an open sky, or even a high ceiling or dome like she'd so taken for granted on Transluna. She thought of her bedroom, high in the Taglioni tower; it had an infinity ceiling that mimicked an endless vista of reflected light, stars, or clouds depending upon the programming.

Turalon might have been a high-security penitentiary for all the freedom Falise had. True, she might be able to leave her cramped quarters, but her travels were, for all intent and purpose, limited to Crew Deck and the even more restricted Command Deck. She wouldn't have allowed herself to be caught dead down on the Transportee Deck, Shuttle Deck, or in the pressurized parts of the cargo hold.

Some standards had to be maintained, even in this miserable burrow.

Crossing her arms, she ambled slowly down the corridor, passing

Chad Grunnel's quarters, with Cinque's door directly across the hall. In the beginning, having her rivals so close had been distinctly uncomfortable. Like being boxed into cramped catacombs, forced every day to be face-to-face with venomous human serpents, all of whom were dedicated, in the end, to your downfall.

That was due to Derek, of course. If he hadn't sent that foul Dan Wirth creature back under Taglioni protection, she'd have never found herself in this position.

So, she wondered, *what do I do about Derek?*

The question had preoccupied her for months. Now that she needn't worry about dying somewhere in the black, she could turn her full attention to the problem of Capella III and her renegade brother.

Though no formal statement had been made by the Board, the importance of the Inspector General was obvious. If he found conditions on Cap III required it, by the power of his Board appointment, he had the authority to dismiss Kalico Aguila and replace her with anyone he might choose. It would be an interim appointment until approved by the Board, or until they chose someone they considered better suited to the position.

And from what pool of candidates will he choose?

The answer to that was obvious: Inspector General Soukup would choose either Falise Taglioni, Cinque Suharto, Chad Grunnel, or Bad Bart Radcek. One of the four—representing as they did, the powerful families—would take Aguila's place. Become the administrator for the richest planet in the known galaxy.

No wonder the IG avoided socializing, having stuck to his quarters through most of the seemingly endless nineteen months they'd been trapped in this sialon hell. He understood. Would not be compromised by any claims of favoritism or conflict of interest.

That reality settled home with effect as she passed the IG's quarters where he and his Four resided. Falise paused, considered the locked door. Wondered what went on behind it. Soukup and his Four—the genetically and technically designed individuals who assisted his investigation—remained a mystery. A completely self-contained social unit.

The future of Capella III lay behind that closed portal. Everything hinged upon that one individual and the decisions made inside that single skull.

"I wonder," she mused under her breath, "if dear old Derek figured on the vigor of the Board's response?" Let alone what it might mean to him. Aguila wasn't the only one subject to the IG's judgement. Her brother, too, could be drawn into the IG's net.

Depending upon what Derek's game on Donovan was.

That he'd been cozy with Dan Wirth—a recognized scum—was bad enough. That he'd given him Taglioni protection? Didn't matter that the family had been well-paid in the process, the very association was questionable, especially given the propaganda machines controlled by the other families.

Walking on, she passed the captain's quarters, and then those of the first officers.

Rounding the bend to the observation blister, she slowed. The sounds coming from within were unmistakable. The rhythmic intakes of breath, the deep-throated moans.

"Oh, God, yes," a female voice almost purred.

Then a male groan steeped in pleasure was followed by yipping female cries of delight.

Well, well, right on schedule. Falise cocked an eyebrow. Stepped back into the recessed doorway leading to an equipment closet.

Heavy panting and a deep sigh followed.

"That was marvelous," the woman said.

Falise placed the voice: Charlotte.

Pus and ions, there was a distinct chance that all of her clever planning over the last nineteen months might work.

"How much time do you have?" the man asked.

With recognition of that deep baritone, Falise smiled. Cinque!

"I should be going." Charlotte gave off a sigh. "He'll probably sleep straight through, but the soporific I slipped into his sherry will be wearing off. He can't know I've been gone."

"Too bad." A pause. "You'll be free of him soon enough."

Clothing rustled, bodies shifting.

Charlotte said, "I'll hold you to that."

Cinque's soft laughter was followed by: "Oh, we'll hold each other. Call it the first of Capella's opportunities."

"We dare not do this again," Charlotte warned. "Not this close to the planet. Duty schedules will be changing. Too many uncertainties."

"Of course." A pause. "Makes the waiting even more delicious, don't you think?"

"See you soon, love."

Falise flattened herself in the recess as Cinque emerged, his black garments like a shadow in the dim lights. Then, as he vanished down the hall, Cinque's soft utterance. "Ah, the sweet rewards of victory!"

Falise waited as Charlotte emerged, pulling a soffiber wrap tight around her lithe body, a satisfied smile on her face.

As she passed the dark recess where Falise hid, the woman asked, "I take it my actions meet your approval, Lady?"

"They do. Serve me well, and you shall have everything you desire."

"Consider the deal done, Lady." And Charlotte continued on her way, the fabric rustling around her long legs.

16

Word had spread. Talina was shocked at how quickly all of Port
Authority was aware that Kylee Simonov was in town. That
Tip Briggs was in surgery.

She wondered if going to Inga's was the right call. All eyes were
on her, Kylee, and Dek as they descended the worn chabacho-wood
stairs to the tavern's lower level. She could feel Kylee's building
panic. The kid was a wild thing after all, more at home alone in the
bush than even sitting at Madison's and Chaco's table. In the recent
past, her only interaction with humans had been among the Unreconciled out at Tyson Station, and they'd been scared to death of her
and Flute. Did everything they could to keep their distance.

Inga's tavern was just the opposite. From the reaction of the sixty
or so people crowding the tables, each and every one wanted a look
at the famous Kylee Simonov. Dya's daughter. The quetzal girl
who'd bonded with Rocket and rode through the forest on Flute.
The girl who had saved Kalico Aguila and Private Briah Muldare out
in the forest at Tyson Station. They gaped, pointed, and said things
like, "There she is." "Wow, look at her face." "Check out those
eyes, quetzal, I tell you." "Look how long her legs are." "She moves
like a hunting cat." "Think she's more human or quetzal?"

Talina shot a narrow-eyed warning at those who would have
leaped to their feet and approached for a better look. Well, all except
Hofer, already half soused, to whom she ordered, "Later. We're here
to eat in peace."

And through it all, Talina kept a firm hand on Kylee's shoulder,
feeling the crackling tension running through the young woman's
body. "Easy," she muttered from the side of her mouth. "Sometimes, being a celebrity really sucks, huh?"

"Famous? I keep hearing people say that." Kylee almost trembled when both Lee Marston and Pete Morgan doffed their hats, bowed, and gave her nods of recognition.

"Get used to it," Dek told her easily as he waved to friends and led the way to the far end of the bar.

To Talina's irritation, both Shig and Kalico were already seated. She led Kylee up to the bar as Kalico and Shig moved down to open the seat next to hers. Dek had stopped to run interference, politely explaining to folks that Kylee, Talina, and Kalico had business to discuss. In PA, that pretty much bought privacy.

Kylee dropped her packs and rifle on the floor, before she climbed uncertainly into the chair.

Kalico, with a smile, said, "So, Kylee, welcome to PA. How's Tip?"

"Dying," Kylee said bitterly.

"In surgery," Talina corrected. "Now we do the hard part. Sit and wait."

Shig reached across Kalico, offering his hand. "Hello, Kylee. Good to see you again. Been a while since Rork Springs."

"You still killing quetzals?" Kylee asked, a smoldering behind her eyes. She gave Shig's hand a puzzled look, and he withdrew it.

It hit Talina that Kylee had no clue what the gesture meant. Have to deal with that.

"Only when they kill us first," Shig reached for his half-glass of wine. "We have learned a lot since those days, and much of it because of you. But perhaps, with you here for a time, we might benefit from your experience. We have had people killed in the last week. Whitey is back. Maybe his entire lineage."

At the mention, the Demon quetzal that lived behind Talina's stomach chortled with delight, hissing, *Good!*

Kylee asked, "So, what? You want me to hunt him down?"

Down inside, Demon hissed his disapproval, then added, *"Get this abomination away from here."*

"Yeah, you'd like that, wouldn't you?" Talina muttered under her breath.

From his perch on her shoulder, Rocket chittered in amusement, but then he'd been relieved ever since Kylee had stepped down from Dek's airplane.

"We want the killing to stop," Shig told her.

Kylee shrugged dismissively. "It's a lineage vendetta. The only thing you can do is kill him and exterminate the lineage. I've tasted their knowledge. They kill humans. No other way they think. Sorry."

"Got the same problem down at Corporate Mine," Kalico said. "Two attacks in the last six months. I'm hoping I can send IG Soukup out into the forest to investigate. Maybe confront said quetzal." She turned her laser-blue gaze on Kylee. "Speaking of quetzals, how are you doing?"

"Scared. Creep-freaked to be here." Kylee told her. "This thing in Tip's leg, well, he'd be dead if it wasn't for the quetzal molecules and proteins in his blood. Raya's his last chance. I had to come."

"Slug?" Shig asked.

"Don't think so." Kylee frowned. "Tip said it was something he'd never seen before. It came out of a hole in a cliff he was climbing. Said he cut it in half, but the part that bit him just kept eating its way inside."

Inga—approaching in her rolling stride—already had Talina's glass filled with stout, calling, "What'll Dek have? What's Kylee want?"

"Dek'll have the special and an IPA," Dek called from the knot of people who'd gathered around him.

"Kylee?" Inga asked.

"Whatever Talina's drinking." Kylee pointed at the stout.

Inga shot Talina a questioning glance.

"Yeah," Tal told her. "Kylee's no stranger to Chaco's homebrew. She might be sixteen, but she's smarter and more mature than half the drunks in here. I'll vouch for her. And bring us another two plates of the special."

"My tab!" Kalico called.

"You got it." Inga turned, hustling away as she called, "Three specials!"

"How is Flute?" Kalico asked. "He still rising in the ranks out there?"

"Second elder now, still orange. Tip and I, we helped the lineage with a chamois trap. Works on roos, too. Flute runs it and we share food. But it comes with its own problems. Nutrition is up, which means more young. Population's getting out of balance."

"How does that create imbalance?" Shig asked, still rotating his wineglass.

Giving him a skeptical glance, Kylee said, "When quetzals hunt, they burn up a lot of calories running down prey. There's not much spirited chasing when a herd of chamois run into a corral trap. There's no energy expended let alone depleted nutrients to be replaced. Means that those resources can be freed for the reproductive system. Fat healthy quetzals translate into lots of little quetzals." She frowned. "Flute, Tip, and I, we're going to have to give this some consideration. Otherwise, there's going to be plague of young rogues out stirring up trouble with the neighboring lineages."

"And I thought Port Authority was challenging at times," Shig noted.

Inga came bustling down the bar, took a swipe at the stained chabacho wood with her towel, and thunked two mugs down, all the while giving Kylee a hard-eyed appraisal. Then, as quickly, the woman was gone.

"She doesn't like me," Kylee said with an ominous tone.

Kalico laughed it off. "You're new, and the stories told about you are fantastic. Suddenly, here you are. Instead of looking like a demigod riding into town on a fire-breathing quetzal, you look like a really exotically proportioned copy of Talina, but with long blond hair and striking blue alien eyes, all dressed in trimly cut chamois leather with a rifle strapped on your back."

"Not to mention," Shig told her, "that you were behind one of the biggest bar fights to ever break out in Inga's."

"Muldare was right in the middle of that," Kalico reminded as she rubbed a finger down the scar on her jaw. "She said something about you saving our lives out in the forest. That we'd be dead but for you and Flute. Hofer shot off his mouth. Called her a liar. Said that no freaky little girl could ride a quetzal. And then Muldare hit him. Of course, everyone picked a side, and by the time Talina got it broken up, half the furniture was splintered, six people were in the hospital, and it took Inga two days to clean up the mess."

Talina added, "People still blame Hofer for that." She glanced at Kylee. "Not starting the fight, you understand, but that the bar was closed for two days as a result."

"And Inga raised her prices to cover the broken bottles, wasted liquor, and cleanup," Shig said with a sigh. "The ripples ran through the entire economy. Meant I had to raise the price of my squash."

"Wasn't all bad," Kalico said thoughtfully as she turned in her chair and glanced around the room. "These paving stones hadn't been that clean since the day they'd been laid. Hell, who would have thought they were really light gray? I always assumed they were black to start with."

Kylee shot an uncertain look Talina's way, shook her head in disbelief; she sipped at her stout. Smacked her lips. "Tastier than that stuff Chaco makes."

"Where are you staying?" Shig asked Kylee. "I have a most comfortable futon out in my study, and it's not more than a two-minute walk from the hospital."

"What's a futon?" the girl asked.

"Medieval torture device," Kalico said with a grunt. "Sort of like sleeping on a board."

Shig's beatific face fell. "I have spent many nights of restful sleep on that futon."

"You're an ascetic who follows all that Buddhist and Hindu searching-for-enlightenment crap. You think that suffering, *dukkha*, in this life will make the next one better," Kalico shot back. "You'd make the same claim about a bed of nails."

For the first time, Talina saw Kylee's lips bend into a smile.

"Dek and I will put her and Madison up," Talina said. "That will give them a bit more privacy."

Kalico agreed, saying, "Not often that a living legend comes to town, Kylee. Half the people here think you walk on water, the other half consider you to be devil's spawn."

"Fuck that!" Kylee muttered as Inga came charging down the

bar, three heaping plates balanced with extraordinary dexterity. "Hey, I'm just me, okay? All I want is to get Tip out of the hospital alive and get back to Flute. It already feels like half of me is missing."

"Sort of like walking on one leg," Talina amended, having her own familiarity with quetzals in her mind.

"Yes," Rocket whispered from her shoulder.

Talina watched the plates set down, Dek's on the end of the bar. No sooner had that happened, than he excused himself from his conversation, taking a position on the end of the bar as he reached for the fork.

Dek said, "Quetzal sign out by Muley Mitchman's claim. Muley climbed out of his hide to take a leak at first light. Happened to catch a silhouette on the ridgetop. He made a mad dash for his air-car, and flying out, said he saw four quetzals staring up from the between the trees."

"That's ten kilometers out," Talina said thoughtfully as she toyed with her fork.

Kylee, without inhibition, had dived into the stuffed poblanos, diced crest meat, and recado-flavored beans. She was eating as if half-starved.

"Like the food, huh?" Talina noted.

Kylee wiping her mouth with a sleeve, said, "Best thing I've eaten in weeks." Then she forked another mouthful and began chomping away.

Kalico squinted at her whiskey. "Ten kilometers is nothing. They could be scouting out the north gate while we're talking about it."

Talina activated her com. "Two Spot? You heard that Muley Mitchman spotted quetzals this morning?"

"Roger that. Farms are battened down. We're being extra vigilant on the gates. Sent a heads-up out to Bernie Monson at the mine. They're taking precautions."

"So weird," Kylee muttered as she finished off the last of her meal and studied the fork. She pulled a pressed-steel one from her belt pack, stuffed Inga's into the pouch, and laid her old one on the plate.

"What's weird, and why are you stealing Inga's fork?" Talina asked.

Kylee looked up, clearly puzzled. "It comes with the food, right? Or am I stealing the food, too?"

"You bought the food," Dek told her. "The fork—along with the plate—belongs to Inga. Put it back."

"How do you tell the difference?" Kylee remained skeptical, as she dug out Inga's fork and returned her rather pathetic item to her pouch.

"Good question, Wild Child," Kalico told her. "PA's not the bush, and it's not Mundo Base. Everything here belongs to someone. It's taken, claimed. Get it? That meal you just ate, I'm giving Inga the SDRs to cover it and the beer you're drinking. Inga just puts the food on *her* plate, and lets you use *her* fork to eat it. Same with that mug you're drinking out of. You only get to keep the beer. Inga wants her mug back so she can use it to sell other people beer."

Shig had a most amused look on his face.

Kylee gave a slight nod. "Got it." A pause. "I think."

"Good," Dek added, "because they shoot thieves here. It's called crime. Surely you remember that from your lessons at Mundo."

Kylee looked around suspiciously. "So, how do I know what belongs to who?"

Talina told her, "If it's not yours, it's someone else's. Listen, kid, you've never lived in a city, so, figure it's just like unfamiliar bush. Anything you touch here belongs to someone else. If you take anything for granted, you're going to get in trouble because you don't know the rules."

"Hey, Tal," Kylee made a face, "your memories are in here. Like a sort of hazy patchwork of dos and don'ts." She tapped her head. "So, all right, I'll ask."

Kalico gave the girl a glance from the corner of her eye as she cupped her whiskey. "You're not alone. Took me a while and a couple of figurative bloody noses to figure out how these crazy libertarians think."

"Yeah," Kylee climbed off the stool. "Well, for the moment, I've got to pee."

Talina wiped her lips, and said, "I'll show you where and how—"

Kylee arched a chastening brow. "I lived at Mundo, Ta Li Na. We had plumbing. I know how to use a stool. Don't worry, I won't pee on the floor. Just point out where the toilet's at."

"There," Talina pointed to the back of the room. "It's behind the stairs. Through the aquajade-wood door. It's communal. Stalls on the right, urinals on the left."

Talina saw Kylee's sudden hesitation as she realized that she'd be crossing forty meters of open floor by herself. Sort of like walking a gauntlet of staring strangers. Talina said, "You sure you don't want me—"

"Hey, I got this," Kylee half growled as she set off across the paving stones.

Talina muttered, "Maybe I ought to—"

"You'll embarrass her," Shig noted, beneficent gaze following the young woman as she strode purposefully down the aisle, head up, eyes fixed straight ahead.

"Got to give her credit," Dek said. "She's doing better than I thought she would."

"She tried to steal Inga's fork," Kalico reminded.

"Trade," Talina corrected, seeing Kylee reach the door to the toilets. "And we're going to have to teach her what a handshake means."

"What do you hear from *Turalon?*" Dek asked, turning back to his plate and forking a cube of roasted crest.

Kalico took a sip of her whiskey. "They're about four days out. Tallia O'Hanley's been getting a steady stream of messages now that the delay is down to a couple of minutes. She records them, sends a reply that the Supervisor will take them under advisement, and piles them in a stack. Anything that's really important, she sends a query to Two Spot, and he lets me know. Most of the stack is filled with demands and interrogatives that are just plain silly."

"That's what we were discussing when you arrived," Shig said. "Obviously, they're going to have to make planet here. PA is the only place with housing and amenities. For once, the cargo is moderately useful, things we need to fix some of our broken equipment. Given that most of what they carry is meant for PA, we'll broker an equitable compensation in siddars that will pay for their lodging and provide spending currency for the crew and transportees."

"That's going to be fun to figure out. Just how many SDRs is a starter motor for Artie Manfroid's caterpillar worth?" Dek asked. "And what about things like light bulbs? Now that Tori Ashan at the glassworks and Sheyela Smith have gotten proficient at making light bulbs, what happens to their market when *Turalon* unloads a shipping container of bulbs?"

Shig said, "Most of the fixtures have been rewired from the Corporate-style bulbs to Tori and Sheyela's. And it's not like they don't each have more than enough to keep them busy. But I'm sure there will be dislocations. We'll just have to think our way through them."

Kalico adopted a wry smile. "Things have gotten a little murky over the years. My beautiful Corporate Mine and my once-inviolable people have all been infected. It sort of crept in, but everything at Corporate Mine runs on crass PA capitalism these days." She propped her chin, gaze distant. "That toilet-sucking inspector general is going to just love unraveling *that* ball of twine."

Talina narrowed an eye. "Hard to see what he could charge you with. You were given Board authority to determine Donovan's fate. Ultimately, everything you did was in The Corporation's best interest. You sent them two starships full of plunder."

"I've got fifty people coming up on contract who want to space back to Solar System on *Turalon,* and each of them is taking a sack of plunder back with them that's worth a fricking fortune in Corporate SDRs or yuan." A pause as she shared a glance with each of them. "Do you know how much trouble I would have spared myself if I'd just nuked you people from space the first time I arrived here?"

"Of course, Supervisor," Shig said mildly, "but to have done so would have changed your tao, sent it down a path that would have left you drowning in *tamas* and *dukkha*. It's just my opinion, but I suspect that with all you have learned on Donovan, you have saved yourself countless reincarnations into a bug's liver to achieve the same *sattva*."

A crash and a scream carried over the usual sound of conversation and rattling dishware. The room went silent.

Talina whirled—pinpointed the origin as coming from the restroom. In a wink, she was off her stool, sprinting for the rear. Even as people were rising from their seats, Talina raced down the aisle, dodged the stairs, and hit the aquajade door with both arms straight.

Blasting through, she found Kylee, one knee on Hofer's chest, arm back, fist cocked. And whack! she smacked the builder in his already bloody face.

"Kylee! Stop, *God damn it!*"

Crimson-smeared fist raised for another blow, the girl continued to glare down into Hofer's face. The man had both arms up to block the assault. Hofer's nose was already gushing red, and his eyes were terror-wide. He was coughing, a spray of blood accompanying each racking convulsion.

"What the hell?" Talina demanded, striding in and reaching down to grab Kylee's arm. She plucked the girl off Hofer's chest as, between wrenching fits of coughing, he screamed, "Get her off me! She's a stinking animal!"

"Slug fucker!" Kylee snarled back.

With Kylee's weight off Hofer's chest, he curled into a ball to grab his testicles, still coughing, blowing blood across the filthy flagstones. Talina thought he made the most pitiful sounds.

"Want to tell me how this all went cucking frazy? Thought you were just going to pee?" Talina was aware of the crowd plugging the door. Somehow, Dek wiggled through, stepping off to the side, a hand on his fancy pistol.

Kylee thrust a hard finger at the wheezing and suffering Hofer. "I was. And that pus sucker poked his head in my stall, cocked it kind of funny like, and said, 'Looks like a normal slit to me. You'd think it would be bigger after all the quetzal screwing you've been doing.' So I jumped to my feet, pulled up my pants, and hit him."

At the sound of snickers coming from the door, Kylee twisted around in Talina's grip, dropping to a crouch, ready to strike again.

Her eyes had that deadly look—quetzal-wide and pupils black to gather all the light—which gave Kylee an even more alien appearance. That she'd bared her teeth didn't help matters in the slightest. Quivering in rage like she was, she'd have launched herself into the whole bunch.

"Ease down," Talina told her. To Hofer she said, "That true? You said that? And don't you fucking lie to me, Hofer. You tell me the God's-rotted truth or I'll finish what Kylee started. Now, did you tell this girl she'd been fucking quetzals?"

"I . . . I . . ."

"*Hofer?*"

"Yeah." The man now cupped his balls with one hand. The other massaged his throat where it was turning red from bruising. Hoarsely, he admitted, "I might have said that."

"Oh, for fuck's sake," Talina muttered. "You have to be the dumbest piece of shit on the planet."

"So, I can kill him now?" Kylee asked, still struggling against Talina's iron grip.

"No!" Talina turned, ordering, "The rest of you? Party's over. Back to your beer and chili. But pass this around: Kylee's a guest here, and she's new to town. Yeah, she's half quetzal, but so are Dek and I."

Shig, being short, had also managed to squirm his way through the crowd, adding, "This young woman is special to me. She doesn't know our ways, so please be polite. If you take the time, I think you will find she is most remarkable."

And in an instant, the mood changed, as if Shig's benevolent words set the tone.

"Go on now." Talina made a shooing motion with her free hand.

Shig crossed his arms, looking down at Hofer. "You do get yourself in the most remarkable messes. Do you need to go to the hospital? Raya's in surgery, but perhaps after she resets it Vik could find a cold pack for your nose."

"Go to hell, Shig," Hofer rasped through his swelling larynx.

Kylee took a deep breath, sighed. Gave Talina a disgusted look. "You can see into the ultraviolet, too, right?" She gestured around.

"You ever notice all the dried urine splashed around in here? And look. Right there where Hofer landed. Like, yuk!"

Dek had stepped close, voice low. "Yeah, but humans can't see it, so don't go saying anything to Inga, okay?" Then he reached down, giving the whimpering Hofer a hand. The man tottered on his feet as Dek pulled him up.

Slapping the man on the back, Dek started him for the door, saying, "You know, if I were you? I think I'd forget this ever happened."

"Why?" Hofer asked hoarsely.

"Do you really want the whole town to remember that the rough, tough, brawling, and randy Hofer we all know and love got beat up by a sixteen-year-old girl? And her, just a little slip of a thing?"

17

Kalico hated having to take the time away from Corporate Mine and Southern Diggings, but here she was, back aboard *Vixen*. Shig, Yvette, and Talina really couldn't conceive the nature of the threat that Soukup posed. Dek did, but while he might be worried about her, he wasn't about to lose everything based on a Corporate IG's whim.

In fact, he was in an enviable position. No matter what message his sister might be carrying from Miko, Fabio, or his father Claudio, Dek had already accepted the fact that he was going to tell them to fuck off. Lucky Dek. These days he considered himself a Wild One.

Ultimately, Kalico Aguila was the Board Appointed Supervisor on Donovan and subject to The Corporation's rules and governance. A position that put her right in the middle of Soukup's crosshairs. That the IG, too, was Board Appointed? That translated into almost unlimited authority that in many cases exceeded her own. Kalico's best option was to blunt as much of the threat as she could, as rapidly as she could.

If her meteoric rise in the Corporate ranks back on Transluna had taught her anything, it was to seize the initiative. So here she sat, back in the command chair on *Vixen*'s AC. The dot from the photonic com glowed like an evil red eye as she waited.

From Seesil Vacquillas' usual seat, Captain Torgussen watched, ready to confirm the photonic link. Other than that, only Second Officer Valencia Seguro was present at the sensor array. Most of *Vixen*'s crew were either off duty, or down-planet on leave.

"Got a signal coming in," Torgussen called. "Fixing now."

The red dot vanished to be replaced by the image of a fiftyish man, bald, long-faced, with cunning hazel eyes. The man's nose had been smashed sometime in the past and never fixed. He wore a marine colonel's dress uniform, which probably explained why he had kept her waiting. Upon Captain Abibi's summons to the AC, instead of hustling to the Command Deck, he'd stopped to don his formal uniform.

"Colonel Stanley Creamer, I presume?" Kalico asked. "I do hope that whatever kept you, it was pressing."

His first reaction was to stare, a slight twisting of his pursed mouth and a tightening of his eyes proof of his reaction to her scars. "And you are?" The disdain filled his voice. He was taking in her quetzal-hide cape, the embroidered claw-shrub shirt, her pulled-back hair.

"Corporate Board Supervisor Kalico Aguila, I am in control of all Corporate assets in the Capella star system, which includes *Turalon,* and, more to the point, your command, Colonel. Or do I need to quote you the Corporate Code regulations covering the powers of a Board Supervisor's authority?"

"I, uh, no, Supervisor. I am fully versed in Corporate regulations, including Article One, Sections Thirty-eight through Forty-one."

"Then as the ranking officer within the system . . ." She paused. "I am correct in assuming you are the ranking officer?"

"Yes, ma'am." His expression had gone perfectly blank, voice controlled. He'd played this game before. Saying nothing. Admitting nothing, thoroughly aware that somewhere down the line, a board of review might dissect the recordings looking for any misstep.

Kalico gave him a smile, the one she knew rearranged the scars on her face. She could barely detect the tightening at the corners of his mouth. "Colonel, I understand that you have a detachment of twenty-nine marines." She held up a copy of his orders. "It is also my understanding that you are here to assist me in the managing and performance of my duties. I see the usual wording, here, 'To protect and support the colony. To ensure the peace, orderly conduct, prosperity, and the common good.' After that we have the usual paragraphs regarding conduct, dedication to duty, performance, training, and rapid force engagement. Am I correct?"

"Yes, ma'am." Creamer was beginning to stiffen in his chair, no doubt sensing a trap.

"And you have no other field orders?"

"No, ma'am."

"Very well." She glanced at the ship's chronometer. "According to Captain Abibi's calculations, *Turalon* is currently about thirty-six hours from achieving a standard orbit over Donovan. From your record, I see that you are familiar with a maneuver called a 'hot pre-orbital insertion.'"

"Ma'am," Creamer was doing all he could to keep from squirming. "For the record, you should know that my team has been in transit for the last year and seven months. We'll need time to get our equipment—"

"*Excuse me?*" Kalico leaned forward, narrowing an eye. "You have been in space for a year and seven months, preparing to enter a star system that might be in God-knows-what circumstances, for which you have *no* information regarding the status of its people, and you haven't even got your equipment online? Is that what you're telling me?"

Creamer went bolt upright. "Ma'am, I—"

"You will address me as Board Supervisor, Colonel. And, starting this instant, you will jump your lazy ass into the harness. Even Captain Max Taggart was ready for a hot pre-orbital insertion on arrival at Donovan, and he was supposed to be dead weight."

She glanced at the clock again. "You have four hours to have your teams on shuttles and deployed for a hot insertion. You will receive the coordinates for a team of nine marines under your command to insert within ten kilometers of Port Authority. Once dirtside, you will be under the instructional command of Corporal Mohammed Abu Sassi for survival training. An additional ten of your marines, under Lieutenant Tomolo, will be inserted at the smelter complex at Corporate Mine. There, they will be placed under the operative command of Private Dina Michegan for instruction in forest survival. The final team of ten, under the command of Corporal Tran, will set down at Southern Diggings, and, under the command of Private Briah Muldare, will reinforce the security force there. All three shuttles will dust off, rendezvousing with *Turalon* at the same time she achieves orbit."

"Excuse me, Corporate Supervisor? You want to place my officers under the command of—"

"Under the command of Donovanian veterans for *survival* training, Colonel," Kalico snapped. "Or are you familiar with the best way to kill scimitars and how to avoid nightmares? Let alone where slugs lurk?"

"No, ma—er. Corporate Supervisor." He seemed to be having trouble swallowing.

"Further," Kalico continued, "all personnel will be armored, equipped, and rationed for a ten-day deployment with all necessary tech and support. Especially the team under Corporal Abu Sassi's command that inserts ten kicks from PA. And, Colonel, pay attention here: The bush surrounding PA *is* hostile territory. We're on quetzal alert here. Everything out there will kill you and your people." She pointed a scarred finger his way. "So I recommend that you pay very close attention to everything Abu Sassi tells you."

"Ma'am, I—"

"Board Supervisor."

"Board Supervisor, with all respect, I'm going to need more time to assemble my people and equip them for—"

"Then rather than sitting there thinking up excuses as to why you can't accomplish your mission, your time might be better spent achieving it." Her grim smile stretched her facial scars. "Or would you rather that I relieved you under the incompetence clause and placed Lieutenant Malanda Tomolo in charge?"

Creamer—face like a wooden mask—jerked to his feet, saluting. "Deploying now, Board Supervisor!"

He clicked his heels as he rotated and stalked out of the photonic com's reception.

Kalico leaned back, laced her fingers together with a sense of satisfaction. Soukup, even if he realized the implications, couldn't stop the deployment. Nor could he question her reasons for training *her* marines in survival skills.

Wasn't more than ten seconds before Margo Abibi settled herself into the command chair aboard *Turalon*'s AC, an amused smile on her lips. "Did you just commandeer three of my shuttles?"

"I'm sending the coordinates. If you could have your pilots drop *my* marines at the locations indicated, your shuttles should rendezvous with you by the time you're in orbit." Kalico gave the woman a slight shrug.

Abibi glanced off to the side; a ship-wide alert could be heard in the background. "Creamer's marines are being placed on alert."

"You heard my orders?"

"I heard."

"Think they can deploy from *Turalon* within four hours?"

"I doubt it."

"Please document their performance."

"Yes, Board Supervisor."

Kalico grinned. "I'd forgotten how formal that sounds."

Abibi arched her questioning eyebrow. "OTR?"

"Sure," Kalico told her.

"What are you doing?"

"Playing a very dangerous game of three-dimensional chess." Kalico tilted her head slightly. "First you have to disrupt your opponent's pawns. Then you can figure out how to tackle the king on the back row."

I t didn't matter that the ship alert was for the marines. Falise—
Ednund hot on her heels—jammed into the hallway with all the
others. Room—never at a surplus, even in the corridor on Command Deck—was cramped. She was reduced to shouting, "Out of
my way" and letting Ednund, with his muscular two-meter frame,
punch a hole through the press of crewmen and staff. But they made
it to the AC, only to find the heavy door closed. A knot of curious
transportees and crew were crowded before it, shouting questions
to each other.

Within moments, Second Officer Madra Arapava appeared, calling, "Break it up! Back to your duties! The marines are conducting
a surprise deployment. That means it's a drill, people. This is not an
emergency."

Falise crossed her arms, backed up against the sialon hallway, and
waited while people dribbled away, all talking among themselves
about what it meant.

When most had gone, Falise stepped up to Arapava asking,
"What are the marines doing?"

The woman had never been forthcoming, but always aloof and
the epitome of a professional officer. "You'd have to ask the captain
or Colonel Creamer." A forced smile. "If you will excuse me."

Falise glanced skeptically at Ednund, who kept his expression
featureless. Then she led the way to the Crew's Mess for a cup of
tea. The room—not counting the kitchen off to the side—barely
measured ten by eight meters, but for *Turalon* standards, it was the
equivalent of a ballroom. True, the Transportees' Mess two decks
down was larger, but who wanted to rub elbows with *them*? It was
bad enough to share space with the crew, but at least that carried a
hint of status.

She had barely seated herself, Ednund standing a half-pace be-

hind her, when Chad Grunnel came stomping in with his valet,
Charlotte, a customary half-step behind. He fixed on Falise, his
amber eyes lighting as he turned her way, demanding, "What is the
meaning of this?"

"From what I gather, the marines are conducting a surprise drill.
The good second officer told me to ask the captain or Colonel
Creamer, but then you'd know better than I when it comes to him."

"We discussed no drill." Chad had a bitter twist to his lips as he
seated himself across from her. Charlotte took up position behind
him, her eyes locked with Ednund's.

During the long transit from Solar System, Falise had made a
study of Charlotte. She was an exquisite thing, perfectly designed,
with fine features and an Olympian wrestler's body, as deadly as she
was beautiful, and having been trained by the guilds. Falise wondered if Charlotte might not have been an even better conquest than
Kramer. Wondered what Chad would do to the woman if he discovered that Cinque had been slipping his cock into Chad's prized
valet.

That was a risk Falise was just going to have to take.

From behind her cup of tea, Falise gave Chad a challenging
smile. "Then perhaps the colonel is keeping some of his cards to
himself. Thought you two were past secrets?"

Chad's expression quickened as he considered. "He's not that
clever. I'd have to say that this is the captain's work. But then, what
purpose would it serve for her to call up the marines? We're only
day and a half from orbit. All this does is create confusion."

"Unless it's an actual emergency." Falise juggled the pieces.
"Trouble with the transportees?" She discarded the thought. "No,
Arapava would have been more concerned, preoccupied. She passed
the whole thing off as within the scope of routine."

"Then, what was Abibi's purpose?"

Charlotte spoke, her voice that perfect pitch of musical and elo-
quent. "First in authority is Board Supervisor Aguila. Then Captain
Abibi, but only within certain situations or conditions. Third would
be the colonel himself."

Chad made a sign with his fingers, some clue that Charlotte read before adding, "My assessment of the man is that he would not conduct a surprise drill this close to our arrival at Capella III. Doing so would be out of character and perceived as contrary to his interests."

"Which are?"

Charlotte fixed Falise with her deep-purple designer eyes, a slight smile on her full lips. "Colonel Creamer would prefer to be prominent among the nobility upon de-boarding. In a position where he would be noticed and perceived as party to the elite."

Chad nodded, his frown deepening. "Aguila? Our mysterious and oddly missing Board Supervisor? To what purpose would she contact Creamer, have him run a drill?"

Falise turned, caught Ednund's eye. "Take a turn through the Transportee Deck. See what kind of drill the marines are running down there. Most likely, it will have something to do with the cargo hold. That's about the only place with enough room to conduct maneuvers."

"Hardly," Chad grumbled as Ednund hurried out. "It's packed tighter than atoms in a carbon lattice down there."

"Outside? Something in freefall?" Falise tapped at the corner of her jaw.

"While we're accelerating against Delta V at one-and-a-tenth gravity?" Chad shook his head. "I'm not much of a space guy, but I'm sure they'd go flying off into the black."

Falise noticed that Charlotte's expression had gone blank. In the time Falise had been on *Turalon*, she'd managed to learn the woman's tells. "Chad, your valet has hit on something. Do have her share."

Again, the flick of Chad's fingers; Charlotte immediately responded, "Assuming that she did indeed order this drill, now we know why Aguila has been noncommunicative."

Chad asked, "And that is because?"

"She believes she is acting from a position of strength. She is denying IG Soukup's ability to use them against her." Charlotte's expression cleared. "That is to be expected."

"But?" Falise asked.

"But she assumes that we're all playing according to Corporate rules."

Oh, clever indeed. Cinque—given his personality—couldn't help but make a play for the woman. But what was Charlotte's deep strategy? And, more to the point, was Chad too stupid to sense what was happening right under his nose?

Chad's expression had sharpened, and he spread his hands wide on the table. "How many times in reports do we read the phrase, 'Donovan does not adhere to Corporate norms,' or 'Corporate doctrine does not apply here?'"

Falise sipped her tea, smiling to herself. Chad, to her relief, had been the first to accede to a change in the rules. Couldn't have suited her better. Nevertheless, she said, "But it does." A beat. "When it relates to IG Soukup and Board Supervisor Aguila."

She was still smiling when Ednund came rushing in fifteen minutes later, declaring, "You won't believe it. The marines are scrambling around down on the Transportee Deck like frazzled chickens. And they're going to Capella III!"

"Aguila," Falise and Chad said in unison.

" I just took him down. I don't think the toilet-sucker had any clue. I mean, he's supposed to be some kind of tough guy. Gets in fights all the time. He never so much as laid a hand on me." Kylee nodded righteously as she talked. "You would have loved it. I just up and kicked him in the balls. As he jerked forward, I hammered him in the nose with a knee. When he staggered back, I smashed a fist to his throat, and he went down. Wham! Right on that filthy floor."

She could feel the Rocket part of her chortling in delight. She liked that about Rocket. He had a sense of humor. Like when they used to play. Or the time that . . .

No. Concentrate. This was about Tip, not the joy of reliving old memories.

Kylee resettled herself in the chair, double checking that Tip was breathing easily. He lay in the hospital bed, an oxygen tube running to his nostrils. His eyes were closed, chest rising and falling, but his color was off, and with her IR vision, she could see that his temperature was about forty Celsius. Definitely fevered.

Tip's leg, where it stuck out from under the blanket, was restrained, swollen, and still discolored. A drain tube ran from the incision to weep foul stuff into a glass beaker on the floor. The incision in Tip's calf looked pretty gruesome. Stitches held it together, a thin line of dried blood like a perverted smile. Another tube snaked out from under the blankets to a graduated bottle. This one ran from a catheter and caught Tip's urine. She'd checked it out, having never heard the term before, and decided that she would have been better off not knowing.

What mattered was that Tip was still alive. If she were a quetzal, she'd be glowing in blue and pink bands of gratitude.

She glanced around the hospital room. Outside of the bed and a toilet, it had one working light in the ceiling. Mold could be seen where the window in the dome wall leaked. And beyond it was the chain-link fence that separated the hospital from the landing field. Also depressing was the pale green paint on the walls. Like, what was wrong with something bright and refreshing? Or maybe they used these drab colors so that people would choose to die faster, freeing up the beds and cutting the workload for Raya and Vik Lawrence.

Vik, now there was an interesting woman. She'd been trained as a microbiologist and geneticist. She'd been a member of the Maritime Unit, its only survivor. She, too, was infected with TriNA, but hers had come from some sort of slime that lived in the oceans. It had left the woman's skin a curious green tone. To a quetzal, the color represented boredom, which colored Kylee's reaction to the woman. Right up until she came to understand that Vik had the Donovanian version of chloroplasts in her cells. She could partly live on sunlight.

"Funny thing," Kylee told the somnolent Tip, "but I'd gone quetzal, right? I could have killed him. Would have, but I think it was part of me that's Talina. Some element of restraint that cropped up in my head. Like a whispered voice in the back of my mind that said, 'This is not the bush.'"

She glanced at Tip, seeing his eyes flickering behind his lids. He'd always had the most amazing long lashes. Probably inherited them from Madison.

Kylee leaned forward, rubbed her eyes. Piss in a pot, but she missed Flute. This whole ordeal would have been so much more bearable if she could curl up against the quetzal's side, feel the warmth and safety. "Part of me's scared, Tip. Alone like I've never been. I mean, first there was Rocket. Then Flash. Then the Rorkies, followed by you and Flute. So, here I am. For the first time in my life, I don't have a quetzal around. I feel like, I don't know. Scared? Adrift? Fucking naked and defenseless. Like most of me is missing, gone suddenly silent and empty."

She lifted her gaze, desperate to see some sign that he'd heard her. Nothing.

"Your mother said that they had you knocked out. But, hey,

better to be sitting here with you than being stared at by these fart suckers who live here. And you can bet it's going to be worse after what I did to Hofer. Don't these candy-dicked bastards have any better sense than to shoot their mouths off like that?"

She rubbed her long-fingered hands together, seeing where the abrasions on her knuckles were already healing. TriNA had its advantages. She wondered what Flute would say when she got back and shared the memory with him.

She heard the steps out in the hall, figured it was Madison coming back. After standing vigil for most of the night, she'd finally taken up Talina's offer of a bed and gone to catch a couple of hours of sleep.

Instead, it was Raya Turnienko who stepped into the room, asking, "How's he doing?"

"If unconscious is good, he's got the planet by the balls." She shrugged. "But he's sure one hell of a poor conversationalist."

Raya laughed at that, glanced at the wall monitor that displayed Tip's pulse, blood pressure, and oxygen. "Temp's a little elevated. I could probably bring that down, but for all I know, it's helping with inflammation and immune response."

Kylee gestured at Tip's leg. "At least the smell's better. What was that thing you took out of him?"

Raya crossed her arms, leaned a shoulder against the puke-green wall. "Cheng and Shanteel Jones are dissecting it now. They're not sure it's a predator. At least, not of larger organisms. The gut's more designed for digesting plants. Dr. Jones thinks that it might have just been afraid, somehow threatened, and was trying to protect itself, but that's just a hypothesis."

"Guess that didn't work out so well for it."

"Or Tip," Raya noted. "But that's the bush for you." She fixed Kylee with her curious eyes. "How's the hip and leg? Any pain? Any lack of mobility? Things got so busy I didn't get to ask."

"Leg's great." Kylee extended her left leg within the cramped limits of Tip's bed. Flexed it. "I can't tell the difference between my left and right."

"Never bothers you?"

"Nope. You do really good work, Dr. Turnienko. For that, I owe you like, a whole lot."

Raya's flicker of a smile at the compliment died as quickly. "If that's the case, could I run some tests? Take an image of your hip and femur? Maybe a blood sample?"

Kylee felt that cold caution slip into place. "Why?"

"Because you're the future." She gestured at Tip. "So's he. You've grown up with TriNA. Part quetzal." Again the flicker of a smile. "And, besides, you live in the bush. Chances are good that you might wind up in my care again someday. Like Tip, I want to give you the best chance to make it that I can."

Kylee pursed her lips. "Yeah, that's always a possibility, huh?"

And she did owe the woman. Not to mention that, even though Tip was still hanging on by a thread, he was alive. That was something, especially since on the flight in, she wouldn't have given him a chance in hell.

20

From the com room in the admin building in Port Authority, Kalico Aguila monitored the progress of the three shuttles flying in. Heard them report as they broke formation and split up for approaches to their respective landing sites.

Little more than oversized closet, this was Two Spot's domain. The skinny com jockey, in his late thirties, practically lived here in the clutter of inoperative and mothballed photonic and hyperlink units, wrapped as they were in plastic. Instead, Two Spot ran his empire from the desk in the back of the room, dominated as it was by his radio.

Kalico checked the time; Margo Abibi was going to be disappointed. Her shuttles were so far behind schedule, they were going to be hours late for their orbital rendezvous with *Turalon*.

"What have you got, Abu Sassi?" she asked as she lifted the mic and shot the lanky Two Spot a "who knows?" look.

"Got my bird on visual, Supervisor. It's coming in from the west, taking a turn to the north now. They're kind of hovering. Curving more to the north. Wait . . . uh . . . Shit, yeah. They're setting down maybe a klick and a half north of here. Up on that ridge. But, ma'am, I swear. I'm standing right on the dot. One foot on each side of the coordinates you gave them."

"Figures." Kalico curled her lip at the mic. "All right, Corporal, go find your errant charges."

"Yes, ma'am. You sure we shouldn't have brought them in on a beacon?"

"That wouldn't have taught us that whoever made the final decision on that landing spot was a dickhead, would it?"

"A big fat gagging roger on that, Supervisor. Abu Sassi out."

Kalico shifted the frequency, asking "Corporate One, where are you? Your contact is standing on the coordinates you were given for deployment. Repeat: What is your position, Colonel?"

"About a kilometer and six hundred meters north of the LZ, Supervisor. I made the decision to set down on a rocky prominence that gave us better visibility and—"

"Colonel, you will deploy your marines and their tech, and you will re-board that shuttle. Your people will wait for Corporal Abu Sassi's arrival and will continue the mission under his command. After dust-off, you will present yourself to me, here, at Port Authority within the next fifteen minutes. Is that understood?"

A silence.

Then, the bitter words: *"Yes, Supervisor!"*

From the corner of his eye, Two Spot gave her a wary look.

Kalico lowered the mic, arched an eyebrow. "We were going to bump heads anyway, right? Might as well knock him on his ass with the first head-butt."

Flipping back to her military net, she asked, "Briah, report."

"My team deployed without issue, ma'am. Textbook. Shuttle's on its way to rendezvous."

"Roger that. Proceed with the exercise."

"Roger that."

"Dina? Report."

"My team is down, shuttle's dusted for orbit. My, but they have some nice equipment! All clean and shiny."

"Well, go get them dirty, but try not to get any of them killed."

"Roger that, Supervisor!" And in the background, Kalico heard Dina Michegan holler, *"Come on, marines. Let's hump it. Tech up, weapons hot. And welcome to Donovan!"*

Kalico cut the connection, still aware that Two Spot—slumped back in his chair—had curiosity written all over him. Not that he'd ever dare to overstep his bounds and ask outright.

"Strategy," she told him. "Doesn't matter that they're marines. They're soft meat. I want them out in the bush with my veterans. I want them smack up front with Donovan. Eyeball-to-eyeball with the forest, death, roots, sidewinders, and fear. And when they come staggering out of the bush, you can bet they're going to have a whole different level of respect for my veterans and Donovan."

"What about Colonel Creamer?" Two Spot asked.

Kalico smiled. "That scum sucker couldn't have been more accommodating." She cocked her head. "Do my ears deceive me? Or is that a shuttle approaching?"

"Shuttle, Supervisor." Two Spot tapped his ear. "Oh, and on com, I've got *Turalon*. Captain Abibi reports that she's made an orbital insertion. Once the ship's secure, she'll be awaiting permission to begin the process of shuttling her passengers and transportees down."

"Roger that." Kalico rubbed her jaw. "Sucking snot, Two Spot, but it's getting busy around here. Be sure you work out a safe rotation with *Vixen* before they link up with *Turalon* for that refit. Hard to believe, but the day is coming when we're going to need traffic control."

With the sound of the approaching shuttle getting louder, she shrugged on her quetzal cape, pulled the brim of her hat down tight, and headed for the door. Just out of good sense, she made sure that her pistol rode loosely in its holster. She didn't expect Creamer to be *that* much of an idiot, but on Donovan, stupid was dead.

21

I n all of his days in the Corps, not since he was a boot, had Stanley Creamer known such a rage. Enclosed in his combat armor, he sat in the right-hand seat on the A-7 shuttle's command deck as Ensign Schulyer made his approach to Port Authority.

Creamer boiled, seethed, and stared balefully out at the scrubby trees and weirdly blue-green vegetation they flew across. This was the supposed bush, as the locals called it. Reminded him of parts of Africa, or maybe the mesquite country in south Texas. Wasteland. Not a house, road, or sign that a human being had ever passed this way. Virgin fucking wilderness. And now, coming up, was a collection of hovels that looked like it could qualify for a refugee camp in Hell.

That was the fabled Port Authority?

He'd expected rustic. This looked like something out of a medieval history book. Not a single building was over three stories tall. Nor, but for the aging domes, was there any sense of architectural conformity. Not to mention that appalling and cobbled-together monstrosity of a fence.

And then there was Aguila. He clenched his first, thumped it angrily on the armrest, and let every vile curse word he knew roll through his head. What the hell had possessed him? He should have told her to suck vacuum and stayed with his marines. Called her bluff. Dared her to tromp out from this insane squalor of a town and relieve him.

Chad Grunnel would have backed him, spoken on his behalf if it ever got back to The Corporation. And that was a big if, given that a Board Appointed Inspector General was coming planet-side hot on Creamer's ass.

But at the last instant—despite the worried looks from his marines—he'd turned and trotted back into the shuttle.

He'd spent too many years in the Corps following orders. Even orders that made no sense. If he'd learned anything, it was that obedience was safety. Following orders without objection had taken him right up the chain of command. Until it had landed him on this *peach* of an assignment.

Never, ever, had a *civilian* questioned his judgment.

Now, he'd already suffered *two* reprimands from this woman. The implication that he was incapable of making a hot insertion was bad enough. To be *relieved* of command because he'd chosen a safer landing spot? That was absolutely unconscionable!

He ground his teeth as the shuttle maneuvered over the high wall of shipping crates, found a space on the heat-baked red soil, and settled.

Dust blew out from the thrusters. Dust? The frigging landing field wasn't even paved?

"We're here, sir," Schulyer told him. "Spooling down. I'll drop the ramp for you as soon as it's safe and dust off as soon as you're clear of the thrust, sir."

Yeah, right. His ride was leaving. Stranding him here in this shithovel of a town.

Creamer leaped to his feet, helmet swinging where it was clipped to his equipment belt. On the way off the command deck, he pulled his rifle from the rack and ducked through the hatch to stalk across the hold. Even as he did, the ramp began to drop; daylight appeared around the seams as it fell.

Creamer considered clamping on his helmet, not just as protection from the stink of burned fuel and dust, but to face Aguila. Let her get the full effect of what it meant to stare a real marine in the face.

Instead, he clumped down into the bright sunlight and squinted against the dust. There, that was the gate. A huge thing, it swung open to let a giant hauler roll through, red dust swirling around the lumbering vehicle's tires.

People were standing in a cluster before the gate. Creamer, driven by rage, thought, What the hell? He sprinted his way across the field at the double-quick. His powered armor made quick work of it as

he charged up to the woman and her two companions. Behind
them—in the confines of the gate—a guy with bushy hair, a flat
nose, and leather clothing stood with a rifle over his shoulder.

Creamer had studied the briefing materials, seen images of
quetzal-hide clothing and chamois leather, but to see it up close,
dazzling in luminous rainbow colors? Not to mention the crude cut
of the clothing, the ugly technicolor boots, the oversized floppy
hats. It was all he could do to keep from bursting out in laughter.
Circus pirates. These two women, dressed in quetzal, with their
hands on belted pistols? It was beyond comic.

To his dismay, up close Aguila's scars were even more appalling.
Like someone had taken a knife and viciously crisscrossed her face
with back-and-forth slashes. Then he met those hard eyes, laser-
blue, with no give in them.

Nevertheless, he barreled into her personal space, his armor giving him the advantage of height, imposing, shining, as he craned his
head forward and snapped, "Do you know what you just did . . .
Board Supervisor? You pulled me out of an operational situation you
had no—"

"Shut the fuck up, Colonel." Aguila lifted her chin, anything but
cowed by his invasion. He would have expected her to step back, to
have yielded ground. Instead, those stony eyes bored into his from
mere inches away. "You are one of two things: Either you're an
incompetent who can't locate a simple set of coordinates on the
ground, or you're incapable of understanding orders. Either way,
soft meat, you're a screw-up."

Creamer blinked, those first fingers of doubt beginning to slip
around his guts. Something about Kalico Aguila wasn't right.
During his career, he'd met Corporate Observers, Directors, and
even a handful of Supervisors and a couple of Board Supervisors
along the way. They might have been arrogant and puffed up with
themselves, but this woman? She stirred his sense of self-preservation.
And if Stanley Creamer was ever good at anything, it was saving his
hide.

Heart thumping at how close he was teetering to disaster, he
lowered his voice, saying, "Board Supervisor Aguila. With all due

respect, to insert yourself into military decisions that you might not fully understand. That could seriously impact mission integrity. I am sure that you had the best intentions, but you need to rely on my expertise . . ."

She raised a hand in a gesture to desist. To his surprise, he could see the lacey pattern of thin white scars on her palm and fingers. What the hell?

He glanced sidelong at the woman standing off to the side. Gaped. Stared.

Not as tall, with thick black hair, she looked like . . . like . . . Hell, how did he describe those almost pointed cheekbones? The oversized alien eyes? Like she was a caricature of human. A mocking smile made a curl of her lips. His sudden shock seemed to amuse her. If anything, her quetzal-hide dress was even more outlandish than the Supervisor's, right down to the knee-high boots and worn rifle hanging from its sling.

"Security Officer Talia Perez," the woman told him dryly. "If you can press your eyeballs back into their sockets and close your mouth, Colonel, I believe the Supervisor would like to finish chewing on your ass so that she can be rid of you and get back to meaningful work."

Creamer turned his angry gaze back to Aguila. "I'm a decorated colonel in the Marine Corps. Not some contracted transportee that you can—"

"Oh, but I can," Aguila told him flatly. "I think you could probably quote by rote the exact Corporate Code, article, section, and paragraph that gives a Board Appointed Supervisor that authority."

He lifted his hands in surrender. "You know there will be an inquiry. That capriciously removing a marine colonel from his command will be questioned. And, Board Appointed Supervisor or not, I have rights under the Corporate Military Code to seek redress."

A wicked smile bent Aguila's lips. "You do indeed, Colonel."

He stiffened to attention, snapping off a salute. "Then, with your permission, Board Supervisor, I will take my leave and present my case to Board Appointed Inspector General Soukup."

"That is your prerogative, Colonel. Have a good day." And with that, Aguila turned on her heel, striding purposefully back into Port Authority.

The freak-looking woman remained, studying him with those eerie oversized eyes. "Yeah," she concluded. "You're about what I expected."

Behind her, the bushy-haired, brown-skinned guy in leather had watched the entire interchange with amusement.

"I haven't a clue about what you expected," Creamer told her bitterly. "Now, if you'll direct me to the Corporate offices, I'd like to see about billeting for me and my marines."

The Perez woman's smile grew even wider. "Come on, Skull, I'll show you around. Not that I'm wild about it, given what you did to Max Taggart, but maybe I've got a twisted sense of humor."

Unsure what that meant, he followed her through the gate, ignoring the brown man who regarded him with knowing, almost sympathetic eyes.

Pus in a bucket, inside the fence the place was even worse than he'd imagined.

People were staring at him as he walked down the graveled avenue, his armor shining mirror-bright. Okay, change the description. The people were more like circus-cowboy-medieval-pirates, all of them carrying weapons.

"Did you read any of the briefing materials during the transit here?" Perez asked him.

"Of course. I had to know what my people were facing upon arrival. Do you think I'm an idiot?"

"Think? No. At this stage we're well into the realm of established fact." She shook her head. "There is no Corporate office. No spacer's lodging. Kalico keeps a barracks just over there in that two-story stone building. That's for her people rotating through on R& R from Corporate Mine and down at Southern Diggings. But you'll have to ask her for a bunk assignment."

"What about . . ." He struggled for the right words. "I mean, well, there's got to be something. The Corporation—"

"Doesn't exist here. Get it? We *bought* Port Authority from The

Corporation. We trade with them. They need us, we need them. It's survival, Skull. But if you're looking for The Corporation to give you a place to stay, something to eat, or whatever, you'd better go see the Supervisor. You're her responsibility. Not ours."

Creamer blinked. Trying to understand. They'd reached a wider, north-south avenue that transected the town. Now he stopped short, fully aware of the people staring at him as they passed.

"But how am I supposed to get back to *Turalon*?"

Perez crossed her arms, considered. "Well, that's easy. Two Spot can call them on the radio. Given you're Corporate, he'd probably do it for two siddars."

"What are siddars?"

"Local term for SDRs. Our coinage. We're a bunch of what you'd call filthy capitalists as well as libertarians. Cash economy."

"And where do I get siddars?" Creamer had the feeling reality was slipping away from him. Worse, the snot-sucking woman seemed to be enjoying it.

"You could get a job. The Jewel is right there. Yeah, that one on the corner. Wearing full armor, Allison might hire you as a bouncer. Or you could gamble for it. Probably something in your kit that someone would wager you for a bit of plunder. And finally, there's prospecting. In full armor? Not even Whitey could take you down."

"Who's Whitey?" Creamer wondered.

"Local badass quetzal." She checked her wrist com. "And, unless I miss my guess, your nine marines are a couple of klicks into their sweep. Hope they find the toilet sucker. He's about as tricky as they come."

With that, Perez called, "You have a fine rest of your day. Oh, and don't try the gates after dark. Sure, armored up, and with tech, you could force your way out, but you'd never set foot in PA again."

He watched her walk away, and even her stride was somehow alien. Almost a floating pace, balanced and powerful. Lions walked like that. What he'd call a supple slink.

"So, here I am," he told himself. "Turned loose in an insane asylum and surrounded by . . ." Then he chuckled, shook his head.

"Idiot." He reached up, accessing his battle com. "Private Mingo. Respond please."

"*Mingo, sir.*"

God, had Creamer ever heard a sweeter voice? "Patch me through to *Turalon*, Private."

Creamer waited, watching the locals pass, wincing every time they called some inane greeting his way, answering their waves. Who cared if the lunatics were friendly?

"*Turalon. This is the AC, Com Officer Cissi speaking. How can I help you, Colonel?*"

"Thank God. Cissi, I need you to dispatch a shuttle to pick me up. I'm at Port Authority."

"*One moment, Colonel.*" Silence. Then, "*I'm sorry, sir. Nothing's headed dirtside until tomorrow.*"

"This is an emergency."

"*Sorry, sir. Captain's orders. We'll have our first bird on the ground to-morrow morning 07:30 your time, Colonel.*"

He wouldn't beg. Nope. Absofragginglutely not.

"Roger that."

Taking another glance up and down the gravel-packed street, he turned his steps to The Jewel. He sure as hell wouldn't ask Aguila for a bunk.

When he stepped into the place, it was plain to see just what kind of establishment it was. The joint—mildly abuzz with conversation and laughter—turned instantly silent. All eyes on him in his combat armor. Made him feel silly and out of place.

But the long-legged blonde in a silky and close-fitted dress stepped out from behind the roulette table, striding up and taking his measure. "Can I help you?"

Creamer chuckled under his breath. Damn, she'd be a sight on any world. "Well, I'm kind of stuck here for a day. Colonel Stanley Creamer, ma'am. That Perez woman pointed me this direction."

The blonde arched a golden eyebrow. Creamer wondered if every woman on this accursed planet was tough as sialon.

"Tal did, huh?" she asked. "That's about as much imprimatur as you can get in PA. Come on, have a seat." She arched the eyebrow again. "Okay, maybe shed that heavy armor first. Enough of the furniture gets broken in here as it is. You got cash?"

"Well, I just got here. Perez said I could trade? Is that right?"

A man dressed in quetzal leather had stood from one of the back tables where a card game was in full swing. "Colonel, come on back. I'll set you up for a round."

"He's all yours, Dek," the blonde called. "Just keep him out of trouble."

"Oh," the man called Dek returned, "You can bet on that, Ali."

God! The guy called Dek was another freak. He brought to mind Perez, with his too-large yellow eyes, long hair framing a diamond-shaped face, and full beard, and like Aguila, the Cretan had a glaring scar under his left eye. Something about the man—a primal kind of intensity—was coiled in his movements. Hard and unbending. But, hey, any port in a storm, as the old saying went.

Five minutes later, his armor piled in the corner, Stanley Creamer lifted a glass of whiskey to his lips and sipped. "Wow. I expected rocket fuel. This is good."

"Not everything on Donovan is without its refinements, Colonel," Dek told him.

The other man at the table—big, looking like a ruffian—said his name was Step Allenovich. He gestured at the cards on the table and asked, "You play poker?"

Cards? Talk about old-fashioned. But even some purists in the barracks insisted on using them.

"Been known to," Creamer told him. At last! A little bit of luck. Here, finally, was his route to siddars and a night's excellent entertainment. He'd been good enough at the game that some of his fellow officers still refused to play him for stakes.

Poor fucking circus freaks. Vengeance for all the ills inflicted on him. He'd skin the bumpkins for everything they had.

Lifting the whiskey, he took a big swig, and said, "Deal!"

22

They called it "the bush." A term Private Keeko Ituri had never heard before. This was just awe-inspiring. Beyond a doubt the most phenomenal patrol she'd ever participated in.

In her youth, Ituri had spent some time in the deep forest in Congo. Her ancestors had raised plantains there, done some mining, and she'd wanted to gain an understanding of what their lives might have been like. What they'd seen and smelled. Making that tie to the past had been important to Ituri. So she'd visited the re-wilded areas where the rainforest was being introduced with regenerated species.

Wasn't nearly as freaking incredible as being on a quetzal hunt on Donovan. Granted, this wasn't deep forest, but it was a whole lot more remarkable, strange, and wonder-filled. For a poor kid from the slums of Kinshasa, it was about as unbelievable as a dream could get. Ituri had enlisted in the Corps because it was a way out of the endless cycles of poverty. She'd scored high enough on the Corporate aptitude tests to get her to boot camp. She'd never worked harder—figured she'd die before she failed to make the cutoff for service—and had passed. Until Donovan, that first trip off-planet to Transluna had been the high point of her life.

Being picked for the Donovan mission had scared her and her fellow marines half out of their wits. Deep within was that knowledge that they could end up lost. Die out in the black, never to be found. But here she was. Alive, walking her patrol transect through an alien landscape, her armor shining under an unfamiliar sun. The colors and shapes of the plants and trees, the sound of the chime, all the funny bushes and creatures, they were all miraculous in Ituri's opinion.

She kept an eye on her bearing, staying right on one hundred and twenty degrees as she rounded one of the aquajade trees. Her HUD was keeping track of her position vis-à-vis the rest of her squad as they searched the bush for any sign of a quetzal. Supposedly they'd pick up an IR trace or be cued by the drones flying on their flanks.

Best of all, despite Corporal Abu Sassi's constant chiding, she felt invincible. Sure, she could see the thorncactus and claw shrub as she strode through. The stuff kept trying to snag her feet and legs, the spines sliding harmlessly across the gleaming armor surface. Same with the bite ya bush and gotcha vine. She got the biggest kick out of the tooth flower. She'd poke her rifle barrel into a pod. Watch it snap shut around the steel. With the advantage of her servo-powered armor, she'd yank the gun free, breaking spines from the pod in the process.

The only real concern so far was news that Colonel Creamer had been relieved of command by Supervisor Aguila. What was that all about? Not that she or the others cared so much. The Colonel had been a pain in everyone's ass for the nineteen months they'd had to live under his alleged leadership. Sunny Valdez had called him "Colonel Cob" once. An allusion to the fact that Creamer had a corn cob up his ass. It had stuck, to be whispered around the gun room.

"*Head's up, people,*" Abu Sassi's voice came through the helmet com. "*Got a stream up here. Keep your orientation as you cross. Don't linger. Bottom's soft.*"

"*Crap!*" came Sasna Firiiki's irritated reply. "*Bottom's muddy. And there's something that looks like a leech clinging to my boot.*"

"*That's probably a slug,*" Abu Sassi replied. "*Nothing that will get past your armor. But people, listen and learn. If we were out here without thick boots or armor, we'd be cutting that thing out of Firiiki's leg with a combat knife. No anesthetic, no wait to evacuate. You cut it out immediately. Believe me. The pain and blood is easier than being eaten alive from the inside.*"

"*No shit?*" Bambo Asaana queried from his end of the line.

"*And to think the Colonel kept telling us that duty on Donovan would be like a day on the farm,*" Huac Than could be heard muttering into his com. "*Almost sank up to my ass in the creek. Gonna have to scrub armor for an hour to get the shine back.*"

Ituri pushed through the scrubby bushes around the creek;

branches reached for her, trying to get a hold. Weird shit, plants that moved. She watched thorns and suckers slide off her armor, one reaching out to slap itself across her face shield. Tearing loose, she made the creek crossing—narrow here—in one long leap. Grinned. So much for having to scrap mud from her armor.

"*Something's up people,*" Abu Sassi called. "*Do you hear the change in the chime? How it's gone slightly off key?*"

Ituri didn't, but then she'd never had a musical ear. Still sounded like a sick symphony to her.

"*Got a signal!*" Zhao Chin called from his position in the line. He was following his transect fifty meters south of Ituri's.

"*What kind of signal?*" Abu Sassi asked.

"*I, uh, don't know, Corporal. I mean. I had it. Reading an IR source about sixty meters ahead. Then, poof. Gone.*"

"*Thought I had one, too,*" Bambo Asaana announced. "*But mine was behind.*"

Ituri wondered what would radiate a thermal signal and then go cold. "You seen this before, Corporal?"

"*Negative on that. Quetzals usually give us a solid IR. While we talked about their ability to camouflage in the visible spectrum, IR always gives them away.*"

Ituri powered up a slope, weaving her way through the chabacho and aquajade, delighted when a couple of scarlet fliers burst from the treetops. Coolest looking flying things Ituri had ever seen, with their four wings and neon-bright blood-red color.

She noted the barest flicker register on the IR sensor in her heads-up display. Just as quickly, it was gone. "Same ghost that Chin saw?" she wondered. But this one had come from behind. Maybe ten or fifteen meters, if the fleeting signal could be trusted.

Cresting the terrace, Ituri kept her bearing, ensuring she was still online.

"*Got movement!*" Huac Than screamed. "*Front and back!*"

Ituri lost the rest, drowned by the other cries, all of them mingling together on her com. She was too busy with her own HUD, images of a blur coming right at her. A half second later, her armor was flashing an attack from the rear.

Ituri, by instinct, brought her rifle up.

And then the impact. Something hit her from behind, smashing her forward. Off-balance, she was reeling, trying to catch herself, when a creature burst from the screen of trees. The thing, giant, burning crimson, might have been a dragon. Ituri had the momentary sight of a great triangular head. Open jaws filled with rows of serrated teeth and a flared collar like a sail.

Then it smashed into her, hit her high. The impact blasted her off her feet.

The armor cushioned her body as it slammed into the ground.

Ituri, too panicked to move, stared up as two nightmarish monster heads loomed over her. One was standing on her armor. The second reached down with those gaping and tooth-filled jaws.

Keeko Ituri wasn't the only person screaming into her com as those rows of serrated teeth fastened around her helmet and began to twist.

23

So this was it. *Turalon*'s shuttle was inbound carrying Board Inspector General Suto Soukup. The moment of reckoning was finally coming. Approaching from somewhere out of that partly cloudy early morning sky.

Kalico Aguila gave a nod to Wejee as she approached the great gate. For the moment, it was open to allow passage of a hauler. Pamlico Jones and his crew had shifted some of the containers, and the PA shuttle had been towed off to the south a bit, leaving room for *Turalon*'s bird to set down. Kalico glanced around at the crowd, nodding to people, exchanging greetings. It wasn't just every day that a Corporate IG set foot on Donovan. She'd have an audience.

Step Allenovich—wearing a Dushku-fabric shirt, knee-high boots, a quetzal hat clamped on his head and a cape thrown over his shoulder—sported a nasty and swollen black eye. He gave Kalico a crooked grin that exposed yet another broken tooth. With a finger, he touched the brim of his hat, saying, "Hey, there, Supervisor. Looks like a whole new load of soft meat's on the way. Heard they're sending you an Inspector General."

"So it would seem." She gestured at the sky. "Guess I'll know what it means anytime now. He's supposed to be about ten minutes out."

Step glanced around, indicating some of the others crowding the gate, Tyrell Lawson, Terry Mishka, and Toby Montoya among them. "This inspector, Supervisor, if he gives you any trouble, you let me know. There's a bunch of us here, and, well, we're not letting any pus-sucking Corporate maggot mess with you. Don't you think that if it comes down to scratch and spit, your people won't back you. You need us? We'll send that white-assed Corporate inspector packing."

"And holding his balls to boot," Lawson growled as he gave her a squinty-eyed look.

When the light was just right, Kalico thought she could see a bruise on Lawson's cheek. What the hell had they all gotten into last night?

"You've had our back," Montoya added as he clenched a fist. "We've got yours."

Her heart warmed at the thought that a bunch of Port Authority hard cases were going to protect her from IG Soukup.

Kalico chuckled in delight before she said, "That means more than I can tell you. Seriously. But pay attention here: *Don't* interfere with a Board Appointed Inspector General. Especially Soukup." She met their eyes, shifting from man to man. "I mean it. And pass the word. It would end in a disaster for all of us if something happened to the man. Like, if IG Soukup was mysteriously shot, or disappeared without a trace. Or was found half-eaten outside the fence. And for God's sake, don't—under any circumstances— threaten the man. Any of those things occur, and it'll be like sticking your hand into a ball of mating invertebrates. We'll all end up bitten and stung."

"What do you need from us?" Step winced when he tried to frown. Reached up to dab tenderly at his eye.

"I need you to trust me." She gestured toward where the shuttle would appear. "I didn't get to be a Board Appointed Supervisor just by my good looks. This is *my* game. I have to play it by Corporate rules. On my turf. It's all strategy and tactics, sleight and feint, and the last thing I need is having to stop in the middle and try and apologize for, and explain why, some Donovanian tried to beat the shit out of the IG over a perceived 'matter of honor.'" She arched her scarred eyebrow. "Does that make sense?"

Step's grin was still crooked. "Yeah. We'd still rather feed him to a nightmare, but you've got our word. We trust you. We'll back you however you want to play it."

She reached out, slapped him on the back. "Now, what the hell happened to you?"

"Some of us had words with a fellow last night. Something about a lady's perceived matter of honor." Step touched his hat again, the grin widening.

Then the others laughed in some shared conspiracy, and they wandered off down the fence for a better view of the landing field.

"What was that all about?" Dek asked behind her shoulder, seeming to have just appeared from the crowd.

Kalico chuckled softly to herself, then turned to stare past Wejee at the eastern sky where the shuttle should be appearing at any moment. "Thinking about change, Dek. The first time I knew who Step Allenovich was, he was coming across the bar at Inga's to kill me. And here we are, how many years down the road? And he's telling me that he, Montoya, and the rest, will sandbag a Board Appointed IG and dispose of his body just, as they say, 'to have my back.'"

Dek stepped up beside her, thumbs in his belt next to his fancy pistol, his quetzal-hide cloak pulled back over his shoulders as he squinted up at the morning sky. "The day I arrived here, you asked me why I had come. Told me the old saw about finding myself, dying, or just coming here to leave. I found myself, but that's not nearly as fascinating as your story. You came, determined to leave. Then, afraid you would die, you found yourself when you weren't even looking."

He gestured around. "All of these people? They remember that you fought off mobbers, that you took your place on the line during Whitey's raid, and that you drove Benteen out. You made Corporate Mine happen from sheer guts and determination. You take the same risks they do. Put your life on the line side-by-side with them. The colony on Donovan is alive because of you."

She squinted up at the sky, wondering where the shuttle might be. "There have been too many failures mixed in, Dek. The Maritime Unit, the three attempts to drive the No. 3 into the mountain. Good people dead."

"Nothing's free, Kalico. And part of what they love about you is that you know what has to be done; and when it costs lives, you grieve just as much as they do." Dek gestured. "How's Step's eye this morning?"

"Someone left him with a hell of a shiner."

"Yeah, Creamer."

She turned. "Excuse me?"

Dek crossed his arms nonchalantly. "Creamer came stalking into The Jewel yesterday afternoon while I was running my game. I let him sit in, staked him to fifty SDRs. Bought him a whiskey. And while he was no mean poker player to start with, the more whiskey he drank, the larger the errors in his judgment. He'd already gambled away most of his armor, having convinced himself he was going to win it back on the next hand. When someone asked how you would react to that, he said the most unkind and vulgar things about your female anatomy."

Kalico felt her anger begin to brew. "He *gambled* away his armor?"

"Like I said, the more he drank, the higher his regard for his poker skills. But after he made that rather rude comment about your anatomy, the whole casino went dead silent. Can you imagine? The Jewel? At that time of night? You could have heard an invertebrate fart from thirty meters. Never seen the like."

Dek had that self-bemused look, made a chiding sound with his lips.

Kalico shook her head, pinched her nose. "Sucking vacuum. I've got an IG landing at any moment, and you're telling me a marine colonel gambled away most of his armor?"

"Well, all of it, actually. He had an outstanding tab that he couldn't pay. And he wasn't exactly conscious to object to the settlement Alison imposed. Especially given the broken furniture."

"What happened, Dek?" She thrust a finger under his chin.

"Why, when Step told the good colonel that he'd best damned well apologize, the colonel launched into what a . . . Well, better if I don't repeat the words. The takeaway was that you were not a very nice person. That there was some mucky muck inspector general coming, and the good colonel was going to personally see you fucked over and . . ." Dek frowned. "We never got to find out what he was going to see happen. That's when Step hit him."

"Step hit a marine colonel?" she asked coldly. "That's assault on a Corporate military office that could lead to—"

"Whoa!" Dek cried. "The colonel got in his licks. You know, he was trained in close quarters combat, hand-to-hand and all that. But he made the mistake of saying that anyone who'd lick the shit off your shoes was just as much a cunt." Dek winced as if he'd said too much. "Well, the whole place piled in." A smile. "Even Kalen Tompzen, can you believe it? He threw the final punch."

Kalico closed her eyes. "What part did you play?"

"Do you think I'm as dumb as I look? I got out of the way." Dek inspected his fingernails. "Wasn't like any of our people needed help. And despite my first inclinations, I figured you wouldn't want the good colonel's body to be discovered outside the fence and at the edge of the bush all covered with invertebrates."

"Where is he?" Kalico asked woodenly.

"My place. As badly as he was hurting, I gave him a healthy dose of the blue nasty. I mixed it with some of Dya's anesthetic paste. He'll be out for hours."

"Shit!" Kalico knotted a fist. She could hear the shuttle in the distance. "That's IG Soukup now."

Dek had pinched his lips, which pulled at the scar on his cheek. "My suggestion is that you turn your attention to the IG. Let me deal with Creamer."

"Dek, he's a Corporate marine colonel. That's playing with fire and—"

"Why, Kalico." He gave her his winning smile, the one that formed dimples in his quetzal-modified face. "Yes, he's a colonel. One who's been relieved of command, gambled away his armor, and gotten the shit kicked out of him in a brothel brawl. And me? I'm a Taglioni. And a really rich one."

She could see the shuttle now, glinting silver in the sunlight. "You be damned careful. This isn't just an IG. The Board sent him here. In a lot of ways, he's now the most powerful person on the planet. He can take you down just as easily as he can destroy me."

"Nothing comes without a little risk," Dek said evenly, his eyes on the shuttle.

The roar deafened as the sleek craft sailed in over the containers, thrusters down, landing struts deployed. The pointed nose gleamed

silver in the light as it swept around and set down on the fired clay.
Dust swirled and blew away. With a whine the engines began to
spool down.

"Let's hope this moment doesn't mark the end of an era, Dek."

"Yep."

Kalico stepped up to the gate, nodded to Wejee, who motioned
her past. She forced a knowing smile onto her lips. Well, what the
hell? This was the kind of fight she'd been born and trained for.
Matching wits with one of the most clever and suspicious men alive.
Not to mention his Four. The First was the recorder, the techno-
logically enhanced individual who concentrated on the witness or
subject being interviewed to determine their veracity and motive.
The Second was the monitor, an engineered human being with
chips integrated into his brain who stored evidence. The Third was
the analyst, who compared and evaluated data. And the Fourth was
the enforcement officer who carried out the IG's will, subdued or
arrested suspects, and acted as personal security.

Kalico was halfway to the shuttle before Shig appeared, having
come at a trot to be at her side, and there, too, was Talina Perez,
dressed in a semblance of a security officer's uniform. Not having
the fine fabric used for the real thing back in Transluna, Kalico
thought that Talina's locally crafted wear came off rather tawdry,
but she'd sure never tell Talina.

"Thought you were going to face the tiger alone, did you?" Tal
asked.

"This is Corporate politics," Kalico snapped, tone betraying her
tension.

"Of course," Shig said amiably. "But it would have been so rude
of us not to bid the good inspector welcome. I intend to extend an
invitation to my house for tea, should it please him. And I have
brought him a squash. Freshly picked from my garden just this
morning."

Kalico vented her anxiety. "Shig, do you really think a Board
Appointed IG gives a damn about a squash?"

Shig's beneficent smile belied the sharp intent behind his eyes.
"We are about to be in conflict, Supervisor. In many ways, our own

Kurukshetra. Families and lineages from our version of Ganhara are set to do battle over Donovan, and the IG may well be our Arjuna. That being the case, it would be well for him to realize that I might be the divine ambassador of the Pandavas. The squash is offered in that spirit."

Kalico glanced at Talina. "Any of that make sense to you?"

"Nope. But over the years there's been talk that Shig was dropped on his head a lot when he was a baby. On the other hand, we always seem to come out of it in one piece when Shig starts spouting Buddhist crap."

"The analogy to which I allude was Hindu," he said with a sigh.

Kalico watched as the airlock opened on the shuttle's side, the passenger stairs dropping.

"Here goes," she said, striding forward.

As expected, a man emerged. Dressed in a high-collared medium-gray jacket over slim-fitting white pants and footwear, he had a black sash of office draped from his left shoulder to right waist. Close-cropped silver hair, high forehead, piercing black eyes, and a strong jaw added to his authoritative expression. Taking the rail in a gloved hand, he carefully descended as if each step was considered and studied.

Behind him came the First—male, tall, close-cropped light-brown hair and hazel eyes. His head immediately began scanning back and forth as he descended. Recording every detail of the landing field for later analysis.

The Second might have been in his thirties, bald, his silver eyes looking mechanical, expression pinched. Like the First, he was dressed in gray, the tunic and pants featureless.

When the Third emerged, she had long white hair, though she, too, had the appearance of being in her thirties. When she reached the bottom of the ramp, Kalico could see that she had blue eyes, delicate features, and a slim figure.

And finally the Fourth emerged, squinted around in the light, and bounced down the steps like a dancer. The man was built like a human wedge, thick-shouldered, narrow-waisted, his face mostly flat planes around a knobby nose.

Kalico led the way, announcing, "Inspector General, welcome to Donovan. I am Board Supervisor Kalico Aguila."

Soukup tilted his head, that dark-eyed gaze sweeping her from head to toe. "You are dressed like a local? Have you nothing official to wear?"

"Not these days," Kalico told him with faked wry humor. She was achingly aware of the recorder and analyst, their gazes fixed on her with a stark focus. Reading her expressions, pupil dilation, skin flush, and temperature. "Come. Let me introduce Shig Mosadek. I'm sure you're familiar with his file."

"My pleasure, Inspector General," Shig said in his most amiable voice. "Welcome to Port Authority. As soon as your duties allow, I would like to have you come to my residence for a cup of tea and conversation. And, in the meantime, allow me to present this acorn squash, picked from my own garden. If you need cooking instructions, I would be delighted to offer some of my own recipes."

Shig extended the squash. The Fourth stepped forward placing himself between Shig and the IG.

Soukup stared at it, then back at Shig. "What do you expect in return, sir?"

Kalico fought the urge to rock her jaw, extended a restraining hand Talina's way when she started forward.

"Ah," Shig continued to smile benevolently, his squash still extended. "Alas, in Port Authority, no gain or obligation is implied. To offer a gift to a guest upon arrival is merely considered courtesy. The roots of the gesture are old, dating back to the origins of human society and symbolic of the establishment of goodwill. Much as I bid you welcome, and hope that your stay in Port Authority is enjoyable."

"I don't think enjoyment is on the IG's list of pursuits here," Talina announced.

Kalico added, "May I present Talina Perez? Tal takes care of security at Port Authority."

"Pleasure," Tal told him. If she was bothered by the sudden stares, the fixed attention of the Four, or even the quiver of Soukup's lips when he really fixed on her face and eyes, she didn't let it show past a slight narrowing of her large eyes.

"While you are with us," Shig said matter-of-factly, "we will be delighted to answer any of your questions to the best of our ability. While Port Authority is an independent community . . ."

Kalico lost the rest when the military channel on her earpiece announced, "*Supervisor? Abu Sassi, ma'am. We just had a fight with quetzals.*"

"Where are you, Corporal?" Kalico bent her head, raising a hand to her earbud to hear better.

"*Bout three klicks out, west of the aircar field. Damnest thing. Six of them. Hit us from front and rear. But for the armor? They'd have killed us all.*"

"Which way are they headed?"

"*Right toward town, ma'am. And moving like a chamois riding a rocket.*"

"Roger that."

Kalico ignored the rapt attention the IG and the Four fixed on her as she switched frequencies. "Two Spot? Quetzal alert. Six of them, three klicks west of the aircar field. Alert the farms. Prepare for a lockdown."

"*Got it!*"

Even as he said it, the sirens went off. The people waiting at the gate to see the newcomers broke like scarlet fliers as they left at a run.

Talina headed for the shuttle where a crewman was standing in the open hatch, calling, "Either dust off and head for orbit, or get off, lock up, and get inside the gate! Quetzal alert!"

Kalico growled a curse under her breath. Shot Soukup a disgusted squint, and said, "Welcome to Donovan. Now, get your asses inside the wire. Now, people, *move!*"

24

F alise took one last look around. Her crates, personal effects, and possessions had all been packed and sent to the shuttle while she had been in the Crew Mess eating her last meal aboard. Hard to believe, but these featureless walls had imprisoned her for the last nineteen months. The cabin almost looked spacious now that it was down to bare sialon and the built-in bed.

While she would have preferred making planet on the first shuttle, it was understandable that the Board Appointed Inspector General would take first preference. She and the rest of the families had to be content to take the second. Which, truthfully, was just as well. This way there would be no playing second fiddle after the IG when it came to making a first impression.

Falise turned, thankful to leave the wretched confines of the cabin behind. Nothing had prepared her for such hardship, confinement, and boredom. Well, there had been the thrill of seducing Kramer, and doing it right under Bartolome's nose. That would go down as one of the greater triumphs in her life. Too bad it had been so short-lived.

Striding into the hall, she found it vacant, the others having already taken their leave of Crew Deck. Good. She liked arriving either first or last, but never in the middle. The fine luminshift-fabric gown she'd chosen for the occasion rustled as she walked, having the same consistency of an antique taffeta; the stiffness allowed for the most pleasing extensions at the shoulders and hips. She'd chosen it for the stunning impression it would make upon arrival on Capella III. For the moment, she left it radiantly golden, but would let the colors bleed into violet after she and her staff had boarded the shuttle.

Ednund, of course, had suggested the dress, while Clarice had argued for one of the pantsuits. Something more in keeping with a frontier world.

"I want to make a statement," Falise had insisted. "The only Taglioni these wretches have ever known is my disaster of a brother. I want them to witness Taglioni elegance and superiority, a statement of fashion that no one on this ball of rock has seen before."

Passing a couple of the Tech IIIs, she ignored their greetings and stares, and stepped into the lift, ordering, "Shuttle deck."

A faint smile curled her lips. Falise had timed it perfectly. She'd make her entry a mere ten minutes before the scheduled departure. Her staff having arrived a half hour past, people would be wondering where she was. What was keeping her. When the lift stopped and opened, her appearance couldn't have been better. She swept into the departure room with its seats to one side and airlock on the far end. Even as she entered, Ensign Schulyer was opening the hatch and bowing as Chad Grunnel and his entourage were the first to board.

Cinque—from where he stood to the side—sent a smile and a nod her way. Acknowledgment of her triumphant entry. Using that as her cue, Falise triggered the luminshift to begin its transition to violet.

In slowly timed steps, Falise approached her staff. Ednund smiling his approval, Clarice inclining her head. Shoto bowed so deeply, the lights played on the back of his bald head. Fig and Phredo, of course, just stood with their eyes downcast, hands clasped obediently before them.

"Are we ready?" Falise asked as she joined them.

"All of the luggage is stowed, Lady," Ednund told her. "I have arranged for our seats to be next to the door. I got to Schulyer before the others thought of it. We'll be the last ones on, the first ones off. Much to Bartolome's chagrin. Cinque implied that he didn't care what order we disembarked, which, of course, is a misdirection. Chad accepts his being first to depart *Turalon,* and first to board the shuttle as his due and a Grunnel accomplishment."

"You are my miracle worker, Ednund," she told him.

"Ah," Clarice announced. "Lady, if you will allow us to precede you, we'll take our seats so that you may enter last. It will be you, seating yourself, that signals our readiness to depart the ship."

"Then, do precede me." Falise extended a hand, then took her place last in line.

As Falise passed through the airlock and into the shuttle, her dress had shifted into iridescent violet. She pulled the fabric out to its best display as she lowered herself into the seat beside the airlock. As she was buckled into the restraints by a crewwoman, she triggered the crimson program that began turning the fabric a ruby-laser red.

Head forward, eyes on the bulkhead, she barely heard the announcements from the command deck. Would they never depart?

And then it happened: the clang of the grapples, the sudden flip of the stomach as she was momentarily in freefall, and finally, the thrust that pushed her into her seat and returned a feeling of normalcy.

Falise—through force of will—kept her expression blank. She hated this. Nothing to see. Just the featureless sialon bulkhead between her and the command deck. Then the g-force shoving her into the conforming cushions. The roar of atmosphere and the thunder of the thrusters could be heard. She was tugged down into her seat, detesting the effect and worried that someone would see her face or breasts sagging.

God, would this never end? Though it couldn't have been more than twenty minutes, just when she thought the g-force interminable, it let up, a slight tremor running through the shuttle as the craft came to rest and the thrusters began to spool down.

"Ladies and gentlemen, we're dirtside. Welcome to Capella III." Schuyler's voice came through the com.

As the thrusters dropped to a soft whine and died, the crewwoman stepped over, unfastened Falise's restraints and gave her a hand up, asking, "You all right?"

"Perfectly so." Falise told her with a deadly smile as she struggled to keep from staggering in the planet's increased gravity. A Taglioni was always "all right."

Another crewman opened the cabin airlock and extended the stairs. A shaft of daylight came shining through. Light from Capella.

For the first time it sank in: *I am on a planet thirty light-years from Solar System!*

Falise walked to the door with carefully placed steps. How long had it been since she'd stood in planetary gravity? Five years, six?

She stopped at the hatch to stare out and get her bearings. A haze of red dust was vanishing, and the first thing she saw was the high patchwork of ugly fence backlit by an afternoon sun. Before people could pile up behind her, she made her way down the stairs in mincing steps so as not to trip. As she did she triggered her dress to shift from crimson to blaze orange.

But where was the reception committee? A line of planetary dignitaries should be at the foot of the stairs. Instead, there was just bare dirt. Only the crewwoman stood waiting, ready to offer assistance.

At the bottom, she stepped firmly onto the heat-glazed red soil of Capella III. Striding forth in her elevated shoes, it was all she could do to keep from wobbling on the uneven clay. She shot furtive glances in all directions and dared not windmill her arms for balance.

If I were to fall. . . . ? The humiliation would be unbearable.

The stacked containers, the parked equipment, the remarkable darker blue sky with its clouds. And the smell. Through the stink of burned fuel, she could detect a cardamom, saffron, vanilla scent. Something almost musical filled the air. Had to be the famous chime.

That's when she realized that her net had gone quiet. Try as she might, her implants couldn't access anything. A switch in her skull might have been flipped. And all that was left was silence. It was one thing to be told that she could access the memory in her implants, but that they couldn't communicate with the net? In an instant, access to a universe of knowledge had just vanished.

So, this is what it's like to be alone inside one's own head.

To Falise's amazement, a line of armored marines—facing outward—had weapons at port arms as if to guard the approach to the gate. And then she fixed on the lone woman standing in front of the main gate. Dressed in what Falise understood to be a quetzal-hide cloak, knee-high boots, a Donovanian-style wide-brimmed hat, and wearing a chamois leather shirt and britches, she held a battered looking and polished rifle at the ready. At first glance, Falise took her to be some genetically engineered caricature of a woman. The oddly proportioned face and too-large eyes, they sent a shiver of unease through Falise's blood. Something about the musculature, the almost feral grace, bespoke an alien quality. And danger. The woman narrowed those oversized eyes, was giving Falise—in her flaring and glowing luminous gown—a distasteful appraisal. The alien bitch's mouth pressed into a thin line, and a muted chuckle trapped in her throat.

The woman said, "You've got to be Falise. Bit overdressed, don't you think?"

"You will address me as Lady. And whatever license you might think you—"

"Lady? We're in the middle of a quetzal alert, so you'll get your bright-orange ass through that gate and follow directions on the way to the cafeteria so that we know for a fucking fact that you're not being eaten alive. Now, *move it!*"

Falise, started, stunned that *anyone* let alone this comically dressed cartoon figure of a woman . . .

"Lady?" Ednund whispered in her ear, taking her arm. "Let us not make a spectacle that the others can use against us. Rather, let us deal with this in our own way, in our own time."

"Yeah, try it, pretty boy," the Donovanian muttered. "Now, move it, you're holding up the freak show." The tone she used was absolutely intolerable. But how could she have heard Ednund's barely uttered words?

Falise made her hand sign for agreement, and forcibly ignored the woman, striking forward on her elevated translucent shoes, raising her hem so that they reflected the auburn light from her dress. Not that walking wasn't a challenge. Dirt! Not even concrete, let alone sialon.

Fuming—and in a rage like she'd never known—Falise stumbled her way forward. A gust of wind blew her glowing tangerine hem up past her knees and whipped it around. She stumbled, clutching at the light fabric of her gown. Strands of her perfectly coiffed hair were torn loose, flapping in the breeze. She would have fallen but for Ednund's quick hand on her elbow.

"Steady, lady. Steady," he told her.

With his hand on one arm, and Clarice's on the other, she made it to the gate, there to face a dark-skinned sentry with bushy red hair poking out from under one of the wide Donovanian hats. The fellow looked like a holo-vid villain, an oversized rifle in his hands. She fixed on his dark eyes, read the amusement in his expression.

"Down the road. Take a left at the main avenue," the man told her as she stormed through the gate. "Shig'll point you to the cafeteria. Orientation's there. And if the quetzals try the gate, the cafeteria will be our final refuge."

"Quetzals will try the gate?" Falise asked, staggered by another gust of wind that blew down the graveled avenue and pelted her with grit. She got her first glance at the buildings. But for the junked equipment parked between them, she might have stepped back into the Middle Ages in Europe.

"Hope not." The bushy-haired man gave her a grin that flashed large white teeth. "Steaks and leather if they do."

Ednund and Clarice keeping her steady, Shoto hurrying behind, with Phredo and Fig bringing up the rear, Falise stumbled ahead. Asked, "When have I *ever* been this humiliated? And why are we *walking?* Don't they know who we are?"

She avoided the gaze of another of the barbaric locals. Bearded, wide-brimmed hat pulled low on a mane of long blond hair, the rude fool had the kind of scar under his eye that hearkened to some barroom brawl. Something wasn't right about his face. Too broad, the cheekbones flaring. He was dressed in scuffed quetzal leather, and the only thing elegant about him was the ornate hunting rifle he gripped by the barrel, the stock balanced over his shoulder as if it were a working tool.

A young woman, same misshapen face, daughter, perhaps? stood beside him, whispering what had to be unkind comments. Her weird blue eyes—must have been a genetic defect—tracked every movement Falise made. Like a predator's gaze.

Suck vacuum, but if that girl, her bearded companion, and the handful of ruffians behind them were any indication, Falise figured she'd be better off back in that cramped cabin aboard *Turalon*.

"We're not doing so badly, Lady." Ednund shot a look behind them. "That freak of a woman is locked in one hell of an argument with Grunnel back on the other side of the gate. Cinque is watching from the rear, enjoying every moment of it."

"If there's a comeuppance for that insubordinate slit," Clarice noted, "you may have to race Chad to beat him to it."

"And Bartolome?" she asked, unwilling to take her gaze from the irregular gravel surface lest she trip and take a tumble on her high shoes. Bad Bart, if he saw her, would realize how distraught she was, and that was untenable.

"No sign of Derek, Lady," Ednund noted. "You'd think he'd make himself present at your arrival. He is your brother."

"Is he, Ednund? Look at this hovel. He's been living in this squalor for how long? I'd say it's rotted his brain. Turned him into one of these rudimentary dirt crawlers. My bet? He's drunk and enjoying the wares in the local brothel. Probably so inebriated, he's unaware of our arrival, let alone the day of the week."

Somehow she made it to the end of the avenue, was waved to the left down a broader street, past what looked like businesses housed in a variety of domes and crude stone-and-timber edifices. At the doorway to a weathered duraplast dome, a short man—of Indian ancestry if Falise was to guess—met her with a smile.

"Welcome to Port Authority. I am Shig Mosadek. If you would be so kind as to step inside, as soon as we have you all here, we'll begin our orientation. Again, welcome, and we hope your stay here will be enjoyable."

Falise bit off her response. *Don't even say it. If this deluded Cretan thinks there's enjoyment to be found here, he's either drugged or mentally deficient.*

"Thank you," Ednund told Mosadek, knowing full well the measure of Falise's rage and embarrassment.

The mutant-faced wretches from the gate had drifted along behind them—as if Falise and her entourage were the finest entertainment they'd seen in years. The way they moved, the powerful grace, just added to her fluster.

Clarice artfully steered her through the doors and into the dome. Shabby as it was, the place looked more like a repurposed warehouse. But at least the floor was level, and she wasn't wobbling on her feet.

"If I have to move heaven and earth," Falise vowed, "If I have to sell my body and condemn my soul, I will see the day when a Board order ensures that this hive of scum and vulgarity is scorched down to bedrock! I am a Taglioni!"

"Shhh," Ednund urged as they encountered a tall silver-blonde woman. Thin of build, she was wearing what looked like a crudely made stroud-fabric shift rustically embroidered with flowers and weird creatures. She had a long face and what Falise interpreted as weary green eyes.

"Welcome." The woman fixed on Falise's glowing-orange dress, stared, and couldn't suppress the twist of a disbelieving smile. Another common-born wretch to add to Falise's list to break, humiliate, and destroy.

"If you'd take a seat up at the table up front and to the left, we'll begin the introduction as soon as all the others have arrived."

Again, it was Ednund and Clarice who flanked Falise, got her to the indicated table. "This has to be a joke," Falise hissed. "They expect me to sit . . . in one of those?"

She grimaced at the collection of chairs around the table; mismatched, made of molded duraplast with tubular frames, they not only looked wretchedly uncomfortable, but as if they hadn't been washed in decades.

"Lady," Clarice said softly, "the others are entering. This is a moment for craft and guile. After the unfortunate impression on the landing field, we must play defensively. As if this were of no concern."

Falise took a deep breath, ground her teeth, and forced herself to rearrange her luminshift gown to best effect, choosing the laser-like crimson as she seated herself on the molded plastic seat. Then she got a good look at the place. A low stage rose against the back of the dome. Upon it, a podium had been shoved off to the side. An industrial kitchen was open to the room on the left side. There, a middle-aged woman in a smock was tending a serving line of steaming trays. The old hag didn't even bother trying to be surreptitious, but openly gaped at Falise, and then Bartolome, the boiling-mad Chad Grunnel, and finally Cinque as the others arrived with their entourages.

Falise's overwrought senses caught the odor of the food. After nineteen months on *Turalon* she wondered if it was the finest thing she'd ever smelled. Cooked by a contractee though it might have been.

In the rear, the doors were pulled shut with a bang. And down the aisle, between the tables, walked the freak-woman in her rustic quetzal garb and high boots. Rifle slung over her shoulder, one hand on a large service pistol at her belt, she climbed up on the low stage and faced them. Hat hanging behind her back, she shrugged her cape over her shoulders, the shimmering effects iridescent in the overhead lights.

"Welcome to Donovan," she snapped, glaring particularly at Chad Grunnel. "I'm Talina Perez. I'm in charge of security in Port Authority. That means my word is law."

A series of chuckles, all low, could be heard around the room.

Up on the stage, Perez's smile went cold and the feral planes of her face seemed even more alien. The woman's eyes expanded, somehow dark and depthless. She said, "Laugh all you want. You're what we call soft meat."

"How dare you," Chad muttered. "I'm a Grunnel. A member of a family who's—"

"You're jack shit, soft meat," Perez barked in disgust. Then she raised a hand. "Let's back up. Here's how reality works here: On Donovan, no quetzal, no slug, skewer, or BEM gives a flying fuck who your family is back in Solar System. You digest just as well as some poor slob who's been exiled to the Belt. Get it? You're a meal waiting to set foot out past the wire."

To Falise's surprise, it was Cinque who stood, raising his voice.

"Officer Perez, I am Cinque Suharto, duly appointed representative of my family." He gestured at Chad and then—to her disquiet—at Falise. "I realize that some of my companions, well, let's say they were inadequately prepared for the realities of Port Authority. Please do not judge them too harshly. They will most assuredly realize the short-sightedness of their folly. In the meantime, understand that there are those of us who are anxious to learn of Port Authority's opportunities. For myself, and on behalf of my family, I will be grateful for any advice or instruction that you can give me."

"Artfully done," Clarice noted.

Falise closed her eyes, a churning of embarrassment, anger, and frustration in her gut. "How did this all go so badly! We look like fools."

"Welcome to Donovan," Ednund whispered under his breath.

As Talina Perez launched into her "orientation," Falise wondered if she wouldn't be better served taking the next shuttle up to *Turalon*.

25

By the time Dek made his way into the cafeteria, Talina had finished her lambasting—as he called her introduction to Donovan for soft meat and Skulls. As had long been the custom, Millicent Graves had prepared a feast for the new arrivals. Yvette and Shig were both up on the stage, taking questions from the various valets and staff. Shig, still smiling amiably, and Yvette, glaring stiffly, were pretty much down to answering the same questions over and over.

"Yes, Corporate Mine will be covering your meals and lodging for the time being." "No, we do not have universal com here like you were used to in Solar System and on *Turalon*. So, your implants can't access *anything*." "No, you cannot go outside the fence at night. It is too dangerous." "Yes, you must pay for everything with SDRs. Nothing will just be given to you." "Yes, you will have your own domes." "No, there is no hotel." "Yes. The quetzal alert is real. This morning six of them attacked a party of marines on a training exercise." "Yes, your personal luggage will be delivered to your place of lodging."

Kylee led the way to the food line, Dek close behind. The part of him that was quetzal felt warily on edge. Filling their plates, they seated themselves at a table in the rear. The dish was a mixture of black, Anasazi, and pinto beans mixed with poblano peppers, chili spices, and chunks of chamois meat. Cherry pie was the dessert.

"You going to go say hello to your sister?" Kylee asked.

"You going to go say hello to any of yours?" Dek shot back, referring to the Mundo family Kylee had adamantly refused to see.

Chewing a particularly tough and stringy chunk of chamois meat, Kylee made a face. Swallowed. Her eyes on Falise, she said, "I got an idea. We could put your sister up on a tall pole out at the aircar field. With that glowing dress, she could be a navigational beacon we could see all the way from the Wind Mountains."

"It's called luminshift." Dek gave his sister an amused glance. "Fabric that changes colors has been around for a long time, but not with the luminosity, let alone the implant link that lets a person think a color change, and then it happens. What that dress cost back on Transluna would have housed and fed a hundred families for a year."

Down inside, Demon hissed, as if the beast could have cared. Or maybe he did it just to raise Dek's hackles. The evil little son of a bitch had come close enough to killing him out at Two Falls Gap.

"Well, the only thing it did for your sister was make her look like a fucking moron." Kylee pointed with her spoon. "You sure you're really related to her?"

Dek heard Rocket's chittering amusement as it filtered through his head.

Talina, arms crossed, her hat hanging down her back from its strings, walked over, hard eyes on the four nobles and their entourages at the tables up front.

"So that's the cream of the Corporate crop? And *she's* your sister? Did you see how she came off the shuttle?" Talina made a face. "Maybe your mother was having an affair with someone smart when you were conceived?"

Kylee snickered, used her sleeve to rub her mouth where it dripped chili.

"That seems to be a recurrent theme at this table." Dek took a bite, chewed. "To set both your minds at ease, Taglioni genetics are very carefully monitored. Little sister, up there, in her colorful carnival tent of a dress and absurdly impractical transparent shoes, has the same genes I do." He swallowed. "The difference is that where I grew up to be a cad and bounder, she grew up to be a spider. She likes webs, intrigue, and camouflage before she kills her prey."

"She walked right past you at the gate," Talina noted. "Like she had no clue who you were."

"She didn't." Unlike Kylee, Dek used a napkin. "It's the beard, the scar, the fact that, like you and Kylee, the facial bones and eyes have changed. Oh, she looked at me, all right. What she saw repulsed her, and—being the kind of local riffraff that we are—she didn't bother to hide her disgust. And then she turned her attention to fuming over the comic disaster that her arrival turned into."

"You could have warned her about what to wear." Talina was still watching the room, flickers of irritation playing at the corners of her mouth as she studied the nobles and their hangers-on.

"Not a chance." Dek shrugged as he took another spoonful. "Wouldn't have made any difference had I tried. You have to understand: Falise might not be right, but sure as clap-trapping hell, she's *never* wrong. She'd have done it her way no matter what."

"She really that dense?" Kylee asked. "That's the kind of stupidity I'd expect from Dortmund Short Mind."

Talina told her, "If all you've ever known is the inside of an artificial bubble, where everything is provided for you, decisions are made for you, and you do what you're told, how can you even conceive of a place like Donovan? These people don't have a clue."

"Yeah. Thought you were going to lay fancy Falise out flat when she mouthed off to you out there." Kylee used a piece of bread to sop up the drippings in her bowl.

"Wouldn't have been smart," Tal said. "Too many repercussions. And I heard the pretty boy whispering that they'd get even with me later. So, Dek, what's with the golden-haired guy fawning at your sister's side? He looks too beautiful and perfect to be real."

"That's Ednund. Her valet. He's her political and social advisor, errand boy, bodyguard, bed companion, spy, killer, and jack of all trades. The stately woman who looks like a reincarnated Egyptian queen is Clarice. Think of her as a sort of human computer and analyst, but also capable of performing most of the tasks Ednund handles. From birth, they've been trained, molded, tested, and prepared to perform any task my sister might require of them."

"Maybe Donovan will corrupt them like it did you," Talina noted. "Maybe I'll make them an offer."

"Don't," Dek warned her. "Talina, they *belong* to Falise. They are property, raised, engineered, and designed to serve her. It's their sole purpose in life."

"You mean they're slaves?" Kylee asked as she stared thoughtfully across the room. "The kind I read about in the history books? Thought slavery was illegal in The Corporation."

"They are, and it is." Dek felt his smile turn grim. "The families are, shall we say, above the law."

Talina drew a deep breath. "Chad Grunnel was within a hair's breadth of getting himself laid out back on the shuttle field. I got the feeling that eye-candy woman was going to launch herself at me. She as good in a fight as I think she is?"

Dek said, "That's Charlotte, Chad's valet. And yes, just because she looks like a holovid wet dream, she's just as deadly as Ednund, and as competent. Keep in mind, none of the families would have sent these people if they weren't capable, clever, and important. *Turalon* and *Ashanti* tantalized the families with what was at stake on Donovan. Kalico got Soukup. We got my sister, Cinque, Chad, and Bad Bart in return. From here on out, the game gets started in earnest."

"What does that mean?" Talina asked, the expression on her face leading Dek to think that, in her imagination, she was beating the snot out of Chad Grunnel.

"Means we're going to have to be careful from here on out."

"What did you do with the colonel?" Talina asked.

"Wheeled him out to that shuttle on Fred Han Chow's cart after you started your lecture. He's still hungover, high on the pharma I gave him, and really messed up after the beating Step and the rest gave him in The Jewel. In fact . . ."

Dek stopped as a roar built, grew to the point that it overwhelmed talk in the cafeteria, and slowly faded. "Ah, yes, I'd say he's on his way to *Turalon*'s med bay for treatment. Wiring the guy's jaw will be first on their list. The broken ribs will heal over the next couple of months."

"And now," Shig's voice carried over the fading sound of the shuttle's thrusters, "if you will follow your guides, we will escort you to your places of lodging. It is my understanding that Supervisor Aguila has taken the liberty of delivering enough currency to cover your immediate expenses during your stay in Port Authority.

And, should you have any questions, please do not hesitate to ask. You will find our people most helpful."

Dek laid his spoon down, saying, "There's my cue."

Talina gave him a twisted grin. "You're really going to do this?"

"Damn straight," Dek told her, rising. "I wouldn't miss it for the world."

"If pretty boy, over there, kills you, I'm going to rip his lungs out and use them to beat him to death in front of your sister," Talina promised.

"Want to come?" Kylee asked. "Should be quite a show."

"Sorry," Talina told her. "I've got quetzals somewhere close by out in the bush. Given my choice of dangerous monsters, I'll take my chances with Whitey and his pack of killers."

"Coward," Dek muttered.

"Smart," Talina noted, bending down to kiss him on the lips. "Be careful."

"You, too."

26

In the admin dome, Kalico, Allison, and Step huddled shoulder-to-shoulder over the town's quetzal map. Unrolled beside it, and covering the other half of the table, was an aerial view of the bush surrounding Port Authority as far out as the mine. Not that it told Kalico much. An X had been penciled in to mark the spot where the marines had been attacked that morning.

In the back of the room, closely packed, like some curious organism, the Four stood. IG Soukup had seated himself at the far end of the table and watched the proceedings with dispassionate black eyes, no expression crossing his face.

Step kept throwing scowling glares in the direction of the Four. "Bastards give me the creep-freaks," he muttered. "It's like they're not even human."

"They aren't," Kalico told him, heedless of their attention. "The First, Second, and Third are engineered for a specific function. All part of the evidence-gathering process. They don't care what you think of them. Don't have feelings that you can hurt. They're just tools to help the IG in his investigation."

"Doesn't that bother you?" Allison whispered.

"Not particularly. I've called on the IG's office before. Back when I was Supervisor of Transluna. Not Soukup, but several of his colleagues. They're very good at what they do. Unbiased, totally efficient, and absolutely dispassionate."

Step, dabbing at his swollen eye, asked, "So, what's worse? Quetzals sneaking around in the bush, trying to tackle marines, or these guys, staring at us like we're a freak show?"

"Quetzals," Kalico told him. "I say that because none of this makes sense. Why hit the marines?"

"Whitey knew the marines were looking for him and his lineage?" Allison suggested.

Kalico lifted a scarred eyebrow. "Before this morning, Whitey's quetzals have never directly attacked human beings wearing armor. I'm not sure he knew what they were. I mean, yes, we've used armored marines during quetzal hunts, but even during Whitey's last raid, three years ago, he was never in direct contact with armor. Tal shot him up, killed one. But Benteen blew a hole in the fence before my marines could take him down with tech."

Step kept prodding at his swollen eye. "That's a point. Abu Sassi says three attacked from the front, three from the rear. It happened so fast, the poor marines, even with their helmet displays, barely saw it coming. Then, wham, they were on the ground being savaged."

"Must have shit themselves inside out," Allison agreed. "One minute they're bored out of their skulls on a nature hike, the next jaws are being clamped around their helmets."

Kalico studied the map, wondering where the quetzals had vanished to. Despite crisscrossing the area, the drones were coming up with nothing. "I wanted the new people to get a feel for the bush, for the dangers. Somehow, I'm willing to wager that all of a sudden, they've had an epiphany."

Step slapped a hand to the map. "So, where did they go? With a drone, we've always been able to pick up a quetzal. They can't hide that infrared signal. And once we had a hit, it was just a matter of tracking the fart-sucking beast down."

"Beast," Allison added. "Single. There are six of them out there. Changes the whole calculus. You and Tal going out in an aircar to start tracking? Knowing that even if you close on one, or two, or maybe three, there's another three? Lurking . . . where? To do what?"

"Why can't we get an IR reading?" Kalico asked again.

"Maybe because they know?" Talina said as she stepped in the door and set her rifle to one side.

"How's that, Tal?" Step asked.

"Just a bad thought," Talina told them as she walked over the table. "But consider this: Quetzals are used to camouflaging in the visible spectrum. They're so good at it, people hunting them have stepped on them."

"But they still give off an IR signature," Step reminded. "And usually they've been running, burning energy. That's what makes tech so good when we're hunting them. They glow."

"Quetzals also control their infrared, use it at night the same way they do color during the day." Talina shot Soukup a wary glance. "At night, they communicate through IR patterns. So, it's not like they can't modify their signatures. Maybe they've figured out how the drones locate them?"

"What about the body heat?" Step asked. "Metabolism is still a chemical fire. It's not like they can shut themselves off, stop digesting, breathing, pumping blood through their arteries."

"Are we sure of that?" Allison asked.

"Well . . . uh . . ." Step made a face. "No."

"There's a lot we don't know about quetzals," Talina said absently. "Even with everything I've been privy to."

"Yeah, something to think about." Talina looked around the table. "The *Turalon* shuttle is skids-up for space. Gates are locked, and marines are standing watch with our people. Motion sensors are on, lights are covering the usual avenues of approach. Shig's sent the overinflated aristocracy off to be horrified by their new lodgings. Unless we've missed something, we're tight for the night."

"I'd better get back to The Jewel," Allison said. "God knows, we barely got cleaned up after last night's free-for-all. And I don't want one of these entitled soft meat wandering in if I'm not there. Costs too much to replace the breakage."

"Appreciate that, Allison." Kalico called. Then she glanced over at Soukup. "You had anything to eat, Inspector? I'm headed to Inga's for the special. I'll stand you and your Four to a meal and a drink."

"That would be considered a compromise of ethics." The IG fixed his black eyes on her.

Kalico stepped over to him, ensuring the First had a good view. "IG Soukup, here's how it lines out: I am not buying you anything, let alone hoping to compromise your ethics. Your meal, drink, and lodging here are being paid for by Corporate Mine. Fact: You're in Port Authority. Everything here functions on a cash economy. If you don't pay for it, you don't eat. If you don't eat, you die of star-vation, which will reflect very poorly on my reputation when the word gets back to the Board."

Kalico wasn't sure. She thought Soukup's lips might have twitched in amusement.

Step and Allison—who'd watched the interchange—left with silly grins on their faces.

"Very well," Soukup extended an arm. "After you."

But as they were leaving the dome, Soukup matched his stride with Talina Perez's, asking, "Security Officer Perez, would you mind if I asked you some questions?"

Kalico saw Tal shoot a wary look over her shoulder at the Four where they followed in matched step not more than a meter behind. "What do you need, Inspector General?"

"According to the records, you shot Supervisor Clemenceau?"

Tal gave the man a squinty sidelong appraisal. "No secret there. You read the transcripts? The good Supervisor here held an inquest."

"I did." Kalico interjected. "Inspector General, if you're fishing for the villain of the piece, it was Clemenceau. He toppled the first of the dominoes, and as the months stretched into years without a ship from Earth, the man turned into a paranoid monster. When the nightmare dragged him up into that mundo tree, Officer Perez did him a favor."

"Favor? A curious word for a bullet in the head," Soukup said tonelessly.

"Don't make the same mistake I did," Kalico told him as they walked up to the tavern doors. "The most humiliating moment in my life was when I discovered what a nightmare on Donovan was." She pointed a finger his way. "Since then, I've had a real education in humility, compassion, and the way reality on Donovan can slap you right in the face."

"And where does Corporate law rank in that education, Super-visor?" The words were spoken mildly.

Kalico gave the man a knowing grin. "It's easy to ask that

question when tentacles aren't weaving their way through your guts and digesting them."

She was fully aware of the attention the Four were focusing on her.

As they started down the stairs, Talina added, "Inspector General, focusing on Clemenceau and the law is going to get messier for you than a mud puddle full of slugs. Let's just say that Corporate law didn't figure much in Clemenceau's thinking there at the end. Unless, of course, the legal code regarding extortion, kidnapping, rape, and murder have changed since I shipped for Donovan."

Reaching the bottom of the stairs, Kalico answered the waves various people sent her way, all of them staring curiously at the IG and his Four. Remembering Step's earlier declaration that they had her back, she chose a table off to the right and in front, the one close to her usual place at the bar. Talina, gave her a "see you" salute and retreated to her stool, calling, "Stout and the special, Inga!"

Seating herself, Kalico leaned forward and braced her elbows on the table, meeting Soukup's emotionless stare. "It seems, Inspector General, that we haven't really had a chance to talk, what with quetzals and all. So, where do we go from here?"

"I want to see all of the Corporate assets. There are questions. Specifically, what is Corporate Mine? What happened to *Freelander*? I want a personal update and inspection of the Maritime Unit. What is the current condition and circumstance of the Unreconciled, as they are called? What, specifically, is your relationship with Port Authority, and was your decision to hand it over to the Donovanians in the best interest of The Corporation? I would also like to interview Captain Torgussen of the *Vixen,* given that there are questions about his transition, not to mention Tamarland Benteen. In addition, there are questions regarding your personal allocation of Corporate property and assets. And, of course, I must pursue any irregularities my investigation might uncover."

Kalico chuckled, glancing up as one of the wait staff appeared. "We need the special, six of them, all the way around. A glass of whiskey with a water back for me. Mint tea for the IG and his aides since they don't drink. Put it on the Corporate tab."

"You got it, Kalico," Ginnie Nagargana called, spinning on her
heel and heading for the kitchen.

"Kalico? That seemed a bit familiar," Soukup noted. "Do these
people have so little respect for your position?"

The intent focus by the First and Second irritated her as she said,
"Look around you, IG. Take in each face, notice the expressions.
The way these individuals interact. Each and every one of these
people depends on every other person in this room. We're all achingly aware that Whitey and five other quetzals attacked a bunch of
marines out in the bush this morning. That's never happened before. At any moment, IG, your life and safety might depend on
someone in this room. I can tell you for a fact: When you're out
there, in the dark, standing over the half-eaten body of someone
you knew, facing the cold realization that at any instant you might
be next, position and titles really aren't worth a smear of shit on
your shoe."

Soukup continued to give her that same flat-black stare.

With a humorless chuckle, Kalico told him, "All right, Inspector
General. Starting tomorrow, I'm going to grant your every wish.
I'll leave it up to you and your Four to carry my nightmares back to
the Board." To emphasize the point, she stared hard into the First's
eyes, asking, "You got that down verbatim?"

But, of course, the First never answered.

27

Having polished off a chamois steak cooked in red chili sauce accompanied by baked squash, Talina nursed her glass of stout. She sat on her usual stool in Inga's, glancing back at the crowd. Of course, the place was packed. A ship had arrived—even if, so far, the shuttles had only landed the IG and his robot-like entourage, and then the fricking aristocracy. So everybody had come to Inga's, hoping to learn the news. Not to mention that the town was on a quetzal alert.

She could feel Demon squirming around behind her liver. When he did that, it usually meant trouble.

For the moment, all eyes were on Kalico Aguila and the Board Appointed Inspector General and his Four. Word had run through town like wildfire. Speculation was rampant. What did the man's presence mean for Kalico? For Corporate Mine and Donovan's future?

Yeah, well, lot of that going around. The fact that he'd asked about Clemenceau right off the bat suggested that the sly sidewinder would eventually pick the scabs off a lot of old and somewhat healed wounds.

As she reflected on the day, her thoughts kept returning to Chad Grunnel and Dek's sister Falise. Both were going to be trouble; she'd seen it in their eyes. There would be a reckoning. She'd never dealt with people like these. Entitled. Arrogant. Who had never been corrected by someone they considered a lowly menial.

She was musing on that when the normal volume dropped.

Turning, she saw Cinque Suharto as he descended the stairs. Every eye in the place fixed on him.

The guy was still dressed in that remarkable black fabric that tricked the eye into thinking it was looking into a hole in midnight. The fabric worked well with the man's completely black eyes, complexion, and sleek black hair where it was tied back in a pony-tail that hung down his back. As he picked her out and crossed the paving stones with a leonine walk, a slight smile—one that reeked of challenge—bent his fine lips.

Without hesitation, he walked up and climbed onto the barstool beside hers. She caught his subtle scent, thick with pheromones. Ah, so that was the game. Dek had explained that the nobles born to the families could excrete chemicals that would influence their prey. Her quetzal-improved nose figured it was some kind of male musk meant to increase his sexual allure.

She arched an eyebrow, meeting his designer-black eyes. They reminded her of glass orbs set in his handsome face. Might have shaken someone who hadn't spent time with quetzals.

"Mind if I join you?" he asked pleasantly.

"Danger," Rocket whispered from behind her ear.

"Where's your valet and entourage?" She asked. "Bit adventurous, wandering in here on your own, don't you think? And unescorted when there's quetzals about."

"But, you're part quetzal, right?" He paused while he really inspected her face, concentrated on her eyes. "That's the exotic look. Almost as if you were drawn as an enhanced image of a beautiful woman."

"Yeah," she told him. "I used to be a lop-jawed hunchback with an oversized nose, and ugly enough to crack a mirror until I got cell-fucked and genetically impregnated with TriNA. Aren't I lucky that I've transformed into such a stunning piece of pulchritude?"

He laughed, looking actually amused. "You're not what I expected, Talina Perez. And, got to tell you, it's a vacuum-sucking relief after nineteen months in that cramped warren of a ship."

"How're your quarters?"

"Those are really the best beds on the planet?" He stopped as Inga came stalking up.

The big woman gave Cinque a disapproving squint. "Those eyes of yours? They do that on purpose?" she asked as she slapped her towel down and took a couple of swipes at the battered chabacho wood.

"They did," Cinque told her tonelessly, his black orbs fixing on the buxom woman.

Tal slipped her hand down, fingers lacing around the grip on her pistol. If Cinque went after Inga, she figured she could whip the pistol out, smack him across the bridge of the nose, and have him on the ground before he could recover.

But to her relief, Cinque asked, "And who are you?"

"Meet Inga Lock," Tal introduced. "If you ask around, you'll find that most people consider her the most important person on the planet. This is her tavern and restaurant, and she makes the best drink on Donovan."

At that, Inga grinned. "What'll you have, mister?"

Talina said, "Bring him a special. And what are you drinking, Cinque?"

"That stout?"

"It is."

"That, then."

"My tab," Talina said, throwing a five-SDR coin out on the bar as an example for Cinque.

He watched Inga depart in her rolling gait. "Does she know who she was talking to?"

Talina leaned forward. "Learn something, soft meat: Compared to the people in this room, you have no skills, no particular worth. Sure, the Suharto name buys you a certain amount of protection. It would reflect poorly on Kalico if you got eaten or were shot dead by a local in a barroom fight. After word was carried back, your family might take umbrage and cause us all trouble down the road. Because it would be a pain in the ass, we'd just as soon avoid that."

"What about Derek Taglioni?" Cinque shot her a look that she couldn't read, which added another layer to those opaque black eyes.

"That why you sought me out?"

"I heard that you and he are close."

"Yeah? What of it?" She felt the quetzal stir in her blood, knew her eyes were enlarging as the IR and UV kicked in.

Cinque seemed to ignore it. "I'd like to speak with him. Funny thing, he seems to be missing. Last I was aware, not even his sister had heard from him. Can you get word to him?"

"I can." Talina took a sip of her stout.

"Tell him I'd like to discuss some business dealings with him."

"I will."

Cinque studied her, the only tell being a slight tensing of the muscles in his forehead. "How did Derek, being a Taglioni, prove his particular worth? Like me, he would have arrived being, how did you say? Soft meat?"

"The transit on *Ashanti* had already beaten the arrogance out of him." Talina watched as Inga set a sizzling plate of chamois in red sauce with steaming squash before Suharto. Then scooped up Tal's five SDR-coin before lumbering back down to where Sawyer was belly-up to the bar with Sheyela Smith.

Cinque picked up his fork, cut off a piece of steak, and tried it. After chewing, he nodded, smiled. "I guess that woman can use whatever tone of voice she wants with me. This is the best I've eaten since Three Spires."

He appeared thoughtful as he ate, washing down the largess with healthy draughts from his mug of stout. Finishing, he shoved the plate away, shot her a black stare, and said, "I would learn. The same way Derek did. What will it take to get you to show me?"

"Dek beat the odds," she told him. "He made it through sheer dumb luck, grit, and a willingness to surrender himself to Donovan. Somehow, Cinque Suharto, I suspect that's a price you're not going to want to pay."

His stone-black gaze didn't waver. "Why don't you let me make that choice? When do I start? I want to know everything there is about Port Authority."

She swallowed the last of her stout. "All right, soft meat, I've got to go make my rounds. You want to follow along?"

"Lead forth," he told her, stepping down from the stool.

I'd be safer walking out into the dark with Whitey.

28

D ek and Kylee rolled Fred Han Chow's two-wheeled cart up to the door of the residential dome and set the braces. Turning to where Falise and her servants followed, he extended a welcoming hand. "This is it," he called. "You'll be staying here until Kalico Aguila makes up her mind about where you'll end up. This one's for the Lady. Next door, there's extra beds for what's left over."

Falise, her gown now shimmering pearlescent gray—probably in an attempt to look a little less like a navigational beacon—gave the dome a glacial stare. Granted, the place was a little weathered, and way down at the end of the residential district. Across the narrow dirt street, it faced one of the warehouses where tanned chamois, crest, and other hides were stored. The perimeter fence stood less than a meter from the dome's west wall. Beyond, across the moat, glazed by sunset, the Mishka fields, rich with corn, beans, squash, wheat, cabbage, and broccoli stretched in pastoral splendor to the distant bush where the aquajade and scrub chabacho were haloed in silhouette.

"This is intolerable," Falise said, expression bitter with distaste.

"Bout the best you'll find," Dek told her reasonably. "No one's been living here for, oh, I don't know. Probably since *Turalon* was here last. You can do pretty much anything you want to when it comes to fixing it up. Talk to Hofer about that. But you'll have to get the SDRs to pay him."

Falise ignored the horrified look on Ednund's face as she wheeled on Dek. "If I need advice, I shall ask someone in authority, mister . . . mister?"

"Folks around here call me lots of things." He grinned, his quetzal vision noting the heat that rose in her face. "Mister is pretty good for an old toilet scrubber like me."

Kylee was grinning, shaking her head, which earned her a wrathful glare from Falise.

"Well, certainly, there are better accommodations in this pigsty of a town." Ednund was still wincing as he took in the dome.

"Sure," Dek said offhandedly, "The finest, of course, is Allison Chomko's place. Three stories, opulent. Dan Wirth built it before he shipped off to Solar System to wow the fancy wancies with his wealth." A beat. "But you'd have to dicker with Allison about staying there."

"Where else?" Falise asked, clearly boiling.

"Shig has a study that he lets out. Only room for one, and the futon that he's so proud of is sort of like a medieval torture rack. Ah, and then there's the rooms that Inga lets out to itinerant Wild Ones."

"What's a Wild One?" Clarice asked, fixing her nut-brown gaze on Dek.

"We're Wild Ones," Dek told her with a facetious grin. "Kylee and me. We mostly live out in the bush. I have a claim out past the Briggs place. Kylee, well, she's in town because Tip had some creature eat its way into his leg. He's in the hospital, recovering. Raya says he'll live, but whatever proteins—"

"Fascinating," Falise's voice dripped acid. "What about the Corporate housing? I heard something about that."

"If you want," Dek told her, sharing a glance with the delighted Kylee. "But there's not much privacy for fancy folks. Just beds in cubicles. But there's always room these days. You see, the crew down at Corporate Mine? Most of them have bought houses. Or married partners with housing here."

Ednund climbed the three steps, opened the door, and entered. Falise, with lifted upper lip, followed. As did the rest.

"She has to be kidding," Kylee muttered.

"Having fun yet?" Dek asked, unable to hide his smile. "Grab one of those crates. Let's carry their crap inside. After that, it's their business."

"Can't believe they don't recognize you. Even with the changes."

Kylee grabbed one of the heavy trunks. Quetzal-strong, she headed up the stairs.

Dek lifted one of the wardrobes, found its balance point and carried it up the stairs. Maneuvering it through the door, he found his sister and her people clustered in the middle of the living room, staring in horror at the kitchen on the other side of the breakfast bar.

"I'd rather return to the ship," Falise said. "I wouldn't put contract workmen in a hovel like this."

"Shuttle's gone," Dek called gaily as he wrestled the wardrobe into the bedroom. "Um, I think I heard that Yvette had blankets put in the chest of drawers. You'll have to make your own beds. Couch folds out in the living room."

He paused while Kylee struggled under another of the boxes, then he was out the door.

"Don't they have grav-lifts?" Ednund asked. "Seriously? Two-wheeled carts?"

"Hey, you're lucky I got this. Perfect for moving things. Normally, Fred Han Chow uses it to carry corpses up to the cemetery. Kylee and me, we thought it would be just great for moving your luggage."

Falise, arms crossed defensively, scowled, eyes a glacial green. The muscles in her cheeks were jumping with anger.

"Are the others being treated this way?" Clarice asked Falise. "Or was this done because of that vile woman you encountered on the landing field?"

"If it is, you can bet Chad is face-to-face with an even more wretched hole." Falise closed her eyes, seemed to sway.

"Nope," Dek told her, noting that Fig and Phredo had ventured into the kitchen. "Talina Perez is a lot of things, but never vindictive." He gestured around at the dome. "It's not that bad. The roof doesn't leak. The kitchen works, so you can cook. And best of all, the door locks in the event quetzals get past the gates. Beats sleeping in the rain where a slug might get you."

The fire behind Falise's emerald glare grew hotter. She stepped forward, a lance-like finger pointing at Dek. "You piece of gutter-born trash! I want you and your genetic freak of a sister out of my sight."

"Oh, you'd be surprised at just how despicable my parents were. Probably about as manipulative and self-serving as the ones who whelped you, lady. So, me and my little sister, here . . ."

Ednund struck. Quetzal reflexes truly were remarkable. Even better than Ednund's training and implants.

The valet barely caught himself. Stopped short, Wide-eyed, arms outstretched. The rail ends of Dek's pistol came to rest just inches from the man's nose.

"Don't even think it, pretty boy," Dek's voice dropped as his emotions went quetzal. "You either, Clarice. Kylee, keep an eye on her and the rest."

"Fucking right," Kylee murmured, stepping over and glaring at Clarice. She had her own pistol out, eyes turned quetzal-black.

"So, *Lady* Taglioni," Dek said conversationally, "keep in mind that I don't owe you slug shit. But I'll give you an SDR's free advice. As of the moment you stepped off that shuttle, you're a guest here. The only person on this planet that your Taglioni name carries any weight with is Kalico. Me, Step, Yvette, and the others, we could care less. You're just shit on our shoes. A pain in our collective asses."

"I swear you piece of pond trash—"

"I'm not finished yet." Dek kept his deadly stare over the pistol's sights. "If you treat the locals here like you treated Kylee and me, they will kill you. And it will be ruled justified. Now, I can imagine what the family sent you here to do. The woman I see in front of me? She's doomed."

"Oh?" Falise asked coldly. "A thug with a fancy pistol tells me this? Where, pray tell, did a wretch like you become such an expert on success or failure?"

"Scrubbing toilets, Lady. I made it all the way up to Tech Class III."

"Can I shoot this one?" Kylee asked, as Clarice tried to shift her balance and ease within grasping distance of Kylee's pistol. The move would be to slap the pistol barrel to the side with a right hand, while Clarice struck for the throat with a left.

"I'd rather you didn't," Dek told her, backing away. "Come on, little sis, let's you and me go check on how Talina's doing with the rest of these idiots."

As they backed to the door, Falise—shaking in anger—snapped, "This isn't over, you pathetic fool."

"Nope," Dek agreed amiably. "Probably because you're not smart enough to know when you're ahead."

Dek closed the door behind him, as Kylee went skipping down the steps.

Through the duraplast, he heard Falise order, "If I ever see that genetically aborted horror of a human being again, I will leave him gutted in the street!"

"Little sister?" Kylee asked as she took the handles of Fred Han Chow's cart.

"Gotta love the irony, don't you think . . . sis?"

29

With Capella's morning light streaming through the high window, Talina set two plates of beans, smoked poblanos, and red sauce on the breakfast bar. Dek was halfway through his cup of coffee. The beverage was still a rare treat, the first bean-bearing trees having been grafted. An entire grove was now maturing down at Mundo Base. There, conditions were the closest to terrestrial regions where coffee flourished.

Dek set aside his coffee. "You should have seen their faces. Ednund was frozen, having never had a menial threaten him. But Falise, I swear, it was like she could have chewed uranium into fission."

"It worries me that Kylee had a pistol on Clarice," Talina said, taking her seat beside him. "The kid's not always what you'd call rock stable."

"She might be just what Falise's people needed. Tal, they've been top dogs, untouchable and privileged to the point of idiocy. One second, Ednund was going to do me severe harm before heaving me out the door. The next, before he and Clarice could comprehend, they were staring at pistols. To them, it's incomprehensible that mere gutter trash would dare. If we're lucky, that little demonstration has given my darling sister enough of a shock to cause her to reflect on some of the things we've all been trying to tell her."

"Cinque gets it." She lifted a forkful and chewed thoughtfully. "He accompanied me on my rounds last night. The guy listens, learns. He's still too damned cock-sure of himself, but he's taking Port Authority seriously. Spent time talking to the guards on the gates. Made me give him a complete tour of the town."

"Then he's a heap smarter than my idiot sister."

"He also asked about you. Wanted to know if it was true that I had a more than passing acquaintance. As soon as I told him I did, the inquisition began. I told him he'd be better off asking you in person. He wants to meet you."

"Aw, the perils of celebrity." Dek arched an eyebrow.

"Seriously, someone's going to point you out. You're going to have to deal with it."

"I know."

"*Tal?*" Two Spot's voice announced in her ear. "*Just got notified. Mac Hanson stepped out back of the foundry to wheel in some metal stock. He says there's a dead man under a pile of tarping that wasn't there last night.*"

"Roger that. Dead guy back of the foundry. On the way." Talina sighed, shoveled as much as she could into her mouth, picked up her plate, and headed for the sink.

"Dead guy?" Dek asked. "Can I come along?"

"Sure." She dumped the food, rinsed the plate, and belted on her pistol. Grabbing her hat, she clamped it onto her head. When she swirled her cape around her shoulders, it sent rainbows of color across the quetzal hide. As Dek hurried after her, she plucked her rifle from beside the door.

Outside, Dek locked the dome, and they set off down the graveled street. The first rays of Capella's morning came streaking through the high clouds. On the shuttle field, a roar built, Kalico's A-7 rising on thrusters to catch the light and curve off to the east.

"Headed to the Maritime Unit," Dek said. "According to the rumor last night, IG Soukup wanted to see the site. Word is that he was a bit perturbed that it was a complete loss. Apparently he asked that Vik Lawrence accompany him on the way out to look at the wreckage so that he could get her testimony."

They were passing The Jewel. Demon shifted in Talina's gut when she walked on the spot where she'd killed Spiro.

Yeah, you'd have liked it if that bitch had blown my brains out, wouldn't you?

Rocket, perched invisibly on her shoulder, chittered in delight. But then, his TriNA considered it simple justice.

A half block south, Talina led the way between the narrow gap to the stack yard behind the foundry. Here Hanson kept his raw metals on stands that his forklift could access. Small items were cast or drop-forged here. Hanson was in the process of building a larger foundry down at Corporate Mine on land adjacent to the smelter, which would allow him to cast even larger parts and frames.

Mac Hanson, Step Allenovich, and Raya Turnienko were standing just back from the line of pressure tanks full of fuel for the blast furnace. These came from Ollie Throlson's oil wells out west of the Winds. For some things, like melting metal, solar cells just weren't as efficient.

"What have we got, people?" Talina asked as she and Dek walked up.

Before the heavy pipe racks with their rollers and flat lengths of metal stock, a pile of tarps lay atop a duraplast crate.

Mac Hanson, a distasteful look on his face, stepped over to the pile of woven-fiber tarps, saying, "I might have walked right past this morning, but it hit me. I didn't leave these tarps here. Too easy for the wind to catch them, you know?" He pointed. "Last time I was out here, they were over next to the lumber, stacked neatly, with that length of pipe to weigh them down."

Hanson lifted the edge of the tarp. "So, seeing this, I walk over and lift the corner, like so . . ."

Hanson raised the tarp high enough that Talina could see the two feet and the lower legs, tucked beneath.

"I think there's some idiot sleeping here, so I lift the tarps off." Hanson ripped them away with a flourish, "And I yell, 'Hey, what kind of fool are you? Sleeping out when quetzals . . . ' I don't finish." He pointed at the dead man tucked into a tight curl atop the duraplast crate. "I jump half out of my skin when I realize it's dead soft meat. So I hustle my butt over and tell Two Spot."

Talina stepped up, looking down at the mussed blond hair, the half-lidded amber eyes and dark-brown skin. The clothing was like nothing she'd ever seen, filmy, silver-red, and soft looking. The shoes had an exotic style, soft-soled, and reminded her of liquid metal. Bending close, Talina sniffed, her augmented senses identifying perfume, a curious body odor, and something else, foreign, that she couldn't place. Even though the chin was tucked down close to the chest, Tal could see the bruising on the throat.

"Suffocated," she said to herself.

Dek bent down beside her. Stopped short and groaned, saying, "You know who this is?"

"Yeah," Talina straightened. "That's Chad Grunnel. My irritating hot head from yesterday."

Raya, unabashed, pulled the head back, taking effort. "Rigor is setting in. I need to get him back to the hospital, get a core temperature. That, along with lividity, should tie down the time of death with greater accuracy, but I'm thinking six, maybe seven hours."

Talina straightened, looked around. "Mac? You see anything else out of place here?"

"Not so's you'd notice, Tal," Hanson told her. "Graveled and packed like this place is, there's no tracks. The only thing I can see that's out of place are the tarps."

"Maybe we can get fingerprints off them?" Step suggested. "Maybe skin cells, fibers, hair? Something. I'll bundle them up and get them to Iji over at the lab."

"So," Talina mused, "Who'd want to throttle Chad Grunnel? And on his first night dirtside?"

Dek had a strained look on his face. "We'd damned well better find out. You get it don't you? He's a Grunnel. And as soon as the family hears about this, they're going to be wanting blood. And, people, that's the kind of trouble you really don't want to have."

30

Kalico stared out of her battered A-7's side window as the shuttle flew out beyond the shore where the crater bottom gave way to the Gulf. She could see the white strip of beach curving northward before arcing toward the northeast. From this elevation, the surf line was thin, the shallows greenish-azure before surrendering to the royal blue of deeper water.

To Soukup, sitting in the middle seat, she said, "We built a pad just up from the beach so that we could recharge airtrucks. The Maritime Unit wouldn't support the weight of the shuttle, and none of the airtrucks had enough range to make the trip. We never got the chance to start the rotations. The slime was killing people, subverting the children."

"Why didn't you take measures when it was first apparent that the research base was in trouble?" Soukup gave her a piercing look.

"I had been asked to leave, not to mention I had other priorities at Corporate Mine. Specifically, the Number Three."

"We'll get to that," Soukup told her. "You are the Corporate Board Appointed Supervisor. Your word is law. Even if you were asked to leave, you have the authority to dictate behavior. Why didn't you?"

Kalico felt that little worm of doubt begin to wiggle in her gut. "I told them that. In hindsight I would have ordered the base evacuated, cut it loose, and used the A-7s to carry it to the mainland. Probably set it at the Southern Diggings. It would have made a hell of a lot better base to start exploiting that deposit. If the Number Three hadn't caved in, I might have."

Then Kalico fixed on Soukup's evaluative gaze. "Or maybe I wouldn't. Making decisions after the fact is an easy exercise. That they, and I, underestimated the slime might be readily apparent at this moment, sitting in these seats. It wasn't that day I left the

Maritime Unit. You'll get a better idea when you depose Vik Lawrence. She'll let you inspect Felix's body. We've got it in cryo."

"Why have you not had your scars repaired?"

The question—seemingly out of the blue—left her puzzled. With a shrug, she said, "Dr. Raya Turnienko is many things, but she is no plastic surgeon. Until such a specialist comes to Donovan, I'll deal with the scars." She held up her hand, displaying the white lines that crisscrossed her skin. "And in the meantime, they serve as a reminder that Donovan is always ready to kill you."

Again that probing look. "You don't seem the least bit reticent when talking to a man who holds judgment over your life."

Kalico replied with an amused laugh. "Inspector General, I could give a damn. I know Miko Taglioni and the rest of the players on the Board and how they think. *Turalon* and *Ashanti* arriving like they did fractured the status quo. Miko and Claudio—having Dan Wirth dropped into their laps—would have immediately realized the threat Donovan poses to Corporate stability and the social order. Obviously, so did the Radceks, Grunnels, and Suhartos, all of whom got their people aboard *Turalon*. And then there's you. Board Appointed. With the authority and power to take whatever actions you deem necessary to ensure control of the Donovan problem."

"You assume Donovan is a problem before you admit that it is an immense opportunity?"

"Problem." Kalico insisted. "It threatens the status quo, defies predictability, tantalizes the hopes and dreams of people who had been satisfied with their lot under Corporate control. But most of all, it terrifies the aristocracy. The families have reached their day of reckoning. The one they never thought they'd see. On Donovan, a sewer rat like Dan Wirth can accrue enough wealth to catapult him right into the highest social circles. And he's rich enough that they have to endure rubbing elbows with the loathsome creature." Kalico lifted a finger. "And that, Inspector General, is intolerable. So here you are."

"You seem unconcerned that I might interfere with your position, Supervisor."

Kalico gave him a grim smile. "I don't think there's any 'might' about it. The Taglionis, the Grunnels, the Suhartos, and the Radceks read the between the lines. Or were faster than the others. Each sent a candidate. The person they thought most likely to be named as my interim replacement when I was found to be corrupt, incompetent, rebellious, or wanting in some manner, shape, or behavior."

She shot him a scathing glance. "So, which one do you have in mind for my replacement?"

He shifted his gaze ahead to what little he could see of the deep blue gulf's surface. "My mandate is to discover the facts, determine where The Corporation's best interests lie. And I will do exactly that, Supervisor. Does that concern you?"

"Not a bit, Inspector General. Falise, Chad, Cinque, and Bartolome? They were all specialists in ensuring that systems ran smoothly for the families. Enforcers, strong arms, the specialists sent in to quell dissent, enforce obedience, and make sure quotas were met. They're masters of Corporate efficiency. Donovan is going to eat them alive."

"I find that a harsh judgment for people you don't know."

"I know Donovan, Inspector General."

"Coming up on the Maritime Unit, Supervisor," Juri Makarov called from the pilot's seat. "I'm slowing to hover. Let me know how you want me to maneuver."

"Thanks, Juri," Kalico called, rising and stepping to the side. "Here, Inspector General. Juri will hold. You can get out of your seat for a closer look."

As the shuttle hovered a hundred meters above the waves, the view through the side window was of crystalline water so transparent the spotty patches of vegetation could be seen where the reef lay so closely beneath the surface. Even as the IG pressed against the glass, a long torpedo–like shape raced across the rounded bulk of the Maritime Unit's sialon hull. It lay on its side, perhaps seven or eight meters below the surface, and just at the edge of the dropoff where the water turned a most remarkable deep and translucent blue.

"You say that the slime ate the duraplast pylons?"

Kalico pointed. "You can see where the foundations were drilled into the reef. Life on Donovan has evolved a carbon polymer as an analog to terrestrial bone. So, yeah, most Donovanian life can digest duraplast. The Maritime Unit disregarded what they called algae. Made the mistake that it was like algae back on Earth. What they didn't get was that the green slimy stuff was intelligent, and it wanted the Maritime Unit for its own purposes. You can see a bit of it, especially around the windows. That's the green moss-like stuff."

"You're telling me there's an intelligent organism living inside that sunken station down there?"

"We could seal you in a hostile-environment suit and drop you down there on a cable, if you'd like. Your choice, but I wouldn't recommend it. Even if we got you back, there would be decontamination, and even then it's not a sure thing that you wouldn't be somehow compromised."

"According to your report, you tried to salvage the station?"

"Brought two shuttles out, but it was already collapsed. And after what we learned from the boy Felix's body, we're not sure that any kind of recovery wouldn't end in an unforeseen disaster."

"But you don't know for sure? With the combined lift from additional shuttles available from *Turalon,* you might still—"

"Inspector General," Kalico said pointedly. "Look down there and pay attention. You are about to make the same mistake I and the Maritime Unit made. You're underestimating the threat posed by the slime. See how easy it is? Like the rest of us, you're thinking it's just a simple algae."

"Perhaps."

"If that's your take away, Inspector General, you're already doomed."

"But I—"

"Supervisor?" Juri jerked around in his seat. "Got a call from Two Spot. It's that guy, Chad Grunnel? They just brought his body into the hospital. Raya confirms, he was murdered last night."

Kalico took a breath and glanced at the IG. "But then, not all deadly life forms on Donovan are indigenous."

31

"**M**y people and I were asleep." Falise pointed around at the dome's interior. "None of us have left this hovel, though we're about to. That slop left in the refrigeration unit might have been fit to dump into the hydroponics, but not for two meals in a row."

Talina Perez, standing with feet braced, wearing one of the quetzal-hide cloaks and a shoddy black-fabric uniform, was studying Falise with those unsettling oversized black eyes. The way the woman watched her, it was as though she was seeing more of Falise than she cared to betray.

"So, you don't know anything about Chad Grunnel's death? None of your people could have been involved? Even the ones who bunk down next door?"

"Was the body found outside our door?"

"No."

"If it wasn't on our doorstep, where was it? And why would you think we had anything to do with it?"

"Behind the foundry." Perez glanced behind Falise at Clarice and Ednund. "No one went out last night?"

"I told you, Security Officer," Falise said coldly. "We were asleep. You might, however, try Cinque Suharto."

"Cinque? Why?" If the revelation was in any way interesting, the Perez woman seemed to miss it.

"Perhaps Chad discovered that Cinque and Charlotte were involved? And Cinque has always been rather envious of Charlotte's skills. Particularly since he's availed himself of the woman's charms on occasion."

Behind her, Ednund and Clarice stood to either side, watching, silent.

"Funny," Perez murmured. "It was my understanding that the

families shared, what did you call them? Charms? Yes, that's it. I've heard you all swap charms without a second thought."

Falise endured that building cold rage in the pit of her stomach. It was enough of a shock to learn that Chad's body was in the hospital being examined for clues. As if these bucolic savages had the capacity for such a thing. Let alone the new calculus for how power would be distributed between her, Cinque, and Bartolome.

Now we're down to three.

New rules. Beyond Corporate scrutiny. Though the Inspector General was never to be underestimated.

"I have also heard," Perez continued, "that you are familiar with the arts of assassination, that you have employed those skills on behalf of your family in the past."

Falise allowed only the slight tilt of a shoulder. "There are many silly and absurd rumors floating around out there. Pay attention to all of them and you would assume I could fly or scry the secrets out of the dead."

"So, no truth to that?"

"Dear God, do I look like an assassin to you, woman? Ignorance is the greatest conjuror of imagination, and those who know the least spin the most fantastic of tales."

Time to redirect the freak woman to different fields of investigation. "However, Officer Perez, as distressing as it is to learn that Chad finally met a bad end, I have my own complaint to make. Yesterday, my people were threatened at gunpoint by one of the local ruffians and his sister. Said I could call him mister. She was called Kylee. Shouldn't be too hard to find. He was the bit of human flotsam delegated to deliver our luggage from the landing field to this hovel. I want them arrested and charged with brandishment, threatening behavior, assault with a deadly weapon, intimidation, malfeasance, and anything else you can find in the legal codes here."

Perez's lips twisted in what might have been amusement. "According to the version I heard, your valet Ednund was about to inflict a beating, and the only reason weapons were drawn was to allow them to depart the premises without violence." Perez pointed a finger at Ednund. "Is it true that your valet here was acting upon your orders?"

"Hardly!" Falise cried. "The sewer-born wretch was acting insolently, insulting. No doubt seizing the first opportunity to vent his displeasure and resentment of his betters."

"You want to press charges, that's fine." Perez told her with sigh. "I'll schedule an inquest as soon as we can get around to it. Meantime, you don't have anything to offer on Chad Grunnel's death?"

"Nothing."

"He had no enemies? No one who will profit from his death?"

Falise barked a bitter laugh. "I didn't say that. Every Grunnel with a pulse has enemies. We all do. And just about everyone here will profit from his death in one manner or another. Cinque, Bartolome, and myself are minus a potentially dangerous rival. Grunnel assets on Capella III have been dealt a serious blow."

Falise narrowed her eyes to deadly slits. "But then, even you, Officer Perez, are a suspect, are you not? Didn't you have words with Chad at the landing? Didn't we hear him threaten you? Perhaps, Dear Officer, he might have stewed on his rage. Unable to sleep, he went stalking out into the night, fit to pay you back for the indignity you inflicted so publicly. And, well, alas, when he found you, things just got a little carried away?"

Perez barely reacted. "Nice try."

"Ah, was it a try? Or a direct hit?" Falise pressed fingers to her cheek, expression thoughtful. "Wonder what we'd find if we dug into your records, Officer Perez? Didn't I see somewhere in the briefing materials that you'd not only killed people on demand but even murdered Supervisor Clemenceau when you put a bullet in his head?"

Perez fixed those chilling and unearthly eyes on Falise. "Did you specifically come to Port Authority to make enemies? Because you're off to a real good start."

"No. I came specifically to conduct family business, yet my brother seems to have vanished from the planet. You should be in a position to know something about him. Do you have any idea as to his whereabouts?"

"Yeah, I'd guess he's at the hospital about now. He's close to a child over there who's recovering from a parasite wound."

"You'd think he would have had the courtesy to meet me at the shuttle field."

"Falise, did it ever cross your mind that he might not want to see you?"

She let her glare thin to slits. "My family's business is no concern of yours, Officer."

"You got it," Perez said, abruptly turning on her heel and heading to the door. "Don't leave town. I might have more questions relating to Chad Grunnel's murder."

And then she was gone, the duraplast door banging behind her.

Falise placed a hand to her breast. "We need to think this through. With Chad off the board, the entire dynamic is changed. Our opportunities have increased."

"Only two left," Ednund agreed with his wily smile.

Falise took a deep breath. "Be that as it may, Perez was right about one thing. We're not making friends while we're sulking inside this hovel. Nor are we learning anything that will allow us to capitalize on Chad's elimination from the game. I'm hungry."

"The food in the cafeteria was outstanding," Ednund offered. "Well, at least it was after these last months aboard *Turalon*."

"Inga's," Clarice said. "Shig Mosadek said it was the best place for news. Supervisor Aguila left us fifty of the SDR coins. If we're to understand how to exploit this economy, we have to learn the rules."

"Sucking vacuum," Falise muttered under her breath, "I'm starting to see why Dan Wirth wanted out of here so badly."

Falise let Ednund take the lead, not that it was difficult finding the tavern. Walk to the main avenue and turn south. Inga's was the large dome three blocks down—weathered to be sure—with two benches out front. Several hide-clad men, hard-bitten types with well-used rifles propped beside them, hats pulled low against the too-brilliant light, sat with their booted feet shimmering in laser-like effect as the sunlight played on the thick quetzal leather. The look they gave Falise, in her fine cadmium-yellow soffiber pantsuit, was both amused and dismissive.

Fucking gutter trash, back on Transluna she would have had them arrested for vagrancy and shipped off to the Belt to spend the next twenty years breaking up asteroids.

As she entered the double doors, any hopes for relief crumbled. If this was the high point of Port Authority's amenities, it would have been an act of mercy to nuke the entire planet. The Corporation could just as easily mine Capella III of its wealth while wearing radiation suits and living in shielded shelters.

She let Ednund lead the way down the worn wooden stairs to the lower level, the place being perhaps a quarter full. All eyes were on her and her people as Ednund picked a table on the far side, opposite the kitchen and against the curve of the wall.

Benches. Fucking alien-wood benches. That's what she was supposed to sit on? And the battered table—hewn from the same curious wood—might have been left over from the Middle Ages. At least it looked like someone had dragged a wet rag over it sometime in the past month.

"Can you believe this place?" Ednund asked, glancing around, taking in the stares, the obvious interest as the other occupants discussed their arrival.

A young man, dressed in the local hand-woven fabric, but still wearing boots, came trotting up. Falise wasn't sure if his smile was amused or just falsely friendly as he asked, "What will you have?"

"How does this work?" Ednund asked, producing some of the coins Aguila had left for them.

"Got crest chili with green peppers, crest steak with potatoes, fresh fruits from Mundo, and oatmeal now that Terry Mishka's harvest is in."

Ednund gave Falise a questioning glance.

"We'll take one of each for each of us. Coffee for all."

The young man shrugged. "That's a lot of food, but you got it." And wheeling, he left at a trot.

Falise was studying the place, inspecting the bar in the back, the kitchen excavated into the earth on the far side. And, of course, the locals with their outlandish prismatic quetzal hide, the weapons they'd laid nonchalantly on the tables beside them.

"It's like we've stepped into another universe," Clarice noted.

"Here comes Bartolome," Ednund noted with a tilt of his head toward the stairs.

The Radcek agent hit the bottom step, glanced around, and, catching Falise's eye, headed in her direction. If there was anything reassuring about his arrival, it was that the locals followed him with every bit as much attention, talking in low voices as they did.

"May I join you?" Bartolome asked, his yellow eyes—with a floating gaze—taking in the room.

"Have a seat," Falise indicated. "You've heard about Chad, I suppose?"

"Your work?" Bartolome asked as he grimaced at the bench, then carefully lowered himself. As he did, he rearranged his silk trousers and slipped the neon suit jacket from his narrow shoulders before carefully folding it. Wiping the seat beside him first, he laid it on the wood as tidily as he could. "Ghastly place, this."

"Sorry," Falise told him. "Given that they found Chad's body behind a foundry, I had him figured for your doing. If I'd killed him, I would have hung him from the shuttle field gate, prominently, so as to cast suspicion on Talina Perez."

"Vile woman." Radcek pulled the ruffles on his white satin shirt straight. "That freakish look? It's quetzal TriNA, you know. She's infected with it. They say it's an intelligent molecule and it talks to her. That's what's wrong with her eyes and face."

"Ah." Clarice seemed to have found an epiphany. "The same with that wretch and his sister yesterday. That's why they look so much like Perez."

Falise nodded, feeling the pieces slip into place. Probably explained how their weapons appeared as if by magic. Holstered one second, drawn in the blink of an eye.

Falise asked, "You've had a visit from the lovely Officer Perez already?"

"First thing. She had the audacity to think I might have strangled Chad."

"Strangled?"

"You didn't know?" Bartolome's inquiring yellow gaze, like always, seemed slightly unfocused. But that was one of his ploys. The man never let an opponent think he was paying attention.

"No more than you knew he was discovered behind the foundry." She paused, well aware that either disclaimer might be misdirection.

Three cups of coffee arrived, and the youth shot a measuring look at Bartolome, asking, "He on your tab?"

"He's on a bench," Ednund said cautiously. "And it belongs to the tavern."

The kid looked confused, then burst out laughing. "Yeah, that's a good one. So, you picking up his breakfast?"

"I think he's asking if we're using our SDRs to pay for Bart's food." Clarice had those little worry lines deep in her forehead.

"I'll buy my own, thank you. And bring me exactly what these people are having." Bart turned his attention to the young man. Smiled indulgently.

The kid looked puzzled again, shrugged his shoulders, and left mumbling something about "Hey, what do I care? It's their money."

Bartolome turned wistful. "I will miss Chad. There was something delicious in baiting him. He always took any kind of offense seriously."

"The day will come when the Grunnels are going to want answers," Falise told him. "That's assuming that the good Officer Perez can find the culprit."

Bart smiled as if in subtle amusement. "Indeed. Would it interest you to know that Officer Perez spent part of last night giving Cinque a tour of the town? Spent nearly three hours escorting our old friend around the various attractions Port Authority has to offer. While there's no telling what they might have been exploring in the darker parts of this benighted village, the lighting being as poor as it is, Cinque would have most assuredly been shown the better places to divest himself of an unwanted body."

Falise leaned forward, mind racing. "Now, there's a fascinating revelation. I wonder if she's given him the same interrogation we've been subjected to. I considered it my duty to remind the officer that in her vigorous pursuit of the miscreant, she needed to remember that she and Chad had bitter words yesterday at the shuttle field."

"As did you," Bartolome reminded.

Falise arched a brow. "You know how Cinque is with women? How he uses the pheromones, exudes that reassuring male personality? When he turns on the charm, radiates that reassuring magnetism, more worldly and experienced women than some back-planet security officer have fallen for his schemes. Am I the only one, Bartolome, or do you, too, wonder if perhaps a word whispered into a suggestible Officer Perez's ear might have motivated her to chastise Chad for his bad behavior at the landing?"

"Sometimes these things do get out of hand," Bartolome agreed. "And Chad could be so abrasive. Might have said the wrong thing. Thrown fuel onto the flames, so to speak."

"And Perez—tough Donovanian that she is and unused to being lectured by a superior—strikes out." Falise nodded. "I like it."

"For the time being, I suggest we keep that to ourselves," Bartolome said in that oh-so-reasonable voice. "Might be worth having it in the toolkit on the day when the Grunnels show up demanding answers."

"Yes, indeed," Falise agreed, seeing the possibilities.

"Heard from your brother?" Bartolome asked. Seeing her expression, he added, "No? Well, my people have stumbled upon some interesting information. Seems your brother Derek runs a poker game at that tawdry excuse for a casino. According to my sources, he's playing this evening. Might be your chance to finally run him down. As to why he's been avoiding you? Word is that he's gone entirely native. What they call a Wild One. Lives out in the bush when he's not in town. Has what the locals call a 'very productive claim.'"

"The poker game I'll believe. But my brother? The strutting peacock of vanity, living in the bush? He doesn't have that kind of fiber. You should have seen him the time Father sent his Guild girl away. He was in tears for days. Always the weak one. A true disappointment. I think, for a while, Father was considering whether

Derek should have an unfortunate accident. For a year my brother's life hung by a thread."

Bartolome's wispy smile broadened. "You more than make up for any shortcomings on your brother's part. Believe me, with the new dynamic we face here, I would rather have you as an ally than an adversary."

Falise chuckled, knowing it for the fucking lie that it was. Bart would slit her throat and never burden himself with so much as a sigh while he did so.

She looked up, seeing no less than three of the serving people, followed by a large, big-boned woman. All of them carried plates heaping with food. When they arrived at the table, the plethora of bowls and platters were set down, crowding the space.

"What in the name of hell?" Ednund asked, glancing up in bewilderment.

The kid, looking nervous, said, "Hey, you said one of each for each of you. Then this guy"—he pointed at Bartolome—"said he wanted exactly what you three had. So, here it is. Just like you ordered."

"Now"—the big woman with washed-out blond hair, a towel over her shoulder, crossed her arms—"I know you're soft meat. But that's forty-eight SDRs. You got it? Or am I taking the food back?"

Hot words rose in Falise's throat. Then she really got a good look at the woman, and that old sense of warning kicked in. She forced a smile, told Ednund, "Pay the woman."

Inga shot her a glance that might have sliced meat from the bone, nodded as she counted out the coins. Handed only two back, and said, "Welcome to Donovan. Eat up."

And then, her entourage following, the woman headed back for her bar.

"Better be good," Bartolome said.

"If it's not," Clarice said softly, "you go tell her. I'm not pissing that woman off to save my soul."

32

The marks on Chad Grunnel's throat were plain to see. The way he lay naked on his back on the autopsy table, there wasn't much to show for being one of the most powerful and prominent men in Transluna. Nothing about his body looked outstanding. Just a man who might have been in his thirties, though with the kind of Corporate medicine a Grunnel could afford, who knew? And, but for his long blond hair and dark skin, about as unassuming as a male body could get.

Kalico shot a measuring glance at Raya, who stood with gloves on, masked, and wearing a lab apron. The doctor raised an inquiring eyebrow, glanced at where Inspector General Soukup stood back by the wall, the Four crowded beside him. "We ready?"

"What have you got, Raya?"

"Male, age indeterminate, but my guess is that he's in his fifties from dental wear and trabecular bone morphology. Looks like really expensive med, and his implants were top of the line." She pointed to the chips where they'd been extracted from Grunnel's brain. "Without comnet, we're not likely to recover any information from them. *Turalon* could take them back to Solar System for a download."

"Cause of death?" Kalico asked.

"Asphyxiation by manual strangulation." Raya pointed at the marks on the throat. "Not only is that supported by the hematoma, but the hyoid is broken, the trachea is crushed, and the petechiae support COD. Blood is anoxic."

"Time of death?" Kalico asked.

"Implants register 01:14." Raya cocked her head. "Body temp, lividity, and rigor support that."

"Any clue as to who might have done it?" Kalico asked.

"Not much." Raya shifted, reached for her scalpel. "The killer was right-handed, strong. There's some evidence on the victim's fingernails that he scratched, flailed. We've got fibers from under his nails. Cheng's got them in the lab. My guess? They'll turn out to be something utilitarian and common like duralon. But Corporate manufacture, definitely not local."

Raya glanced uncertainly at the IG. "You want the big surprise?"

"And that is?" Kalico asked.

"The guy was drugged. Polyphysorate fentanine. That's a surgical anesthetic. We use it here when we have it in stock. From the amount in the blood, it wasn't enough to knock him out, but it would have really slowed him down. Inhibited his reflexes. Probably affected his cognitive abilities."

Kalico sighed. "Any of your supply missing?"

Raya had that hard-eyed look. "We haven't had any in stock for the past year and three months since we used the last on Artie Manfoid's knee surgery after he fell off his bulldozer."

Kalico shot a look at Soukup. "So someone brought it down from *Turalon*?"

"Had to be," Raya told her. "That's not to say that someone couldn't have nipped a couple doses from the hospital a couple of years back, put them on ice, just waiting for the day a high and mighty Grunnel set foot in Port Authority, and thawed them out so they could slip it into his drink and kill him, but Occam's razor says it came down with one of the *Turalon* shuttles. My meds aren't scheduled until later this afternoon."

"That's pretty conclusive. Narrows the list of suspects considerably." Kalico crossed her arms.

"Can I start my autopsy?" Raya asked.

Kalico glanced at Soukup. "IG? You have any comments or concerns?"

"Not at this time."

"Then, you may begin, Raya. I would ask that the IG accommodate us and allow the First to step close. If ever there was a need for a rock-solid record, this will be it."

At a nod from the IG, the First stepped up beside the table.

Raya gave him a wary look, then bent, starting her Y incision.

It didn't take long before Kalico decided that autopsies weren't going to qualify as one of her favorite pastimes.

As ribs were cut and Chad Grunnel's face was peeled back over his forehead, she made herself concentrate on what Raya had said: The guy had been partially drugged with pharma from *Turalon*, fought weakly, while he was strangled by a right-handed assailant. And then left behind the foundry.

Could be anyone, she realized.

Even—she glanced sidelong to where Soukup stood—the IG.

33

D ek stepped in the door, taking in the nightly crowd at The Jewel. Something was in the air. Demon was stirring inside him, hissing, changing colors and patterns, as if Dek could feel the angry quetzal burning a bright and incandescent red. The beast was fit to burst his chest.

Rocket, too, was whispering warnings in Dek's head. Words like *"Careful"* and *"Danger"* slipping around in his mind. He could feel the young quetzal's presence: tense and wary.

He had spent most of the day at the landing field as the first of the *Turalon* shuttles set down and began offloading cargo and contractees. The only oddity had been when he'd encountered Charlotte. He'd almost run into her as she hurried down the ramp from Kalico's shuttle. The woman had looked oddly satisfied. Hardly the expression even a well-trained valet might have, given the proximity of Chad Grunnel's death.

"Can I help you?" Dek had asked.

The woman had fixed those designer-purple eyes on his, her smile triumphant. "I rather doubt it." Her voice had dripped disdain. "Now, be on about your business, or I shall have you whipped." And she'd made a shooing gesture with her hands before hurrying off, an empty bag dangling over the shoulder of her gleaming indigo suprasatin suitcoat.

He'd paused, glanced curiously up the ramp, wondering what business a valet with a dead master might have been pursuing, and with whom, in Kalico's shuttle. Maybe Chad had given her instructions before his death? Some delivery for the IG?

It had been a busy afternoon processing people. With Talina investigating a murder, and Kalico in and out with the IG, Dek had pitched in to help Yvette and Shig process the soft meat and helped with the orientation. Then came the process of showing them their new quarters and delivering their luggage.

All of it more complicated given the heightened security necessary with quetzals roaming around somewhere in the vicinity.

Talk of the town revolved around the murder of Chad Grunnel. Every speculation under the sun could be heard—even that it had been a quetzal. Though why a quetzal would reach out and strangle someone instead of ripping them in two and eating them had never been clearly articulated.

Made Dek wonder how Talina was doing with her investigation.

Standing inside the door, he could hear the approaching thunder. Clouds had been rolling in from the Gulf. The night had the feel of a storm, that antsy electric sensation that foretold rain. The way Demon kept repeating *"Yes!"* in his sibilant tones sent a shiver down Dek's spine. Didn't matter that it was a quetzal night; he'd personally checked out the armored marines guarding the gates.

At his table in the rear, Step Allenovich was dealing cards to Tyrell Lawson, and yes, right there sat Falise. As usual, Ednund and Clarice stood behind her chair, backs to the wall, keeping watch on the room.

Well, well, she'd finally run out of patience and taken steps to run him down. He beckoned Kalen Tompzen over. The ex-marine—wearing a crest-hide vest, high boots, and a claw shrub fiber shirt—gave Dek a smile, saying, "Looks like rich soft meat at your table."

"Yeah. Do me a favor? Ask Step to meet me at the bar. Do it on the sly without mentioning my name."

Kalen's gaze turned conspiratorial. "Sure thing."

Dek kept his hat pulled low, grunted at greetings from old friends, and elbowed up to the bar, saying, "Tall whiskey, Vik."

As Schmenski poured, Dek tossed out a five-siddar, saying, "Keep the change."

A moment later, Step Allenovich sidled up next to Dek, asking, "What's up?"

"How much have you and Lawson told Falise about me?"

"Just about nothing," Step said carefully. "She asked if it was your night to play at that table. We told her it was. Mostly, it's like she really doesn't want to talk to Lawson and me. Like we're the sort of people she really wishes would go away. Any time we try to be friendly? Ask about the trip here? What news there is from Solar System? She shuts us down. Only time she opens her mouth, it's about the game."

Falise glanced their way, her emerald eyes turned to green ice. His vision already shading into the infrared, Dek could see the heat and disgust rise in her neck and face. Fascinating. He'd never been able to read her this well.

Dek said, "Let's go play poker. Call me Mister. Any questions that come up about Derek Taglioni? Leave them to me."

Dek led the way to the table, pulling out a chair opposite from Falise, waving Lawson down as he glanced up and opened his mouth to say something.

"What are *you* doing here?" Falise demanded, both Ednund and Clarice coming off the wall to take positions at her shoulder.

"Figured I'd ask Derek Taglioni if he had any objection to an old friend sitting in on his game." He glanced around. "Assuming he gets here tonight."

"Get out or I'll call . . ." Falise seemed to realize there was no one to call. "I'll have my people remove you, you bit of—"

"Tut tut," Dek interrupted, emphasizing a clipped Donovanian accent. "One of the first things, as a good Taglioni, that you would have been taught, is that you *never* make a humiliating spectacle out of yourself."

He glanced at Lawson. "You mind sitting in on a grudge match? The soft meat across the table and I seem to have gotten sideways with each other. Could get a little bloody, and I don't want you caught in the crossfire."

"Mister, I'm in!" Step declared, a grin widening on his face and squinting his already black eye. Figured. Step was always ready for trouble.

Lawson, now cautious, said, "I'll bail. Maybe find a quieter game at Betty Able's."

Dek gave him a two-fingered wave as the man departed. To Tompzen, he called, "Closed game tonight, Kalen. Just me, the soft meat, and Step."

"Whatever you say," Kalen agreed, shooting a suspicious glance at Clarice and Ednund, who still stood protectively at Falise's shoulders.

"What's your limit, Lady?" Dek asked as he took the cards and shuffled. "I assume you have plunder?"

"You assume I'd deign to play cards with a mongrel-bred half-breed freak like you. It's quetzal TriNA, isn't it? That makes you look so misshapen?"

"Give the soft meat a point. Wait. No, better idea." Dek tossed a five-SDR coin across the table. "There. Now you've got something to start with."

"I refuse to involve myself with the likes of street cur such as yourself." Falise leaned forward, her eyes green ice.

"You're already involved," Dek said. "It started when you told Ednund to break me up and toss me out on the street. Now, you willing to put your vaunted Taglioni superiority on the line? Or is my old friend Derek the only Taglioni within sixty light-years of this rock who's not afraid of a little card game?"

Step looked like it was all he could do to keep from gaping. As it was, the big man was half-choking the guffaws that tried to rise from deep in his belly.

Falise might have been entirely out of her element, but she sensed the trap. Was trying to figure where it lay. More to the point, she was really looking at him, now. Seeing him for the first time, some fingers of doubt stroking her innate caution.

Dek began dealing the cards, saying, "Nothing fancy. Five-card draw. Five SDRs to ante."

Step tossed out a coin from his belt pouch, his curious gaze going to Falise.

"Oh, and soft meat? Have your people stand back against the wall like they were. Dan Wirth taught us all the trick of having a spotter.

Surely you met Dan in Transluna? This used to be his table. His game. Think of it as coming full circle."

Falise waved Ednund and Clarice back and took her cards. Glanced at them.

As they played the hand out, Allison Chomko appeared from the back, noticed the growing crowd that Kalen was monitoring. She crossed over, and Kalen whispered in her ear. She nodded, stepped up to the table, asking, "Can I get anyone anything?"

"I'd take a whiskey," Step declared as he studied his cards. "And I'll raise five."

Falise, with sudden understanding, smiled wickedly. "Ednund. I need those two coins."

When he handed them, she studied them. Tossed out the five, saying, "If your plan is to embarrass me for a lack of physical SDRs—"

"I'll stake you," Dek told her. "That means I'll advance you what you need to play. I think everyone in the room knows that Taglionis don't welch on debts."

A murmur went around the room. Falise noting it with a flicker of her eyes.

Falise won with two pair.

And then the game began in earnest.

Falise won enough hands to prove herself competent. Step, turning cautious too late, dropped out after a half an hour, having bled nine hundred, most of which had gone to Falise.

The crowd had grown, news having traveled around that Dek was playing his sister. Seemed that—but for Falise—the entire town knew.

None of this was lost on Falise, of course. She had to be achingly aware that people didn't flock to The Jewel just to watch a poker game.

Time to end it. On Falise's deal, Dek lost a good-sized pot. Falise, ever more confident now, had that old familiar glint. The one she got when she was about to triumph.

Of course, she had the same implant he did. Top of the line. Unlike him, she was relying on the skills and card memory it provided. Dek had been playing for a decade on *Ashanti,* and then running his weekly game on Donovan. His ante was a nugget the size of a robin's egg. Falise's eyes widened. She hesitated, pushed out part of her pile of coins.

Dek controlled the shuffle, dealt, checked his cards, to find them exactly as he'd planned. Falise should have two jacks. He had three spades.

He raised with a pigeon-blood ruby. Let his stare burn into hers. For a second, she fixed on his eyes, then shook it off, as if seeing things. "What's that worth here?"

"About six hundred. Which is about all that you've got on the table."

She considered her two jacks, pushed the pile in. Took three, which he'd anticipated. If his deal was as good as he hoped, she was staring at three jacks, backed by an AK.

Dek discarded and took two. He reached into his belt pouch, tossed out a bar of silver metal.

"What's that?" Falise asked.

"A two-pound bar of rhodium, but if you don't think it's enough, I'll back it with another eight pounds. Just didn't want to carry it around with me."

A mumbling went up from the crowd.

"As a new arrival, I don't have anything of nearly equal—"

"I'll take your slaves as equal value, Lady." He glanced up, seeing the shock in Ednund and Clarice's faces. "They've been trained all of their lives to do your bidding. Rhodium is a rare element in Solar System, but it's the most corrosion-resistant metal known. Not to mention the most valuable. How about I up my bet? A half metric ton. You could buy Taglioni Tower with that. It would put you in good with sour old Claudio. A real one up on Suharto and Radcek. I can have it delivered right to your dome. You can sit on it and have a holo taken before we ship it up to *Turalon.*"

God, how he loved this. Demon was squirming in his chest, almost bouncing off his ribs. The quetzal sensed blood, the kill. Dek could see the seething behind Falise's eyes as she stared down at her three jacks. Wondering all the while at what he held. Torn between the remarkable wealth he promised, or the unthinkable shame of gambling away her personal servants.

"How do I know you really have such a fortune in rhodium?"

"I've heard that a Taglioni never lies, never welches on a bet. Is that true?"

"It is, not that a gutter-born Cretan like you would know."

That elicited a chorus of gasps around the room; Falise ignored them, her hard green gaze weighing her predicament. If she folded, she lost everything, all the wealth sitting in that pot that she'd built. That Dek had staked her for. And that placed her in debt to him.

So, now that you're trapped, what are you going to do?

In a coolly dispassionate voice, he told her: "As a Taglioni, I give you my word that I have more than a half metric ton, in my possession." Then he smiled and added, "So, if a Taglioni never lies, that should end the matter."

In all of his life, Dek had never seen Falise look so horrified.

34

Dek stared into his sister's disbelieving eyes. Behind her, Ednund and Clarice both looked as if they were going to be sick.

"But . . . what happened to you?" Falise finally asked.

Dek supposed that for the first time in the place's history, The Jewel was quiet enough to hear an invertebrate fart.

"*Got her.*" Rocket's TriNA whispered in Dek's ear.

"I grew up," Dek told her. "People come to Donovan for three reasons: Most come just to leave again. Many come to·die. And some come to find themselves. I did that last thing. Found myself. I suggest you do the first. Leave."

"But your face?" she wondered. "I mean, I can see it in your eyes, but Derek's were yellow-green. Yours are . . . feral. And your face? Like it's misshapen. And, Gods almighty, that horrible scar. When did you grow a beard? How could you? Genetically, you shouldn't be able to."

"I'm part quetzal now, Falise. That's what changed me. You might have seen that if you'd been willing to look. But I'm afraid that you are nothing more than the heartless tool that Father and Mother have shaped you into. Your only purpose here is to serve the family."

He gestured at the pile. "So, serve it. Will you call, or fold?"

The faintest frown lined her forehead. "Let's table this and take family business behind closed doors where it belongs. Making a scene—"

"Call or fold."

Step eased sideways in his chair, which exposed his pistol butt to an easy reach where it hung in his belt holster.

"Derek, this isn't funny." Falise closed her cards, laying them face-down on the table.

"You have a bet on the table, little sister. I've just raised it. By laying your cards down, do I take it that you've folded?"

He could see the raging turmoil. As much as she wanted to believe in those three jacks, her sense of self-preservation was getting the best of her. She couldn't help but glance at Ednund and Clarice, both of whom had turned a shade of pale and looked stricken.

"Doesn't matter," Step said in the most mild voice Dek had ever heard him use. "Dek, she still owes you, let's see." He reached out, fingering through Falise's share of the pot. "Looks like about twenty-seven hundred after you figure in the gemstones and nuggets."

"And a Taglioni never stiffs someone over a debt." Dek kept his gaze locked with Falise's "But then, I recall some of the things you have been saying about my parents. Gutter slime? Filth? Lowly trash? Not that I don't disagree with the sentiment. I promise you, however, that one place our dear mother, Malissa, never gave birth to either you or me was in a gutter."

"You've had your fun," Falise told him with deadly intent. "I'm not playing any longer."

"How about cutting the deck?" he asked. "High card takes all. Step, here, can shuffle."

"Not a chance." She stood, and back straight, marched for the door. People leapt out of the way, staring in disbelief as Falise, her servants following close behind, vanished into the night.

Dek cut out Step's nine hundred and threw in a half-ounce platinum nugget for good measure. "Thanks. Wouldn't have missed that for the world."

Step leaned back in his chair, tilted his whiskey to his lips, and wondered, "Maybe you were a changeling? Switched at the hospital?"

Dek took a sip of his own whiskey. He reached over, turned her cards upright, and stared. Impossible! How the hell had he screwed that up on the deal?

Step reached out to flip Dek's own hand over, exposing the spade flush. "Goddamn, Dek! You bluffed her! While she was holding four jacks!"

And, as The Jewel began to return to normal, people making for the tables and bar, Dek threw his head back and laughed until his sides ached.

35

The way the shoring ran, the entire roof of the Number Three was enclosed. No way that IG Soukup could see the shocked rock that the bore had been drifted through. Kalico, Desh Ituri, and Arobindo Ghosh, dressed in protective suits with helmets and breathers, took a position in rear. Soukup, also covered in a protective suit, stared up through a transparent facial shield.

They stood in the tunnel—rails underfoot where the ore cars carried the rich quartz, schist, and metal-laced rock mined above, out to the haulers that in turn trucked them down to the smelter. Occasional lights—sometimes flickering—illuminated the tunnel. Even with the shoring, water dripped on them as if it were a healthy rain, while on the floor, the "water make"—heavy metal-rich water draining from the mountain—ran in a fast rivulet to one side.

Kalico pointed to where the ore from above fell through the hopper and into the cars. "That's the payoff. Took us three years. We're still using the tram above, removing ore and metal with the skip, then carrying it down in buckets. If we had a bigger smelter, we could triple production."

Soukup winced at the droplets spattering on his helmet and face shield. His voice came out tinny through the speaker. "And you say this is all toxic?" It had been necessary to leave the Four at the tunnel mouth, not having enough protective suits.

"Many of the metals we mine, like beryllium, arsenic, and cadmium, are toxic. Not to mention the uranium, polonium, thorium, radium, and the rest. We have had to innovate. The really hot stuff is unprocessed. We load the radioactive ores directly into containers and ship them up to L5. When *Turalon* gets around to it, those containers can be strapped to the hull and can make the trip back to Solar System in vacuum, and on the other side of the ship's radiation shielding."

"You said it took you three tries to dig this tunnel? That it took you two years during which time, the mine was only running at partial capacity?"

Ghosh stepped up, saying, "We had to learn as we went. Had to develop the technology, design the shoring. Drilling through the shocked rock necessitated new techniques. And then there were the safety issues when it came to the metals. Dealing with the mercury alone caused us a month's worth of delays."

"And it cost us five people," Kalico added. "Five lives we couldn't afford."

"You all seem unusually preoccupied with safety," Soukup noted. "Even to the detriment of meeting production quotas."

Ituri started forward, fists clenched, but Kalico motioned him to desist, saying, "Inspector General, my people aren't expendable. There's only sixty-five of us left, not counting the children, and we're producing more wealth and rare Earth elements than the entirety of the Belt. Even with the delays, breakdowns, and setbacks. But my people come first. Period."

She could see his eyes as drops of water ran down the face shield. "Indeed." His tinny voice conveyed no emotion.

"Inspector General," Ghosh said, "it doesn't matter what our production might have been, even if we'd been running at full capacity. As it is, *Turalon* can't transport what's already up in orbit, even if they stripped out the Transportee Deck and strapped a container to every square meter of external hull. My guess is that it would take her two and a half trips, just with what we and Port Authority have stockpiled."

"But it could be so much more efficient," Soukup noted as he stared up at the bottom of the hopper. "How many people would it take to excavate this entire mountain?"

Desh laughed. "That depends on how you mine it. What kind of equipment you bring in. With enough explosives, and properly placed, your rock fragmentation could be so thorough that you could strip it from the top down with draglines. This is the twenty-second century everywhere but on Donovan, where we're handicapped by the equipment at hand, and whether we can keep it running." He pointed up. "Like these lights. Made in Port Authority. Just like they would have been in 1920. But that's the best we can do with the resources we have at hand."

Soukup took one last look around. "I've seen enough at Corporate Mine. I want to see *Freelander*."

Kalico shifted, water spattering on her helmet. "All right. I'll have Juri have the bird ready to go up first thing in the morning. It's—"

"I would like to go now," Soukup said tonelessly.

Kalico wheeled on him, stabbing a gloved finger into the man's chest. "It's the middle of the night. Ensign Makarov is asleep. I'm tired and hungry. We're heading up top to the compound for a meal and a night's sleep. Sorry, but you and the Four are in the barracks with the rest."

And with that she turned, stomping down between the rails, splashing water as she went.

Hurrying behind her, Ghosh asked, "You think that's a good idea? Pissing him off like that?"

"Hey, I've got a crew of soft meat landing at Port Authority. Replacement contractees who are looking for some kind of leadership. There's a dead Grunnel lying on a slab in Raya's morgue, and three conniving nobles who are up to God-knows-what-kind-of mischief. Six quetzals, *six* mind you, are skulking around PA. And I've got a marine colonel—bearing one hell of a grudge—up in *Turalon*'s med bay who was beat up at The Jewel. Not to mention his command scattered over half of Donovan. And"—she jerked a thumb over her shoulder—"he wants a guided tour of *Freelander*?"

"No one *wants* a guided tour of *Freelander*." Ghosh's shiver could be seen through his protective suit as he plodded along.

"Ghosh," she told him, "here's how I see it. I've got two choices. I can babysit that Corporate candy ass, taking him here, showing him this or that, acting like his personal taxi service until something goes clap-trapping wrong and we're in a real mess. Or I can wave bye-bye, and send him and his Four off on their own with Juri as the guy's private chauffer, and let IG Soukup stumble into whatever mess he finds himself in."

"Sounds like a recipe for disaster," Ghosh growled before glancing back to ensure that Soukup wasn't close enough to hear. "Either way, you'll be blamed."

Kalico raised her eyebrow. "I've been thinking about it ever since he stepped off the shuttle. Ghosh, I don't think there's a way out of it. The only way I save my ass is face-to-face with the Board. They're thirty years away and two years out of touch. Their reality is so different from ours, they can't conceive. You know the old saw? It's like they're living on an entirely different planet? Well, they are."

"So, what are you going to do about Soukup?"

"Haven't a clue, Ghosh. But you're a smart guy. Put yourself on Transluna. Look back at our record on Corporate Mine and throw in Southern Diggings. Think about what that's worth to The Corporation. To the Boardmembers who are going to profit from the richest find in the galaxy. Got that in your head?"

"Constantly." His muttered reply was barely audible through the helmet.

"Now, if you wanted to take Supervisor Aguila out of the picture, and put someone else in charge, do you think, looking back over our record here, that you could find enough mistakes to justify my replacement? Policy decisions that were not in The Corporation's best interest? Violations of Corporate rules and regs?"

"Like letting us make our own plunder? Giving us a percentage of the profits? Allowing us to buy property in PA? Stake our own claims?" Ghosh shook water from his sleeve. Shot another look over his shoulder. "Yeah, Supervisor, they could dismiss you over that."

"Putting Corporate contractees out at Tyson Station despite their rights?"

"They were cannibals!"

"Where does it say in the regs that a Supervisor can justify exiling people just because they're cannibals?" She vented an irritated breath. "It's coming to a head, Ghosh. One way or another. It's just a matter of how hard they want to take me down."

"Can Soukup decide that? Here? Now?"

"He has that authority. While I can't know for certain, he may already have orders to do so."

"With your replacement to be chosen from among the nobles?" Ghosh guessed correctly.

"Yeah, so what does that mean? Think, Ghosh. Chad was the most likely choice. He was the one with the most experience ensuring quotas were met in the Belt. Cinque Suharto is a logistics specialist and strike breaker, head breaker, and muscle for the Suharto industries. Bartolome? Systems management, behind the scenes. And then there is Falise; she could have something on the IG. But, hey, I'm ten years out of the loop. Any one of them might have qualities I don't know about."

"Maybe that's Soukup's game." Ghosh kept glancing back to be sure they weren't overheard. "His orders are to come, see, and choose the one who's the best fit to take over Corporate Mine?"

"Might be."

She could see the end of the tunnel, the doors closed at the decontamination chamber.

"So, what are you going to do about it, Kalico?" Ghosh asked.

"Haven't a clue."

36

What the hell just happened? Falise tried unsuccessfully to bring it all into focus. Worse, she really wanted a drink, hard liquor, like a whiskey. And all she had was a two-SDR coin. Was that enough?

She stomped down the main avenue, rain beating on her bare head, hating Port Authority with a passion she'd never known she was capable of. Not only that, this miserable toilet sewage of a town didn't even have working lighting. Only one out of every two or three streetlights cast a feeble cone of illumination down on the street. The rest of it was all shadows. Her feet, shod in expensive Son-Tay shoes, were soaked, and worse, the expensive fabric was now filthy.

Behind her, Clarice and Ednund didn't utter a word, but kept pace, no doubt consumed with situational awareness as they scoured the shadows for danger. Even as they, too, had to be reeling from the events in The Jewel.

That that bearded, bug-eyed, flat-faced ruffian dressed in quetzal hide had been her brother? Not in a million years would Falise have believed that Derek, spoiled, shallow, whining, and craven, could ever have descended to such a brutish creature. That *couldn't* have been her brother.

But it was!

And he'd played her masterfully.

I owe him money.

Pus in vacuum, but why hadn't she played that last hand?

"Because he was too sure of himself." That much of the old Derek, she'd recognized in the set of his lips, that almost-glow of satisfaction that reflected from his relaxed shoulders, the slight curl of his body. Even those now-alien eyes had gleamed in anticipation.

"The pus-sucker was going to break me with an impossible hand. From the very beginning, he played me!" She lifted her face to the rain, let it patter on her nose and cheeks. "If I could, I'd burn this misbegotten abortion of a world to slag! And Derek with it!"

"Lady?" Ednund called from behind. "Where are we going?"

"Where is there to go, huh?" Falise whirled on her heel, heedless of the water running down her face. "Perhaps Three Spires? Solar Elan? Tiboronne? Or were you thinking of the spa at the Heiman? Perhaps a relaxing evening at one of the Guild houses?"

"Lady," Ednund began.

"Where the fuck were your eyes? Clarice? You're the one with the data. Why the hell didn't you see that coming?"

Clarice, her form upright in the wet darkness, said, "Lady, consider. It's been thirteen years. Your brother has been genetically modified by an alien intelligence. That man . . . he was . . ."

"Unrecognizable," Ednund finished. "You could not have known."

She blinked, hating the water running down her face, at a loss like she had never been. "He claimed to have a half-metric ton of rhodium. All those jewels, the nuggets, those coins. Who knows what the worth of a Port Authority SDR is compared to the Corporate monetary unit? Clarice? Do you have any idea?"

"No, Lady. The Corporate SDR is a digital fiat currency. It's only used for calculating credit and debt, which is why yuan are still in use among the lower classes. The value of the PA SDR would have to be calculated against the various metals and the worth of the gemstones. Diamonds have different value per carat than rubies. I cannot compute a reliable value without access to current exchanges in Solar System."

"He said that his rhodium could buy Taglioni Tower." She stared down at the dark puddle she was standing in.

"He might have been correct, Lady," Clarice told her.

"I folded that hand while holding four jacks." God, she closed her eyes, almost reeling at the implications.

"Was it because of us?" Ednund asked softly. "Because you would not risk losing us?"

Falise bit back the truth. Tried to think what to . . . But it had taken her too long. Screw vacuum, she owed them nothing. They *belonged* to her. Period. One didn't spend time thinking up soothing words to reassure one's property.

To herself, she said, "Derek played the game perfectly. Yes, I have the same implants. The difference is that he demonstrated a mastery gained by experience. Right down to using that fool Allenovich as a shill. He runs that game every week. I expected us to be equally matched."

Blinding white flashed overhead. A moment later, the thunder cracked, deafening, almost a physical blow. Falise cowered.

"Lady?" Ednund asked. "Did you have a destination?"

"How about the estate on St. Lucia?" She lifted a fist. "Damn you, Father, for sending me to this cesspool of a place." A pause. "I was thinking I wanted a drink."

"That would be the tavern." Clarice's wet face gleamed in a flash of distant lightning.

"I've got a two-SDR coin left."

"That will buy you a single glass of whiskey." Again, Clarice's voice held no emotion.

"And then what?" Falise wondered as she started down the partially lit avenue.

What the hell have you done, Derek?

37

Kylee stepped out of the hospital and into the rain. Tip had been too drugged to talk, let alone carry on a conversation. Bored, she had left Madison seated in the visitor's chair, her head nodding, eyes closed.

Kylee figured that it wouldn't be another five minutes and Madison would be snoring.

Stopping in the light under the double doors, Kylee sniffed the wet wind. Pulled up her hat, and let her eyes adjust to the darkness. She caught the odor of crops, the sweetness of corn, the barest whiff of mint, the smell of the pepper plants. And yes, a taint of quetzal blowing in from out beyond the fence.

In that moment, she was hunting, leaping scrub, reliving the fast pursuit of a darting chamois. Her senses expanded, delighted with the flashes of white lightning and the hollow booming of thunder.

Quetzal scent from beyond the fence. Had to be Whitey's lineage.

Ought to tell Talina.

Kylee took a deep breath, turned her feet toward Inga's, figuring that's where she'd find Tal. Especially after a day of searching for a killer. Fancy soft meat, no less. Strangled. The story had been all over the hospital. Kylee herself had snuck into the autopsy room. Not much to see. Just a brown-skinned man with nothing much going for him but a quickly sutured Y incision and loose facial skin.

Even Tip had a better body.

As she went, her gaze searched the shadows. Had to remind herself that humans were night-blind. Unable to distinguish the things she could with her IR and UV vision. And they pitied her?

A smile cracked her lips.

She'd thought she'd be home by now. Back to sleeping against

Flute's warm stomach, hunting, living the paradise that was the Briggs homestead.

But Tip just kept hanging in limbo. Sometimes more lucid. Others, like tonight, drifting off as Raya tried to manage his pain. And the fucking wound in his calf? The thing just kept leaking pus. Some kind of single-cell Donovanian version of a bacterium. Cheng—when he wasn't working on the crisis of the moment—had cultured it. Vik Lawrence was in the process of coding its TriNA. A process a hell of a lot more laborious than was possible with the machines that cataloged DNA.

At Inga's, Kylee glanced up and down the avenue, seeing but a few people scurrying about their business in the rain. Then she stepped inside. And, of course, the first person she ran into had to be Hofer, who was talking to one if his friends.

"Oh," Hofer growled. "It's you."

"Never figured myself for anyone else." She gave him a menacing smile. Or what she hoped passed for one. "Glad to discover that you don't forget a face."

"You know, kid, if I hadn't been drunk that night . . ."

"You sober now?"

"Mostly."

"Wanna step outside where Tal can't break it up and give it a second try?" She shot a side glance at the second man.

He smiled, offered his hand. "Toby Montoya. We haven't met."

Got it. Shake the hand. A form of polite greeting. Dek had made her practice. She thought she did a pretty admirable job for a first for-real handshake. "Kylee Simonov. I hear good things about the stuff you build. Chaco says you're the best."

Montoya's grin was honest. "High praise, even if he's an old friend."

"Shit on a shoe," Hofer growled. "Old home week."

"Lighten up, Hof," Montoya told him. Looked at Kylee. "You heard about Dek?"

"No. Thought he had a game down at The Jewel."

"Game of the century. You know that sister of his? Falise? She went down to find him, didn't recognize him behind that beard and all. He set her up, broke her. She folded on the last hand rather than take a chance on losing those people she owns. I mean, slaves? Really? Should have seen her stomp out of there, like someone set fire to them fancy clothes she's wearing."

"Would have loved to see that for myself," Hofer said wistfully.

"Where's the sister?" Kylee asked. Figured that it wouldn't be past the silly bitch to set up and ambush Dek on his way home. Especially with all these nobles killing each other. And, who knew, maybe it was Falise who'd taken out that Grunnel?

"She's down at a table against the wall," Hofer muttered, still giving Kylee an askance look. "Trying to nurse a glass of whiskey for all she can. Looks at it more than sips it."

"Hey," Montoya added, "it's all she's got left. Dek took the rest."

Okay, she wasn't laying an ambush for Dek. "Gotta go. There's quetzal smell coming from the south. Need to tell Talina."

Hofer squinted. "What's that to you? Thought you'd be on their side."

Tall as she was, she leaned, eyes within inches of Hofer's. "Learn something, dick brain. This is Whitey's lineage. I don't owe him jack shit to start with, but he's tried to kill Talina too many times. That makes it personal."

She slipped past the men, her sharper hearing letting her catch Montoya saying, "And you really picked a fight with her? Damn, Hof, you got a death wish?"

"Aw," Hofer muttered self-consciously, "maybe the kid's all right."

That brought a twist of smile to Kylee's lips. Rocket chirped inside her as she practically danced her way down the stairs. Suck a skewer, the place was packed. Lots of soft meat in the most remarkably clean and new-looking overalls Kylee had ever seen. The shaved skulls, the wide-eyed expressions, the pale complexions stood out like oil from Donovanian water, given that the locals were dressed in quetzal, chamois, and claw shrub fiber.

At the bar, Talina's stool was empty, as was Kalico's.

But where . . . ? Ah, yes. There she was with her tall golden-haired male companion and the sloe-eyed black beauty crowded almost defensively close.

Kylee was aware of the gazes cast her way as she seated herself on Talina's stool. Sacred ground. Claimed territory. The quetzal inside her reveled at the transgression onto a venerated elder's domain.

Didn't take long before Inga came trooping down, her towel over her shoulder. The look on her face might have frozen Leaper. "You know whose chair that is?"

"Yeah, Aunt Talina's." She flipped a ten-SDR gold coin from her pouch. "How much whiskey does that buy?"

"Five glasses. But I don't serve kids. Not even you, Kylee. And if Tal finds out you're trying to—"

"Five glasses." She pointed Falise's way. "For them. Falise and her two stumbling sycophants."

"How'd you ever know what a sycophant was?" Inga was shooting a wary glance at Falise.

"Dya was my mother, along with Rebecca and Su. I don't get much use for words out in the bush, but it seems they come in handy when a person is in town. Now, there's ten. You gonna let me take five whiskeys over to Dek's sister?"

"I'll send someone. That good enough for you?"

"Absafuckinglutely."

The look Inga gave her might have cowed a quetzal, but she took the ten and lumbered her way back down the bar.

Kylee waited, sitting on Talina's stool, aware of the glances cast her way. It took a bit for her to realize that not only was she on Tal's sacred seat, but she'd added to her reputation by pummeling Hofer in the public toilet. Funny fucking place, this Port Authority. But not as vile and full of quetzal-hating scum as she'd expected it to be. It was one thing to know that these folks had a low tolerance for quetzals. And totally another to realize that Whitey was out there, motivating an entire lineage to kill humans.

Sure, there were plenty of Hofers here, but so, too, were there Montoyas, Shigs, and Raya Turnienkos. Some of what she'd considered to be Talina's incomprehensible memories began to make more sense.

That's when Inga, casting a sidelong and narrow-eyed glance Kylee's way, carried a tray bearing five whiskeys to the side table where Falise and her glowering servants huddled.

Inga placed the tray, which raised eyebrows at the table, and pointed in Kylee's direction. As Falise and the others turned surprised gazes her way, Kylee slipped off the stool and nodded to Inga before ambling her way over to the table.

"So, I hear you had a little bad luck at the poker table," Kylee said by way of introduction. "Of course, the big news is that you finally figured out who Dek is. Are you people congenitally stupid, or what?"

At the words, Ednund rose, a glittering in his eyes as he dropped into a combat crouch.

"I wouldn't," Kylee said softly, her vision expanding. "It's a quetzal night, what with the storm, and my blood is already up. Besides, I may be from the bush, but even I know it's bad form to attack someone who just bought you a round of drinks."

Clarice was watching her with the most fascinated dark gaze, as if trying to find some explanation for her behavior.

"What do you want?" Falise asked, motioning for Ednund to sit.

As the golden boy took his seat, and that deadly gaze locked on Kylee, she dropped onto the bench beside Clarice and opposite Falise and Ednund. "Guess I'm curious." She tapped her head. "Got some of Dek in here. Shared TriNA. He's lineage. But then I meet you. Like, fucking wow. Talk about different. Makes for a fascinating study. Same genetics, same enculturation, but you're like a total waste of skin."

"*What* did you call me?" Falise's eyes had narrowed to slits.

"Comes from living in the bush with quetzals." Kylee lifted one of the glasses of whiskey. Took a sip. Made a face and tried to keep from coughing as she swallowed. "People actually drink this stuff? On purpose?"

Falise remained expressionless, coldly focused.

Kylee indicated the glasses. "You might take a drink. Don't know if you've noticed, but we're, like, the center of attention. Not sharing a drink someone's bought for you? I'm told it comes across as particularly rude."

"Now why would I, of all people, have the slightest interest in being polite to a sewer creature like you? And what are you? Some hybrid freak with your too-pointed face? Those bug-big eyes? And Derek called you his sister? Really? Or, as I would guess, is it that my mutant brother can't find companionship? He's so desperate he's warming his cock in your too-willing slit?"

"Nice try." Kylee set the glass down. "But you really aren't very smart. You keep making mistakes, even when presented with easily interpreted data. How can I be Dek's sister? You, Manilla, and Al-lise are the only sisters he knows about. Unless good old Claudio spread his seed far and wide." She narrowed an eye. "And Dek's already landed the most fantastic woman on the planet."

"Then," Falise said with a frown, as if struggling, "What are you to my brother?"

"I'm lineage. Lineage is an entirely different thing. Dek, Talina, Tip, Flute, even that pus-sucking Whitey out there. We're all linked. Can't say that I'd mind sex with Dek, but he and Talina are remarkably monogamous."

"Talina Perez? And my brother?" Falise's eyebrow lifted in distaste.

"Shit on a shoe, woman, you keep making my point. You've been on Donovan for a couple of days, and you don't have the foggiest clue about the simplest of things." Kylee leaned forward, propping her chin. "Whatever Claudio and Miko sent you to do, how do you expect to do it when you don't have the first fucking notion about how things work here? For a supposedly superior Taglioni, you come across as a laughingstock."

Falise put a hand on Ednund as the man started to rise, his teeth grinding, eyes flashing blue hatred. She actually had to struggle to drag him back down.

"Don't," Kylee turned quetzal eyes on his. "I know you're trained. Dek told me all about what you and Clarice do for Falise. Problem is, you'd be up against quetzal reflexes and strength.

Doesn't matter which of us might win, all it would do is further damage good old Falise's image. It's a no-win for you, pretty boy. Even if you killed me, Dek, Talina, Tip, or Flute would kill you."

"Why?" Falise asked.

"You really don't get this lineage thing, do you?" Kylee sighed. "Now, pick up the whiskey and take a drink. It's your first step toward repairing your image."

Falise shot some kind of meaningful look at Ednund and then Clarice. The three of them took glasses, lifted and sipped.

"Why are you here?" Falise replaced the glass next to her empty one. "What do you care if I succeed or fail?"

Kylee played with her glass of whiskey, tipping it back and forth until the liquid barely reached the rim. "Dek figures you're here in response to him sending Dan Wirth back to Solar System. If you're the best the Taglionis have, you better get on that starship and run. Dek's got half the planet by the balls, and so far all you've done is make a mess of your end."

Falise, for the first time, stopped glaring, cunning filling her emerald eyes. "Go on."

"If you killed Chad, Talina's going to find out."

"What if I did?"

Kylee shrugged. "I'd say steal an airtruck and get the hell out of PA. It wasn't a fair fight. He was drugged. From what I've heard, they'll have an inquest. Shig, Yvette, and Talina will have the proof they need, and one of them, probably Talina, will shoot you in the back of the head."

"Hey, idiot child, I'm a Taglioni, get it? I don't—"

"That means quetzal shit in PA, *get it*? This isn't the fucking Corporation. The Taglioni name only means anything here because Dek made it. Look around. No one in this room gives a flying fuck. Well, maybe but for the spacers down on leave from *Turalon*." A beat. "So, did you kill Chad?"

"No."

Kylee shrugged. "That makes things a little easier. But not much." She took another sip of the whiskey. "Shit on a stick! People really drink this? On purpose? That's as bad the second time as the first."

"What do you get out of this?" Falise asked.

"Pay attention here: Dek's lineage. That means if you try and retaliate against him for the humiliation, or blame him for your failure, and send Ednund, here, or Clarice after him. Tal and I will kill you all. That's what lineage means."

"Why would I—"

"Shut up and listen: You're nothing but a sister he doesn't even like. Right now, you're even a bigger laughingstock than Hofer, and from what I've learned, that takes a lot."

"And you would have me do what?"

"Stop acting like a Taglioni. On Donovan, stupidity is a death sentence."

Kylee stood, reaching into her belt pouch. "I heard that Dek cleaned you out, left you in debt. Here. There's a hundred siddars and a bit of plunder to keep you going."

She tossed the coins, a couple of nuggets, and some uncut opals and sapphires on the table with a clunk.

Falise and the others blinked. "And what is my obligation to you in return?"

"Nothing," Kylee told her. "I'm not here for that long, and there's plenty more where that came from. Now, go apologize to Dek for being an idiot."

Turning her back on them, Kylee propped her hand on her pistol, striding for the door. There was still Talina to find. And Whitey out there, somewhere, in the storm.

alise sucked down the last of the whiskey, feeling the burning rush as it hit her stomach. She fumed, Kylee's final words as fiery in her memory as the whiskey in her gut. Around her, Inga's roared with laughter, the clink of glasses, curses, not to mention the bedlam of too many people shouting over each other. Worse, the dome overhead acted as an echo chamber, blasting the sound right back down. That made people yell louder to be heard over the din. Infuckingtolerable! Even the rudest joint on Transluna would have had privacy cones.

As she picked up the gold nugget, and glanced around, it was to find the place filled with locals, all looking like rejects from a bad holo. And then there were the contractees, the first of the new specialists and laborers shuttled down from *Turalon*. Here and there, mixed in with the crowd, were uniformed crew from the ship. All were eating, drinking, laughing, telling the news, answering questions.

The whole place seemed to reek of a joyous carnival celebration.

On the far side, Bartolome sat with his servants, engaged in a conversation with Shig Mosadek and Yvette. Planning what? Angling for what?

The merriment, noise, and laughter just added to her misery and the sense of total and complete isolation.

Go apologize to Derek for being an idiot? In a pig's ass.

"Learn the rules," she sneered in as close to a mimicry of Kylee's voice as she could muster. She lifted the nugget, seeing bits of rock still stuck in the crannies. Looked like it had come right out of the ground. Next, she picked up one of the coins, while Clarice studied the other nugget. Ednund was frowning down at the sapphire pinched between his fingers, muttering, "There's more where that came from."

"What kind of person would just give away gemstones of this value?" Clarice wondered. "What's her purpose? Is she trying to impress us?"

"I don't think so." Ednund set the gemstone on the table, picked up one of the coins, inspecting the design. "No, my reading is that her concern is for Derek. She kept going back to lineage, trying to get us to understand its importance. Letting us know that if we act against him, she and Talina will retaliate."

"She's definitely not afraid of us." Clarice lifted the silver-colored nugget, frowned. "I think this is one of the rare Earth elements." Her eyebrows rose. "Do you suppose this is rhodium? It has the same vitreous luster as the bar Derek bet at the poker game."

"He said he had a half metric ton," Ednund mused.

Falise closed her eyes, feeling the whiskey running in her blood. She pinched the bridge of her nose, as if it would enable her to think better. "That irritating little gutter slit is right about one thing. We need to get smart about Port Authority and how Donovan works. My fucking brother is sitting on a fortune, and I've just made a fool out of myself."

She chuckled bitterly. "What did the freak-child say? Only Hofer was more a laughingstock? Who's Hofer?"

"Doesn't matter, Lady." Clarice took a deep breath. "Cinque is out working with Talina Perez. Bartolome is over there ingratiating himself with Mosadek and Dushane. We're sitting here, looking defeated, while the tale of how your brother humiliated you travels like wildfire. The last image people have is of that skinny wisp of a girl buying us whiskey and giving us money." She made a face. "Like it was charity for the indigent."

"Finish your whiskey," Falise told them. "The freak-child told the truth: These people play by a different standard. Everything we know. Every cunning advantage we count on. All of our skills don't apply. We've got to learn the rules, because we're losing here."

Clarice upended her glass. Made a face and choked down the strong drink. "So, what are you planning?"

"We're going back to find Derek. He's the key. I don't know how, and I will hate every pus-gagging second of it, but I will apologize. I will grovel if I have to. And I fucking well want to do it while I'm full of whiskey, because I'd vomit if I had to do it sober."

With that, she got to her feet, realized that she needed to hurry, before the last glass had a chance to hit her bloodstream. She managed the transit of the irregular paving stones, led the way up the steps, ignoring the hundreds of gazes that followed her departure. Was especially conscious of the half-smile on Bartolome's face.

Fine, let them talk.

She'd forgotten the rain. With no other recourse, she pulled the willowy fabric of her pantsuit tight about her, ducked her head, and started purposely north along the avenue. As she went, her previously soaked shoes kept feeling looser and looser on her feet. In the light of one of the few working streetlights, she glanced down, horrified to see the seams separating from the delicate fabric.

"Will this horror never end?"

"Lady?" Ednund asked. "Want me to run to the dome? Find you better attire? Different shoes, something to keep the rain from—"

"No, damn it. I want to get this over with before I talk myself out of it."

She hurried forward, Ednund and Clarice following dutifully, getting just as wet as she was. So, how was she going to do this? Her hair was a mess, already hanging like a saturated mop down her back. Her pantsuit, made of the fine, almost sheer fabric, was clinging to her body like a second skin. Not that a Taglioni minded, genetics had given her a *hetaira*'s body, but the drunken louts in that maggot-choking casino would be thinking of her the same way they thought of the prostitutes working on the floor.

"I'm not sure it would work, but I could try and seduce him away from this Talina Perez." Clarice's voice was full of uncertainty. "Though the man I saw in the casino hardly spared me a second glance. Even when I posed myself as available."

"No, he didn't. Not even when he wagered for us," Ednund agreed. "And didn't the freak child say he and Perez were monogamous? Curious use of the word, that."

Ednund might be Falise's way out of this. She'd send him in

while she waited. Maybe somewhere out of the rain. Ask him to have Derek step outside. Keep her humiliation to the minimum.

"But will he do that?" she asked herself as rain trickled down her face. "Or, knowing me, will he suspect a trick?"

"Lady," Clarice said from behind, "you know that he hates Claudio and Malissa, so no appeal to family loyalty will work. But I have been thinking about that man you played poker with. About the things he said. How he acted. It is a risk, and humiliating, but from my study of his behavior, and knowing who you are, the most likely chance for success is if you walk in, looking just as you do now, and tell him you have made a mistake and ask him if he will forgive you."

"Ask him to forgive? When I look like a fucking drowned dog?"

"Of course," Ednund said as if in revelation. "I see. Lady, think of it. He's expecting retaliation, scorn, dismissal, some counterattack completely in accord with your personality. Even the Derek we knew—and there must be something of him left inside—would be surprised, curious, and even satisfied by what seemed a complete capitulation. What was the word you used? Grovel?"

"It's so totally out of character, he can't help but take it seriously." Clarice reached around to wring out her hair as she stumbled along on the uneven surface.

"The danger is that the riffraff will forever hold it over me. I'm a goddamned Taglioni! It's bad enough I have to humble myself in front of Derek. I'll be damned if I do it in front of an audience of gutter trash."

"Not even for a half metric ton of rhodium, who knows how much gold, or the wealth of Capella III?" Ednund asked. "Once you win, take command of the wealth and wield the power, the act will be forgotten. The narrative will change to 'Can you believe that, wet and bedraggled, she once pleaded to get back in her brother's good graces?'"

"We talked about new rules clear back when we were aboard *Turalon*," Clarice reminded her as The Jewel came into the view. Slanting rain shone in silver streaks in the light over the door.

"All that matters is winning in the end." Falise sighed, then laughed. "What the hell am I thinking? I've debased myself far worse than this. Played more pathetic roles. If I could endure the things I did in Vincent Xian Chan's bed—and for a far lesser prize than Capella III's wealth, I can do this."

She made a face. "It's just that it's Derek. And this place."

"Only results matter in the end, Lady," Ednund told her.

She took a breath, hated the water leaking down her face, and started forward, only to hesitate as a staccato of sound erupted in the night behind her. Something about it chilled her worse than the rain. Couldn't be fireworks. That crackling and popping. Gunfire?

A scream sounded. Then a shout.

What the hell? This didn't sound like revelry. She turned, lifting a hand to shield her eyes from the rain. A flicker of lightning strobed white in the clouds, momentarily illuminating the avenue. In that instant, she saw something coming. Just the quick glimpse. Long bodied, running low, like some . . . And then it was gone.

"Did you see that?" she asked.

"Something," Ednund agreed. "Like a creature that . . ."

The blaring of the siren almost made Falise jump out of her skin. The damn thing was so loud, painful, she clapped hands to her ears.

Ednund had taken another step, his head forward as he used the flat of his palm to shield his eyes against the downpour. As the siren continued to blare, he shouted, "I thought I saw it." He pointed with his other hand. "Something between where we . . ."

A piece of the night—swelling darkness—came alive. Midnight moved, blotting the light down the avenue. Falise tried to make sense of the inky shape that came barreling out of the rain. In the flickering white of distant lightning, she caught the momentary image of a great triangular head, wet and gleaming in the black. Something like a sheet flared wide behind the head, faintly red in the reflected light from The Jewel. Big. Fast. Three shining orbs, widely spaced eyes, glinted.

And then the jaws opened, shadowy in the midnight rain. The casino lights gleaming on wet serrated teeth.

The huge head slammed into Ednund, lifting, crushing his hips and stomach as the monster twisted him up into the air.

The scream torn from Ednund's throat was like nothing Falise had ever heard. The pain, terror, and horror would ring in her soul forever.

An impossible monster slung its rain-black head back and forth, like a terrier savaging a rat, water slinging silver in the casino lights.

Falise could hear the snapping of bone, the whimpering shrieks going silent as Ednund's severed legs were flung to the side.

A bolt of lightning overhead flashed as the great beast tossed its head up. Swallowed. The lump that was Ednund engorged the throat, caused the frilling expanse of collar to ripple and swell. The three lightning-lit eyes fixed on Falise. She gaped, frozen, every muscle and nerve paralyzed.

She couldn't breathe. Couldn't think. Could only stare at the thing, her body electric in panic.

As the ruin of Ednund's body pulsed wide down the beast's throat, it started forward, reaching out with two short, clawed arms.

She tried to draw breath. To scream.

And then her brain turned off.

She felt herself falling . . .

Thought there were the banging sounds of gun shots.

Her last sensation was the pattering of rain.

Hitting her face.

From a long way away.

39

Talina could sense them. She still hadn't caught their scent, but with the rain, the flashing lightning and rolling thunder, she could close her eyes and almost see through Whitey's. She didn't need Demon down in her gut to know they were close. The quetzal kept squirming around down there. Agitated. All the more reason to know she was right.

And on her shoulder, Rocket continued to shift nervously. In her imagination, the little quetzal kept sweeping the darkness in search of danger.

"Yeah, I know," she whispered as she stared out past the Mine Gate at the inky darkness, rain, and lightning flickers. The gentle shishing sound of the falling rain, the patters as it dripped from her hat and cloak and streamed down the chain link from above, obscured everything but the rumbling thunder.

"Know what?" Cinque asked from behind.

"Don't mind her," Wejee told the Suharto. "She's just talking to her quetzals."

"Wish someone would explain that to me sometime." Cinque shifted, boot dragging across the wet gravel.

Talina—search as she might—could see nothing out in the scrubby trees lining the road. Once, back in the Clemenceau days, the Supervisor had ordered all the trees cut down within a quarter mile of the haul road. That was back before people learned just how fast Donovanian vegetation could move. Within a fortnight, the trees were lining the road again, kept back only by the constant traffic of the haulers crushing their roots when they tried to wiggle their way onto the road.

Talina sighed, turned back. "It's like having a second and third being inside you. A total lack of privacy and an invasion of who you are as a person. You lose part of yourself, and nothing is private. All those hidden memories, the ones that you're so ashamed of, the ones you hoped would die with you? All the shitty stuff you wish you'd never done? Never thought? They're now shared with aliens. Doesn't stop there. Quetzal memories are constantly flooding your thoughts. Like tonight. I won't sleep. It's a quetzal night. I want to be out hunting. And that's what I'm going to do. Tonight, I'm quetzal."

"What keeps you from going crazy?" Cinque asked as he stepped closer. She could see the water sheeting from his slicker and the quetzal-leather hat he'd acquired from somewhere. Like Wejee and herself, Cinque now cradled a rifle under his rain gear. Something fancy with an engraved stock that had been in his luggage. She wondered if he knew how to use it.

"I did." She gave a shrug. "Then I figured out how to put myself back together. Well, me and Rocket." To Wejee, she said, "Stay frosty, old friend. I can feel it. They're planning something."

"If I see steaks and leather move out there, I'm blowing a hole in it," Wejee replied. "You don't worry about me, Tal."

"You're the last guy out here I worry about." She gave him a slap on the shoulder and turned for the avenue. As she led the way, her night gaze scanned the warehouses, the parked and disabled machinery. "Wish we could haul half of this junk out of here. It would sure make life easier when it came to hunting quetzals."

"Then, why don't you?" Cinque asked. "None of the reports going back to The Corporation are exactly glowing when it comes to Port Authority. They call it a junkyard, a slum, a collection of hovels and dirt."

Talina gestured. "Because . . . okay. See that broken-down track hoe beside the pipe racks? That's one of three on the planet. The one that still works is running on parts scavenged from this one and the second one that's broken down out at the mine. I know for a fact that the functioning track hoe is working on the last clutch. When it goes, everything out at the mine stops until Lawson and Montoya can make a new clutch. Maybe they can use some of the old parts, maybe they build it from scratch. Given that, like every other specialist, they have a list of emergency repairs as long as their arms, it might be weeks before they can get around to it. But, if it's a driving sprocket? There it sits on that defunct track hoe. Bernie Monson can have it unbolted and ready to install within hours."

"So, do you reuse everything?"

"Pretty much. Oh, eventually something's stripped down to the frame. But you'd be surprised. Mac Hanson used two chassis from worn-out haulers to make the framework for his first dropforge. We're innovative here. Something The Corporation should consider should it ever decide to break us or shut us down."

"Would you go back if you could?" Cinque was peering at her with his totally black eyes.

"Not a chance. I'm Donovanian. Back there, I'd be a laboratory specimen."

"Any progress on Chad's murderer?" he asked casually.

"Nope. Why? You kill him? You've got the body strength."

She saw his clever smile. "I suppose I do. And, yes, eliminating him would have been a prudent move."

"Why's that?"

To her dismay neither his expression nor facial temperature betrayed a misdirection when he said, "In many ways, Chad was the best successor to Kalico, should anything happen to her. He had the most experience when it came to mining, processing, and transporting extractive resources. More to the point, he knew it. Hence his cultivation of Colonel Creamer." A pause. "Where is he, by the way?"

"Up on *Turalon*. Seems your soft meat Colonel got crosswise with half the crowd at The Jewel when he made disparaging remarks about Kalico. Dr. Tyler, up in *Turalon*'s med bay, was wiring his jaw back together last I heard."

Cinque stopped short, rain pattering on his hat. "You're telling me that a mob beat up a marine colonel? Why weren't the rest of us told?"

Talina tried to make sense of the irritation on his face. "Not our business. Get it through your head. You're in Port Authority. If you've got Corporate concerns, take them up with Kalico. Ah, but she's playing handmaid to this IG. The one you, Falise, and Bartolome are depending on."

Cinque resumed walking, face thoughtful. "Question. Let's say he dismisses Supervisor Aguila for some reason. How will that affect Port Authority? What will the ramifications be?"

She stopped, pointing down at the puddled water at her feet. "See this spot? The night Tamarland Benteen took down the fence, and Whitey led two other quetzals into PA, I found Kalico Aguila, standing right here. She was the link holding Step's line to the west, and Abu Sassi's team to the east. Unlike this nice gentle rain, it was fucking coming down in buckets. Kalico had just found Dube Dushku's body. People were dying all over town. And here is Kalico, a rifle in her hands, her ass on the line."

Cinque stared down at the mud. Would have been barely visible to his normal eyes. Not that he'd understand.

"My question to you, Suharto, is not what PA would do if Kalico was dismissed. Kalico's earned our respect. And she'd probably resign without causing a scene, because, damn her for a lunatic, she's still got this fart-sucking loyalty to the Corporation. I want to know why you, soft meat and ignorant as you are, think you could run this colony?"

"It would take . . ."

"Tal?" a voice called.

Talina looked up, saw Kylee trotting toward her. "What's up, Kylee?"

"You looking for Whitey?"

"You find him? Know where he's at?"

"Caught a scent, faint, coming in from the south when I got out of the hospital. Anything out there they can get into?"

"Sczui farm is south of the moat." She accessed her com. "Two Spot? Is Szong Sczui keeping an ear on the radio?"

"Should be. What have you got, Tal?"

"Give him a heads up. We think Whitey's somewhere in his vicinity."

"Roger that. Damn. If it wasn't raining, we could put a drone up."

"Yeah, I know."

She turned to Kylee. "You said a faint scent?"

Kylee was looking back down the avenue to the south, her nose twitching. "Not strong, but good enough to identify the lineage."

"Tal?" Two Spot said in her earpiece. *"No answer from Sczui. What do you want me to do?"*

"Not much you can, Two Spot. Just let Mishka, Miranda, and the rest know that Whitey's out there in the night. We'll see if we can track him in the morning. After the rain, it shouldn't be that hard."

"Roger that."

Kylee was giving Cinque a curious inspection. "What's with the pheromones?"

"Makes him attractive to women," Talina replied as if Cinque weren't there. "He's supposed to be winning my confidence while he's plying me for information."

"Makes him smarter than Falise. Dek just put her more than two grand in debt before she finally figured out who he is."

"Is that whiskey I smell on your breath?"

"How do you think İ got Falise to drop her guard and betray her plans for the future?"

"Suck an ion," Cinque muttered, irritated. "Who are you people?"

Talina said, "The ones who will either save your ass, Suharto, or let the quetzals eat it."

Kylee stuck a thumb out, asking, "So, does the man in black, here, know that you're in Derek Taglioni's lineage?"

"Excuse me? Taglioni's *lineage*? What's that mean?"

"Guess he's no smarter than Falise, huh?" Kylee cocked her head water streaming from the brim of her hat. "Think the Bad Bart character's any better?"

"Don't know," Talina said. "He's supposed to be the tricky one."

Cinque threw his head back and laughed. "I'm turned loose in the midst of lunatics."

"You sure you want the IG to appoint you as the new Supervisor?" Talina asked.

Cinque smiled in the darkness. "What does *in the Taglioni lineage* mean?"

Talina stared south, trying to see past the fence, past the moat to the Sczui farmstead. The house was more like a fortified blockhouse, complete with loopholes, reinforced door, and sensors. If Szong and "Mother," as his wife was called, had holed up, no quetzal was breaking in. And there would have been the sound of gunfire.

Kylee told him, "Talina and Dek live together when he's in town. They have what's called a monogamous sexual union."

"Think you can make it sound any less romantic, Kylee?"

The girl shrugged. "Probably. How about a mutual companionship including non-productive copulation that—"

"Give it a break, kid!"

Cinque was studying her with a new intensity. "So, are you Taglioni assets?"

"Just the opposite," Talina told him. "Taglioni? Suharto? Grunnel? I could give a clap-trapping slug's ass. My loyalty is to the people on Donovan. As to what that means for Corporate plans for our future? You're welcome to tag along, Cinque. And hope I don't get you killed in the process."

They froze as fusillade of shots could be heard from over by the shuttle field gate. Then screams.

Which was when the siren went off. That long and dreaded wail that meant quetzal in the compound.

"Steaks and leather," Talina called. "Load your weapons. Let's go." And she started up the avenue at a run.

40

Something warm and wet was being sponged across Falise's eyes and forehead. For the moment, she lay quietly, thinking the sensation was most pleasant. But her reeling senses insisted on wailing that this wasn't right.

Opening her eyes, Falise blinked, reached up to rub the moisture away. A woman—dark brown hair and amusement behind brown eyes—pulled the warm washcloth away. "You back with us?"

"What happened. I was on the street. Something . . ."

She clamped her eyes again, seeing Ednund lifted up and twisted, shaken back and forth as if he'd been a toy. The legs . . . Oh, fucking God, the legs . . . How they flipped away into the night to slap soddenly on the wet gravel.

"That didn't really happen, did it?" she asked. "That . . . *thing* appearing in the night. That's not real. It's the whiskey, right? I was drunk. Imagining—"

"Yeah, Falise. He's dead." The woman's expression reflected simple fact. "Tal and that girl Kylee got the quetzal. The fucker's lying out there on the street. Steaks and leather. Sorry about your slave."

"He's not a slave." How could she say it so callously? "He's . . . He's . . ."

She swallowed hard, looked to the side. Couldn't think about Ednund. Not now.

She lay in a bed, in a small room. Weird knickknacks on a shelf, a quaint dresser, a small sink with folded towels to the side. The coverlet looked like something out of a history book, homemade, with embroidery. Local designs.

"Where am I?"

"My room," the woman told her, standing and taking the washcloth over to the sink where she rinsed it out. "It's not like I'm working anymore tonight. Dek said to bring you back here. Your other slave, Clarice? She's out at the bar. Been in tears. Said she didn't want you to see. Angelina's keeping an eye on her and that weird Suharto character." She paused. "They do that to his eyes on purpose?"

"They did." Falise sat up, swung her feet to the floor.

"Wow. Somebody really didn't like him, did they?"

"He's one of the most powerful men in the Suharto family." She rubbed her face. Sitting up had turned a raging headache loose inside her skull.

"Then why doesn't he fix his eyes? Makes him all creepy. Like he's a psycho murderer in a holovid. If he wanted to buy a trick, I'd turn him down flat. Don't think I could take those eyes, staring down at me. Think I'd freeze up like ice, trying not to shiver while he did me."

"Oh, for fuck's sake," Falise said through a pained whisper. She had to be in The Jewel. She was sitting on a whore's bed. No wonder the woman wore that form-fitting wrap. Quick to put on and take off.

"I saw you earlier. What's your name?"

"Dalia."

"Thanks, Dalia." She stood, winced at the headache, and walked to the door. Hesitated. "Why'd you do this? Take care of me?"

"Dek asked me to." She smiled wistfully. "I owe him. He's always treated me right."

"Client?"

"Who, Dek? No. Not that I'd mind, let me tell you, but he's never even fucked Allison. And he's one of the few she'd take these days. Naw, he's pretty much dedicated to Talina." Her gaze went wistfully distant. "Gotta admire a man like that."

Falise grasped the doorknob. "Yeah, well, I'm going to go pull Clarice off her barstool, have a friendly chat with my dear brother, Derek, and wander my way back to that miserable dome so that I can wish I was off this pestilent disaster of a planet."

"Nope." Dalia turned, crossing her arms, which pulled the warp tight across her round breasts. Advertising, no doubt. "You're stuck here. We're on lockdown."

"Oh, joyous," Falise muttered to herself as she stepped out into the hall and made her way on unsteady feet to the main room. God, the whiskey was still running in her blood.

The place was empty of clientele. Cinque Suharto sat at one of the high-top tables by the door, an expensive rifle laid across the chabacho wood beside him. His every attention seemed to be on the door, as if he didn't want to miss whatever stepped through it.

Clarice, at the bar, had her head bowed, face in her hands, bedraggled hair hanging around her like a soggy veil. The old man, Shin Wong, was behind the bar, washing glasses. The whore called Angelina—wearing a low-cut shift that exposed a lot of cleavage—had propped herself on the stool at the end, kept staring worriedly at the door.

Falise walked over, seated herself beside Clarice. "Are you all right?"

"No." Clarice's voice sounded small. "There are still pieces of him. Severed legs, laying out there in the rain next to that dead . . . *thing.*"

"That's a quetzal, lady," Wong told her, no emotion in his voice. "Welcome to Donovan."

"How did it get in?" Falise asked, desperately trying not to think, not to remember. Didn't help the hideous replay that kept running in her throbbing head. She'd actually seen that. The creature looming out of the darkness, as if formed from the night itself. How it snatched Ednund.

She swallowed at the knot of grief—felt it pull tight into an ache that paralyzed her tongue and brought tears to her eyes.

No. Block it. You're a Taglioni.

She turned her attention to Wong. "So, how long does this last?"

"Until they search the town."

"But the quetzal's dead, right? Lying out in the street?"

"One," Wong told her. "Word is there's more than one. Maybe all six."

Clarice began sniffling again.

"How long to search the town?"

Wong set his glass down. Leaned forward to glare into her eyes. "Until we know we got 'em all. You get that, lady?"

"Yeah." She pushed off the stool, walked over, and seated herself at Cinque's table. "What do you know about all of this?"

He turned his pitch-black eyes her way. "What little I overhead was that Whitey forced some farmer named Sczui to call out that he was hurt, needed to be let in the shuttle field gate. Couple of the new marines were on guard there. They opened the gate, Sczui came staggering up, and the quetzals piled through. Four of them. Knocked the marines flat and ran right over the top of them. Wasn't a complete loss, they recovered enough of their senses to shoot two of the beasts. The third is out there on the street. Another is somewhere on the loose."

He shook his head. "I was with Tal and Kylee when it all happened. We were coming up the street. They just up and lifted their rifles."

He snapped his fingers. "Bam. Bam. Bam. Just like that. And Tal calls over her shoulder, 'Stay close!' We come pounding up the street at a run. I can finally see in the casino lights as they split and go wide. Each one shoots the dead quetzal. You're lying on your side in the mud, Clarice is screaming." He frowned. "I mean, that *thing* was reaching down for you when they shot it."

"I don't know what happened," she told him. "Like it came out of nothing. I saw that horrible creature appear out of the darkness, grab Ednund. Rip him apart. You get that, Cinque? It tore him in two!" She heard the terror rising in her voice. "And then it started for me. And . . . and . . ."

"The world just faded?" He gave her a knowing glance. "You can read the reports all you want. Think you understand. But until you're face to face with it?"

She rubbed her nervous hands together. "Ednund had been with me all of my life."

"Yeah." He sniffed, ran his fingers down his rifle's stock. "I'm taking Charlotte. She needs someone. The rest of Chad's people can go home."

"What about Tamala? She's your valet. Been with you for years."

"We got tired of each other. She understands." Cinque smiled. "It was being cramped up in *Turalon*. Like you and Kramer . . . things happened."

She nodded, figured he knew it was calculated on her part. "So we wait here?"

"That's what Talina told me. No uncertain terms: 'Get your ass in there. Lock the door. Shoot anything that isn't human that comes in after you.'" He chuckled. "And then she, that girl Kylee, and Dek, they charge off into the darkness. Just the three of them. Going quetzal hunting. Out there in the dark, can you imagine?"

"What about the vaunted plan?" Falise asked. "The organized search they made such a big thing of at that supposed orientation."

"That's happening, too. Allison left at a run to get to the Admin dome. They start at the south end of town. Sweep north." He wiped a finger under his nose. "Wong told me that with the new marines, it's going to be a lot quicker. Maybe even more so if Tal, Dek, and that girl don't get eaten."

"My brother is out there in the dark, hunting one of those *things*." Her reeling thoughts—after taking too many hits and still whiskey-fogged—struggled to understand.

And Ednund is dead?

She wanted to hang her head and weep.

"What kind of hell have we gotten ourselves into?" she asked.

"They have a saying, Falise. People come here to leave, to die, or to find themselves."

"Yeah," she whispered while her heart ached. "What's left of Ednund is out there on the street. Guess we know which one he came for."

41

As the airtruck settled on the aircar field by the west gate, Kalico checked her pistol in the morning light that shone through the side window. Port Authority had been conducting a quetzal hunt for half the night and was still in the process of searching for any of the beasts that might have managed to elude the sweeps.

She shut down the fans, killed the power, and took a moment to study the lines of junked aircars out by the bush. Then she scanned the still-running ones parked closer in and the four airtrucks backed against the fence. Nothing seemed out of the ordinary. No irregularities. Nothing that looked like an innocent pile of dirt or a mound where flat ground should be. She checked the shadows cast by Capella's slanting light, seeing regular lines, nothing with a watery look or shimmer as would be projected by a hiding quetzal.

Only then did she pull her rifle from the rack, check the chamber, and open the door. She took another careful scan of her surroundings. Stepping down, she locked the door behind her, walked warily to the gate, rifle at the ready. When quetzals were in the vicinity, she cursed evolution for not giving her eyes in the back of her head.

At the gate, Sean Finnegan—wearing his battered armor with its make-do powerpack, rifle in hand—told the shiny new marine with him, "Keep an eye out, Aberash. Rifle up, ready to shoot."

"Yes, sir," the young woman told him, every ounce of her looking like she was ready for the shit to come down.

"How you doing, Sean?" Kalico asked as Finnegan unlocked the gate and swung it open, his attention remaining fixed on the aircar field behind her.

"Long night, ma'am. Four dead, three of them soft meat. Killed four quetzals. The teams are wrapping up the search on the north end. Working through the warehouses now." He swung the gate shut behind her, still keeping his eyes on the field and its approaches.

"Two Spot said they came in through the shuttle field gate? Used a hostage?"

"Yeah. Sczui. He's in hospital. I guess it will be a close thing." Finnegan gave her a wry grin. "Privates Ituri and Asaana were on the gate when Sczui came staggering up. Figured they'd just slip the gate open, drag him in, and close it right quick. They got a lesson in how fast quetzals move. Knocked them flat, but, by damn, ma'am, they rolled over, pawed their rifles around, and from prone, smoked one. Hit a second one hard enough to slow it down. But the two in the lead got scot-free into the town."

"Whitey one of them?"

"Nope. More's the pity. That tricky son of bitch is still out there, somewhere."

Kalico told him, "Stay frosty."

"You got it, Supervisor."

As Kalico walked away, she heard him saying, "Now you know why that woman rates so high. She might be in charge of Corporate here on the planet, but she's one of us first."

It brought a smile to her lips, but she wondered what Soukup would make of it. Call it a "cult of personality" and use it as grounds to dismiss her? Consider it fraternization with menials? Or accuse her of blurring the lines between social classes?

Screw it. The IG could enjoy his day on *Freelander*. She'd slipped out of Corporate Mine early, left orders for Makarov to take the IG up in the A-7. She'd assigned the task of tour guide to Fenn Bogarten—who knew as much as anyone about the haunted wreck. Fenn could accompany the IG on his investigation. By now they'd be most of the way to *Freelander*, with Fenn wondering what he'd ever done to deserve being sent back to one place in the universe he hated more than anywhere.

On the other hand, it was nice to think of Soukup—and especially his Four—walking the eerie black corridors, feeling the hair rise on the backs of their necks, and recording the "dome of bones" in the Crew Mess. When those recordings were finally replayed for the Board, Kalico hoped it would creep-freak them with a real feeling for walking those haunted hallways.

Maybe, Soukup—being who and what he was—would order the door of the AC to be cut open, answering the question whether Tamarlind Benteen was alive or dead.

She rounded the corner onto the main avenue. In the middle of the street, hanging from a forklift, a quetzal swung slowly in the morning light. Rude Marsdome carefully skinned the hide from the beast. Ripples of iridescent red, yellow, blue, green, and violet rolled across the folds of loose hide lying on the avenue surface, the insides rosy with splotches of the creature's caked blood. Bullet wounds could be seen in the pink flesh on the naked carcass. People with long knives were waiting for the last of the hide to be cut loose. Then they'd tackle the task of butchering.

Allison Chomko stood at the door of The Jewel, arms crossed, wearing a much-too-slinky red gown for this time of the morning.

"You look dressed to kill," Kalico observed. Then she got a look at the woman's face: drawn, tired.

"Just got back from the Admin dome. Been up all night with Shig and Yvette coordinating the hunt. Vik and Kalen are still on the line, but they're down to the last hiding places. Drones are up, so it's pretty much over."

"Heard we lost four." Kalico indicated the hanging quetzal as Marsdome cut the last of the connective tissue free and the heavy hide collapsed into a pile.

"One was right there. One of that Taglioni woman's slaves. The blond boy toy. Happened right in front of the woman. Shocked her so bad she passed out. Fainted like in those old movies. Thought Taglionis were made of tougher stuff."

"Don't underestimate her, Allison. Over the span of her career, she's cut a lot more throats than Dan ever did. You follow me?"

Allison nodded, her golden hair shining. "Just FYI, Dek took her to the cleaners at his game before all of this happened. Humiliated her. Not sure how that little bit of family drama might affect the rest of us, but I thought you might want to know."

"Got it. Inga's open?"

"Never shut down. Rather than send all the soft meat running out into the night to get eaten or ripped into bloody bits, someone made the smart decision to just lock the door."

As the forklift growled to life, Marsdome and two others dragged the heavy hide to the side. A sterile tarp was laid out, and the quetzal was slowly lowered. The knives flashed, chunks of meat being stripped off as it came into reach.

"What's that?" Kalico gestured at a yellow-and-blood-smeared tarp that lay pushed up against the stone warehouse on the other side of the avenue.

"What's left of the blond boy toy. The legs were easy. They landed where those blood stains are out in the avenue. The rest had to be pulled out of the thing's gullet with a come-along. The woman servant, Clarice, had to take the Taglioni away before she fainted again. I'd call it six, two, and even that they're on the next shuttle up to *Turalon*. Their happy Donovanian vacation isn't going so well."

Kalico grunted her assent. Falise would be devastated. Didn't matter that—no matter what the fictions—she might have owned Ednund. He'd been an integral part of her life since she was a child.

Along the way, Kalico nodded to people she knew, sharing that hard-eyed acknowledgment. Like them, she walked with her rifle at the ready, fully aware that search as they might, declaring the town quetzal free was never a sure thing.

At Inga's, Kalico raised a "way to go" thumb at the Wild One sitting on the bench, smiling into the morning sun, a mostly empty bottle of what looked like wine at his feet. A battered-looking bolt-action rifle, one of Freund's, lay across his lap.

Then she opened the door, crossed the foyer, and squinted in the tavern's dim interior. Took most of the way down the stairs before her eyes began to adjust from the morning brilliance. To her surprise, Tal, Dek, and Kylee were seated at the end of the bar, plates of food before them.

Kalico made her way over, rested her rifle against the bar, and climbed onto her stool. "How did you do last night?" she asked.

"Got two," Talina said. "Tagged the first one in front of the Jewel. Popped the second down in the lumber yard after the lines started to close. Marines got one just inside the gate, and Step and his team took out the fourth back of the assay office."

"When I came through the gate, Finnegan told me Whitey wasn't one of them." Kalico waved to get Inga's attention, made the sign for the special. She had the distinct impression there was going to be way too much quetzal on the menu in the coming days.

"Nope." Talina pursed her lips. Kylee was watching carefully from where she'd pulled up a chair at the end of the bar.

"New tactics," Dek said. "They got Sczui. Roughed him up and sent him staggering up to the gate."

"Yeah, I heard. What about Mother and the kids?" Kalico asked.

"No word yet. That's next on the list. As soon as the all-clear's sounded." Talina gave Kalico a dark look. "Thought we'd eat before we go out to the Sczui place. Drones don't show anything. But we're going to be tracking that snot sucker. Put an end to this, once and for all."

"Where's your shadow and his four human robots?" Dek asked.

"Headed to *Freelander*." Kalico sat straighter as Inga set a plate of broccoli, beans with garlic, and mashed purple sweet potatoes in front of her. Kalico tossed out a five-SDR coin and picked up the fork sticking out of the potatoes. "I've got a planet to run. Soukup doesn't need me chauffeuring him from one mine to the next. Bogarten, Ghosh, and Shimodi can do a hell of a lot better job. And they won't be tempted to strangle his chapped ass every couple of hours like I was."

Talina shot a warning look. "Isn't that a bit dangerous? Letting a Corporate quetzal like Soukup out of your sight?"

With the first mouthful, Kalico exhaled in delight. She loved the way Inga cooked the purple potatoes. "I've been thinking a lot about why he's here. My take is that we're too dangerous for The Corporation to leave alone. We're worth too much, and we're too destabilizing to the status quo. The Corporation was established by the mega-corporations in the middle of the twenty-first century and built on the Chinese model of population control. Conformity and uniformity were the key to keeping the masses in line. Punish individuality. Abolish personal wealth, provide the baseline needs, and direct the whole process through the algorithms. Manage humanity with the same principles you would if they were sophisticated livestock."

"But for the few mega-rich and powerful at the top," Dek reminded.

"When it comes to Donovan, they now know they don't control all of the resources," Talina said. "We're outside their nice tidy system. A wild card. We represent a dream. Hope that, like Dan Wirth, anyone can come here and get rich."

"Yeah, we're a bad influence, all right," Kalico said. "My suspicion is that Soukup has figured out that I'm not a good Corporate player anymore. I'm corrupted by my association with the pestilence of libertarian anarchy. He'd probably suffer from night sweats if he ever listened in on one of my conversations with Shig about political philosophy."

"But what about everything you've built?" Talina asked. "Corporate Mine, Southern Diggings, the smelter. All that incredible wealth that you've funneled out of PA and sent up to orbit for shipment back to Solar System?"

"How much more productive would it be if it were all put in Cinque's hands? Or Bartolome's? They have reputations for streamlining extraction, processing, and shipping." Kalico lifted her scarred eyebrow.

"Notice you didn't mention Falise," Dek noted.

"She was supposed to use you to her advantage when she arrived. If what Allison tells me is true, that's not panning out for her."

Dek frowned, grunted.

Kylee said, "Some of us think that if that's what being a Taglioni is all about, Dek was adopted."

That brought the first chuckle to Kalico's lips that she'd had in a while.

"Seriously," Talina asked. "What happens if Soukup appoints Cinque or Bartolome as the new Supervisor?"

Kalico chewed thoughtfully. "I haven't a clue. My day of reckoning may come in a matter of hours."

"You could tell them to fuck off," Kylee said as she wiped up the last of her beans. "What could they do?"

"Turn the marines loose," Talina said. "They still have twenty-nine of them on the planet."

"If they'd follow the IG's orders," Dek reminded. "By now—"

"Kids," Talina interrupted, "I hate to break this to you, but there's a marine colonel up on *Turalon* who'd be only too happy to have Soukup put him back in charge. And, believe me, after the manhandling he was put through, I don't doubt but that he'd love to come down here and flatten a big chunk of PA, starting with The Jewel."

Kalico took another bite, swallowed. "My best strategy was to break up the marines, split them up, get them dirty and give them a reality lesson. At the same time, my veterans could reeducate them about who called the shots on this rock. Figured that was my only chance."

"That's a lifetime of indoctrination to the Corps that you're hoping to overcome in a matter of days," Dek said.

"It's happened before," Kalico told him. "Just ask Talina. Cap Taggart resigned his commission and half my marines revolted rather than space back on *Turalon*. By now the FNGs have not only heard that story but had time to really think about it. It's one thing to be assigned to a post in Transluna and a whole different thing to be out here, peeling sidewinders off your boot, shooting mobbers from the sky, and all the while a ghost ship is orbiting overhead."

The wailing blast of the all-clear could be heard; everyone in the room, including the tired-looking soft meat, began to cheer and clap. People were rising from their benches, the babble of relieved speech rising in volume.

"That's my cue," Kalico said, and turning, bellowed, "Hey! Your attention!"

When nothing much happened, Talina turned in her chair, thundering, "*Shut the fuck up and listen!*"

Instant silence, all eyes turned their way.

"One of these days, you're going to tell me how you do that," Kalico muttered, then to the room called, "For those of you who don't know, I'm Board Supervisor Kalico Aguila. My apologies for not meeting with you sooner, but we've had some complications. I need all new contractees to assemble in the cafeteria at 08:00. I'll address you then. As soon as I have your contract information, we'll begin placements. If you have any questions or complaints, any issues regarding contract, bring them to me in the cafeteria. See you there."

Talina, Dek, and Kylee were slinging their rifles, looking ragged and tired.

"Where are you off to?"

"Sczui's," Dek told her. "And my guess, given what we're probably going to find, we'd rather be attending your meeting."

Kalico watched them go, nodded her agreement. "Yeah, bet it's going to be nasty."

Falise thought she'd suffocate in the confines of her dome. A shabby excuse of a habitation, it seemed to suck the air out of her lungs. Dark, dingy, with its dirty windows. Even worse, she'd found to her dismay that the water that she'd thought was supplied by pipeline from a city facility, was from a cistern. Rainwater, fallen from the sky, that ran off the dome and was collected for future use.

Heaven alone knew what sort of filth might be in that tank.

The miracle was that, so far, she hadn't gotten sick.

Sitting on the old couch, she stared sightlessly at the door and tried to breathe. Suck in a lungful. Exhale. But grief beat with every contraction of her heart. Ednund? It shouldn't be this hard.

But it was. Like she'd never take a full breath again.

Clarice sat, back slumped, on one of the stools at the breakfast bar; her eyes focused on some impossible distance. Expression dull. As if that remarkable analytic brain of hers had turned off.

Fig, Phredo, and Shoto had been dismissed to their dome. Partly because there wasn't much to do, and second, Falise didn't want to endure their expressions. Fuck them, but they kept looking at her with pleading eyes. Expecting her to do . . . what? Make it better?

If there was a dismal way to exist, she was living it.

And behind it all, the constant memories of Ednund being snatched up from the darkness. Being savaged and torn into pieces. And then the sight—in the first rays of morning light—of his body. How the wet and lacerated remains were being winched out of the creature's gullet. Limp, torn, bloody meat and splintered bone. Unrecognizable, but for the fact that she knew. Had seen.

She closed her eyes, shook her head.

Get it the fuck out of your system!

Her father's words—from sometime in the past—echoed hollowly: "*You are a Taglioni. You have been given every advantage. Not so that you can waste yourself like your pathetic brother, but so that you can use those advantages to triumph over any adversity."*

"Yes, well, Father, you should come to Capella III." She closed her eyes, bowed her head, and pinched the bridge of her nose. Father had broken her of the habit when she was a child. Why was she doing it now? Why didn't she care?

Her pathetic brother—freak that he now was—had somehow become the victor.

For a tantalizing moment, she considered ordering her things packed. The walk to the landing field would take ten minutes. She'd listened to the shuttles roaring and booming as they made the trips back and forth to *Turalon*. She could be back in that safe cabin, walking those sterile white sialon halls, eating in the comfort of the cafeteria, her every need . . .

"That's failure."

Dek owned a half-metric ton of rhodium? Hadn't blinked as he tossed coins, gems, and precious metals onto that poker table?

She reached into her pocket. Pulled out the nuggets Kylee had given her. *"There's more where that came from."*

As though to mock her, she could hear the roar of another approaching shuttle. A half hour turnaround time as it unloaded and reloaded before powering up and rising, the thrusters driving it back to space and *Turalon*.

Jaws clenched, fists knotted, hot tears began to leak from behind her clamped lids.

Torn.

God, she wanted to be on that shuttle.

A half metric ton of rhodium.

She fumbled her way to her feet, rubbed a sleeve across her cheeks to wipe her face, and sniffed to clear her nose. Taking a deep breath, she started for the door, ordering, "Stay here."

"Yes, Lady." Clarice's dull voice could barely be heard.

Outside, Falise glanced through the fence at the low-hanging sun in the west. It cast the silhouetted lines of crops in a glow, burned a rime of gold on the distant treetops that marked the edge of the bush.

Turning her steps down the street, she passed the line of domes, occupied now with contractees. At the main avenue she turned south, made her way to The Jewel.

Inside, she found Allison, talking with the bartender, Vik, and Angelina the whore. People were playing pinochle at a table in the back. A couple of quetzal-dressed, bearded ruffians let out a howl as Dalia spun the roulette wheel.

Marching up to Allison, she met the woman's curious blue-eyed stare. Given her figure and quick mind, Allison could have been a guild courtesan. In another time and place, she'd have been exactly the kind Derek would have demanded.

"I'm looking for my brother," Falise said.

Gaze still level, Allison told her, "Last I heard Dek was up at the cemetery. It's been a tough day. Lot of graves to be filled. He and Tal brought in what they could find of Mother Sczui. Not a sign of the kids so they're probably quetzal shit. You might catch him at the hospital. If not, try Inga's in an hour or two."

Falise turned on her heel, wishing she had something on her feet besides these ridiculous translucent designer shoes. The wrap-around sari was bad enough. Perfect for an evening at Three Spires, it looked garish, out of place for this rustic backwater, even if it did have the same laser-like brilliance of quetzal-hide.

She kept her eyes averted from the spot where Ednund had died. Felt a wave of relief run through her when she noted that the place they'd left his tarped remains was vacant. Well enough, she supposed. She needed to make arrangements for his body.

But . . . what? Ship the pieces up to *Turalon?* If she chose *Turalon,* would Abibi insist Ednund's remains be dropped into the hydroponics along with everything else organic? Or should Falise order that they be frozen for return to Transluna? And then what? Have them cremated and put in a jar? If he'd been killed on Transluna, she'd have simply ordered Clarice to dispose of the corpse.

What made it so different here? Now?

She kept her eyes forward, ignored the stares as she passed people on the street. Made her way to the hospital. Opening the double doors, she stared around.

This was a hospital? A shabby waiting room filled with mismatched duraplast bench seats was off to the left. A single long hall ran to the far end of the building. No one was in the reception office. From the dust and piled boxes, it looked like it hadn't been used in years. The next room on the left would have once been a nurse's station. A woman with a sickly green complexion—and even after blinking, she was still green—was studying something on a notebook.

Next came what had to be the doctor's office; no one there.

Pushing open the door to the first room Falise came to, it was to find Kylee, sitting on the foot of the single bed. Some brown-haired boy was propped up, looking drawn and emaciated. He had those same quetzal eyes—though sunken—as Kylee and Derek. Another half-breed freak.

"Where is Derek?" Falise asked. "I need to speak to him."

"Wow! And a happy hello to you, too," Kylee told her. Then she glanced at the boy. "You get some sleep. I've been here long enough."

"That her?" the boy rasped.

"All five feet nine inches of her," Kylee said as she stood and slung her rifle over a shoulder. "Can you believe something like that is Dek's sister?" A half beat. "Love you. Get well."

"Love you, too," the boy whispered, closing his eyes.

With a hostile stare from her weird blue eyes, Kylee got Falise to back out of the room and closed the door behind her.

"Who is that?"

"That's Tip Briggs. He's lineage. Some kind of creature ate its way into his leg. Don't know how, but somehow Raya's managed to keep him alive. We're trying different antibiotics brought down from *Turalon*. Even if the invasive proteins can be whipped, it's still nip and tuck if Raya can save his leg."

"Oh."

"Oh? That's it?" Kylee crossed her arms. "Hey, I might have been raised in the bush by quetzals, but even I'm more human than that."

Falise pinched her nose again, wondered if she'd wear through the skin over her nasal bones. "Listen, I just need to find my brother."

"Why?"

"That, child, is none of your business."

Kylee laughed, the sound of it bitter. She leaned close, big eyes fixed on Falise's. "Are you dumber than rocks? Must be, because you don't seem to learn. Dek's lineage. He's got me, Rocket, Flute, and Talina in his head. All you've got is some shared DNA and the fact that you both slipped into the universe through the same vagina."

With unusual grace, Kylee slipped past her, starting down the hall.

Falise exhaled her frustration, started after the girl. "Just tell me where I can find Derek. Dek. Whatever."

"Best bet? Somewhere in PA. Why the fuck should I tell you? You're a waste of skin."

"Because I need help!" Falise gritted her teeth, then added, "Please."

Kylee turned. "Fuck me with a skewer, bet that cost you."

More than you will ever know, you vile little half-breed.

Kylee was giving her that disgusted look again. "Listen, I don't know where Dek's off to. It's been a tough day putting pieces of friends into graves up on the hill. Toughest was Mother Sczui, not to mention your boy . . . um, what's his name?"

"Ednund? You buried him?"

"Duh. You weren't going to leave him lying on the street under that tarp, were you? God, don't you people have any respect?"

Falise closed her eyes, sagged against the wall, whispered, "It's just this place."

Kylee seemed to be looking past the expression Falise tried so hard to keep wooden.

"Come on," Kylee relented. "You got a weapon?"

The last thing she'd tell the urchin about was her knife. "No."

"Wandering around like that, what would you do if Whitey leaped out of an alley? Get eaten like whatshisname?"

"Ednund."

"Right. You need a rifle." Kylee straight-armed the doors, stepping out into the sunset. "We've just got time. And those shoes? Better than those falling-apart disasters you had on last night. But damn! If they hadn't poisoned most of the slugs in PA, after last night you'd be screaming full of them all ready."

"Slugs?"

"Yeah, like Tal told you about at the orientation?"

Falise tried to remember. It seemed an eon ago, but she'd been busy plotting Chad's and Bart's downfalls. "Listening to that was Clarice's responsibility. She'd tell me if I were at risk."

Kylee's too-large eyes seemed to expand, then she shook her head as if in disbelief. "Adopted," she muttered under her breath. "It's the only explanation."

43

When she wasn't being Falise Taglioni, the woman could actually listen. And, Kylee had to admit, after what Falise had been through—fucking arrogant Taglioni though she might be—she did have a functioning brain. She hadn't made a single protest when Kylee led her into Marsdome's for boots, hat, and cape. Especially with rain clouds brewing in the east again. Nor had Falise pitched a fit when—next door at Freund's—Kylee had pointed out a .375 caliber, variable velocity semi-automatic-action rifle with a slim laminate chabacho-and-aquajade stock. That the ammunition was locally made was an added plus.

So, what do I make of her? Kylee wondered as they sat at the table closest to Talina's stool at the bar.

Kylee had her glass of stout, Falise a glass of Inga's latest petite sirah. Technically, it was partly Kylee's petite sirah, since the vines grew down at Mundo. This whole property thing was starting to sink in. Maybe it was time to go back. For her to claim her inheritance. Mundo wouldn't be a bad place. Especially if she had to take care of Tip.

She lifted her right hand, studied it. She'd pulled the trigger on two quetzals. Made killing shots on both. Not that she hadn't been party to killing quetzals before—like when she acted as bait for that rogue the Rorkies killed. But this was the first time she'd taken full responsibility.

These days, Leaper and Diamond didn't pose the threat they once did. Not to Kylee Simonov, at sixteen, with Flute and Tip, not to mention the .33 caliber high-velocity rifle that Dek had gifted to her. After being in PA, she was finally beginning to understand that she had other options than just the Briggs claim.

Kylee leaned back as one of the young women who waited tables brought plates over. She might have been in her late teens, had curly black hair, dark-brown eyes, and a pointed chin. The look she was giving Kylee was curious, intense.

"You gotta problem?" Kylee asked softly, picking up the fork, *Inga's* fork, she reminded herself.

"Damien's wondering if you were going to stop by. He's back from Southern Diggings. Said if I saw you, to tell you that Su and the rest of your family would like to see you."

"And who are you?"

"Janeese. I'm Damien's wife. We got married a couple of months ago. I guess that means you're my sister-in-law. So, hello."

"Hello back," Kylee told her warily.

Looking really uneasy, Janeese said, "So, maybe you'll drop by the house?"

"Yeah, well . . . I'll see." Kylee indicated Falise with a tip of the head. "Got some things to do."

Janeese shot a suspicious glance Falise's way, took the coins Kylee offered, and hurried away.

"Family?" Falise asked dryly. "Not lineage?"

Kylee pointed a hard finger. "*Not* lineage." Then she added, "It's complicated."

"Isn't it always?" Falise murmured, taking the large knife Kylee had bought for her at Freund's and slicing off a bite of steak. Falise had insisted that her idea of a knife was something used at a dining room table, or maybe to slip between someone's ribs, or to open a box. She'd complained that the twenty-centimeter blade on this thing was too short to be a sword, too big for a dining implement. Impaling the steak on her fork, she popped it in her mouth and chewed.

"Curious taste. Sweeter than pork, almost a cross between beef and chicken? No. Something that defies easy categorization."

Kylee started to say something—was smart enough to figure that Falise might not have the stomach to handle it if she discovered she was eating the quetzal that had eaten Ednund.

Finally Falise said, "Part of the problem between Derek and me? I mean I never would have guessed *that* was my brother. He's not the same petulant whiner that I last saw in Taglioni Tower. That Derek . . . ?" She seemed to be struggling for the right words.

"Dek says he was a loathsome beast back then." Kylee attacked her own steak. Pointed with her knife. "It's not my place to tell his story. But, lady, there's a lot you could learn from it."

"You don't act like a sixteen-year-old." Falise was studying her through those perfect emerald eyes. Designer eyes, like Dek's had been before the TriNA had remodeled them.

"Got too much of Talina up here." Kylee tapped the side of her head. "And down at Mundo, I was treated like an adult. All of us were. My mothers had me doing genetics and molecular biology by the time I was six. And then I bonded with Rocket. After he was killed . . . well, the shit just kept coming down." She gestured around the room with her knife. "Once, I was dedicated to coming here and killing them all."

Kylee paused. Smiled. "And here I sit." A beat. "So, see, fancy lady? If I can learn, so can you."

That stone-green gaze was still wary as Falise gestured at her hat, tapped the rifle with an insistent finger. "You bought all of this. Paid out almost a thousand SDRs. What do you expect to gain in return?"

Kylee waggled her fork in Falise's direction as she chewed the piece of meat. "See, here's the thing: I don't really give a fuck about you. But Dek's lineage, and you're on Donovan because he's your Taglioni brother. So here's what you can do as payback for buying you an outfit. I don't want you fucking up Dek's life. And, shit, like I said, I'm curious. Never met a fancy Transluna noble before."

"You always have such a foul mouth?"

"Yeah, picked it up from Talina. And, out in the bush, Flute and Tip don't care. Madison and Chaco tried their best to 'make a lady' out of me. But times like this, when I'm face-to-face with soft meat I don't trust? It just comes natural." A beat. "And you remind me of Dortmund Weisbacher. That didn't end well."

"The scientist from *Vixen*?"

"Yeah, he was a real shit bag. I don't want you doing to Dek what he did to Talina."

"Whatever that was, it wasn't in the records."

Kylee leaned forward, took a swig of the beer. "So, give. What do I have to do to keep you from fucking with Dek? What does dear old papa Claudio want? If you give it to me straight, maybe I can help you. If you're here to fuck Dek over, and I find out, I will kill you. Dead. On the spot. That's where it stands between the two of us."

A genuine amusement flickered behind the woman's gem-like eyes. "Kill me? Really? Child, I don't think you have any idea who you're dealing with."

"Yeah, you're the Taglioni assassin and dirty tricks master." Kylee grinned, cut another piece off of her steak. "This is what Kalico calls a 'dick swinging match', but I saw you laid out cold in the street last night. Didn't exactly inspire the kind of fear that would shiver my bones."

"That was the whiskey. The whiskey *you* bought."

"Sure, we'll go with that if it makes you feel better. But, assassin lady? You're on my ground. Just an example, wearing those shoes you had on last night? I could have walked you through a puddle down at the Mine Gate, and by now you'd have fifteen slugs eating their way up your leg."

Falise seemed to consider. Then she said, "Derek really owns a half a metric ton of rhodium?"

Kylee leaned back. "You're not just interested in his plunder."

Falise stared thoughtfully at the length of her new knife, the polished blade shining in the tavern lights. "The nuance of this might be beyond you, but there's an Inspector General sticking his nose into all kinds of things on the planet."

"Damn it! Does it have to be nuance? I've always been pretty short on that given that I'm just a stupid Wild One with a bad reputation when it comes to quetzals. Simple as I am, I couldn't possibly understand, but there's a good chance Soukup will try to replace Kalico. Right?"

Kylee ran her long thin fingers down the smooth barrel of Falise's new rifle where it lay on the table beside them. "By the way, when it comes to replacements, you're in last place. That guy Cinque has been learning everything he can from Tal. Bad Bart? He's spending his time quizzing Shig and Yvette on how things work here. You've been stumbling around in really weird shoes watching your people getting eaten."

Falise tensed, seemed to talk herself out of whatever she'd been about to say. "How do I catch up?"

"We have a saying here. It goes something to the effect that stupidity—"

"Is a death sentence. Yes, child, I've heard it. How do I stop being stupid?"

"You afraid of dying?"

"Until last night, I would have told you I wasn't. What happened to Ednund . . ." She lowered her gaze.

"Wow. Honesty at last." Kylee leaned forward, gesturing with her knife. "So, pay attention. To come out of this in first place, you're going to have to face Donovan. By that, I mean the planet. On its rules. Out in the bush." She paused. "And you're going to back Kalico, no matter what comes down."

Kylee saw the hesitation, especially at that last. "I mean it, Falise. If you can't do that? Even if this IG appointed you the new Supervisor? You're dead in a week. Same with Cinque or Bart."

"And what are my chances doing it your way?"

"Maybe ten percent, if you listen and learn."

"Ten percent? That's . . . that's . . ."

Kylee smiled. "Welcome to Donovan."

44

Of all the jobs he did for Kalico Aguila, Fenn Bogarten *hated* going to *Freelander* the most. That was saying a lot, since he'd worked in the shadow of cave-ins while they drifted the Number Three through shocked rock and into the mountain under Corporate Mine. He'd been lost and alone in the forest down on the smelter floodplain. Barely escaped with his life. Fenn had faced mobbers and even murderers. He'd been one of the men who had Kalico's back when she braced the ex-marine, Kalen Tompzen, and declared him a spy and a traitor. He'd survived gunfights and quetzal attacks.

He'd have traded any of those threats to have avoided this current duty. *Freelander* scared him down to the marrow in his bones; visits to the ship left him haunted by nightmares for weeks afterward.

Seated as he was—right seat in the row of three behind the pilot and copilot's chairs on the command deck of Kalico's shuttle—he should have been enjoying the ride. This was the elite seat. Normally, Kalico herself sat in this chair where she could look out the side window. Bogarten had always ridden in the back. That was the cargo/passenger hold. No windows. And nothing like the plush seat his butt was now planted in. The thing conformed to every curve, was comfortable as all get out.

Didn't matter. Looking out the window, he couldn't miss it: *Freelander* loomed before them like a giant gray-white ball, its crew and cargo tori like fat rings atop the globe.

Just the sight of its corroded hull sent a shiver down his spine.

"That's it?" IG Soukup asked, leaning over and pointing.

"That's it."

"What's that slight shimmer?" Soukup asked, still leaning close for the view. "It looks . . . I don't know. Watery? Grungy?"

From the pilot's seat, Juri Makarov called back, "The crew on *Vixen* have studied it, Inspector General. The hypothesis is that *Freelander* leaks light and energy back to whatever universe it was stuck in for those missing hundred and twenty-nine years. Some of us speculate that sometime in the next tens of billions of years, our universe will be completely drained into wherever *Freelander* passed through on its transition to Donovan. Like having a pinhole puncture in a fuel tank. Leave it long enough, and eventually it's going to be empty."

Fenn made a face. It was bad enough having to go there, walk those halls. Feel the ghosts and see that dome of human bones. Last thing he needed to know was that part of him might be leaking away in the process.

Kalico's words echoed inside his head: *"Fenn, I need you to escort the Inspector General to* Freelander. *You know as much about that ship as anyone. You're an engineer and a scientist as well as trained in physics. You can explain what happened on* Freelander *in terms I never could. Make him understand. And, this is critical. The man is a Board Appointed Inspector General. That means you will follow his orders. No matter what they might be. Do you get that?* Anything *he asks, you will comply."*

Fenn had gritted his teeth and said, "Yes, ma'am."

But why the hell did it have to be *Freelander*?

The ghost ship disappeared overhead as Juri Makarov changed the shuttle's pitch and rolled it onto its back. This was the final approach.

Fenn felt the g-force as Delta V slowed them to match *Freelander's* orbit. To Fenn, in his seat, it seemed like it was the ship that lowered itself onto the shuttle. He could see the expanse of hull that appeared like a horizon against the stars, the line of shuttle bays disappearing around the derelict's curvature. And then the great ship seemed to slip down around them. Dark, threatening, the walls of the shuttle bay barely visible where cables, tubes, and ducting hid in the shadows.

"And . . . full stop," Makarov called. A clang could be heard, vibrations through the floor. "We have hard dock. Grapples engaged." A moment later, Makarov added, "We have the lock engaged." A pause. Then, "Hard seal. Welcome to *Freelander*, gentlemen."

That old uncomfortable feeling, like a prickling wave, rolled through Fenn's body, his vision detecting a shimmer, like a smearing of light, that passed only to leave an indistinct waver in his retinas.

"At your pleasure, Mr. Bogarten," Soukup said, rising from his chair and tugging his gray jacket down. Doing so pulled the flaring shoulders higher and straight.

Fenn made a face, climbed warily to his feet, and headed for the hatch to the back.

He heard Juri Makarov mutter "Have fun" under his breath.

"Yeah." Fenn barely mouthed the words. "I'd rather stick my finger in a light socket."

He led the way to the hatch, stopping only to procure hand lamps from the storage locker. "Going to need these," he told Soukup as the Four rose from their seats and took positions behind the IG.

In Fenn's mind, *Freelander* was spooky enough without those weird human cyborgs trailing along behind. All but the Fourth. The guy reminded Fenn of an assassin in search of a victim. It was something about the packed muscle and flat planes of his face around that knobby nose and stone-cold eyes.

Nevertheless, he swallowed hard, led the way to the lock, and powered it through the shuttle, explaining, "There's no power on the other side. The shuttle deck is mostly dead. There's still power to a couple of the lights, but that was jury-rigged by the *Turalon* crew on their last visit."

"Why hasn't it been fixed?" Soukup asked. "That would seem a priority for the Supervisor."

"It was," Fenn snapped. "Didn't last. And you can't get anybody to work up here."

"Kalico Aguila is a Board Supervisor. Her word should carry enough weight." Soukup had his flat stare fixed on Fenn. The First, recording it all with that distant gaze, turned Fenn's stomach cold.

"Yeah, right." He cycled the hatch, leading the IG into the

waiting room beyond. Overhead, the sole working light panel flickered. The flashing came randomly, out of sync with reality, to illuminate the lines of seats off to the side and cast jumping shadows in
the murk. The floor had that same thin layer of filth scattered with
bits of trash. In the corner was a moldering rag that had once been
overalls. The air carried the unforgettable dank odor of dust, decay,
and decomposed sweat. But most of all, Fenn disliked the corners.
A simple joining of the walls, why were they always darker than the
rest of the room?

Tagging along, the First was scanning back and forth, recording
the room. Soukup's expression had pinched; his usually composed
face showed the first trace of doubt.

At the far hatch, Fenn pointed out the control box. "Don't
bother. Ship's AI is dead. *Freelander's* crew cut it out with a torch.
Chopped the N-dimensional qubit matrix up with an ax. Whatever. Fact is, being condemned to this hulk for what they thought
was eternity, they went kind of crazy."

"So, there is no interaction? No communication with records?"
Soukup asked.

"Nothing you haven't already seen. When *Turalon* went back the
first time, she took everything known. Not that anyone's wild to
look, but there have been no journals, diaries, or hidden records
recovered." Fenn winced. "Not that anybody's been keen to search
this hulk for them."

Then he led the way into the corridor beyond, flicking on his
hand lamp to illuminate the dark corridor. "Stay close," he ordered.
"Weird shit happens from here on out."

Even as he said it, his hair was standing on end.

"Huh!" Fourth cried, leaping and spinning. The man kept staring off into the black behind them. "Who's there?" To the others,
he asked, "Did you see that?"

"See what?" Soukup asked, staring into the black distance down
the hallway.

Fenn shone his light, kicking up the illumination and narrowing
the focus. Nothing but abandoned hallway could be seen. "This
entire deck, along with the Transportee Deck, was opened to

vacuum when Captain Orten and First Officer Sakihara realized just how screwed they were. First, they let the transportees suffocate, and then they froze the corpses to preserve them. Added them one by one to the hydroponics over the years as the organic molecules broke down."

"Fascinating," Soukup whispered. "And so terribly efficient."

Fenn rolled his eyes, catching movement. Like a reflected glisten, it flickered and vanished into the corridor wall. "Fucking phantoms," he muttered. "Come on. Sooner I can get you to the command deck, the sooner I can get off this shit-sucking wreck."

Fenn led the way, past the stained and brown-streaked sialon walls, the dark inspection ports, and dead holo stations. At the companionway, he climbed, catching the odd flickers and enduring the feeling that time was moving sideways, siphoning parts of his soul away.

At the hatch, he stopped. "This is the hatch they kept closed. Beyond is the Crew Deck, and above it, the Command Deck."

He physically undogged the hatch, leading them in. Lights flickered, then cast a dull urine-yellow illumination. Pointing at the wall, Fenn said, "There's the famous writing. Line after line of cursive written atop other lines of cursive. How many thousands of hours did they spend here? What in hell was in their minds as they wrote these phrases? Like this one." He indicated with a finger. "What does this mean? 'With each breath, we inhale the lifetimes of the Dead.' Or over here, 'I am vacuum. A cloud of emptiness.'"

"It covers the entire wall," Soukup whispered to himself, reaching out to run a finger along the chaos of overwritten script. "So thick it's almost solid."

"And the floor and ceiling," Fenn pointed out, noting that Soukup's First was scanning, bending close to record the scrawl.

"Malfunction," Third said in a monotone, straightening. "Data . . . incongruity." She seemed confused, not that her face projected anything, but her eyes had slightly crossed.

"Elaborate," Soukup said, turning to the white-haired woman.

"Potential malfunction. Observed a female. Age early thirties, black hair." The Third's head tilted slightly. "Image . . . projection? Partially there. Walked into wall. Confirm, Second?"

The Second, the monitor, who was supposed to keep track of the entire team, said, "No woman walked into wall. Malfunction confirmed."

The Third seemed to freeze, paralyzed, her hand partially lifted.

"What's that about?" Fenn asked.

Soukup, looking perplexed for the first time, told him, "She's running a complete diagnostic. Whatever it was, she thinks she saw it. A partial image of a woman who walked into the wall."

"Yeah, no shit." Fenn grabbed Soukup by the sleeve, fully aware that it was probably a death sentence. "Come on. Let's get you to the Crew Mess so you can see the dome of bones. I mean, they made a shrine out of the people they ate. Built this—"

Soukup started, gulped. Staring down the hall. "I would have sworn . . ."

"Yeah, I know. I'm telling you, come on." Fenn started down the hall, hearing Soukup tell his Third. "Diagnostic override. Malfunction explained. Catalog and reference for future analysis."

Climbing the next companionway to Command Deck, Fenn led the way to the AC hatch. Welded as it was. The willies were getting worse. His stomach was flipping, and the wavering light at the edges of his vision was playing tricks on him.

"So, here's the famous AC. Beyond is where Jem Orten and Tyne Sakihara blew their . . ."

"Screaming," the Second said with a start. "Corroborate."

"Unable to corroborate," the First replied, his head swiveling this way and that, ears cocked. "Silence."

"Silence," the Third agreed, eyes unfocused. "Describe screaming for analysis."

"Male voice," the Second told her. "Uttering the words, 'For God's sake, let me out of here' with high emotional context. Then screamed, 'Don't get close to me' and 'They're picking at my brain.'"

"Did you hear that?" Soukup asked Fenn.

"Nope." To the Second, he asked, "Where did the voice come from?"

The Second blinked. Raised his hand, pointing at the welded door. "Inside. There. Again. Listen."

Soukup swallowed hard. "But . . . there's no one in there, right?"

"Only the corpses of Jem Orten, Tyne Sakihara, and good old Tamarland Benteen. Maybe he's still alive, but if he's kept up the hydroponics and water recycling, I'd say that by this time, he's as insane as the rest of this place."

Soukup jerked, spun around, asking, "Who touched me?" and found empty space.

"She will kill you, you know," the Third said, eyes still unfocused.

"What? Who?" Soukup demanded.

"Drive a knife right through your heart," the First whispered.

"But only after she severs my carotid arteries," the Third said in a monotone.

"Mister Bogarten," Soukup told him nervously, "Return us to the shuttle. Immediately. Whatever the field effect is, it is affecting my Four. This is intolerable. Second, note: We will interrogate Supervisor Aguila concerning negligence concerning *Freelander*. Whatever is affecting my people, surely she should have detected it on previous visits."

To Fenn he asked, "Are we being exposed to some electromagnetic field? Some sort of radiation? Perhaps a field generated by—"

"No!" Fenn leaned close. "Get it? It's *Freelander*. And it's fucked!"

"Screaming," the Second repeated. "He won't stop screaming. He can't. It will be forever."

"Malfunction," the Third insisted. Voice listless. "Analytic parameters . . . exceeded."

Soukup's mouth fell open as he stared at the Third's face. "That can't happen," he cried. "She can't do that!"

Fen turned, looked at the Third's delicate face with the fine cheeks and petite chin. Tears were leaking from the woman's blue eyes. "So much . . . pain," the woman mewed in a broken voice.

"Sir!" the Fourth snapped. "Get us the hell out of here. Now!"

"Aguila," Soukup growled as he followed behind Fenn. "Something she should have diagnosed and fixed on this bucket. I'll get to the bottom of this." Then louder. "Mister Bogarten, assuming my

Four come back online, I want to see Tyson Station. Talk to these, what are they? Irreconciled?"

"Yeah," Fenn said from the side of his mouth. "In a quetzal's ass."

That's when he saw himself, just a glimpse, dressed as he was, walking down the corridor, leading the IG, and . . . The image vanished.

Fucking *Freelander.*

45

The ancient chair in Kalico's office in the Admin Dome should have been taken out and burned. In places, the duraplast had been polished to a sheen from posteriors, arms, and thighs dating back who-knew-how far, through various administrators, directors, then Clemenceau's reign, hers, and even a fortunately very short stint by Tamarland Benteen.

A lot of historic asses had contributed to that chair's worn status.

Not that the office, overall, was much better with its dilapidated shelving along one wall. The window—set into the dome's curvature—had dirty glass, a view of the chain-link, and the green streak of terrestrial mold that crept down from the leak in the age-hardened seal.

The floor looked the worst, discolored, gouged, scuffed, and abused by the years.

Nevertheless, this was Kalico's official bastion in Port Authority, though, truth be told, she did more business from her barstool down at Inga's. She studied the com monitor where it perched on the even-more-battered sialon desk. On its screen, yes, screen—the holoprojector had ceased to function a couple of years back—the contractee manifest was displayed along with the duty assignment she'd made for each individual. Thirty-one were earmarked for Corporate Mine, another twenty-nine for Southern Diggings. They'd go just as soon as the fence was up and the prefab barracks and domes were downloaded from *Turalon*'s cargo hold and erected so they had a roof over their heads.

The rest, including the medical techs, electronics technicians, com experts, and the like, she was leaving here, at Port Authority. What good did it do her to put a scanning electron microscopy technician at Corporate Mine when the equipment—long-mothballed for lack of spare parts—was here at the hospital?

Kalico rubbed her tired face as she stared at the list. One hundred and thirty-two contractees. She'd sat down with each one of them in the cafeteria. Looked them in the scared, excited, disappointed, or anxious eyes. Soft meat. Clueless. The quetzal raid had finished what their first glance at Port Authority had started. All but a handful really didn't want to be here. Didn't want to ship up to *Turalon* and face another transit back to Solar System, not to mention that it would leave them in debt for the rest of their lives if they didn't fulfill their contracts on Donovan.

On top of that, I have Soukup out there flying around in my old A-7, coming to who knows what sort of a conclusion?

At the soft knock, she looked up, seeing Shig Mosadek in the door.

"You asked to see me, Supervisor?"

He was wearing a wide-brimmed hat, his quetzal cloak, and knee-high boots. Shig's favorite shirt was one Yvette had made for him; woven from claw shrub fibers, it sported colorfully embroidered squash-blossoms.

Speaking of which, here came Yvette, appearing in the doorway behind Shig. The tall and the short of it, was the old joke. Darkly complexioned Shig stood barely five foot three, and Yvette, at six feet, with her pale skin, silver-blonde hair and green eyes.

"Come in. Pull up a chair. I've been up to my ears in personnel assignments. Normally, I'd just tell them to go to work at whatever they're contracted for, send them a salary for expenses, and call it even. With Soukup out sniffing around for reasons to declare me unfit, I'm going to have to come up with an agreement that can withstand scrutiny. One that justifies leaving seventy-two Corporate contractees in PA. It's an entangled mess."

"I can imagine," Yvette said as she dragged the stained red plastic chair over. Shig chose the faded blue one, his round face pensive.

"Take Salassi Assanti, here. Twenty-eight. He's a medical maintenance tech III, rated on the SEM, the spectroscopes, and whatever they call that big machine that analyzes blood and bodily fluids, the centrifuges, and protein synthesizers. According to the manifest, the parts are aboard *Turalon,* and Assanti assures me he can get our broken equipment working again."

Kalico stopped, stared thoughtfully. "*Our* broken equipment. See how pervasive it is? It's *your* broken equipment."

"To be fixed by a Corporate tech," Shig noted with a knowing smile.

"And that's just one of them," Kalico waved at the list on the monitor. "Xing Hanaan. Aircar tech. *Turalon's* got sixty powerpacks on the manifest that will put at least thirty of the wrecks out in the weeds at the edge of the aircar field back into service. Assuming the other parts on the manifest, like fan motors, can be adapted. Again, a Corporate tech, using Corporate parts, that can repair aircars that belong to individuals in PA."

"Those individuals can pay The Corporation for the parts and hire Hanaan for a set fee to fix them." Yvette gave a dismissive shrug.

"What's a fan motor for a Beta aircar worth?" Kalico asked. "See, what I mean? We're going to have to put a fricking price on every piece of equipment, every spare part." She tapped the printout of the cargo manifest where it lay on the desk beside her. "It's going to be an accounting nightmare."

"Did The Corporation send us an accountant?" Shig asked mildly.

"Hell, no!" Kalico snapped. "Back in Solar System what do you need an accountant for? Inventory and value are all handled by the AI and algorithms. Everything's 'in the system' from starships down to lock washers."

"We can pay for starships and lock washers, assuming Lawson can't make them on his own." Yvette leaned back, fingering her chin. "It's the intangibles. How do we set compensation for services? And worse, what happens when we get into that gray area where we're using a mix of PA and Corporate parts, tools, and know-how? It's all melted together over the past couple of years."

"It's been working fine," Shig said. "We've made progress. It was

Lawson and Montoya, working with Talovich, who figured out how to finally and safely drive the Number Three drift into the mountain."

Kalico leaned back, making the worn chair squeak, and tapped fingers on the butt of her pistol. "Outside of the fact that we were running out of just about everything we need to keep the more advanced equipment running, I'd say we had a pretty good thing going here. Unfortunately, I don't think that IG Soukup is going to be as open-minded when it comes to Corporate rules, let alone leaving seventy-two people in PA."

"You going to house them in the barracks?" Yvette asked. "If you are, where are you going to find beds for your people rotating in from Corporate Mine and Southern Diggings?"

"Not to mention," Shig said mildly, "a lot of your people have bought homes here in PA. They hold title to their property. Has IG Soukup discovered that yet?"

Kalico's nails clicked a faster staccato on the pistol's grip. "No, and no. I'd rather keep the barracks for my R&R rotations. I can build more housing for the soft meat, but in the meantime, I need a place to put them. The empty domes in the residential area would be best, but even though we're using them for the moment, title's a murky area, isn't it?"

Yvette told her, "It hasn't been a problem before, but yes. A lot of those properties belong to dead people. Allison owns about half. Some were never claimed when you allowed people to buy The Corporation out." An eyebrow lifted. "Kalico, I'd say those properties would still be Corporate as long as no one holds paper on them. Fourteen of them, just off the top of my head. But, as you know, they're in pretty rough shape. Need a lot of work."

That brought a smile to Kalico's lips. "So, that settles one problem and raises another. I can put about two thirds of my PA contractees in them, charge them with repairs. Work out some deal with Allison. Sheyela Smith and the three electricians that just came down from *Turalon* can attend the rewiring. And the rest? Some will have to put up at the barracks at Corporate Mine until housing's dealt with."

Shig gave her a winsome smile. "You know that we'll work with you in any way we can, do anything to help you. But seriously, what is your assessment of IG Soukup? How is he going to react to what he finds here?"

Kalico gave him a grim smile. "Frankly, Shig, I haven't just bent the rules. I've smashed them with a double jack. Just between the three of us, I've done everything in my power to dilute his ability to harm us. I got ahead of him by dismissing Creamer and scattering the marines all over the planet. But, when the moment of reckoning comes, if he can control them, there's nothing any of us can do to stop him short of civil war."

Shig laced his fingers together. "Surely, he will come to see that everything you have done has been to ensure the survival of humanity on the planet. Those ships you have sent back have made The Corporation wealthy. No strict application of the rules would have resulted in the success we've had."

Kalico chuckled. "You may be the wisest man I know, Shig. But whatever gave you the notion that anything in politics has to do with reason? The actions we took in the past will be judged by a political appointee following a directive given by the Corporate Board on distant Transluna. Judgment will not be based on what was required of us to survive, only by the strict interpretation of the rules and regulations applicable to a solar system thirty light-years away."

"What was The Corporation's creed?" Shig asked. "To safeguard social equality and justice, maintain social order and stability rather than causing chaos and turmoil, and inspire positivity and appreciation of the good and beautiful in all walks of life."

"Lot of good that does you when a quetzal is ripping you in two," Yvette growled.

Kalico said, "I also remember the Corporate adage: 'No case of corruption will escape investigation, and no corrupt official will escape unpunished.'"

"But you haven't been corrupt," Shig told her. "When have you ever acted in your own best interest instead of the betterment of others?"

"When I tried to put you, Yvette, and Talina up against a wall and shoot you dead?"

"You had not found your tao at that point." Shig's smile warmed.

"Yeah, well, my tao may be headed for a . . ."

In her earbud, Two Spot said, "*Supervisor? Just got a mayday from Juri. He says the shuttle is going down. Everything just quit. Went dead. He's on manual, riding it down on emergency power, but says he's not sure he'll have enough to land.*"

"Where are they?" Kalico stood, staring out the dirty window, as if she could see the ailing A-7 from her office.

"*Not sure, Supervisor. Signal's coming in from the west.*" A pause. "*Wait Juri's down. They're . . . It's gone dead, Supervisor. I mean, nothing.*"

Kalico took a deep breath, closed her eyes. "Let me know the second you get anything."

"*Roger that, Supervisor.*"

Shig and Yvette had both been listening, as had anyone else on the net. Yvette said, "I'll call Bateman, have him prep our bird."

"Why should you?" Kalico asked. "I've got a new A-7 sitting right out there on the field. And as soon as I can get a team on board, we're leaving."

"Assuming we can find them," Shig said warily. "If they've lost all power, can they even broadcast?"

"Depends," Kalico told him as she reached for her rifle where it was leaned against the wall behind her. "If they're down in deep forest? Well, we've never put an A-7's hull integrity to the test when it came to roots, but I don't like the odds."

Shig had accessed his com. "Talina, you read that?" Then, "Yes. The shuttle field. As soon as you can."

Kalico slung her rifle. "Looks like IG Soukup's facing his own reckoning with Donovan, doesn't it?"

"And if Donovan wins?" Yvette asked.

"How many ways can you spell, *We're fucked*?"

alise watched the shuttle lift off from just inside the fence. She had her fingers woven into the chain link, saw the dust billow as the bird rose into the darkening lavender sky. Beside her, along with the other locals, Kylee Simonov was just as hard-eyed.

The news had gone through Inga's like a tidal wave. Everyone rushing to the shuttle field. Falise and Kylee had made it to the fence just as Talina, Derek, Kalico, and five of the marines charged up the ramp. The second they were inside, the A-7 raised the ramp and began spinning up.

Falise turned her head away from the blasted dust. Squinted her eyes and clawed to keep her new hat on her head. She'd never endured the like: pelted by hot gas and bits of grit stinking of burned earth.

As it ascended into the night sky, the shuttle climbed to the east, banked to the north, then roared as it headed westward to vanish in the darkness.

"Wonder where they went down?" Step Allenovich asked where he was standing next to Cinque.

"They don't have a beacon?" Cinque asked.

"Nothing Two Spot can hear. Juri said he was going down somewhere out west. On failing emergency power. They had a term for that in the old days. Called it *dead stick*."

Falise asked, "So, if the impact didn't kill them, it's just a matter of finding them, landing, and rescuing the people?"

In the yellow glow of an overhead light, Step gave her a wary look. "Depends. Without a beacon to home in on? Lady, if they're down in deep forest, they're dead. Roots will get them."

"What do you mean, roots?" Cinque asked.

"The big trees will use their roots to crush the shuttle," Kylee told him. "Crumple it up like it was made of tin foil."

"That's a sialon shuttle, girl. With a hyperalloy space frame." Cinque's totally black eyes were almost as alien as Kylee's. Almost.

"Yeah right, soft meat." Kylee turned to Falise. "See what I mean? You people don't know jack shit about Donovan. That's why you'll lose."

Falise grabbed her by the arm, asking, "Can we go talk?"

The look Kylee gave her hand threatened mayhem and broken bones. Falise turned her loose, asking, "Please?"

Falise led the scowling Kylee back down the graveled avenue, wishing that more of the burned-out streetlights worked. She asked, "Somewhere out west. That's where you and Derek are from, right?"

"Out west can mean a huge amount of territory, Falise. Figure from Rork Springs in the south, clear up to Wide Ridge Research Base up north. And from there, all the way across the continent to the Western Ocean."

"But IG Soukup wouldn't be going to the Western Ocean." Falise gave Kylee a knowing squint. "Word is that he was up at *Freelander*. Consider his mandate: He's here to uncover information about Corporate successes and failures before making recommendations to the Board. After he'd finished with *Freelander*, where would he go out west? What would he want to see for his report?"

"The Unreconciled? They're out at Tyson Station." Kylee shrugged. "After a day on *Freelander*, maybe a bunch of self-mutilated cannibals might come across as mean, median, and mode normal."

"Your homestead and Derek's claims are out there, too, aren't they?"

"What are you getting at, Falise?" Kylee crossed her arms, one foot out.

"Too bad you can't fly Derek's airplane."

"I can. But I won't."

Falise frowned at the girl. "You can fly an airplane?"

"Duh, yeah. But like I said. I won't. It's Dek's. I'd have to call and ask him before—"

"What about the airtrucks? Some are Corporate, right?"

"Yeah, two of them. Used to be four. One's down in the bottom of Best Pass, and the other was torn up by a lollypop tree."

Falise figured she didn't need to know what a lollypop tree was. "Can you fly an airtruck?"

"I have. But just for short hops."

"I want to go to Tyson Station." Falise raised her chin, the action resolute.

"Why would I fly you out there? It's after dark, and we've got a whole night to go before we get to morning."

"Anyone told you that you couldn't?"

Kylee seemed to be considering. "No. But just like Dek's airplane, those aren't *my* airtrucks. Talina and Dek told me. Everything here belongs to someone else until I buy it."

"Girl, have you still not figured it out? I'm Falise Taglioni. And if I want to take a Corporate airtruck, I'll fricking well take an airtruck. If Kalico Aguila, or IG Soukup, or anyone else on this damned rock has a problem with that, they can take it up with my father or Chairman of the Board Miko."

47

Kylee stood at the wheel, her attention fixed on the canyon walls as she flew through Best Pass. Too close on either side, the vertical rock had a ghostly look as the stone reflected in the IR spectrum. The good news was that the winds weren't bad. She'd heard bone-shivering tales about the howling gales that blew through the narrow crevice. If she lost it in here, hers wouldn't be the first airtruck to plummet into the canyon's depths. Even so, the sheer walls rising to either side were scary enough. Imposing, humbling. No wonder people hated flying between these implacable cliffs.

"I can't see a damned thing," Falise said where she stood holding the grab rail and peering through the windshield. "It's pitch black out there. How do you know where you're going?"

"Quetzal vision." Kylee turned the wheel as a gust tossed them sideways. Long distance in an airtruck was easier than she'd expected. "TriNA in your body is a pain in the ass, but there are some advantages to being, what did you call me? A half-breed freak?"

"I may or may not apologize for that. It depends on if I get out of this alive. You say we're flying through a mountain pass?"

"Solid rock walls about thirty meters to either side of us, and they go up another five hundred. That swaying and rocking we're doing? Those are the winds that gust through here. Even then, this is still the best way to get west."

"What if this wind blows us into the rocks?"

"You never have to apologize." Kylee fought to keep them level, Falise, grabbing onto the crash bar, turned a shade more pale, her eyes widening.

"So," Kylee asked, "Like this airtruck. You just walk up to the marine on guard at the gate and tell him you're taking the airtruck.

Then we climb in and fly off? Just like you can do whatever you want?"

"I'm a Taglioni. Might have been different if one of the locals had been on guard. They might not have known when they were talking to someone above their station."

"Every so often, Falise, you start to sound human. Then you spout that shit."

"The Corporation was founded so that every person knew his position in society and would have his or her needs taken care of. You don't know the history. At the last moment, when the national governments would have led the world to destruction through their greed and arrogance, the multinational corporations merged for their own survival. They began dictating to the governments, replacing politicians with Directors and Supervisors to ensure that safety and security were enjoyed by all. Global redistribution of resources, population control, focused and efficient agriculture and extraction, processing, manufacturing, and distribution allowed The Corporation to stabilize the planet for the first time in the history of humanity. Those who would foment discord were removed or denied resources until they capitulated. Tranquility and harmony replaced uncertainty, fear of starvation, or exploitation. The algorithms ensured efficiency of resource distribution on the global level."

"As long as, what did you say, people 'know their station?'"

Falise gave her a sidelong glance. "Would you prefer a world of chaos, strife, and inequality where every nation, led by a petty narcissistic and psychopathic 'great leader,' had his finger on the nuclear trigger? Each of them waiting for the first slight that would justify their use of the weapons based on 'national security?'"

"No way," Kylee muttered, her attention focused as she broke through into the uplifted ridge country beyond the Winds. "You couldn't get me to go live in that slug-infested warren. I might not know my position in society." She gave Falise a knowing look. "And if you, Cinque, and Bart are examples of the best of the best back in Solar System, I'd say the place is fucked."

"I'll have you know that without the families—"

"Shut up and listen, *Taglioni*. We're going to set down at Briggs' to recharge the airtruck, get a night's rest, and pick up Flute. Now, there's not likely to be any threat right there at the homestead, because Flute and Chaco are there. But it's still the bush. They might kiss your milk-soft ass back on Transluna, but once you set foot out of this airtruck, you're lunch. Mobbers won't give a flying fuck about what table they seat you at back at Tiboronne."

Falise tensed, gaze going fiery, then nodded. "Very well." It was said reluctantly.

"That means you'll do everything I tell you to. When I tell you to." A beat. "It's not about swinging dicks, as Kalico would say. When I give you an order, it is about keeping you alive." Kylee pointed a finger. "And saying that, it's no clap-trapping guarantee. You could still walk under a nightmare when I'm not looking or get too close to brown caps. You with me on this?"

"I wouldn't be out here if I wasn't."

"Good. Keep that in your head, and I might actually get you back to PA alive."

Kylee could see the Best River below, a dark line of water twisting and winding its way west through the trellis-pattern drainage created by the hogsbacks. Then they were out over virgin forest. Deep forest, a thick canopy that created a high-piled carpet of blues, greens, and turquoise.

At the confluence of Briggs River, she turned north, sent them skimming over the chabacho, aquajade, stonewood, and what they'd started to call blue leaf.

When the homestead came into view, Kylee turned the wheel, banking around and approaching from downwind. With care, she settled them on the pad just to the side of Chaco's battered old Beta aircar. Not bad, she still had a thirty percent charge left in the powerpack.

With a smile, she let the fans spool down and hit the cabin lights. Her first long-distance trip. Flown solo, without backup. In the middle of the night! How fantastic was that?

"So, how does a Taglioni not know how to fly an airtruck?" she asked. "Dek came with his own airplane."

"My brother was into having a good time. I was dedicated to my duty and family responsibilities. As to piloting an airtruck? I have people for that. Ednund . . ." She smiled wearily, no doubt feeling the ache and loss. "Yes, well, surely there are people who can be appointed when the need arises."

"Appointed?" Kylee unclipped her rifle from the rack. "Good luck with that." A pause. "And don't forget your rifle. Ever."

She opened the door, stepped down onto the pad. God, it smelled so good to be home. The scents from the forest, the smells of the garden, and the sound of the night chime backed by the waterfall down in the canyon.

Rifle held awkwardly before her, Falise stepped down; squinting around in the darkness she asked, "Where are we? What's that sound?"

"That's the night chime. Entirely different from the day chime. Different invertebrates. And what I'm hearing is good. One of the tricks here is that if you hear something different in the chime, it means something's happening. Like, if a bunch of foreign quetzals were lurking out in the forest? The chime would change."

"Oh, sure. Sounds like a broken symphony, and I'm supposed to know there's quetzals out in the darkness."

"You'll figure it out if you live long enough. Meanwhile, don't creep-freak on me, because you've got a quetzal six feet away from you." Kylee told her. "I mean it, don't scream."

"Sure, now you're trying to humiliate me by making me—"

"Hey, Flute," Kylee said, stepping over to hug the big quetzal that had rounded the front of the airtruck. "This is Falise. She's soft meat. Don't expect her to be smart."

Flute blew a harmonic from his vents. Falise yipped, jerking upright.

"Kylee?" she asked. "I mean, I can see it. In the glow from the cabin lights. It's . . . It's . . ."

"Flute. He has a name." To Flute, she asked, "What's happening here?"

Ignoring the petrified Falise, she watched the flashes of IR across

Flute's hide. Mostly images and patterns for "I missed you," "Chaco's okay," and "How's Tip?"

"Tip's holding on." Kylee laid an arm across Flute's neck. Gave him another hug. "I don't know how that's going to come out. He's not healing. Just kind of staying the same. Madison's hovering over him like a mobber over a chamois. Wish I had better news."

Flute's colors shifted to yellow, green, and pink patterns, his vents softly whistling in interrogative as his patterns asked, "Why are you home?"

"Got a rescue mission," she said. "Let me plug the truck in, get the charge back up. Then we need supplies. We've got to find a downed shuttle. Figure it's somewhere between here and the cannibals at Tyson Station."

Flute chirped an affirmative, turning his attention to Falise and intensifying his colors.

"Yeah, she's Dek's sister. And no, she doesn't have his sense. If I had to give her a quetzal name, if would be Tenth Black."

Flute whipped his head around, colors shifting to a kaleidoscope of interrogative astonishment, and the white and incandescent red of amusement. He exhaled a flatulent harmonic that would have translated into a raspberry of disgust. Some sounds really did exceed species boundaries.

"Yeah, it's true," Kylee told him.

"What's happening?" Falise asked. "Is it . . . I mean . . ."

"Come on, Tenth Black," Kylee told her. "It's a little after midnight. It'll take five hours for the airtruck to charge. Tomorrow might be a long day. Let's go get some sleep, load up, and we'll be gone by sunup."

"And where are we going to do this?"

"My house." Kylee started off, glanced back. "You coming?"

"I don't believe this," Falise whispered under her breath as she stumbled along in the darkness. Kylee relented enough to pull her flashlight from her pouch, handing it to the woman.

Falise immediately flicked the beam onto Flute, who expanded his collar frill to shield his eyes.

"It's . . . huge!"

"Oh, yeah," Kylee told her. "And just wait until we get to the house. Flute's going to want to get to know you." She figured that Falise would just have to endure the whole "French kiss" thing. Call it one of her first lessons in Donovanian protocol.

48

Falise had no more than stepped into Kylee Simonov's dwelling than she turned in the half-blinding room lights and froze at the sight of the mind-numbing horror stepping through the wide door behind her. She gaped at the half-meter-wide triangular skull, the flaring collar that expanded in a billowing sheet behind the monster's head. Like living rainbows of translucence, the colors bent into prismatic patterns, out of order, and so laser-bright as to stun the eyes.

Falise's heart stopped in her chest, panic like lightning in her nerves.

And it was so big! Two meters at the shoulder. Maybe six in length with the whip-like tail. It strode into the shabby room on oversized, muscular back legs that sported clawed feet. Smaller forearms ended in deadlier-looking curved talons. And it walked right up to her, three gleaming black eyes the size of midnight peaches fixing on hers. Then the thing had jammed its head into her face and opened its mouth to expose rows of serrated triangular teeth.

Falise opened her mouth to scream.

That tongue—like a striking snake—shot right past her lips and into the back of her mouth clear to the uvula. Tripped her gag reflex. She'd have stumbled backward, but one of the arms snapped out, the talons curling around her back to keep her upright.

Yelping cries died in her throat. Dumbfounded, she couldn't move, couldn't breathe. Could only endure that probing tongue.

Next came a rush of bitter peppermint; the astringent taste flooded her mouth. Saliva running wet, full, trickled down her chin. And that hideous tongue, whipping around like a rude finger, probing her teeth and cheeks. Depressing her tongue. Invasive, violating.

It finally built down in her gut, broke the knot in her throat, and as that wicked tongue snapped back, Falise screamed.

Long. Loud. Like she'd never screamed before.

Kylee said, "Told you" as she threw out some bedding. "You can sleep there."

Falise backpedaled to the wall, tried to brace her shivering legs, turned to spit the vile peppermint taste onto the floor. She'd never expectorated in public in her life, let alone in someone's home. Couldn't care less. Her heart was fit to beat its way through her breastbone.

Staggering, every nerve in her body trembling, she watched the monster curl up on a mat in the corner. The thing took up half the room. Then, impossibly, Kylee settled into the gap between the monster's front and back legs where she could rest against the beast's stomach. As she did, a riot of white and pink colors in incomprehensible patterns seemed to flow across the creature's skin.

"This isn't happening to me," Falise whispered, feeling her stomach flip.

Through slitted eyes, Kylee was watching as Falise placed a hand to her stomach.

She could feel the growing nausea, her mouth still watering.

"If you're going to puke," Kylee warned, "do it outside. 'Cause I'm sure not cleaning it up."

Falise felt the tell-tale tickle in the back of her throat. Spun on a heel, and bolted out the door. She barely made it to the yard. Bent double, while her stomach tried to turn itself inside out.

It pumped. Pumped again.

Wiping her mouth, Falise staggered back for the door, only to hear Kylee call, "Hey, don't forget to turn off the light. And close the door. Never know what kind of unwelcome guest might come wiggling in during the night."

Falise blinked as she stepped inside, stared down at the bedding on the floor. She, Falise Taglioni, was supposed to sleep on the floor? With only those filthy blankets?

She closed the door, aware that Flute was studying her with his left eye. Turned off the light. Then she sank onto the blankets, mouth now tasting like peppermint bile.

Her stomach heaved again, but she kept it down, staring wide-eyed in the dark at where the monster and sleeping girl lay.

"I am in hell," she whispered, and, back to the wall, prepared to wait out the night.

49

" **T** o the west" covered a lot of territory.

Kalico glanced over at Talina Perez and Dek Taglioni where they sat in the row of seats behind the pilot and co-pilot's chairs on the shuttle command deck. Ensign Brian Schulyer kept the bird on course; co-pilot Venus Abena had an eye on the lateral array as they banked tightly to the starboard and began the next transect headed south. On a hunch, Kalico had sent them as far north as the Wide Ridge Research Base. Though the outlying bases had been abandoned for a couple of decades, IG Soukup had mentioned seeing them as part of his fact-finding mission.

From there, Kalico had ordered the search to carry them south to Mundo, then back north on transects that would allow the lateral sensors to search for any sign of her missing A-7.

"Should have traded it out first thing," Kalico muttered under her breath. "It was way over on hours. I could have ordered Abibi to put my A-7 in maintenance, used one of hers."

"Thought you had *Ashanti* give it a refit," Talina told her, leaned back in the reclined seat, eyes closed, fingers laced on her stomach.

Kalico stared out at the topography. "That was three years ago."

She'd never spent much time in the north. From this altitude, she could see snow fields in the distance. Other than that, the land looked cracked, irregular with mesas, the occasional volcanic neck sticking up like a spike—and fascinating, long volcanic dikes that ran like lines across the planet's surface where the overburden had eroded away over the eons. All of Donovan reeked of geological wonders. But for a few small areas, the immensity of it beckoned, unexplored and awaiting a survey, reconnaissance team, and thorough mapping.

To the south was the uplifted strata where the asteroid's impact had thrust deep layers of bedrock upward at a dip of almost ninety degrees. And behind them, the northern arc of the Winds.

Over his shoulder, Ensign Schulyer called, "Anywhere out here, Supervisor, as flat as it is, we should get a hit. We're taking out a fifty-kilometer swath with each transect."

"Roger that." She looked up at the indigo-black vault of the night sky. "Wish we had *Vixen*. Their instrumentation is so much better."

"Figures," Talina said, eyes closed, looking too peaceful. "*Vixen's* in dry dock for maintenance alongside *Turalon* just because it was available, and your old A-7, which was in need of repairs, is crashed somewhere on Donovan."

"I just hope we got the right 'west,'" Dek said. "It'd be a real pisser if Makarov meant 'To the west' of Southern Diggings. That's the sort of place Soukup's going to want to see. Dr. Shimodi says it's the richest couple of square kilometers known to humanity."

Kalico took a deep breath, trying to still the tension in her breast. "If Soukup is dead, killed when my shuttle went down, it's political fodder for anyone on the Board. It looks too convenient. As soon as they hear the news, I will be hauled back to Transluna to stand before a Board of Inquiry. They'll send along another detachment of marines to ensure my 'cooperation.'

"And if Soukup survives, it will be the nail in my coffin. I sent him out on a malfunctioning shuttle. Can't get much more negligent than that. He'll immediately order me relieved and escorted up to *Turalon*."

Dek gave her a warning look, hooking a thumb toward the pilot's seat as he did. A reminder that unfriendly ears were listening in. "Don't be so dire. There's no one on this planet who wouldn't stand up, throw a screaming fit, and demand you be reinstated." And louder, he said, "You kept the colony alive, Supervisor. And you did it through guts, determination, skill, and unbridled competence." A beat. "And *that* will be the official Taglioni report."

Kalico gave him a crooked smile. Turned her head toward the window to watch as the shuttle raced its way south toward the Winds. Sometimes it was good to have friends, especially when everything was headed straight into the toilet.

50

Nothing in her life had prepared Falise Taglioni for Donovan. And, to date, nothing on Donovan had prepared her for that first encounter with Flute. Just the opposite, she'd *always* been in control. In her element.

And just as terrifying, even though the monstrosity hadn't eaten her in the middle of the night, the big quetzal was curled on the cargo deck less than a meter behind her. The creature's three eyes were clamped shut as it fought the shivers.

Falise Taglioni had never felt so traumatized. So vulnerable. What that *thing* had done to her? Talk about *inconceivable* violation! And worse, that brat Kylee had to have heard Falise as she spewed vomit all over the ground.

The humiliation of it was infuckingtolerable!

Falise had a lot of time to dwell on it as the airtruck flew over the lush verdure of blues, greens, and every hue in between. She'd never seen so much thick and dense foliage. This was forested wilderness, without a sign of humanity. It did nothing to sooth her rattled nerves.

Images from the night before kept playing in her head. Back in Solar System, she'd never been in proximity to a large animal. Not even a horse. Her first encounter with a quetzal had been watching it eat Ednund.

Falise hadn't slept a wink, had spent the night tasting peppermint and trying not to throw up. Had huddled on the dubious bedding, sure that the terrible creature would sneak across the floor in the darkness to eat her.

Had to have been the most horrible night of her life.

Now, as she was flying across this trackless and unbroken forest, the sense of lonely desolation came crashing down. For Falise's entire life, she'd been surrounded by humanity. Since childhood,

Ednund and Clarice had been her constant companions. The sights and sounds of masses of people had always been with her. She had lived in a safe warren packed with human beings.

The thought hit her as she looked out on the endless forest: *There is nothing here.*

Only Kylee.

And less than a meter behind her, a huddled monster that, at any moment, might decide in its alien brain to leap up and crush her to death between those mighty jaws.

If I die out here . . .

No one would care. No one would race immediately to her aid.

Why didn't I bring Clarice?

Call that laughable. Her servant might be trained in close quarters combat, talented when it came to disarming an assailant or breaking a person's neck. What use were those skills against a quetzal?

Falise fought a shiver, closed her eyes, feeling sick to her stomach. She didn't dare glance over her shoulder at the huddled quetzal, suffering instead to believe that if she ignored it, it might ignore her.

"Coming to the conclusion you made the wrong decision?" Kylee asked where she stood at the wheel, piloting them over a tree-thick mesa that rose tall above the forest. They were skirting tree-clad mountains that gave the timbered heights a rugged look.

"What makes you think that?" Falise ground her teeth, irritated by her fear and Kylee's apparent ability to read her despair.

"Those pheromones you guys use really give you away."

"Most humans can't smell them. Let me guess. TriNA?"

"Yeah, and every muscle in your body is quivering. You're pretty good with the expressions, but you're leaking fear."

"Wonderful." Falise took a deep breath. "What happens if we have a power failure? Have to land in these trees?"

"We do our best to drop down through the branches, causing the least amount of disturbance. Once we set down on the roots, we grab our shit, fling the door open, and get as far from the truck as we can." Kylee pointed at the mountain they were skimming past.

"We head for the slopes. Climb for the high ground. Look for outcrops of rock."

"That doesn't sound so bad."

Kylee gave her a look. "Then you don't have the first clue. The roots are going to engulf the airtruck and crush it. We're going to be climbing over a squirming mass of them. One wrong foothold, a missed sidewinder, slug, or bunch of brown caps, not to mention a flock of mobbers, and we're dead. And this is treetop terror range. Like the one that got Mom and Mark. And there's other things, different predators we've never seen but that I know." She tapped the side of her head. "Quetzal memory. Our only real hope is Flute."

"How's that?" Falise dared a wary glance back at the cowering quetzal. Yellow and black patterns were running like a broken movie across its hide, and those tightly clamped eyes hinted of terror.

"Lots of stuff won't attack us while we're accompanied by a quetzal. And Flute's senses are better than mine." Kylee shot her a look. "Biggest worry is you. Soft meat usually gets killed right off because they don't listen. And I don't know if you have the strength or stamina to make the hike."

If only I had told Father to go fuck himself.

"There," Kylee pointed at a tall, flat-topped basalt ridge that stuck out on the south side of a north-south trending massif. A bend of green river looped at its base. "That's Tyson Station. That's our next stop."

"Thank God, I can see the buildings. Who lives here?"

"Cannibals. They call themselves the Unreconciled."

"Why are we going to see cannibals?"

"See if they know anything about a shuttle going down. If they heard anything, saw anything, or if maybe Makarov had been in contact, telling them that he was bringing this guy Soukup."

"This is the death cult from *Ashanti*. I read the report." Falise squinted distastefully. "Cannibals? Really?"

Kylee shrugged. "They say they're not anymore. Just stay close to me and Flute. Oh, and if they invite you to have a meal with them, politely decline."

"This is a nightmare that never ends." Falise tried not to think about it.

"Oh, sure they do." Kylee turned the wheel, descending toward the now-visible landing pad beside one of the five white domes. "Nightmares never extend beyond the highest branches of a mundo tree."

Falise shot her a questioning look.

Kylee shook her head, muttered "Soft meat" under her breath.

51

As the airtruck set down on the exposed basalt, the barest amount of dust blew from under the fans. Falise bent to the side window and looked out. The flat top of the old basalt flow was home to five sun-bleached ivory domes, a series of sheds, more abandoned equipment, and to the south, agricultural ground that ended in three solar collectors. Beyond, she could see the drop-off where the basalt rim overlooked the forest below. The few trees dotting the rim looked small and scrawny where they kept a tenuous hold on the thin soil, though to the north, the forest picked up, trees rising in height as they dominated the slope leading up to the mountains.

"So, this is the famous Tyson Station?" Falise asked. Then, she jumped half out of her skin as Flute clattered to his feet, blinking, his hide displaying a series of flashing orange interrupted by alternating blue and pink bands. They gave way to white and pink patterns as the quetzal vented a harmonic from the vents at his tail head. He opened his jaws, snapping them shut with a clap that made Falise jump like it was a gunshot.

"Yeah," Kylee told the quetzal, "surprise, surprise, you arrived alive again." She opened the side door. Falise barely leaped out of the way as Flute scrambled for the door and out into the morning sunshine.

"He really hates to fly," Kylee explained as she pulled her rifle from the rack.

"I didn't know terrible predators feared anything," Falise told her, grabbing her own rifle when Kylee pointed to the rack.

"You bet they do." Kylee leaped agilely from the door. "Get them close to deep water, and quetzals go catatonic."

"Why's that?" Falise climbed down using the steps, slung her rifle, and turned. The first thing that hit her was the perfumed scent rising from the forest. Second was the chime, louder, raucous, a different kind of half-mad symphony than she'd heard that morning at Briggs'.

"Quetzals drown." Kylee turned toward the big dome where people were emerging, shielding their eyes from the morning sun as they took in the airtruck. "Their lungs go straight through from the mouth to the vents, right? That's what allows them to run so fast. They can't plug their tracheas or close off their vents. So, drop a quetzal in deep water, and the lungs flood. Poof. Dead quetzal."

"I'll remember that next time one of the beasts is eating one of my people." Falise followed a half-step behind as Kylee and Flute crossed the barren stone toward the waiting people.

"Welcome!" a man out front called as he raised his hand in greeting. "Kylee, Flute, good to see you."

"Hello, Vartan," Kylee replied. "Sorry to bother you. We've got a missing shuttle with a Corporate big shot aboard."

"Is that what happened?" Vartan came to a stop a couple of paces shy of Kylee, and Falise got her first good look at a cannibal. He stood about five foot eight, with dark eyes and black hair that hung down in two braids from under his floppy hat. The scars, however, took her breath away. Long lines of them that ran down the man's arms, across the backs of his hands. Spirals had been cut into his cheeks, and she could see lines of scar tissue that ran down his neck into the loose shirt he wore.

People were emerging from the dome, mostly women dressed only in skirts, all of them bearing the same patterns of scars, especially spirals on their breasts that started at the nipples. Lines of scars ran down their chests and stomachs to vanish into their skirts. Just the sight of it made Falise cringe. Damn! Who'd *do* that to themselves?

One of the women came to stand at Vartan's side, also tall, just as intricately scarified. Her umber-brown eyes fixed on Falise, hard, evaluative. The usual Donovanian hat was tipped back; long brown hair hung down in a ponytail that reached past her belt. She gave Kylee a slight nod, then asked Falise, "Who are you?"

"My name's Falise Taglioni. Kylee's giving me a look at the bush."

"Any relation to Dek?" Vartan asked.

"He's my brother," Falise told him.

"Not much resemblance." The woman crossed her arms.

"Must be the scar," Falise said, instantly on the defensive.

The man laughed. "Yeah, well, I was the one who gave it to him. Hello. I'm Vartan Omanian. This is my wife, Shyanne. Welcome to Tyson." The wry smile clung to his lips as he asked, "Eaten? We've got breakfast on."

"Had a bite at Briggs," Kylee told him, voice off-handed.

Again the laugh. The man gave Falise a wink. "We haven't chowed down on anyone since we threw Batuhan out. Breakfast is just broccoli, peas, and fried corn cakes. But try and convince anyone of that."

Kylee told him, "As much as we'd like to stay and socialize, what do you know about that missing shuttle?"

"Marta happened to hear the radio. Call coming in for Tyson Station. She got to the receiver and answered. The guy on the other end told her he was fourth, whatever that means. Asked her to change frequency to a different wavelength. When she did, Mr. fourth said that the general would like to inspect us." Vartan shrugged his ignorance. "I didn't know we had a general on Donovan. Didn't even know we had an army."

"He's an Inspector General," Falise explained. "Appointed by the Corporate Board to investigate conditions on Donovan. A fact finder. He's kind of like a Corporate detective."

Shyanne, still watching Falise with that hard brown glare, said, "Thought he'd be here around dusk. Heard that roar the shuttles make when they're entering atmosphere. Sounded off to the north. It was loud enough we all came out . . . and then nothing."

Falise noticed that Flute had wandered off and was now standing at the edge of the cliff just beyond the dome; his three eyes were fixed on the forest off to the west. And then his colors changed. Patterns of yellow, green, and pink were broken with bright crimson patches.

Kylee turned, called, "What have you got, Flute?"

The quetzal tooted something soft from his vents, hide rippling into a light blue interspersed with strange yellow-green-pink combinations.

"Son of a bitch," Kylee muttered, breaking away, trotting across the thin soil to where Flute was staring out at the forest. Falise, having no idea what was going on, followed, along with Vartan, Shyanne, and the rest.

Reaching Kylee's side, Falise could see the girl's expression, the hard set of her jaws.

"What is it?" Falise asked.

"The motherfucker's back," Kylee told her in an acidic voice. "Out there. Somewhere. It's like raising hackles, that sense of threat. Flute's got it. I can just barely feel it."

"What motherfucker?" Shyanne asked, narrowing her eyes as she stared out at the billows of treetops and undulating canopy.

"The creature that killed Mom and Mark," Kylee said.

"The treetop terror." Vartan unconsciously took a step back from the rim.

"Or one just like him," Kylee announced.

"What's that mean?" Falise asked, unsure what a treetop terror was.

"Means we'd better be about finding that downed shuttle." Kylee told her. To Vartan and Shyanne, she said, "Thanks for the help. But my advice? Until Dek and I can get back with the airplane? You might want to steer clear of the forest."

"Yeah," Vartan told her. "That *thing* took enough of us last time it was around. Meanwhile, keep in touch. We've got the radio back on PA's frequency. I'll let Two Spot know that you've got a lead on the shuttle and which way you're heading." He paused. "Kylee? If you get into trouble out there, there's not much we can do to help you."

"Yeah, I know." The girl's gaze was fixed on the distant treetops, their image hazy and wavering in the growing heat.

"Come on," Kylee told Falise, turning, as if physically tearing her gaze away from the forest off to the east. "Let's go see if we can find your general before he's skewered and pulled up into the trees."

"Skewered?" Falise tried to keep pace with Kylee as the girl's long legs ate the distance between them and the airtruck. Flute was trotting beside them, and to Falise's amazement, kept rotating one eye to look back the way they'd come.

"Yeah, skewered, and then eaten."

52

Kylee flew the airtruck north, curving around the tree-covered slopes of the mountain. More precisely, it was an old volcano, one of the many that had followed in the wake of the asteroid's impact way back when. Eons of weathering and erosion, not to mention the constant conflict between the trees, had worn the cone down, left a rounded and humped massif covered with varying depths of forest depending upon the thickness of the soil mantle.

Falise kept a hand on the crash bar in the dash, watching flocks of colorful four-winged creatures as they rose above and then dove back down into the canopy. Scarlet fliers, Kylee had called them. And then there were larger flying things that at first hearkened back to pictures she'd seen of pterodactyls. Until she got a good look at them. Call them flying tetrahedrons? No, that didn't work either.

She glanced back. Flute had once again curled himself into a ball, eyes closed hard, the fear colors and patterns back. Seeing the big quetzal so vulnerable almost made it sympathetic. Almost.

Falise noted, "Was it just me, or is there some underlying tension between you and the cannibals?"

"There's tension." Kylee pointed off to the east where the volcano sloped away. "Mobbers. See all the colors in that column? Like kaleidoscope crazy? And how they flock so tightly together and whirl around each other? That's your first clue that they're not scarlet fliers."

"Will they attack the airtruck?"

"Yeah. But we're a good half mile away . . . and yep, they're diving down into the canopy. Got something down there that they're chasing. It's a guess, but the common suspicion is that they don't have good vision at a distance."

Falise watched the swirling column vanish back into the forest. "So, what's the tension with the cannibals?"

"I think it's what you call baggage. From when they got here. They tried to kill my folks, Kalico, and Briah Muldare. Were going to eat them. Chased them down into the forest. Mom and Mark were killed by the treetop terror. People died. Didn't end up warm and fuzzy, even after they cast Batuhan out."

"What happened to him?"

Kylee gave a knowing look. "Flute and I lured him into range of the treetop terror. The pus sucker never knew what hit him. Paybacks are a bitch."

"You play rough." Falise turned her attention to the forest rising to the airtruck's left, wondering at the lumpy-looking slope, seeing patches of stony outcrop here and there where the trees couldn't find purchase for their roots.

Kylee again gave her that appraising quetzal look. "Are you getting it yet?"

As they rounded the mountain, it was to see the land to the north, a series of ridges and mounded hillocks, interrupted here and there by volcanic necks that shot up in spires as they faded into the hazy blue distance.

"Makarov would have had the mountain for a landmark," Kylee told her. "It's the biggest thing . . ." She lifted a finger from the wheel to point. "Whoa!"

Falise followed her point, seeing where the mountain's flank extended to the north before falling off into a series of steeper slopes. Even as Kylee pulled back on the wheel to gain more elevation, the scar in the trees could be seen.

Kylee banked them to the west, still climbing, and Falise got a good look. The shuttle had come in at a low angle, rising at the last instant to clear the outcrop at the toe of the ridge. Then it had torn into the trees, crashing through vegetation, leaving a clutter of sialon debris, shattered trees, and devastation as it slid and skimmed across the thin soil.

The bulk of the shuttle had come to a stop, piles of splintered, broken, and trashed trees wrapped around the leading edge of the delta-shaped fuselage. That it remained in that good of a condition— looking like a broken silver bird—was a miracle.

The next surprise came when Kylee slowed, approaching down the line of smashed trees, hovering maybe fifty meters above the crash site. To Falise's amazement, she could see the branches turning this way and that; the entire length of the wreck site moved. No, it writhed. The sight of it reminded her of convulsions. The ripped and shredded forest suffered in agony.

Then Falise fixed on the shuttle itself. All the splintered debris piled up and wrapped around the shuttle's dented and damaged front was slowly flexing, curling, branches interlocked and wrestling in a slow-motion struggle. The notion hit her that the dying trees were battling to pull free where the shuttle's weight pinned them.

"That's amazing," Falise gasped.

"Yeah," Kylee slowed them to a hover. "Kind of creep-freaks you, doesn't it?"

"What cleared that space around the shuttle?" Falise pointed to the bare soil around the wreck.

"Unhurt trees getting away from the trouble." Kylee changed the airtruck's pitch for a better look. "We call them trees. Consider them plants, but my suspicion is that they're a whole different kingdom, like nothing we know on Earth. We're just not smart enough, haven't done the research, to figure out how trees live on Donovan. You ask me, they are sentient. Like so much of the life on the planet, they think, process information. Probably through TriNA like the animals do."

"Fascinating." Falise studied the downed shuttle. "Think anyone's alive down there?"

Kylee drifted the airtruck closer to the downed shuttle, saying, "Makarov had his shit together. Putting the shuttle down here, on the side of the mountain on this thin soil gives us a chance. If he'd set down in the deep forest, we'd have never found it."

"I don't see anyone. I . . . Wait. The hatch over the command deck is open. Yes, there. Look. See it?"

Kylee backed the airtruck around until she could see the person waving from the open hatch. "Got it." She wheeled the airtruck around again. "No place we can put down here. The clearing around the shuttle's not open enough. And there's no telling if those dying trees down in the scar could get a hold on the airtruck. They foul the fans, we're screwed."

"So, what do we do?"

"There." Kylee pointed up at the slope. "That outcrop. Looks like bare basalt. Let's go take a look."

Falise stared down as the airtruck skimmed the treetops. As it passed, the branches turned to follow them. The effect was as if the chabacho and aquajade were watching them.

At the outcrop, Kylee slowed. "Okay, see how you can make out the patterns? That's where the ferngrass and musk weed can find enough soil to root. Means the dirt's not more than a centimeter deep, and you can see patches of open rock. This will do."

Falise felt the airtruck settle onto an irregular surface, rocking as it did.

Flute was instantly on his feet, claws scraping on the sialon deck. Rudely, he shoved Falise out of the way, trying to maneuver his big head into a position so he could see out the side window with more than just one of his eyes.

"Oh, let him out." Kylee's voice leaked irritation.

Falise—her skin crawling at the sensation—slipped her arm between Flute's warm hide and the side of the cargo bay and flipped the latch open.

Flute clawed and scrambled his way out, riotous white, mauve, and orange patterns flickering and rolling down his hide.

At the controls, Kylee had picked up the mic, dialing the radio up. "Two Spot? This is Kylee Simonov. We've located the downed shuttle. We're on the north slope of the mountain maybe fifteen klicks north and slightly east of Tyson Station. I'm turning on the emergency beacon so you can find us."

"Roger that, Kylee. To repeat: You've located the shuttle on the mountain north of Tyson Station. Any survivors?"

"Yeah, Roger that. Somebody stood in the top hatch and waved at us. Looked like a man. Nobody I recognized. So, listen, we had to set down on a basalt outcrop. We're about six or seven hundred meters uphill. Falise and I will go take a look. In the meantime, there's no place here to land a shuttle. We'll have to ferry the survivors to Tyson if Kalico wants to pick them up with an A-7."

"*Roger that, Kylee. Tal and Kalico should be there within the hour.*"

"So," Kylee told Falise, "this is going to be tricky. It's up to you and me. We're going to have to get whoever's alive down there up to the airtruck here. Then we can ferry them down to Tyson."

Falise shot a look out the door, wondering where Flute had vanished to. "Doesn't sound so bad."

Kylee put a hand on her arm, those quetzal-alien eyes gleaming. "Between us and the shuttle are a hundred things that can and will kill you. I mean it. You do anything and everything I tell you."

Falise pursed her lips, nodded.

Kylee pulled Falise's rifle from the rack, ran a chamber check, and handed it to her. "Do your own chamber check. And let me watch you do it."

Falise pulled the bolt latch back far enough to see the cartridge and let it snap shut. "That's on a high velocity round. Should I change?"

"Nope." Kylee pulled her own rifle down, running her own check, then looked to her pistol. "Let's go."

Falise followed her out of the airtruck, reacted when the odd green vegetation squirmed under her quetzal-hide boots. The effect was like walking on strings of rubber.

Kylee walked around, checking that no roots were near the fans before saying, "All right, let's go. Stay right behind me. Put your feet where I put my feet. Keep as far as you can from holes, crevices, and gaps in the roots. Touch *nothing!*"

"You make it sound like even the air's dangerous."

"Remember that column of mobbers we saw?"

"What happens if they show up?"

"Might have a chance if we can get up off the roots and freeze. Best outcome? We end up looking as scarred as Kalico. Most likely? We die."

53

The call came through on the military com, crackling in Kalico's earbud. *"Supervisor? You there? I need a priority patch to Supervisor Aguila. Repeat. This is Briah Muldare stationed at Southern Diggings. I need an Emergency patch to Supervisor Aguila."*

Kalico straightened in her conforming seat on the righthand side of the command deck. She glanced out the side window, seeing the red sandstone uplift where Rork Springs lay hidden among the anticlines. Capella's light was shining down, casting shadows behind the rising teeth of the Wind Mountains.

So far, progress along the search grid had been remarkably slow, boring, and unproductive. The shuttle's delicate sensors hadn't picked up as much as a peep that wasn't from a known settlement or claim. The radio silence was downright ominous.

Kalico accessed her com, saying, "Briah? Kalico here. What's wrong?"

"I'm missing four marines, ma'am." A slight crackle of static. *"Had something curious . . . a biological trace out in the trees. Corporal Xing Ming and Privates Radagan, Cantos, and Aberash wanted to run a reconnaissance. Figured they were savvy enough about the roots, that they'd learned enough of the field craft, that they could run out and back. Get readings on whatever was up in the trees."*

A pause. *"Xing argued that they were in armor, with tech, so what could go wrong?"*

Outside of the fact that it was Donovan?

"Ma'am, I was listening to their com chatter. Normal stuff. Talk about avoiding roots. Being attacked by plants. Even a swarming by our local brand of mobbers. Then I heard Cantos say, 'Guys, what the hell is this?'"

"And there's some chatter as the rest of the team cuts across to meet up with Cantos.

"Then I hear Radagan say, 'Holy shit! You see that?' And a moment

*later, Xing calls, 'Rad, get back!' Aberash, sounding excited, yells, 'Fry that
pus sucker!'"* A pause. *"Then there's grunts. Sounds like thumps. Then
nothing. I got no response on my inquiries. Nada. Thought I'd better call
it in."*

"Yeah, thanks for the update. You're sure they were armored?
Had a full charge in the packs? All their tech was functional?"

*"Roger that, ma'am. All I can figure is that something's gone clap-
trapping wrong out there. There are four of them, for freak's sake. Someone
should have gotten a report off. Called for a mayday, said something."*

"Roger that, Briah." Kalico sat back in the seat, frowning.

*"Want me to take a squad and go out there? Maybe leave some of the
FNGs to keep an eye on the fence building?"*

"Briah, I don't—"

*"Hold everything! I've got movement on my HUD. I'm on the southeast
corner of the pad, looking down into the forest, and yeah, it's Private Aberash. She's limping, falling . . . shit . . ."*

"Briah. What's happening? Briah, report."

"Running down there now, ma'am" came the reply, mixed with the
sounds of panting. *"Fuck me with a skewer! She's covered with blood,
staggering, helmet's . . . like . . . blasted."*

"You mean as in explosive?"

*"No, ma'am. If you ask me, it looks like Aberash has taken one hell of
an impact. Got her. Packing her up the hill in a combat carry. Her armor's
fritzed, shorting, but she's alive."*

"Roger that. Can you evacuate her to PA?"

"That's a negative. Won't have another shuttle rotation from Turalon
until tomorrow."

Turalon shuttles were making a daily cargo run from orbit, dropping off fencing, dome kits, and other material that Kalico hoped to
use in the construction of her new mine. She leaned back, fully
aware of the questioning looks Talina and Dek were giving her. But
without military com they'd only heard her half of the
conversation.

Kalico knotted a fist, slammed the armrest on her seat.
Considered.

"What is it?" Talina asked.

Kalico explained the situation, adding, "Briah can't evacuate Private Aberash. Nothing down there has the range to reach PA, let alone orbit and *Turalon*'s medical bay."

"So," Dek mused, "what could have possibly taken out four marines? In armor and with tech? That's impossible."

"Is it?" Kalico asked. "Do you really want to say that after what happened to the Maritime Unit?"

"If there's something in the forest outside of Southern Diggings that can take out marines," Talina mused, "we might really want to know what it is."

"How badly is Aberash hurt?" Dek asked.

"Briah doesn't know. Said that Aberash's armor was shorting in and out. Means the med readouts would be fritzed. If it's really that bad, the miracle is that she was able to make it back to the mine."

"So, what do you want to do?" Talina gestured out at the forest they flew over. "You've got a Board Appointed Inspector General lost somewhere. A most important person, and not the kind of high mucky muck you can just up and lose."

Which was when the PA frequency came alive and Two Spot happily announced, "*Supervisor? Got good news. Kylee Simonov reports that she's found the missing A-7. Says it's located on the mountain slope north of Tyson Station. Says we've got survivors. You'll have to meet them at Tyson. She says the shuttle can't put down at the crash site.*"

"Roger that, Two Spot," Talina said into her com. "We're on the way."

On his own initiative, Ensign Schulyer changed his heading, banking to the north-northwest.

Kalico leaned back in her conforming seat. What would it be? A couple of hours? A half day, to pluck the survivors from the downed shuttle?

And all the while, Private Aberash would be what? Dying? Suffering?

If Kalico ordered *Turalon* to send a shuttle, Abibi would have to pull it out of the schedule, change orbital navigation. Might be after nightfall before she could have one on the ground at Southern Diggings. Aberash might be dead.

To com, Kalico said, "Two Spot? Hospital frequency."

"You're on, Supervisor."

"Raya, you there?"

Kalico waited, seeing Dek and Talina's questioning stares.

Finally. *"Kalico? That you?"*

She checked her chronometer, did some figuring. "Raya, can you be at the shuttle field gate in twenty minutes? I've got a badly hurt marine at Southern Diggings. There's a med unit down there, fully stocked. I just need a doctor."

"All I've got here is a freshly sutured knife wound, a slight concussion a soft meat got when his buddy broke a bottle over his head, and Vik's taking a slug out of another soft meat's calf. Meet you at the gate in twenty. Out."

"What are you doing?" Dek cried.

Kalico gave him an evaluative glance. "Those are my people down there."

"And this is Board Appointed Inspector General Soukup who's in a crashed shuttle," Talina reminded. "And you're skating on micron-thin ice as it is. You do anything to piss on his shoes, and he can order you dismissed on the spot."

Kalico arched her scarred eyebrow. "So, tell me, Tal, given the score, what would you do? Attend the VIP who's already got Kylee headed to the rescue? Or bust your balls trying to save one of your people's lives? Especially when whatever Aberash knows might save the lives of even more of our people?"

To Schulyer, she called, "Get us to PA, Ensign. And as soon as Dr. Turnienko is aboard, see just how fast this thing can get us to Southern Diggings."

She could see Schulyer give Venus Abena a sidelong glance before answering, "Yes, ma'am."

54

As the A-7 shot across the Donovanian sky, Dek took one last look out the side window on the command deck. Below, he could see the southern shore of the continent looping away to the west, shallow water giving way to the depths. Ahead, in the distance at the edge of the horizon, a faint green line met the ocean. Southern Continent. Their destination. He felt the slight shift in attitude as the shuttle's pitch changed; it adopted a descending arc that would end at Southern Diggings.

He liked flying. The quetzal part of his brain was quiet.

He stepped back to the main cabin where Kalico and Dr. Raya Turnienko were going over the data radioed up from Southern Diggings by Private Briah Muldare. For the time being, it looked like Private Aberash was barely holding on. The preliminary diagnosis was that she had fractured bones, internal bleeding, and a severe concussion. Possibly with subdural hematoma.

With regard to Aberash, at least, Kalico had made the right call. If the private had a chance, it was getting prompt medical attention.

"Still no word from Kylee," Dek said, seating himself in one of the chairs and clasping his hands. "But then, who knows what they found when they reached the wreck?"

"Why didn't they take belt radios with them?" Kalico asked. "Given that they ran off with a Corporate airtruck, there should have been two radios in the emergency kit in the aft bulkhead."

"This is Kylee," Dek told her softly. "And my soft meat sister, Falise. The last thing Kylee would think of would be why, out in the bush, she'd need, in her words, 'a fucking radio making a nuisance of itself.' Then you have my sister, raised in Solar System, where her implants kept her in constant communication. The net was always just a thought away."

Kalico closed her eyes. "Can this get any worse? For all we know, Soukup is dead or, God forbid, dying. His First is recording every second of it for the eventual judgment of the Board. And Kylee's taking a Taglioni for her first nature walk in the forest around Tyson. Or do any of us remember the last nature walk we went on outside of Tyson Station? The one where Dya and Talbot died? Not to mention the meals the local flora and fauna made of the Unreconciled?"

Dek arched an eyebrow, rubbed his hands together. "Two Spot says that when he checked with Vartan, the man said that Flute was with them." He cocked his head. "Falise and Flute? Now there's a meeting I'd have given anything to see. I wonder if my arrogant asshole sister has broken down into a blubbering wreck yet?"

"What if she has?" Kalico gave him a sober stare with her laser-blue eyes. "The woman passed out when she saw her valet eaten. Like you said, this is Kylee. She doesn't have much sympathy for weakness."

Dek extended his hands, spreading his fingers as he studied them. "Nope. But then, that's Donovan for you. After what Two Spot reported during this last conversation, Falise was the one who orchestrated the airtruck adventure. Told the guard—one of the new marines by the way—that she was a Taglioni, and if he had any questions, to take them up with the Board." A beat. "Hey, that poor marine? She's Corporate soft meat. They're trained to obey when the nobility asks them to do things."

Kalico glanced at Raya, who smiled in sour amusement, and said, "My call? If they're out in the bush, Kylee will either convert Dek's sister . . . if she's got the guts for it. Or if she doesn't, Kylee has absolutely zero sympathy when it comes to fools."

"What do you think?" Kalico asked him.

Dek leaned back, shook his head. "That woman I observed in Port Authority? All full of schemes, blind superiority, condescension, and disdain? Kylee's already fed her to a nightmare."

"Bit far north for a nightmare," Talina said as she stepped out of the lavatory and settled herself in the seat next to Dek. "But there're plenty of the other usual suspects eager to provide an early and most hideous death. I'd put my money on a pincushion. Or maybe a skewer or bem. Something fast and efficient so Kylee didn't have to linger to make sure it was permanent."

Dek gave her a scolding glare. "This is my sister, the heartless assassin, we're talking about. Show a little respect for my close family ties."

Tal grinned. "Oh, I don't know, Dek. If we're going to be serious, you've got to think of it from Kylee's perspective. Why in hell would she, of all people, partner up with your sister? My bet? After the humiliation Falise endured at your poker game, after seeing her boy toy eaten, Kylee figured she might be a threat. We're lineage, and as strong as that feeling is for us, for Kylee—who is more quetzal than you and me put together—it's an imperative. Instinctive."

"How do you know that?" Raya asked.

Talina tapped the side of her head. "Kylee's in here. Along with Rocket and the rest. Even as I said it, Rocket was whispering 'yes' in my head."

Dek could feel it, too. That quetzal sense of agreement. "Hope Falise doesn't try and pull a fast one. Kylee would kill her in an instant."

Talina asked, "Any news about the IG? Anything about the survivors?"

"Nothing that Two Spot knows. He keeps trying. Calls every fifteen minutes trying to raise her. Probably won't hear a thing until Kylee gets back to the airtruck and the radio."

Dek saw the tension lining Kalico's brow, how it contorted the long scar that ran up from her eyebrow. "You made the right call," he told her.

"Yeah." Kalico exhaled wearily. "Funny thing, having Soukup here, spending that first day with him, I kept falling back into old habits. A person doesn't realize how much they've changed. Who I was, who I am now. What's important."

"Like Private Aberash?" Talina asked. "How's that going to go down when Soukup learns you chose to save a lowly marine instead of his exalted Board Appointed Excellence?"

"Probably have him mad enough to suck vacuum and spit ions,"

Kalico answered. "Doesn't matter. Something in the forest outside
Southern Diggings took out four armored marines. What if it decides to give the mine a visit? We've only got a quarter of the fence
up." She frowned, asking, "Does fencing even stop this thing?"

Talina pulled up a knee, gaze distant. "We know about as much
about Southern Continent as we did about the sea. And look how
that turned out."

"My point exactly." Kalico rubbed her brow, eyes slitted.

Studying the Supervisor's face, Dek could see the exhaustion.
The woman had been at it for thirty-six hours, at least. He doubted
that she'd slept a wink as the A-7 followed the search grid. Even
Schulyer and Abena had taken turns sleeping.

"Kalico," he said softly.

She gave him that wary look she always did when he used
that tone.

Dek added, "We're with you. Whatever it is, we'll deal with it.
All of us. You don't have to carry the entire weight of Donovan on
your shoulders."

"He's right," Talina added. "You're thinking from a Corporate
mindset again because Soukup is triggering those brain engrams.
Forget that paradigm. Donovan isn't the Corporation, and it doesn't
function by their rules."

"Nope." Dek agreed. "Think it through: If Soukup orders you
to step down, you can appeal, call an inquest. Your people will demand it, and we'll hold it in Inga's with everyone in the
audience."

"It's all right," Talina told her. "I'll keep Step from leaping across
the bar and strangling the guy. But we'll all give testimony. The
First and Second will record and archive it. The Third will analyze
and come to the conclusion that you have the support of the people and the best interests of The Corporation at heart. Faced with
those facts, Soukup will back off."

Kalico laughed dryly. "You think that's what's keeping me
sleepless?"

"Isn't it enough?" Raya asked, her flat Siberian face amused.

"God no," Kalico tilted her head back. "Well, okay, maybe a

little, yes. But what's got me creep-freaked?" She glanced from face to face. "We're just getting started at Southern Diggings. And now, as we start to move out from the pad, something just took out four of my marines. It's like I've lived this before."

Kalico took a deep breath, adding, "It felt like this when I was out at the Maritime Unit. We had the technology. We had the sense of invulnerability. Don't you see? What if Southern Diggings turns into the same kind of disaster that destroyed the Maritime Unit?"

55

As she followed Kylee, Falise got an immediate and overwhelming education; it happened in the first one hundred meters of her descent. Step by step, she got an in-depth introduction to roots, thorncactus, gotcha vine, tentacle bush, blue linda, cutthroat flower, sidewinders, brown caps, purple burst flower, some spiky thing Kylee didn't have a name for, and balls of colorful invertebrates that Kylee warned her to stay clear of. All the while she was clambering down tumbled basalt, ducking low branches, weaving around vines. Overhead, the garish, turquoise, oddly blue, and viridian-green leaves blocked the midday sun and left the forest floor in a sort of twilight.

The sounds—especially the chime—were almost deafening; but the first time tree clingers hooted just above her head, it almost stopped her heart.

Of it all, the roots might have been creepiest, moving constantly underfoot as Falise kept to Kylee's tracks. "Clap trapping hell," Falise whispered as shadows cast patterns on her face, "I'm starting to get it. If I don't keep moving, the roots start to wind around my boots. What happens if they get a good hold and I can't pull free?"

"They pull you down and sort of roll you into a cocoon. Then they digest you. I think you suffocate first, which is way better than being jacked up into a tree by a nightmare."

"Remind me. Why are we on this planet in the first place?"

Kylee sent a deadpan look over her shoulder. "Does a half metric ton of rhodium ring any bells?"

"Right. Gotta keep that in mind." She paid even more attention to putting her feet where Kylee did, wincing at the rubbery feel beneath the soles of her boots. Then they encountered the first interlaced tangle of roots. A chaotic Gordian knot of them—more than a meter high—where three trees had wound themselves together.

Something white, sinuous, and evil-looking whipped away into the depths of the root ball. "What was that?"

"Never seen the like," Kylee told her. "Step wide. That's bite ya bush."

"Where did these crazy names come from?"

Kylee tilted her head toward the plant hanging from a low branch. "Well, walk up and touch it. After you cut yourself loose with that knife that you said was too big for anything useful, you can tell me what you'd rather call it."

They made another detour when Kylee sniffed, stared cautiously around, and told Falise, "We're going to veer wide. Take another path around to the right. Smells like a bem in there."

"What's a bem?"

"Short for 'bastard evil monster.' You probably can't smell it from this distance, but there's a taint of vinegar odor on the air. It's a dead giveaway for a bem or a skewer. You *ever* smell vinegar? Stop. Back away. Look for anything, especially rocks or stumps, that might be a predator."

"They look like rocks?"

"And sometimes piles of dirt." Kylee leaped gracefully up onto a tightly interwoven cluster of thigh-thick roots. "They depend on camouflage to let their prey get close. Mostly they catch chamois, crest, and roos."

"Why don't those things back off when they smell vinegar?"

"Maybe because they can't. Whole different olfaction here." A pause as Kylee studied the route to the right. Pulling her knife, the girl eased down the slope, and with a blurred slash, severed a climbing vine with crimson tentacles. As she did, the sinuous stalk began whipping back and forth; the plant emitted an ear-piercing squeal while it shot fluid in a spray. The roots immediately reacted, sending thin filaments to suck up the largess.

"Don't get near those whipping tentacles." Kylee pointed with her knife. "Stay close to the trunk of this aquajade. That blood vine's probably got its mind on dying right now, but you still don't want it getting a hold of you."

"Right." Falise eased her way downhill, trying not to touch the trunk of the aquajade. Like a mantra, she mumbled, "A half metric ton of rhodium. A half metric ton of rhodium."

Kylee with her keen hearing, chuckled as she almost skipped her way down the root-thick slope. "For a scary Taglioni assassin," Kylee called over her shoulder "you don't come off as particularly scary."

"You wouldn't say that if we were creeping down an alley in Shanghai. Or if you were selling stolen Taglioni property in Amsterdam." She paused. "Or even if we were having a delightful meal at Three Spires, when all the while you would wonder if I'd slipped something into your food or drink that would wake you up from a sound sleep that night with a severe stomach cramp. One that would let you stagger to the toilet where you could watch in horror as you shit the bowl full of blood and bits of your intestines." She paused. "Well, you could for the few minutes you had left before you lost consciousness."

Kylee pointed with her rifle barrel. "See that thing that looks like a potato? Don't touch it. It's some kind of relative of the slugs. Sticks to your boot and will start eating through it."

Falise waved at a whirling flight of invertebrates that hovered around her; the things chittered and clicked before buzzing their way up into the aquajade overhead. "Lovely place you have here."

"Yeah," Kylee told her in an almost absent voice as she scanned the route ahead. "We could be down in the deep forest, knowing every instant that a spike on the end of a tentacle could come shooting down from above to spear us through the guts. For Donovan, so far, this is kind of warm and fuzzy."

Falise ducked another branch. "Warm and fuzzy? Really?"

Kylee pointed ahead. "If there were anything really dangerous, Flute would be back to warn us."

Falise struggled for balance on a rolling root, leaped to another, and caught herself before falling into the gap. Kylee said that would be bad. "Anything dangerous? Like the roots?"

"Only if you get trapped by them."

"What about that big colorful flower thing hanging from that chabacho limb?"

Kylee didn't even look. "Remember? That's tooth flower. That wicked-looking pod drops down, snaps closed, and drives the spines through your flesh. Then it pulls you up and eats you, crunchy bite by crunchy bite."

"No shit?" Falise gazed up at the blazing red, yellow, and black colors displayed inside the pod. As she hurried around it, the pods rotated on their stems, following her movements.

Maybe fifteen minutes later and a hundred feet down the sloping ridge, they hit the tree band—the chabacho, aquajade, and blue leaf all crowded together, roots intertwined as they reached up the hill, crowding into the upslope trunks as they sought to move away from the crash site.

Flute appeared, his hide flashing a psychotic blend of colors and patterns; at the same time his ruff expanded, and he made a warbling hooting sound from his vents.

"Flute's found us a way around this tangle," Kylee said. "Follow him."

The quetzal led the way down off the ridgetop, skirted the slope, and started back up. Falise saw the sidewinder get one look, feel, smell, or whatever, of Flute before it shot back into the dark recesses under the roots.

She was panting, sweating by the time she climbed back to the top and into the devastated swath left by the shuttle's crash.

Kylee stood out in the sunlight, her blonde hair shining and golden. Beside her, Flute radiated several laser-bright patterns, a rainbow of colors communicating . . . what?

"Stay back," Kylee told the quetzal. "To them, a quetzal's a quetzal, and they'll shoot you on sight."

Yeah, that makes it unanimous, Falise thought as Flute let them pass.

"Try not to touch any of the dying trees," Kylee told her. "And avoid as much of the spilled sap as you can. Chabacho, aquajade, and stonewood won't hurt you, but there's probably a lot of vine sap and other stuff that might eat your skin off and kill you."

Falise side-skipped where she'd been about to put her foot. "Does this shit ever end?"

"So, you'd rather be back at Inga's in third place?" Kylee asked as she started across the obstacle course of cracked, smashed, and splintered timber. The shining silver hulk of the shuttle lay another fifty meters upslope. "You're about to rescue the Inspector General. Ought to set you up just right with the sorry-assed legally constipated prig."

"How do you know what a prig even is?" Falise's legs had started to ache from the exertion; her lungs were starved for breath as she picked her way across the uneven wreckage. This wasn't the first time she'd sweated this much. But last time had been in a sauna, with a cold drink at hand.

"It might not have been by exalted Taglionis on Transluna, but being raised by my mothers at Mundo was sort of a comprehensive education. At least up until I was nine."

That's when Kylee stopped, gaping at the wrecked shuttle. "Wow! Would you look at the size of thing?"

"You act like you've never seen a shuttle."

"Never been this close to one. Hard to believe these things can actually fly."

Falise made her way up a deep scrape in the soil, stepped wide to avoid something wiggling in the dirt, and arrived at the back of the left wing. On the other side, the right was pretty smashed up. Hydraulic fluid was leaking out of a crack in the smooth sialon. And there was a stench. Smelled like fried electronics. A couple of invertebrates—blue-violet shelled things—skittered across the wing's sialon surface.

To Falise's surprise, Kylee set her rifle to the side, bent, and cupped her hands to offer Falise a foot up. To her greater surprise, the young woman practically catapulted her onto the wing, streaked with dried vegetative matter as it was. How strong was that kid, anyway?

Then Kylee grabbed her rifle and vaulted up, led the way to the wing's bent and buckled leading edge where a matting of crushed aquajade and assorted vegetation was desiccating and adding yet another aroma to the hot dense air that reminded Falise of burned ginger. The mass of splintered foliage swarmed with invertebrates that appeared to be devouring the stems and fluids. Beyond, on the fuselage, just ahead of the wing root, they could see the main hatch. Blocked by broken and piled vegetation, there was no way that was going to be opened anytime soon.

"Boost?" Falise asked, pointing to the fuselage's high curve.

Again, Kylee helped to thrust her up enough on the curvature that she could find purchase.

"Here I come," Kylee stepped back on the wing, took a run, and made a leap, scrambling. Falise leaned low enough to catch the girl's hand and pull her up. All of it made awkward because of the rifles they carried.

Together they walked forward to the hatch where it was open over the rear of the command deck.

"Hey!" Kylee called. "Anyone here? We're your rescue."

A woman, white hair, blue eyes, looking thirtyish, appeared. Falise recognized her as the IG's Third. In a toneless voice, the Third said, "Help, please. The Inspector General is hurt."

Kylee glanced at Falise, gave her a way-too familiar wink, saying, "That's our new line of work." She turned, whistled, and Flute seemed to magically appear on the wing before leaping up onto the fuselage with a graceful bound.

Kylee called down to the Third, "Any of you hurt this quetzal, and I'm leaving you behind to be eaten by the forest, you got that?"

The Third just blinked her blue eyes, seemed to be processing the information.

"Keep an eye out," Kylee told Flute, and dropped into the command cabin.

Falise climbed down more slowly, making sure not to bang her rifle on anything. When she reached the deck, the first thing she saw was the blood, and only then recognized that it had to have come from the slumped figures seated in the pilot's and co-pilot's chairs. Next she caught the coppery smell. Oh, she knew that. Had—on occasion while practicing her assassin's craft—smelled it before.

Ensign Makarov and his co-pilot were dead.

56

Talina stood at the edge of Southern Diggings. What they called the pad—the scraped-off and leveled top of a geological dome. Behind her, the lab, stacks of shipping containers, bundles of fencing, portable lights, and a partially built perimeter fence were the center of human activity. The shuttle, resting on landing struts, gleamed in the slanting light as Capella dropped toward the horizon.

She could smell the forest: a rich saffron, ginger, and rose-like fragrance so different from what she knew in her own part of Donovan. Her quetzals, too, found it fascinating and new. She could feel their excitement.

For once, Demon, down behind her stomach, wasn't making a pain in the ass out of himself.

Nor were the sounds here the same. The hoots, howls, screeches, and whistles from the forest beyond the berm hinted at creatures not even her quetzals could place. A completely new world, right down to the peculiar melody of the chime: a deeper, almost bass tremolo. That it sent unease through Rocket and Demon just added to her own sense of foreboding.

She'd already inspected Aberash's armor. Ran her fingers over the dents in the sialon, rubbed at the bloody smears. Whatever had smashed it had done so from two sides. Like a hammer on an anvil. And it had to be big.

Which could be anything. The scope of human knowledge when it came to the planet's biosphere was like a drop in an ocean of the unknown. Kalico had been correct. They should all be scared shitless that Southern Diggings could end up like the Maritime Unit. That creatures—big *intelligent* creatures—could be stalking just behind the line of curious trees. Looking up at her with alien eyes, wondering.

"*Yess,*" Demon hissed down in her gut. "*Danger here. Sniff.*"

Talina tipped her head back, scenting the breeze that drifted in from the forest. Catching . . . what was it? That faint scent of something. . . .

Not even quetzal memory could tag it.

Dek appeared behind her, placing his reassuring hands on her shoulders. "Raya's still in surgery. Kalico's pacing. Never seen her so unsettled."

"She has a right to be," Talina told him. "Down there. Out in the forest. I got just a faint whiff. It tickles the quetzal memory, but it doesn't. That make any sense?"

"Unfortunately, yeah." He did his own sniffing, letting his enhanced sense of smell filter the breeze. "Got to tell you, Tal. It's all new. Maybe that taint? Or what we think is a taint? Might just be some new variety of plant in bloom."

"I think it's animal." She made a face. "No idea why, but I do."

"I'll trust you for that." He rubbed her shoulders, his strong hands massaging some of the stress out of her too-tense body.

She told him, "Part of it is Soukup. Knowing that the IG is second-guessing every decision Kalico's made, she's ready to pull the plug. She may not know it yet, but she is. The disaster at the Maritime Unit is haunting her like the ghosts in *Freelander*. She won't let Southern Diggings suffer the same fate."

"Hard to blame her."

"You know what has to happen, right? The only way we're ever going to know what went wrong out there?"

"Yeah," he told her sourly. "We've got to go out. Find the rest of the marines. Figure out what killed them. And not get killed ourselves."

"There's always a hitch, isn't there?"

"How are we going to do this?" Dek asked.

Talina laughed, turned, and kissed him. As she pulled back, she looked into his yellow-green oversized eyes. "We're going to do this the only way we can."

He chuckled. "Let me guess: Very. Very. Carefully?"

"Always knew you were the smartest man alive."

57

Kylee stared in amazement. She'd never been inside a shuttle before, let alone on the command deck. Sure, she'd seen pictures, but this was for real and magical in spite of the bloody corpses slumped in the oversized seats. She tried to imagine what the instrument panels must have looked like, all filled with glowing holo images, and how the controls worked. Let alone what it must have been like to look through those now filthy-windows—covered with spattered bits of dried blood and vegetation—and see stars. Behind the pilot and copilot's seats she found a row of three plush high-tech conforming seats. She punched one with her fingers, feeling the cushioning sink and flex.

She turned then, stepping out of the way as Falise climbed down the extendable ladder from the escape hatch. Rounding the seats, Kylee got her first real look at the white-haired woman, although she didn't look more than thirty. She was slim, her face perfectly formed, lips thin. Something wasn't right about her blue eyes . . . until it hit Kylee that like Dek and Falise's eyes, they'd been genetically altered.

No expression crossed the woman's face as she and Kylee stared eye-to-eye.

"Who are you?" Kylee asked, resetting her rifle back on its sling.

"She won't answer," Falise told her after having stopped long enough to check the bodies in the command chairs. "She's the IG's Third. She's an analyst, genetically and cybernetically engineered to manipulate data. Think of her as a human computer."

"Wow. Must be really fun on a date, huh?"

"Her only sexual function is to service the IG," Falise said as she pushed past Kylee and stepped through the lock into the cargo compartment.

"That's fucked up." Kaylee stared curiously. The woman didn't seem to care, just looked blankly back with those too-blue eyes.

Falise, taking one last look, said, "It's for the IG's protection. If he restricts sexual activity to members of his Four, he can't be blackmailed, biased, or manipulated."

Kylee waved a hand in front of the Third's face, seeing the pupils react, but no other change in the woman's features. Creepy as that was, the Third turned on her heel to follow Kylee into the cargo cabin. The lights had a dim glow, while most of the illumination came from a long tear in the right side of the fuselage. In the first row of seats, a guy in a high-collared, official-looking, medium-gray jacket, sat with his head back on the rest. He appeared to be in pain. The guy's hair was close-cropped and silver; kind of looked like a helmet the way it was cut. His thick jaw was knotted, lips pinched, and when he opened his eyes, he fixed Kylee with the kind of black-eyed stare that pinned her like an invertebrate on a study board.

Falise knelt by his seat, asking, "Inspector General, are you hurt?"

"Fourth said my collarbones are broken and I have a sprained neck and bruised, maybe broken ribs. Just get me out of here."

Kylee took in the three other men in the room. Two of them wore the same dress as the Third; they shared that nobody-home look and lack of emotion. They were seated off to the IG's right. The guy two seats down on the left, however, wore Donovanian-made coveralls and looked familiar.

Walking down Kylee asked, "Hey, you're Fenn Bogarten. How hurt are you?"

"Broken lower leg." He glanced up with pain-wracked eyes. "Do I know you?"

"Kylee Simonov, and that's Falise Taglioni. Dek's sister, if you can believe. Let me check that leg."

"I'll save you the trouble." Bogarten told her. "It's a snap fracture of the left lower tibia and fibula." He shifted, winced. "Not to mention that every bone and joint aches. We took one hell of a wallop." A flicker of a smile. "Get me out of here, Kylee. I'm ready for evac."

"Yeah, well, that's not so easy. Kalico's on the way with another shuttle, but we're going to have to pack you up to the airtruck first.

There's too much broken shit and danger from the trees to set down here, so the airtruck's almost a klick up the slope." She bent down. "Here, give me your arm."

With Bogarten's help, Kylee got the man to his feet. Well, foot. The other dangled limply.

"Damn that hurts," Bogarten told her.

"We got anything we can use to splint that?"

"You kidding?" Bogarten took a half hop, gasping as his foot flopped. "We stripped the emergency medical kit out of this crate last time we had an accident at the mine. Bet we can make something, though."

"How about I pack you out?" Kylee told him as she set her rifle to one side. "I can rig something. There's enough broken and splintered chabacho and vine laying around out there I could weave us a bower big enough we could sing 'Coming Together' under it."

Bogarten chuckled. "Hey, how are you going to . . ."

Kylee stepped in front of him, thankful she was a half a head taller than he. She backed against him and pulled his arms around her shoulders and said, "Hang on tight. I'll be as careful as I can." Then she hunched and lifted him off his feet. Heard him gasp as she carried him through the hatch to the command deck.

At the ladder, she started up—thought the guy would half strangle her as he held on for dear life—but she made it to the top. Crawled out and laid the panting and sweating Bogarten at Flute's feet.

The poor man looked up, blinked, and almost swallowed his tongue as Flute's big head bent down to inspect Kylee's latest "friend."

"Flute? This is Fenn Bogarten. He's hurt. Broken leg. Keep him safe."

Bogarten stared up with skull-popped eyes and a death rictus. "That's a . . . That's . . ."

Flute turned orange and chirped a tremolo from his vents.

"A quetzal, yeah."

"But he'll kill me," Bogarten squeaked, perspiration beading on his forehead.

"Only if you piss him off." Kylee slapped him on the shoulder. "So, I guess I wouldn't if I were you."

Dropping back inside, Kylee stepped into the main cabin to find Falise and the three aides crowded around the IG. "Thought there were four in the Four?"

"There were," Falise said. "The IG tells me his Fourth was going to stand guard outside the hatch last night. When the Second went to check on him this morning, he was gone."

"Welcome to Donovan," Kylee told her. "How do we want to do this? I've got Bogarten out. I figure that he's fit enough to ride Flute up to the airtruck." She looked at the IG. "This guy? Broken collar bones? I could toss him over my shoulders for a combat carry up the ridge, but he'll be in the worst pain he's ever known. And if there's a busted rib? Could puncture a lung. Best bet is that we build a litter and pack him."

Falise's expression pinched; then she jerked a nod. "Whatever you think."

Kylee leaned down, staring into Soukup's eyes. "Here's the deal: We can't immobilize your shoulders, so I'm going to need you to keep your body stiff as I lift you up the ladder. It's going to hurt worse than you've ever hurt. But it's got to happen, get it?"

Soukup blinked. Gave her a half-dazed nod.

Kylee pointed at the two men and the woman left of the Four. "They of any help?"

"Not for this," Falise told her. "It's not in their programming."

"Programming. Right," Kylee muttered. "Hell, let's program everyone. Make them really fucking valuable in a crisis."

She squinted an eye at Soukup, took in his tailored gray jacket, and reaching down, knotted her fingers in the flaring shoulders. Then she lifted.

Soukup screamed.

And he came right out of the chair.

Kylee didn't relent, backing as she walked him forward through the hatch to the base of the stairs. There, she reached down under the hem of his jacket, got a firm hold on his belt, and ordered, "Stay straight, motherfucker, or you'll get yourself jammed up in the narrow confines of the hatch."

Kylee didn't give him a chance to reply; she flexed her left arm. Lifted the screaming Soukup off the deck and started climbing. Sure, she had quetzal strength, but it took all of it to muscle Soukup's half–limp weight to the top. The whole way, he kept shrieking *"Stop! No! Please!"*

"If it's the pinch from your britches that's got you in a knot, your balls will heal." She'd just made the top of the hatch, muscles trembling, felt her grip giving on the man's pants. Damn it! That fancy fucking fabric. He was going to slip through her fingers. The tumble back down onto the deck . . .

Just as the last of the slippery fabric slithered through her fingers, Soukup rose as if on wings. Kylee twisted her head around to see Flute's big head blocking Capella's light. Soukup's collar was stretched, dangling from Flute's serrated jaws.

After the quetzal laid the squealing IG down next to the still-gaping Bogarten, all Soukup could do was whimper, his face a mask of terror and agony.

"Well," Kylee muttered. "At least we got them out of the shuttle."

Then she glanced up at the sky. Capella was starting its slant to the west, burning hot, white, and unforgiving. But that was the only thing in the sky. Where the hell was Kalico's shuttle?

With both rifles slung, Falise climbed up and out, catching Kylee's expression. "What's the matter?"

"I don't know." Kylee pointed skyward. "Kalico should be here by now. Something's wrong."

There were four of them: Talina, Dek, Briah Muldare, and the soft meat marine, Private Sunny Valdez. They assembled at the edge of the Southern Diggings pad, standing on the berm where it overlooked the forest below. The difference, this time was that Briah and Sunny both carried what the marines called "boom tubes"—though the official designation was Distance Ranging Remote Detonation Devices, or DRRDDs—along with their rifles.

For the first time in years, Muldare was in shining new armor, fully functional with a brand-new powerpack instead of her old suit with its make-do repairs. The look on the woman's face as she clamped her new helmet in place was satisfied. She turned to Tal, saying, "All right, now let's go kick ass" and propped the boom tube over her shoulder next to her slung rifle.

Talina glanced at Valdez. "Given the data in Aberash's armor, we've got a general idea where we're heading. That's about a kilometer to the south." Tal pointed. "That's off the bedrock, in what we call deep forest. The trees are huge, one hundred to a hundred-fifty meters high. It's going to be dark, the root mat's thick. This is unknown territory. Whatever killed your friends will probably still be out there. Our job is to figure out what it is, and if it's a threat to Southern Diggings. That's *all* our job consists of."

"Roger that," Valdez said. She was a young woman, looked to be in her early twenties, short-cut black hair, said her family came from Colombia back on Earth.

"No matter what," Muldare told her, "you don't shoot until you're told. Doesn't matter if it looks like you're about to die, you wait for our order."

"You got it, Sarge."

"Sarge?" Dek asked, checking the charge on his ornately engraved rifle for the fourth time.

Muldare grinned inside her helmet. "Inside joke, Dek. They started calling me that when we were training. Said I was like a clap trapping drill sergeant."

Talina ensured she had a round in the chamber, then slung her rifle. "We get through this, we'll have Kalico make it permanent. Come on. Let's go. We don't have that long before dark, and we want to be back before then."

Talina set off down the slope, soil and rocks sliding under her feet.

Down in her gut, Demon was squirming. She could feel Rocket, tense as a compressed spring as he rode on her shoulder.

"What do you think?" she asked.

"Dangerous," Rocket's voice came from just behind her ear. *"Unknown."*

Talina glanced at Dek, saw that he, too, had a grim set to his expression. He was murmuring under his breath. Meant he was talking to his quetzals, too.

As they entered the forest, it was to wind past a curtain of vines hanging down from above. Talina pulled her knife, ready to slash at anything that tried to snag her, bite, or attack. Then, with the barrel of her rifle, she pushed the closest—a frilly blue-green thing—out of the way. The only reaction was a scurrying of chittering invertebrates as they fled up the stem.

Stepping past, she led the way onto the root mat.

"Sure wish Flute was here," Dek said nervously.

"That makes two of us," Muldare agreed as she stepped out to the side. "Let me take point, Tal. I'd rather that anything we encounter hit my armor first. Trust me. There's things here you won't recognize."

"You got it," Talina said, letting the marine pass.

"Who's Flute?" Valdez asked.

Dek told her, "Our quetzal."

"You have a quetzal?" Valdez was walking warily, scanning. In the shadow of the trees, the reflection of her HUD's glow could be seen on her face. "Thought they were the enemy."

Talina told her, "It depends on the lineage. Nothing on Donovan is ever what it seems."

The difference in the forest here surprised Talina. It wasn't only the almost-grating chime. Or the smell. The trees were entirely new species. She couldn't recognize any of them, though they followed the same trilateral morphology. The roots they trod on, however, were still roots. And still dangerous, especially as she and her team made their way down the slope and the depth of the soil increased.

Didn't matter that it was a different continent, different forest, and different trees, the rules were the same. She discovered that when they came upon the first toppled tree. Its neighbors had managed to rip it loose, uproot it, and cast it down. Muldare led them around the gaping hole in the ground. The surrounding trees had already filled the opening in the sky, were crowding the space their vanquished foe had lost.

"Never understood why the trees fight with each other," Muldare growled.

"Because they can," Dek replied. "Sort of reminds you of people, doesn't it?"

Valdez—stepping carefully on the squirming root mat—asked, "Security Officer Perez, people keep telling me you've got Donovanian TriNA, that it's changed your body. How does that work?"

Talina watched something that looked like a white glowing snake slither into a gap in the root mat. "I'm stronger, my senses are better, and I've got three beings inside me. One wants me dead, the other wants me alive, and the part of me that's me wants them gone."

They encountered the first impressive tangle of interlocked roots as the smaller trees gave way to towering forest giants. One by one, they climbed over the three-meter-high barrier.

On the other side, Briah pointed to a cluster of what looked like purple puffballs. "Don't get close, they shoot out toxins."

As Muldare started across the root mat for the next bunched cluster of roots, Talina whipped her rifle around. The small scimitar had camouflaged itself but fled as they got close. On its paddle-like legs, it scurried up the root cluster and disappeared on the other side.

"Lot of those around here," Muldare said. "Some are huge."

"Yeah," Dek told her. "We ran into the like at Two Falls Gap. Hard to kill."

Carefully, they scaled the root cluster, skirting wide of the various pod-covered vines. And then there were what Talina called spike-ball vines: a blue-green, thick-stemmed, hanging vine with what looked like tennis-ball-sized fruits covered with hundreds of needle-like thorns.

They had made it to the flats, where deep soil gave the trees enough purchase to reach huge heights. Most of the boles here had to be five, even six meters in diameter. The light had grown dim, blocked by the thick, high canopy. In the twilight, four-winged fliers kept darting through the hanging vines, snatching at flying invertebrates. The chime had changed, ominous, deeper in bass.

Talina sniffed. "Wait. Slow down. Smell it, Dek?"

"Yeah," he told her, shifting his hat back, raising his face to scent the air.

"Valdez," Muldare growled, "What did I tell you about roots and stopping and staring around like a five-year-old?"

"Roger that, Sarge. I'm moving."

As she padded forward, Talina pointed between the thick boles of the giant trees. "Just up ahead. But I don't like that root knot. Something . . ."

"What?" Muldare asked. "I'm scanning with IR and UV. I get nothing but background."

"Go around," Dek said.

"Even if there's nothing there?" Valdez was craning her head, scanning the heights.

"Kid," Muldare said, "If Tal or Dek have a hunch, we follow it."

As Muldare led the way to the right, they had to cross an interlaced mat of barrel-thick roots that often had them a couple of meters above the forest floor.

Talina saw the tentacle lash out from below, slap onto Muldare's back, and struggle to jab a line of barbs into the marine's armor.

In a flash, Talina pulled her knife, got her footing, and with a slash, severed the tentacle where it stuck out from the depths. Something down in the darkness issued a piercing squeal, and the tentacle dropped away, twisting and whipping this way and that. In the process, it smacked the toe of Talina's boot, leaving barbs protruding from the thick leather.

"What the hell was that?" Dek asked, looking down uncertainly into the black gaps beneath.

"Haven't a clue. Don't want to find out," Valdez told him soberly.

"Let's get the hell off of this root mat before whatever it is tries again," Talina said as she tried to look down on all sides at once, her knife at the ready.

Muldare led the way, finally clambering down the roots, smashing something mindful of a slug that stuck to her arm as she did. With a gloved hand she wiped the thing's guts off her armor. "Don't make that mistake."

"We won't," Dek promised, carefully picking his route as he climbed down.

Talina followed, rifle in one hand, knife in the other.

"Smell that?" Dek asked as they started across the flat between the trees. The air was coming from off to their right. The odor was distinct.

"Got it," Talina agreed.

"What is it?" Muldare asked, slowing, bringing her rifle up.

"Dried blood," Tal told her. "Human blood. Whatever happened, it's right over there, on the other side of that big tangle of roots."

"I can't smell anything," Valdez said as she walked carefully forward.

Talina's quetzal sense kicked in. "Careful, people. We're close. And there's something . . ."

"Familiar," Dek finished, testing the air. "But not. It's . . ."

"Come on," Talina said as they reached the bottom of the root tangle. "Here's the game plan. Stay low on the thick roots. Just a feeling, but we shouldn't be high. Shouldn't make targets of ourselves."

"What if it's some kind of giant scimitar?" Muldare asked as she started to climb, keeping her feet to the thickest of the roots.

"That's what the boom tubes are for," Talina told her. "You know where to hit a scimitar?"

"Right in the mouth," Dek answered as he dialed up the power on his fancy inlaid rifle. "It's easy. They come at you straight on. When the three blades open, you've got a shot right down the gullet."

"Sounds like you've done this before," Valdez noted.

"Yeah," Dek sounded nervous. "Well, it worked on the one I killed outside of Two Falls Gap."

As Muldare reached the highest of the interlaced roots, Talina said, "Briah? Go over the top. Don't hesitate. And keep low."

"What are you thinking, Tal?" The marine stopped, just shy of the highest of the meter-thick roots.

"I'm thinking . . ." She made a face. "Just a hunch. Something I can't put words to."

"Works for me." Briah crouched, powered her armor, and leaped over the top. A moment later, she called. "Clear. Good footing. Got another of those slug things. I'm working my way down."

Dek looked at Tal, who nodded. He got a good grip on his rifle and scrambled over the top in three rapid steps.

"Go ahead," Valdez told her. "I'll be right behind you."

Talina took a breath, muscles electric as she followed in Dek's footsteps, cleared the highest root, and found her footing on the other side. Then she scrambled down, following where Dek pointed.

Valdez was next, stopping just above where Talina perched on one of the barrel-thick roots. These big ones didn't wiggle around like the smaller ones, though she could feel it writhing beneath her feet.

And then she got a look at the root flat before her.

"Guess we've found my marines," Valdez said from above.

59

The newly erected admin dome at Southern Diggings smelled of fresh duraplast. Construction was fast and simple. The circular base or foundation of the dome was poured on a flat surface. Pre-fabbed walls were laid flat on the foundation. The dome itself was a graphite-fiber fabric that was affixed to the outside of the circle and inflated. Once inflated, crews erected the pre-fabbed walls, raising them into position and locking them in place to create walls, halls, and rooms. Then every surface was sprayed with liquid duraplast, the polymer hardening and cementing the dome into a strong and resilient structure. It had gone up in a day.

Now, with fans blowing the fumes into a tubing, the structure caught the midday light.

Kalico, seated on a stack of bits for the pneumatic drills, waved at a pesky invertebrate that had been drawn to her perspiration. She reveled in Capella's hot light after being in the air conditioned and ad hoc medical bay inside one of the shipping containers they'd used for initial shelter at Southern Diggings. Inside, Raya Turnienko worked on Private Aberash.

Kalico figured she had a strong stomach. Watching the Siberian doctor sucking blood out of the marine's skull, however, had given birth to a queasy unease down in Kalico's gut. So she'd stepped out here, taken a seat, and now was pondering if that brand new dome, smelling of fresh polymers, wasn't already doomed by whatever had killed her marines and inflicted so much trauma on Aberash.

Worse, Talina Perez, Dek, Muldare, and the soft meat Valdez were just out yonder. Somewhere in that thick forest off to the south. Facing . . . what?

The lurking reminder of Maritime Unit remained fresh in her memory. The haunting reality that Donovan had destroyed the entire research base. And it hadn't just been the big terrifying monsters, but the slime that had killed all those people and sank the supposedly impervious sialon complex into the ocean.

So, what's lurking out there, and is it going to kill my friends?

And all the while, she was down here, terrified by what this latest venture was going to cost her. Three dead marines and one wounded? The remarkable promise of Southern Diggings and its unimaginable wealth? Or Tal, Dek, and Briah? Friends. People she cared a good deal about.

"So," she mused, eyes on the striking white dome, "is this how the universe works?" Be just like the perversity of fate to cost her everything. Disaster on all fronts, grief, and defeat, all there to be witnessed by Soukup. Even while Kalico wanted to drown herself in grief, the slug sucker would order her arrested, appoint her replacement.

A weary smile bent her lips. *Could I handle that? If Tal and the others don't come back? Southern Diggings abandoned? Me, locked in a cell aboard* Turalon?

She stared thoughtfully at the lines of scars on her hands, wondering what more Donovan could inflict on her. What greater price she might have to pay.

Which was when Lea Shimodi stepped out of the lab, glanced around and fixed on her. "Kalico? Got Shig on the radio. Says he needs to speak to you. Urgent."

Kalico nodded, stood. She glanced off at the thick forest to the south. "Damn it, Tal. Dek. You come back to me."

Walking across the bare stone, she saw the threads and smears of metal where the overburden had been bladed off. Her boots were treading on more wealth than humans had ever known.

And she'd give it all to have her friends safe and that clap trapping Soukup back on Transluna.

She ducked in through the open door of the shipping container they'd turned into a lab and office. Shimodi, back at her lab bench, pointed to the radio where it sat on an aquajade-wood table in the back corner.

Crossing, Kalico lifted the mic, asking, "Shig? You there? This is Kalico. What's up?"

"Ah, Supervisor," Shig's perfectly articulated speech carried no emotional inflection. *"I thought it prudent to inform you. Bartolome Radcek was brought to the hospital about an hour ago. Vik determined that he was dead when his people wheeled him in. No cause of death is available at the moment. His valet, if I have the relationship correct, has asked that Radcek's body be transported up to* Turalon *for autopsy. I thought I should clear it with you before I released it."*

"Dead?"

"That, I am afraid, is the case."

Kalico closed her eyes, took a deep breath. Damn it, they still hadn't found Chad's killer.

"Does Vik suspect foul play?"

"I thought you would ask. She does not. Nor, she was most insistent to tell me, can she rule it out until she has a cause of death."

Would the blows never cease? What the hell was Soukup going to make of this? At least, for once, he couldn't hold Radcek against her. Unless there was more to this than she was aware.

"Yes, Shig. Clear the body for transport. Put it on the next shuttle up. Tell Abibi I want a full report as soon as her medical team can conduct an autopsy."

"I will do so." A pause. *"I regret being the bearer of bad news."*

"Yeah, well, Shig, let's just hope that's the worst of what's coming down today."

She laid the mic down, dropped into the chair, and braced her elbows on the table. Rubbing her eyes, she tried to place Radcek's death into context. The man's murder, and surely it was murder, considerably narrowed the field when it came to her replacement.

And that left only two: Cinque Suharto and Falise Taglioni.

60

"This is taking too long," Kylee growled under her breath as she pulled the last knot tight on the section of fiber. She'd used claw shrub—cut from crushed plants in the shuttle's debris field—to bind sections of triangular chabacho branch into a crude litter frame. A battered tarp, with holes cut for the litter poles to fit through, had been fastened by long thorncactus spines.

The sun had slid closer to the horizon, the temperature was somewhere in the high thirties, the humidity thick. On the sialon, it was like working on a baking tray with the oven set to simmer.

But at last, they were ready to go. Kylee stood, wiped her mouth. Wished for a drink of water. But it had already been established that the shuttle's small reserve tank had ruptured in the crash.

Falise was giving her a skeptical gaze where she sat looking hot, sweaty, depressed, and fatigued, on the wing next to the perspiration-soaked and panting Soukup. The woman's once-fancy streaked hair was now hanging in an unruly tangle.

"We ready?" Bogarten asked where he was propped on the wing's trailing edge; his splinted foot was dangling.

"Yeah," Kylee told him. "We're barely going it make it by sun-down as it is. We get stuck out there in the dark, we're dead."

"What about Flute?" Falise asked. "Won't he protect us?"

At mention of his name, Flute extended his head out from where he crouched in the shade beneath the wing. Quetzals, it seemed, didn't worry about invertebrates biting them or toxic chemicals from broken vines.

"How's a quetzal going to protect you from roots?" Kylee asked, standing and slapping at her filthy fabric pants.

"I didn't think of the roots," Falise looked away.

"Yeah, well, you'd better. Out here, you get no second chances."

The three left of the Four just watched with those emotionless eyes; they might have been unconcerned. Unfazed by the fact that they could be dead within the hour.

Kylee pulled the litter over to Soukup; the guy didn't look well. He was obviously thirsty and in pain; each breath he took sounded ragged. His normally piercing black eyes lacked luster, seemed to have trouble focusing.

"All right, let's get you on the litter," she told him. When he didn't respond, Kylee reached down, and as gently as she could, started to lift.

"*Stop!*" The scream was torn from his throat. Tears collected like diamonds around the pinched black eyes. Beads of sweat rolled down his sun-reddened skin.

Kylee stuck her face in his. "We don't have a lot of time. I don't care if it hurts like a motherfucker! If we don't get you up to the airtruck, you're dead anyway. You get that, soft meat?"

He jerked a slight nod, and Kylee, with Falise's help, got him laid out on the stretcher.

"Flute!" Kylee called.

Again, the quetzal stuck its head out from under the wing, the three eyes rotating her way.

Kylee bent down, pointed at Bogarten, who sat with his jaw clenched. "Fenn needs you to carry him up to the airtruck. He's going to ride on your back. He's wounded, so *be careful*." She paused, reading his affirmation in orange as the collar flared.

"Fenn, scoot over here. As Flute eases out from under the wing, drop onto his back, just above the front legs. Now, it's going to hurt, but you need to clamp with your thighs."

As Bogarten shuffled his way over, he muttered, "I don't believe this. I'm riding on a creep-freaking quetzal! No one's gonna believe this."

"Yeah, well, I'd take a holo, but we're a little shy on equipment out here."

Like a working radio. One that would tell us where the hell Kalico is.

"Fenn, I see that you've got a pistol on your hip. I don't give a fuck if it's mobbers. Don't shoot it while you're on Flute. He'll drop

you flat. And, given your leg and the roots, that would be the real
shits."

"Got it. No shooting."

She helped Bogarten by supporting his broken leg as he positioned himself over Flute, then clapped him on the back as he slid
onto the quetzal's back.

"All right, Flute. Get him up to the airtruck. And then get your
butt back down and keep us safe. We're on the way as soon as we
get Soukup's litter off the wing."

Flute flashed iridescent orange, white, and pink patterns; then he
carefully eased out, picking his way through the wrecked trees, and
then down out of sight into the forest. Bogarten looked like he had
a corncob up his ass, but kept his seat.

"That's the easy part." She turned, looking at Falise. "You ready
to help lift the litter off the wing?"

The woman—already looking haggard—nodded. "This doesn't
get any easier, does it?"

"Nope." Kylee hopped off the wing, pulling the upper handles
around. "Falise, I can see that you're hot, dehydrated, and exhausted. And it's all uphill. But if we don't make the airtruck, if you
can't find the stamina, you, Soukup here, and these walking brain-
less zombies are going to die. So you reach down into whatever
Taglioni guts you've got and hold up your end."

"And no mistakes," Falise said through a weary exhale.

"Glad you got that." Kylee pulled the litter out as Falise got under
it, managed to lift it off the wing, and not drop it. "Because you
only get one. There will be no second."

61

Talina crouched on the thick roots; she could feel her quetzals going stiff. If they'd been real, they'd have turned yellow and black. Frozen in terror, the beasts would have immediately camouflaged themselves. Their natural response when it came to a predator. That they figuratively did so—went dormant and camouflaged in her mind—left Talina singularly focused as she stared through the gloom. The remains of the marines' crushed armor were just visible in the lacery of roots between the trees.

"Okay," Muldare said in a hoarse whisper. "There's two helmets, smashed. I see a carapace, a couple of thigh pieces. That's a shoulder with its servo over there. And there's no telling what's under those humps of roots. Why the fuck do I think it's more armor?"

"That's armor, all right," Valdez said. "But where did the bodies go?"

"Eaten," Dek muttered from where he crouched beside Talina. He pointed. "And there, off to the side, sticking out of the roots? That's a scimitar blade. I've seen them up close. They're made out of some kind of tough polymer, almost indestructible."

"And there's the broken shell from one of the land tanks," Briah pointed. "Like it's been eaten out."

Talina nodded, her acute vision picking out patterns in the thick carpet of interwoven roots. A lot of lumps. And the smell of it. Yes, old human blood. But there was more, a medley of strange scents. She'd never seen such a collection of . . . Wait. She half rose, peered.

"I have to do something," she said, heart beginning to pound. "I think that's a skull over there. It's kind of covered by roots, but I need to go take a look."

"Are you crazy?" Dek asked. "Whatever killed those marines, left all these bits and pieces—"

"Dek," she said, turning to meet his gaze, "I think I can figure this out. I'll be all right."

The quetzal molecules cowering in her blood didn't think so.

"Trust me," she said, crouching and hopping down root by root. To Briah, she said, "Keep an eye up above. You see movement, yell. But, whatever you do, don't shoot."

"Tal," Briah told her, "there's times you really worry me."

"Yeah? You should see it from my side." Then she was down, setting foot on the slowly writhing root mat. Keeping low, every sense singing with tension, she crept out, trying to keep her pressure even on the slowly stirring roots. At the first hump, she bent, using her knife to dig an armored knee joint and its servo free.

Then, as the roots wiggled, she hurried to the next, but to her surprise, when she cut the thing loose, it was a fractured piece of a scimitar tooth. The next hump was a football-sized skull from some creature she'd never seen. And now, down so close, she could tell the entire forest floor was a mass of humped refuse. The amount of it astounded her.

Then she recognized the rifle butt. Carefully she peeled the rhizomes back, got a grip on the stock, and worked it free from the clinging roots.

"Goddamn it!" Briah cried from where she hunkered on the root tangle. "Fired?"

"Nope," Talina slung it over her shoulder, next to her own. "Safety's still on."

"They never knew what hit them," Valdez said bitterly.

Talina checked the section of carapace armor sticking out of the mass, though a fine weave of roots had laced themselves over the surface. "Says Corporal Xing on the stenciled ID," Talina called.

"Fuck!" Briah snapped.

Talina kept glancing from side to side, keeping low as she carefully made her way to the land tank, seeing how the creature's hard shell had been smashed from both sides. The cloying odor of decomposition tickled her nose. The inside of the shell was crawling with invertebrates who made a sort of high-pitching singing when she got too close.

Talina found the next rifle beside one of the smashed helmets, struggled to pull it free, but too many thick roots had a firm grasp on the weapon. She did get enough of a look to call, "This one's been fired."

"That tells us that whatever happened, it went down here. Come on, Tal," Briah called. "Get back. We've got what we need to know."

Talina took a deep breath. Stood fully upright and stared up, overhead.

If I'm right, there should be a . . .

It came as a blur from both sides. Just the shimmering of the branches at the edge of her vision. Closing in from the right and left . . .

Talina flipped her body—all of her strength galvanized—as she pitched herself forward, landed flat on the roots. Felt them twisting and wiggling at the impact.

As she did, a deafening *bang!* sounded; she felt the hard puff of air. And then she was scrambling on all fours, scampering on the now-excited roots.

For the moment, all she could think of was to get away. Out of the range of those deadly tentacles. Glancing up, it was to see eyes. Three of them, peering down from above. They might have been floating against the background of branches, vines, and diffused light.

She knew those eyes, had looked into their like before. Known this same terror. This was death.

She heard shots, screamed, "*Don't fucking shoot!*" And, as she got a second lungful, "Hold your fire!"

Then she was up, running. Beating feet across the mounds of slippery roots and whatever they were covering. She saw the skull— just a glimpse as she went by. A human, roots like veins wrapping around the cranial vault, weaving their way into the eye sockets, in and out of the nasal sinus, slipping around the teeth and into the foramen magnum.

Then she raced full bore for the high tangle of roots, where Briah and Dek were gesturing to Valdez to get her butt over the top and away. Talina hit the lowest root at a dead run; she barely hesitated, powered by terror, as she pounded her way up, root by twisting root.

I t was the roots. The motherfucking roots. That was the worst part. They wanted to roll underfoot, squirm when Falise put her weight full on whichever foot.

And then there was the heat and humidity.

But the thirst really made her crazy.

Her shoulders ached like they were being pulled out of joint. The knot of pain in her hands—where they gripped the poorly shaped triangular handles—almost brought tears to her eyes. And worst of all, because of the litter, she couldn't see where she was putting her feet.

Which meant she stumbled.

And that excited the roots. Made them squirm more.

Which meant that she staggered, fighting for balance. Felt her strength sapping, her lungs sucking for breath. The telltale burn in her muscles told her that she didn't have much left.

And all around, the harmonics of the chime mocked her, added to her physical and mental misery. The heat made it seem she was working out in a sauna. Several times, tears of pain and frustration broke free to trickle down her cheeks. Lost water, that, along with the sweat that leaked from her hairline, broke out on her back, and sent little beads tickling along her sides, added to her maddening thirst. Never in her life had Falise been this thirsty, this hot, or had her muscles, bones, and joints hurt like this.

They'd made what? Two hundred meters? Was that all?

She considered quitting, dropping her end of the litter. Letting Soukup fall into the fucking roots. Who the hell cared if he died there? Wasn't any skin off her hide. She could go back and write whatever report she wanted once *Turalon* was out of orbit. Bogarten was on his way to the airtruck. What was left of the Four wouldn't leave Soukup. The roots would get them, too.

And if what Kylee said was true, entombed, devoured, there would be no body. No evidence.

Except Kylee.

Prudence suggested that after leaving Soukup to his fate—and Kylee was leading the way up the ridge—Falise could swing her rifle around on its sling the way Kylee had showed her. Before the half-breed quetzal freak had a clue, Falise could blow a high-velocity round through her back. Didn't matter how much TriNA was bubbling in the girl's blood. Nothing survived that kind of terminal ballistic effect.

Falise staggered sideways, almost fell, her breath rasping in her throat. Barely caught herself and jerked her foot out of the tightening knot of roots.

"Gotta rest," Falise pleaded. "Kylee . . . ?"

"Yeah, got it, Falise," the girl called. "Right up ahead. See the tangle? That thick root on the top. It's too big to grab us." A pause. "Just make it that far."

Falise tried to swallow down her dry throat. A simple swallow of water. She'd give Dek's fucking half metric ton of rhodium for a drink of water. Hell, she'd give a ton of it for a couple of liters, a soft couch, and a bowl of Inga's chili.

She barely made it, slipping, staggering up the tangle. Her legs were shaking, her arms like liquid fire. Kylee positioned the litter, sort of balanced on the top root. Then she looked back, met Falise's dull eyes, and damned if the kid didn't smile.

"You're doing just fine, Falise." Something about the way Kylee said it carried weight.

"Glad you think so." Falise pushed her trembling body as far as the highest thick root, found a seat on the waxy bark, careful to rest her shaking feet on the next thigh-thick root below.

"Hey, you Four. Three, whatever. Get up here. You don't just stop!" Kylee barked, gesturing.

Falise tossed a weary glance over her shoulder, frightened at how the two men and woman barely managed to pull their feet free from the writhing mass. Like nothing that day, the sight of those seeking tendrils made it all real. That fast?

But, woodenly, without any apparent concern, the IG's aides clambered up the tangle of roots. And, reaching the top, stopped to fix their eyes on Soukup. For a moment, Falise wondered if he was dead, but then saw the shallow rising and falling of his chest.

Something screamed in the chabacho overhead and was choked off. Like a death squeal. Falise, despite her fatigue, jumped at the sound.

Kylee was looking around, her eyes scanning the forest, the root mat, the hanging vines and low branches ahead. The hard part was that the climb before them was almost a forty-degree incline. "Notice how the light's going? It's getting dark. We're almost out of time, and we're halfway there."

"How can I . . . I mean, I don't have the strength. Kylee? I can't. I'll drop Soukup halfway to the top. Let alone make it up that last steep part."

Kylee glanced back, studied the roots Falise slumped on. Made sure the Four weren't getting entangled. "It flattens out again up top. Can you get the litter up there? Maybe drag it?"

"What about Soukup?" God, was Kylee, too, thinking about leaving the man to his fate?

Kylee gave her a conspiratorial squint. "He's gonna squeal like a bloody bastard, but if it don't kill him, he'll still be alive."

"Huh? That doesn't . . ." She didn't finish as Kylee bent down, grabbed Soukup by his official jacket, and lifted.

And yes, he screamed as if he were being gutted. Kylee settled the man over her shoulders, then picked her way down the root tangle, one careful step at a time.

"Don't forget the litter, Falise. And keep the robot people from doing anything stupid."

It took Falise two tries to stagger to her feet, catch her balance on the now shifting mass of roots, and grab hold of the litter handles. Only then did she start down the other side. The "robot people" were already on the move, following along behind Kylee Simonov and the panting and whimpering load she carried.

Falise wasn't really watching, being more concerned with her footing, with her failing strength. But, by chance, she happened to glance up as the Second, staggering and stumbling on the wiggling roots, went reeling sideways.

The tooth flower. That's what the thing was. It shot a pod down like a blur. Brilliant colors flared inside as it clamped around the Second's right shoulder. The bald man's eyes popped wide, his mouth open to expose a perfect arc of teeth. Then he screamed as the long needlelike spines lining the pod's rim drove deep into his flesh. The way the plant went about reeling the kicking man into the air looked effortless.

The Second was still screaming when another pod clamped tightly on his left shoulder and a third on his hips. Impossibly, the long spines had to have driven clear through the man's pelvic bones given how deep they were.

"What happened?" Kylee called from where she was struggling up the steepest part of the slope.

"Go!" Falise cried. "Just go! It's too late."

She didn't remember dropping the litter. Didn't remember much of anything as she scrambled past the First where he stood looking at the Second's struggling body.

For Falise, the only thing that mattered was the airtruck. And lifting off. Getting away.

When she reached the top, she was blinking away tears, gasping for breath.

"Hey!" Kylee's harsh voice snapped. "Get your shit together!"

Falise turned, sucking for air, wanting to be sick. "Tooth flower. Got the Second. Just . . . just snapped shut and hauled him up into the air."

Kylee, sweat on her brow, damp on her cheeks, nodded. "Yeah, I get it. Where's the litter?"

"Back . . . back . . . I . . ."

"Fuck." Kylee swallowed hard, her throat working, her shoulders bent under the load. "Well, don't just stand there like a fart-sucking idiot, Falise! Check your feet."

When Falise looked down it was to see little tendrils of roots slipping up along her quetzal-hide boots, fingering their way up along the curve of her toes.

"Just get me the hell out of here!" she cried, yanking free.

"Calm down." Kylee's voice carried a soothing note as the girl started off across the flat, the IG's weight draped over her shoulders. "Think, Falise: Panic is stupid. Stupid is dead, and that's a stand of brown caps off to your left. Keep the last two robots out of it."

Yes. Think. Don't be stupid.

Brown caps? That's right. The knee-high standing tube-like things poking up from the thick root mat. Deadly.

And they were only halfway there?

63

"Forget quiet, forget careful," Talina ordered as she and the rest leaped and jumped down the back side of the thick web of roots. "Run! Now."

"What *was* that?" Valdez practically cried as she turned, heading across the flat at a run.

"What the hell were you thinking?" Dek bellowed as he ran full out at Talina's side. "You *trying* to get yourself killed? You knew what that was, didn't you?"

"Had to be sure." She was throwing glances over her shoulder, looking up.

"Treetop terror, wasn't it?" Muldare asked, slowing as they reached the thick netting of roots where the barb tentacle had ambushed them.

"Something like it," Talina agreed, pulling her knife, trying to balance both of the rifles on her back as she tackled the web-work of fat roots. "Different though. The southern version, I guess."

"That's why it didn't smell the same," Dek agreed. "This is nothing our quetzals have ever encountered." He, too, was throwing creep-freaked glances up overhead.

"It didn't have a spiked tentacle," Briah added, following in Valdez's footsteps as she leaped from root to root, her armor whining as the servos powered each step.

"It had two. Blunt-ended," Dek said. "For that moment after they slammed together, the camouflage dropped. Hell of an adaptation. Sit up there in the tree, wait for scimitars, land tanks, and what have you, to come inspect the carrion down below, and wham. Smash them, lift them up, and drop the leftovers to lure in another victim."

"Why the hell did you stop me from shooting it?" Valdez asked.

"With the boom tubes, we could have blown that shit-licking bastard right out of the trees."

"Yeah, we could have," Talina told her. "And maybe . . . *maybe* Dek and I might have made it back to the pad. You and Briah? Despite your armor? You can't move fast enough."

"For what? That *thing* would be lying on the forest floor with big fucking gaping holes blown in it."

"Look behind us," Talina told her. "Back at the roots."

Valdez tossed a glance back over her shoulder. "Screw vacuum! The fucking roots have gone apeshit!"

"Yeah," Dek told her. "Now magnify that by about a thousand times. The entire forest goes bonkers. You should see it from the air."

"Fuck the air," Talina told him. "Nothing, ever, in our entire lives, had Kylee and me as scared as we were trying to outrun that last attempt at killing a treetop terror. Valdez, pay attention here. But for sheer stupid blind luck, we barely—and I mean *barely*—made it out alive. Here, in this forest, unknown as it is? Taking that chance would be stupid."

"And what's stupid?" Briah asked, leaping down off the roots and pelting across the flat.

"Stupid's dead," Valdez snapped. "Then why'd we bring the boom tubes?"

"Because if we'd been after a scimitar, or some big hulking land-lubbing creature," Dek told her, "you and Briah could have blown the sucker in two. We could have backed off, and the roots would have delighted as they chowed down. Blow a hole in the branches up top? The shit hits the fan."

"So, what does it mean?" Valdez asked. "That thing just gets away with killing Xing, Radagan, and Cantos?"

"Naw, we'll get it," Muldare told her.

But Talina could hear the frustration in her voice. They hadn't gotten the last one that had killed their people. Wounded it, yes, but they hadn't seen its corpse.

She barely heard Dek, the words mouthed under his panting breath as he ran. "Nothing in life's fair."

That's when Talina tossed a glance over her shoulder. In the dying light, she could see the high branches. See something moving up there. Something that bent branches, shifted them, and blurred their image as it passed between her and the upper story.

They had to get out of the deep forest. Onto the shallow soils.

"People!" Talina cried. "It's following us! Move it! Or we're dying next!"

"Tell me you've got a plan, Tal!" Muldare called over her shoulder.

"Yeah," Talina muttered under her breath. "I wish I did." Then, at the top of her lungs, she yelled, *"Run!"*

64

Dusk was falling. The Inspector General's Four were down to One. Only the Recorder was left. For Kylee, the trip had become a desperate race. One she was losing. Not to mention that quetzal strength or not, her body was flagging in the unrelenting heat and dehydration.

They had lost the Third when she had stepped mindlessly into a hole in a knot of roots she had tried to climb over. Her leg had plunged in all the way to the crotch. When she'd tried to pull it out, nothing had happened. Her only words were uttered in a dispassionate monotone. "Help here."

By the time Kylee had staggered back and she and Falise had tried to pull the woman out, tendrils were already winding around the woman's free foot, awkwardly placed as it was. The Third kept mechanically trying to rock to the side in the effort to free her foot. Didn't matter that she made no progress. She kept repeating, mumbling, "Help here."

"Kylee, go," Falise had said. "I've got this."

Turning, reeling for balance on the undulating roots, Kylee resettled Soukup on her shoulders, blinked the sweat from her eyes, and started up the slope. She didn't look back. Didn't want to know.

Probably should have been worried about Falise, but by then her leg muscles were burning, her thoughts muddled. Quetzal visions, hallucinations of old hunts, distant memories of exhaustion and thirst kept trickling into her brain. Fooling with her vision.

The ache in her back, Soukup's constant moaning and whimpering, not to mention how hot the IG was, just added to her misery. And they had what? Another two hundred meters to go?

As she went, so, too, did the First. Like a biomachine, the gray-suited man followed along behind. His hazel gaze stayed fixed on Kylee and her mewling burden. The guy never looked at his feet.

Couldn't seem to grasp that giving thought to where he'd step
might make his travel easier.

Flute? Where the hell are you?

The question had no more than formed when the quetzal
emerged from the shadows, his collar flaring wide, rolling patters of
color that informed her that he'd made it.

"Bogarten's safe?" she rasped through her dry throat, gasping for
breath.

Flute flashed an almost neon orange, twittering and hooting
from his vents.

Kylee blinked, staggered; memories of a heat-prostrate quetzal,
collapsing, dying on a hot hard pan filled her. She fought for balance, tripped over a root, and almost dropped Soukup.

Lost the world for a moment, only to have the load lifted from
her shoulders. As it shifted and vanished, she almost toppled. Fought
for clarity and fixed on Flute.

The quetzal had the suffering Soukup by the jacket. The quetzal's
serrated teeth were fixed in the fabric, and the forearms supported
the rest of the man's weight.

The images for *Gone to sky fly. Come back for you.* rolled across the
quetzal's hide, and he hooted, before the interrogative of yellow,
green, and pink asked, *Okay?* Followed by orange for *Yes?*

"Yeah, go," Kylee told him. "Try not to kill him on the way."

Flute made a flatulent sound that Kylee knew mocked a fart,
whirled, and trotted away in the growing gloom.

Kylee resettled her rifle, feeling cool air where Soukup's hot body
had been pooling her sweat. She felt a ton lighter as she sidestepped
on the roots.

To her amazement, the First went trotting headlong after Flute,
stumbling and waving his arms for balance as he did.

"Hey! Come back here! You, First. You're gonna get yourself . . ."
He vanished behind a screen of trees, roots, and hanging vines. ". . .
killed."

"Who?" Falise asked, dragging herself up the hill, one weary foot
at a time.

Kylee got a good look at her. Hadn't really had a chance while plodding under Soukup's extra weight. The woman's streaked hair hung in a damp mass that fell down her back and was tangled with the slung rifle. Her nut-brown skin shone from sweat, and her fabric shirt clung like a second skin. The floppy-brimmed quetzal hat would have been long gone, but for hanging by its strap. The woman's face would have made a photographer's study in exhaustion and defeat. The fire that had once burned in those emerald eyes might be called lusterless and cold.

"Where's Soukup? What did you do with him?" Falise asked woodenly.

"Flute took him." Kylee matched steps with Falise, plodding up the incline. "Bet he'll have him at the airtruck in a matter of minutes. That fool First went running off after him. I tried to call him back but—"

"He can't help it." Falise wiped a blood-spattered sleeve over her forehead. "They're programmed that way. His only goal is to record what the IG sees, hears, experiences. When his implants are full, he would download it to the monitor, who would share the record with the analyst. Don't have a clue what's going to happen with the rest of them dead. Maybe the First's system will just stop when it can hold no more data." Falise made a defeated, tossing-away gesture with a red-stained hand. "They're not designed for conditions like these."

No sense asking how Falise had dealt with the trapped Third. Given the fresh blood, she suspected that Dek's sister had found yet another use for that knife she'd once thought too big to be practical.

"Shit," Falise muttered as she tripped over a high root. "I can barely see. How much farther?"

"Fifteen minutes? Maybe less. Listen, I have night vision. Part of my spooky alien eyes. You follow right behind me. I'll talk you through the dangerous parts. We're going to the left. You remember where we bypassed the bem with . . ."

She heard the distinctive whimpers coming from ahead, there, off to the right of the aquajade tree. Could smell the distinctive vinegar smell.

"Shit."

"What's wrong?" Falise was staring around with that gaping look of a human trying to peer through darkness.

"I guess I know where our missing First is. Ran right into that bem." She reached out. "Here. Take my hand. We've got to hurry."

Keeping a tight grip on Falise's hand, Kylee led the way, talking the woman through the tough parts, keeping her from disaster.

It went on that way for what? Ten minutes?

Through it all, Falise—stumbling and fatigue-stupid—panting for breath, voice cracking with thirst, followed with one clumsy step after another.

Gut it out, Kylee told herself, praying that the woman wouldn't collapse, fold into a heap like she had that night on the avenue in Port Authority.

And then, just as Kylee figured it would never end, Flute came trotting out of the night, his collar flaring in the IR, communicating that he'd delivered Soukup to the "sky fly," as he called the airtruck.

He let out a happy chortle through his vents.

"Relax," Kylee told Falise as the woman's grip tightened. "You can't see him in the dark, but Flute's back."

"How far?" the spent woman asked.

"So, except for falling into the roots, we're made. Five minutes."

It was probably more like four. It was that last climb. The one that necessitated scrambling up the blocks of basalt. Kylee was wondering if she'd need to carry the tottering Falise, or perhaps have Flute pluck her up by the clothes and . . .

The sound was unmistakable. The fans were spinning up on the airtruck.

"What the hell?" Kylee cried.

She didn't know where she found the strength; she manhandled Falise up the rocks, Flute leaping up behind her. Then, as she crested the outcrop, the downwash almost knocked her off her feet.

"Bogarten!" she bellowed through her too-dry throat. "Damn you! Set it down! We're here, you stupid slug fucker! Set it down!"

She let loose of Falise, running forward, waving, blasted by the grit blown out as the airtruck rose, turned, and headed off to the east.

For the moment—Flute standing at her side, interrogatives running across his hide—all she could do was watch the vehicle's outline as it vanished into the night.

"Toilet-sucking piece of shit!" Kylee cried one last time.

"What the fuck?" Falise rasped, dropping onto the basalt. "They just left us?"

"Yeah," Kylee ran a sleeve over her dry lips. "Shit fuckers."

"What's that mean?" Falise looked up with hollow eyes.

"It means they left us to die"

65

The sun was dropping behind the screen of trees that marked the start of deep forest on the horizon. Long shadows were extending across Southern Diggings. A breeze—blowing in from the sea—carried the scents of salt and sand. Kalico sat with her butt on a duraplast container, her back hunched, chin propped on her palms as she stared off at the forest just beyond the pad. Overhead, blue fliers—some sort of distant cousins to the scarlet fliers she was used to—swooped and cavorted as they chased buzzing invertebrates. She could hear the crunch when they caught one low overhead.

Two of the armored marines, Privates Zhao Chin and Ralph Smith, stood just behind her, rifles at port arms, boom tubes—the new standard-issue gear for Southern Diggings—hanging from slings. God knew what might come charging out of the forest to race up and kill every living thing on the compound.

Behind her, the grinding clank made by the drills could be heard as they marched their way across the pad making hole-for-shot charges of magtex. With the arrival of *Turalon*, Kalico had wanted to rush a shipment into orbit. Would have enjoyed the satisfaction of sending a first load of rare earth metals back to Solar System with *Turalon*'s return.

Now, with her position uncertain—with even the future of Southern Diggings questionable—she wondered if it wasn't just delusional to even try.

Were she to look over her shoulder, she'd see a quarter-finished fence and a line of tall posts stretching along the northern edge of the pad. Depending on what Talina and Dek discovered down south, well, there might be no purpose in trying to finish the barrier.

I will not see these people eaten, no matter what the value of the metals and elements we're sitting on.

W. MICHAEL GEAR

Soukup could damned well relieve her. Let another Supervisor pay for the wealth with the blood, lives, and dreams of his workers.

Something made a screeching down in the forest. It was followed by a change in the chime, a bass-harmony that almost became a melody, only to fail.

Like her aspirations for Southern Diggings?

What kind of creature could crush marine armor like that? And after the lobster thing the Maritime Unit had encountered, should she be surprised?

She heard the crunching of gravel, turned, and looked up as Raya Turnienko walked down, arms crossed, expression thoughtful.

"Mind if I join you?" Raya asked.

"Have a seat," Kalico shifted on the crate to make room, propping elbows on her knees. "How's Aberash?"

"She's stabilized but in critical condition. I've got the blood drained from her subdural hematoma, set most of the broken bones. Assanti's keeping an eye on her. If she doesn't take a dive in the next couple of hours, I'd suggest shipping her up to *Turalon*'s med bay. That's her best chance."

"Do it." Kalico returned her gaze to the forest.

"Anything from Tal?" Raya indicated the forest.

"Heard a burst of gunfire. Short. Maybe six or seven rounds. Then nothing."

"Could be anything." Raya rubbed her slim shins, squinted eyes fixed on the forest. "Might have shot a sidewinder, blown away some predatory vine. Given it was just a burst, I wouldn't rate it too highly." She smiled. "You've heard the gunfire when they find a quetzal? You'd think it was a small war."

"That's what I keep telling myself." A beat. "And then I tell myself other things. Ask other questions."

Raya gave her a sidelong inspection. "You remember that first time we met? In your office in PA? You were looking for any excuse to rid yourself of Talina Perez. And now, all these years later, here you sit, terrified that she might not come walking out of that forest. Pain in the ass that she is."

"Yeah. Pain in the ass," Kalico muttered. "Didn't she overpower you, strap you to your own bed once?"

"Never been so humiliated in my entire life." Raya sighed. "My call at the time was that she was headed off to the bush in an attempt at suicide. That she was determined to let Donovan kill her."

"She just came back stronger." But what about this time? Whatever was out there had killed three armored marines and severely wounded a fourth. "I should never have let her, Dek, and Briah go. Hell, Raya, if this goes south, if something happens . . ."

"Stop it."

"Stop what?"

"Torturing yourself. Tal and Dek know what they're doing. Beyond that, they know what's at stake. You haven't been yourself since that IG landed. You're second guessing yourself, suddenly insecure in a way I've never seen."

"Raya, I played the Corporate game and played it fucking well. That's how I got here, you'll recall." She glanced at the doctor. "Soukup *will* find a reason to dismiss me. Assuming he's still alive. When I talked to Two Spot a half hour ago, there was still no word from the crash site. And, if the IG's dead, I've got a reprieve, but only for as long as it takes for *Turalon* to transition to Solar System and whatever ship they dispatch to make it back."

"That's what? Four years for a turnaround?" Raya laughed. "On Donovan, that's like, what? An eternity? Odds are better that you'll be eaten by a quetzal first."

"Gotta love an optimist." Kalico shook her head. "I'm not that lucky."

"Which one would Soukup appoint?" Raya frowned. "And, more to the point, who'd listen to this interim Supervisor? This isn't the same colony that Clemenceau tried to intimidate. It's not even the same one you encountered that long-ago day when you walked off the shuttle in that ridiculous outfit."

"Let's see, after Bartolome's death, Soukup's running out of choices, so I'd say Falise Taglioni has the best chance. She's out there in the bush with Kylee saving Soukup's butt. But never count Cinque out."

"Well, if it's Falise, Dek will probably speak sense to the lady. Cinque? With him, I suspect that some Wild One will get crosswise with him and blow a hole through him." A beat. "Not even Tamarland Benteen, with all his tricks, lasted more than a couple of weeks."

"Doesn't save us in the end," Kalico told her. "There will be a day when The Corporation lands here with . . ."

Kalico saw the flash. A blink of yellow-orange in the treetops down the slope. The detonation made Kalico jump. It clapped out over the forest, a wave of sound rolling away through the trees. More flickers of burning orange. Treetops torn, bits of detritus flying high.

Then a series of detonations—like deafening crackles—sent shockwaves through her. All of it followed by a rattling of automatic fire. More concussions carried on the night, the chime having gone still. Blue fliers and a haze of invertebrates rose from the forest, flying outward, fleeing.

Kalico was on her feet, staring, her heart hammering. She could see the tops of the trees thrashing, the ripples of it rolling out over the forest to the south.

Again, another series of rapid concussions, the sound of it like a battlefield barrage.

"That's about it," Ralph Smith, the marine, said from behind her. "That's a full load. Enough detonations to exhaust both of their boom tubes."

And down in the trees, the rifles kept firing, the chatter unending. Had to be magazine after magazine, including the occasional louder boom that she knew was Dek's high-powered hunting rifle.

The ever-spreading ripple from excited trees kept expanding out like a tsunami, leaving thrashing trees in its wake.

66

In the wake of the explosions—and as Capella dropped behind the distant tree line and shadows fell across the pad at Southern Diggings—Kalico told the two marines, "We're going down there. Weapons hot, on safety. I want those boom tubes charged."

"Ma'am?" Chin frowned. "That's . . . I mean . . ."

Kalico stepped up to him. "Did you hear me, marine? Those are our people down there. Now, button up your yap, get your shit wired, and let's go."

"You sure this is a good idea?" Raya Turnienko asked from where she stood, looking down at the violently thrashing forest. They could hear the trees, the cracking of splintered wood, the lashing and snapping branches. The chime had gone berserk. Occasional hoots, calls, and screeches rose as the wildlife panicked and fled. Several flocks of blue fliers and a horde of invertebrates darkened the air above the treetops.

"Damn straight, Raya. That's Tal, Dek, and Briah." Kalico started down the hill, pulling her pistol from her belt. "Hope we're not looking at more casualties. Last thing I want is for you to have a busy night."

Raya called after her, "You're crazy! And you thought I was being silly when I said that Soukup and The Corporation were the least of your problems? How's being dead suit you?"

Kalico gave her a buzz-off gesture with her fingers. Checked to see that the marines were still behind her. They'd locked their helmets down, had their rifles up, looked ready for action.

"So, Kalico, what are you going to do if you stumble onto a mess of broken bodies?"

If she could get them out of the roots, she'd order the marines to evacuate the worst off. God pray it wasn't Talina or Dek; they hadn't been armored. But, shit on a shoe, who knew? Who'd have thought anything on the planet could pound a marine's armor the way Aberash's had been crushed?

And what would she do if they were dead down there?

"Fucking nuke this forest for twenty kilometers in any direction," she vowed.

Slipping past the vines and stepping under the first of the trees, it was to enter a world of movement. The first premonition that maybe this wasn't her best idea ever began to fester in her gut. She could barely see in the dim light and reached into her belt pouch for the small flashlight she carried. She flicked it on, and the beam illuminated a forest floor alive with squirming roots. Overhead, the branches were slapping this way and that. The chime sounded crazy.

"Ma'am? You sure about this?" Smith asked.

Kalico ground her teeth, jerked a nod, and started across the agitated roots.

Whatever had gone down, it had sparked a wave of chaos that had every tree jiggling and upset. She moved fast, surprised that, disturbed as the roots were, and with the vines and branches flipping and waving, they seemed to ignore her. That rubbery feel underfoot, however, was even more disconcerting than usual.

She did her best to stay out of reach of the gyrating vines, so many of them new, undoubtedly deadly. Several whipped her way so quickly, she couldn't dodge. But for whatever reason—probably too distracted by the shaking and jerking—they didn't attack.

Kalico raised her cupped hands, calling, "Tal! Dek! You there?"

Yeah, right, as if that could be heard over the raucous warbling of the chime and the rasping and clattering of the leaves.

The only thing that encouraged her was that this portion of the forest, sitting on shallow soil atop bedrock, wasn't covered with those giant trees like down below. The pitching of the roots, therefore, didn't knock a person off his or her feet. Only left her careening for balance. More than once, however, she barely avoided getting a foot trapped. The marines had their own trouble, heavy as they were in their armor. Kalico could hear their cursing as they ripped their armored feet loose from the grasping roots.

"Supervisor?" Chin called. "This is getting worse. Do you really think going on is a wise move?"

No sooner had he said it than a crackling sounded. Too loud. Too close. Kalico danced sideways as the footing shifted under her feet. With a tearing from above, one of the taller trees—something with big triangular leaves—tilted, began to . . .

Grabbed from behind, Kalico was lifted off her feet, jerked backward with enough force to snap her joints. Stunned, she watched as the tree smashed down in the space she'd just occupied. Then she was lowered, feet landing in the roots.

"Sorry, Supervisor." Chin kept a hand wound in her shirt and cape. "Figured you'd rather be manhandled than end up lying under that thing."

"Yeah, I guess I would. Thanks."

"I say we call it," Smith said, shifting like a dancer to keep his feet from getting entangled. "I know, ma'am. Valdez is down there, too. She's a friend. But taking more chances? Do we want you dead down there with them?"

"No," Kalico said wearily. "Turn me loose, Private. It's just that I've been where they are: lost, people dying around me. And Talina and Dek came for me. We do that here. Doesn't matter who it is. If there's a chance, even a slim one, we don't leave our people. You get that?"

As she plodded wearily back up the slope, she kept shooting her flashlight down into the growing gloom, searching among the swaying boles, the waving vines. The roots were still shifting and squirming, but the intensity was fading.

Chin and Smith were glancing uneasily at each other. Then Chin said, "Yeah, Supervisor. We get what you're saying."

Smith told her. "Sarge told us how it is with you people. Thought it was weird how Sarge kept calling you Kalico. Insisting you weren't just a Supervisor. We thought maybe that was just an order coming down the chain of command: refer to the Supervisor in these terms. Or else. Like back in Solar System. Hell, for all we knew, Sarge was your lover or something."

"Sarge?" Kalico asked, still shooting her flashlight beam down into the trees.

"That's sort of what we call Private Muldare." Chin was grinning behind his faceplate. "Didn't matter that she was a private giving us orders, even Corporal Xing, he called her Sarge."

"Sarge?" Kalico mused. "Briah would like that."

"Yes, ma'am." Chin made it sound suggestive.

"Private, spill it."

"Pardon me, Supervisor, ma'am?"

Still searching the forest, she sighed. "People stay alive on Donovan by working together. Yeah, I'm a Board Supervisor, and you're two marine privates. But out here, in the dark, we're all the same. Three human beings praying that our friends are still alive. So, spill it."

"Can a Board Supervisor promote a marine?" Chin asked.

Kalico flashed her light toward movement. Thought she saw something glint in the trees; she hesitated, sidestepping. There was so much movement. Especially where the freshly felled tree was thrashing and lashing with its branches. "I guess. I'd have to check my implants for the exact regs."

"Maybe Muldare ought to be a sergeant," Smith said, as if to himself. "Our people? We'd take her orders any day of the week."

Kalico smiled. Well, even if this turned out to be one of the worst days of her life, at least there was that.

Give it up, Kalico. They're not coming, and you can't get to them.

"Well," she told herself, "whatever went down out there, by God, they gave it a hell of a fight." The worst part was that by tomorrow, the roots would have taken them, though some of Briah's or Valdez's armor might be left.

"Never seen such a concentration of DRRDD fire," Chin agreed. "That would have taken out a main battle tank."

"Sure would have," Smith agreed. "Come on, ma'am. We'll try it again in the morning. Sarge told us the trees settle down after a while. Whatever's left, we'll bring them home."

Kalico took one last breath, remembering the crackling detonations. Yep. One hell of a fight.

She nodded, shining her light on the footing ahead, and started back up the slope.

"*Hey!*" The voice was augmented to carry over the forest noise. Had to come through a helmet speaker. "You mind shooting that light back down here? Keeps us from stepping on the bugs."

Kalico whirled, splashing the slope in light. Another glint. This time she could make out the shine from armor, Briah Muldare in the lead. And, yes, beside her came Talina, a hand up against the flashlight's glare.

There they were, all four. Tal and Dek, plodding wearily as they climbed, rifles held by the barrels and balanced over their shoulders like shovels after a hard day's work. And Valdez, her faceplate open, armor stained, wore a grim expression. She, too, carried her boom tube over her shoulder, two rifles slung at her back.

"So, you're alive?" Kalico called.

"Gotta be," Dek yelled back. "The dead don't blow brown stuff into the seat of their trousers like I just did."

Tal reached out with a fist and slugged him playfully in the shoulder as she shook her head.

Kalico started forward and threw her arms around Talina's shoulders. "You scared the shit out of me."

Chin and Smith were clasping Valdez close, talking soldier trash.

Kalico released Tal, slapped Muldare on the armor, then hugged Dek.

Treading on the rolling roots, she asked, "So, what's the verdict? Do I shut Southern Diggings down? Is this something we can handle? And that fireworks show? You turned half the forest upside down."

"Got it," Talina told her, her large eyes squinted. "Some kind of southern species of treetop terror. Take you down in the morning if you want to see what's left. Valdez and Briah got video of it. Three tentacles. The first two have thick keratin–like knobs on the end. Maybe weigh a couple hundred pounds each. Uses them to crack the shells on the local predators like land tanks and scimitars. That's what got the marines."

Dek laid a hand on Kalico's shoulder. "It needs the treetops. You don't have anywhere it can perch to threaten Southern Diggings."

"Well, that's . . ."

Kalico's earbud crackled, Two Spot's voice announcing, "*Supervisor? Just got a call from Bogarten. He's got Board Inspector General Soukup. They're on the way in. Just thought you deserved a heads up.*"

"Roger that, Two Spot. Thanks."

"*And Supervisor, you should know. Bogarten added something. Really soft. Like, it was under his breath. Sounded like, 'Tell Kalico to get her butt back to PA.' Then he signed off. And, Supervisor? Fenn didn't sound like he was any kind of happy.*"

67

F alise wondered at the impossible insanity that she now had to accept as reality. Her dreams had been filled with terror, with bleeding and broken bodies, images of the dead dancing around inside the wreckage of the shuttle that she knew lay just down the ridge.

More amazing, as she came awake, her butt might be aching on the bare stone, but the rest of her was cushioned against Flute's soft belly. Her sleep had been lulled through the night by the reassuring gurgles of his digestive system. Adding to the absurdity, she was snuggled against Kylee Simonov, half spooned with the same intimacy as if they were lovers.

She didn't even like the foul-mouthed brat.

Or did she?

Pondering the question, she scanned the forest, hearing the endless chime, so different in the night.

The last two days had been like a harrowing disaster. Reality turned upside down, inside out, and then shattered. Were she to lift her right hand, it would be to see the Third's dried and flaking blood. She'd been trained on how to cut a human being's throat. Trained was one thing. The act was something else. She hadn't been prepared for the hot spray of blood that blew out with each of the frantic Third's terrified exhalations.

Beat leaving her to be entombed and slowly strangled.

"Who am I?" Falise mouthed the words, eyes on the streak of light that marked the eastern horizon. From the elevation here, she could see the serrations of the Wind Range, a distant dark silhouette above the endless forest.

When it came to answering her question, she had no clue. The impulse would be to state emphatically that she was Falise Taglioni. Daughter of Claudio and Malissa. That her competence and dedication were the budding strength in her line after the shame brought on their side of the family by Derek. That she was the one chosen to ensure the family's access and influence when it came to Donovan's wealth.

That Falise Taglioni, however, had met with nothing but disaster from the moment she'd stepped down from *Turalon's* shuttle.

She glanced at the blonde head leaned against her shoulder. She'd never slept with a woman who wasn't a lover. This, too, was something new. And with it, the notion that this genetic freak of a girl—and the quetzal—were her only hope for survival.

Not victory.

Not success.

Survival.

Falise had been on the point of tears last night, figured she'd be dead of thirst by morning, when Kylee said, "Falise, you stay here with Flute. Don't set foot off the bedrock. Keep to bare stone. I'm off to get us something to drink."

And Kylee had. She'd returned sometime later bearing a young aquajade sapling. Had shown Falise how to use her knife to open one of the three veins in the trunk, and how to prop it so that water drained into her mouth.

"It's not a forever solution," Kylee had said. "The heavy metals will kill you in the end. In, oh, say, a couple of weeks. And heavy-metal toxicity is nothing nice when it comes to ways to die."

To her dismay, Falise's stomach let loose with a loud gurgle. Yeah, it was that empty.

It brought Kylee awake. The girl blinked, shifted, and raised her head, sniffing the morning air, laden with vanilla and cardamom scents from the forest. The chime was beginning to change.

Kylee sat up, rubbed her eyes. Then she slapped Flute on the belly, saying, "Better than a night spent at what's it? Three Spires?"

"That's a restaurant." Falise—crying out loud at the pain her in muscles—climbed to her feet. "Maybe you mean the Solar Elan? It might be the fanciest hotel in Transluna."

"Yep." Kylee leaped spryly to her feet.

The way she did made Falise want to slap her. God, every

pus-sucking joint in her body hurt. The feeling in her legs, arms, shoulders, and back was like every muscle had been pulled loose from its attachment and torn in two.

Flute rose, stretched, his head extended, muscular legs rippling as he raised his tail. Then he made a warbling sound that might have been the horn section from a small band through his tail vents. A plethora of colors streaming down his hide from just behind his wide frilly ruff.

"Yeah," Kylee told him. "Can you go find something to eat? I'll start a fire."

Flute made a chirping sound, patterns of prism-bright orange flowing across his hide. After another stretch, he trotted off up the hill, vanishing between the trees.

"What's next?" Falise asked. "We just going to wait on this rock for someone to come by?"

Kylee squinted her too-large blue eyes as she slung her rifle and stared around. Falise had to admit, there was something feral, capable, and damned attractive about the girl. Here, in the middle of wilderness where people had died within a stone's throw, she looked completely at ease. Almost exuded a calm purpose. A wild thing in its element.

She turned those hard blue eyes on Falise. "You don't leave someone in the bush like they did last night. On Donovan, that's a death sentence. Bogarten knows that. Why he'd—"

"It was Soukup," Falise said flatly. "It's the only explanation. He's an IG. His orders carry more weight than even a Supervisor's."

"Still, Bogarten—"

"You saw Soukup," Falise told her. "The man was half-crazy with pain. Terrified. And a quetzal carried him through a dark forest to the aircar. His Fourth, the strong one, had vanished in the night. His Second had been eaten by a tooth flower. His Third was . . . Well, he knew she was dead. Once Flute set him in that airtruck, Soukup was so panicked and crazed, he ordered Bogarten to get him the hell away."

"But, to leave someone—"

"Stop it." Falise turned, looking at the brightening sky to the east. "He's already back in PA. He'll tell someone to come back and get us."

"Stop it." Kylee mimicked in the same no-nonsense voice. "Step Allenovich, Talina, Shig, would have Soukup strung up by his balls for leaving us out here." She raised her voice. "No way he or Bogarten are telling. We're on our own."

"So, what do we do?"

Kylee pointed south. "It's about fifteen kicks to Tyson Station. We walk."

Falise blinked. "We barely made a single kilometer last night, and you might recall, it didn't work out so well."

"Talina and Cap are said to have made almost forty. And they didn't have a quetzal."

"You ever gone that far, across that much forest before?"

"Nope. Got to be a first time for anything, right?"

Falise took a deep breath, her gaze going back to the trees, hearing the howls, seeing the distant shapes of things flying up over the trees. Mobbers?

She'd been horrified at Kalico Aguila's scars.

"You and Flute. Sure. What are my chances, Kylee?"

The girl shrugged, re-hitching her rifle. "You don't remember well do you? I told you back in—"

"About ten percent."

Kylee gave her a sidelong glance. "Beats dying of thirst here on this rock, doesn't it?"

68

Shig Mosadek was standing at the gate when the airtruck appeared out of the west. Bogarten had already called in, explaining that they were flying on the last reserves of the vehicle's powerpack and could fall out of the sky at any moment.

The two marines at the gate were people Shig didn't know, Keeko Ituri and Sasna Firiiki, both women. Ituri was a tall African with ebony skin and tight hair, while Firiiki's ancestry was Finnish, and showed it in her milk-white complexion, gray eyes, and really blond locks. Both, though soft meat, had taken on the beginnings of what Shig called the "Donovan look," that wary tension and alertness in the eyes.

"Enjoying your stay so far?" Shig asked as he wound his fingers into the chain link, gaze on the growing dot of the shuttle.

"Been a real introduction," Ituri told him. "Firiiki and me? We both got flattened by those quetzals when we were out on that first patrol. Then the raid? And the hunt? Had to cut a slug out of Bambo Asanna's foot when he took his boot off to change socks. Can't say we've been bored, sir."

"And now the IG's coming in, and reports are that he's hurt." Firiiki pointed at the airtruck. It was braking now, sailing in over the agricultural fields. The down draft was flattening the cabbages, barley, amaranth, and chia, all of which had Terry Mishka waving a fist and yelling imprecations, since such low flying over his crops was unconscionably rude and destructive.

At the sound, Shig turned to find Step Allenovich, the two-wheeled cart rumbling across the gravel before him. The big man's black eye was fading to yellow-green, and a grim smile bent his wide lips.

"So, the IG's not feeling well?" Step asked. "Picked a hell of a time to get himself busted up. But Raya's on the way. Word is

Soukup's going to have to take his turn. Raya's got a priority case. One of the marines from down south. She's hanging on by a thread."

Ituri asked, "She's going to make the IG wait while she cares for a marine?"

Shig, with a benevolent smile, said, "Of course, if Raya thinks Private Aberash needs the care first. But don't worry, if the IG is critical, Vik will get him stabilized. Supposedly it's only broken bones and bruising. That's assuming Fenn Bogarten's report is correct."

Ituri's face screwed up. "That's pretty risky, putting a marine's health before the IGs. He's Board Appointed, you know."

Step made a dismissive gesture. "Who the hell do you think is more important? Some *Corporate* appointee, or a marine who can kill quetzals and keep important people like Mishka out there alive?" Then he gave her a ribald wink. "Naw. Just kidding." Then a frown. "Or maybe not. Truth is, Raya will give priority to who-ever's at the most risk. And fuck the Board."

Shig fought a smile as both marines' eyes went big.

He turned his head away as the airtruck spun, its fans blowing dirt, and slammed down. As quickly, the fans were shutting down.

"Here goes," Step muttered, telling the marines, "You can open the gate now. Yank it closed as soon as Bogarten gets in. He'll drag a cable over and plug the airtruck in to recharge first."

As the gate swung open, Shig followed the big exozoologist and the cart out, winding between the rows of aircars and the web-like maze of charging cables.

The door to the aircar swung open, and Fenn Bogarten, looking exhausted, hopped, one-footed, to the door. His other foot was in some kind of jury-rigged splint. The man's face was drawn, his eyes haggard and pain-pinched. "Got the IG here. He's pretty messed up. No telling how serious. Take him first."

"What happened to you?" Step asked.

"Broken leg."

"And you flew in from out at Tyson?" Shig asked. "At night?"

Bogarten's expression tightened. "You'd be surprised what you can do when someone's got a pistol pointed at your back." A beat.

"Kalico said I had to obey the scum-sucker's orders. No matter what." A flicker of a snarl bent his lips. "Now, get him out of my sight."

Step rolled the cart round back, pulled the cargo door open, and with Shig's help, reached in and slid the gasping and mumbling IG across the deck.

"One, two, three," Step counted, and on three, he and Shig lifted the whimpering and panting IG onto the cart. The man—true to Bogarten's word—clutched a large-bore five-shot revolver. Bogarten's belt holster was suspiciously empty.

Step gave Shig a sidelong look, and before the IG could react, peeled the big gun out of his hands. Said, "Want to wheel him to the hospital while I take care of Bogarten?"

"Of course." Shig took the handles, rolling the cart around, and said, "Inspector General, we're delighted to have you back safely. Must have been a traumatic event. You have the honor of being on the first A-7 to go down on Donovan." He paused. "I'm sorry to hear about your companions. It's my understanding they didn't make it."

Soukup winced, fought for breath, as one of the cart wheels bounced over a bump. The man swallowed hard. Eyes flickering. "You know . . . the only difference between hell . . . and Donovan?"

"I suppose that would depend upon your epistemology and eschatology," Shig mused.

"On your . . . what?"

"Your belief system, Inspector General."

"Yeah? Well . . ." He swallowed hard again. "I can't do a thing about hell, but Donovan? I can. I'm going to raze this shit-pit of a planet, and we can mine it in radiation suits if we have to."

Shig knit his brow, doing his best to roll the cart as carefully as he could. Pushing the medical cart wasn't his best skill. Nor did he have much body mass to do it well.

"Inspector General, in your voice I detect a surrender to *tamas*. Or is it just that you are drowning, lost in the illusions of *maya*."

"What the hell kind of crap is that?"

"Oh, no 'crap' as you would call it. Rather it is the way in which we delude ourselves from seeing the truth. I suspect that you have never truly embraced your *atman*. Perhaps that is why you have come to Donovan. The reason you have suffered the misfortunes you have. This is your opportunity."

"That's insane!"

"No, on the contrary, that is Hindu."

In reply, the Inspector General ground his teeth at the pain and clamped his eyes closed. "Just get me to medical care. I'll deal with the rest as soon as they've given me something for the pain." A pause. "And get me a line to Colonel Creamer."

69

The sensation dazzled Falise, an experience that transcended anything she'd known. Or even dreamed. She was riding a quetzal! Her perch was just ahead over the beast's forelegs, Flute's shoulders giving her legs support. A sense of total awareness and awe filled her. Call it frick-fracking magic, the reality of *riding* being totally surreal.

Such a thing would never have crossed her mind. She hadn't conceived that such a relationship was possible—not just with a giant, deadly predator, but with a sentient alien being. Falise needed only to reach down and run her hand along that warm, slick hide—fingers tracing chevrons of color—to feel the creature. Solid. Muscles working. This wasn't a dream; her body swayed with each stride, with each step. The world continued to pass by as she ducked occasional branches. Though periodically, that flaring collar expanded into a sheet of riotous color that blocked all forward vision.

"It's how he fine-tunes his hearing," Kylee had explained the first time Flute sent the membrane unfurling before Falise's face. "Think of it like the tympanic membrane in your ear. The frill reacts to sound waves as they bounce on the surface."

Falise had only nodded, surrendered herself to the moment, trying to suck in every bit of the experience as Flute strolled effortlessly down a forest trail. Chimes sounded in all directions. And here, on the mountainside where the trees weren't as tall, shafts of golden Capella light shone through breaks in the branches overhead. Scarlet fliers flushed from hiding places behind giant leaves to flutter off into the maze of vines and colorful plants. What Kylee called tree clingers could be seen up in the branches, alien, with three eyes, peering down at her before fleeing into the foliage.

The way Flute moved, he understood where the dangers were,

making a hollow whistle with his vents when Kylee needed to step forward and use her long knife to slash a particularly noxious vine that blocked the trail.

But mostly Flute had the lead.

Falise caught more than one glimpse of odd creatures fleeing into the foliage, ducking into holes in the root mat, or shooting out of the quetzal's path in a panic of flight.

She burped, placing a hand to her stomach. Her *full* stomach. Didn't matter that Kylee had sent Flute out to find food. A quetzal? Oh, sure. How was that supposed to work? Falise had surrendered herself to the notion that her hunger would only get worse until they reached Tyson Station. Then Flute appeared out of the pre-dawn gloom with some dead thing hanging from his mouth.

"Crest!" Kylee had cried, used a strike-a-light from her belt pouch to start a fire, and began cutting the creature up with her big knife.

Falise, aghast at the sight of the dead creature dropped so heedlessly onto the stone—let alone that it had been in Flute's mouth—had sworn she'd not touch a bite. Until the smell of sizzling meat had overcome her revulsion. She'd justified the feast by telling herself it couldn't have been worse than what came out of the hydroponics aboard *Turalon*.

And then Kylee had ordered her to ride Flute. That they'd make better time. Might even reach Tyson Station by nightfall if they had a little luck. This was better than dreams.

She watched in amazement, when what seemed to be a tumbled boulder by the side of the trail shape-shifted into a three-eyed beast that extended two suction cups on feelers and shot a long, needle-like spike out from its middle. The thing backed away, uttering moaning and clicking sounds.

"Did you see that! It looked like a rock! It *was* a rock! I'd swear."

"Smell that odor?" Kylee called from behind.

"Yeah," Falise answered. "Vinegar. And wow, strong."

"That's what we call a spike. Now, you catching on to just why I wanted you to ride Flute? You'd have walked right up to that thing, wouldn't you?"

"Yes," Falise said wearily. "What would have happened?"

"Those two suckers would have shot out, grabbed you, and yanked you onto the spike as it speared its way through your guts. Then it would have pulled you close and enveloped you. They engulf their prey to digest it."

"Dek knows all these things?"

"Yeah, he's pretty good in the bush. Of course, a lot of it is quetzal knowledge. Some of it is just plain luck, and a lot of it comes from sheer guts. Worst fix he was in was with mobbers out on his claim. Should have died, but through cussed willpower, he crawled out of the canyon, and Talina rescued him."

Falise shook her head. "You talk about my brother like he's . . . I don't know. Someone I can't recognize. Back in Transluna, he was what you people would call 'shit on your shoe.'"

"Your dad shouldn't have sent that woman he loved away. Broke Dek's heart."

"Kalay?" Falise chuckled. "She was a Guild girl. Her only job was to train him in sexual proficiency. They both knew that. Knew the rules."

"You got trained in that, too?"

"Of course, I'm a Taglioni. From birth we're trained to master a great many skills."

Kylee was walking at Flute's side now. She looked up with those oversized blue eyes. "Did anyone tell you that you people are really fucked up?"

"No one would dare tell a Taglioni such a thing. Not to their face. Not and live."

"Got news for you, *Falise*: You people are really fucked up."

Falise stared down in amazement. "You'd never say that in public. Not where anyone could hear."

"Try me."

Falise balled a fist. "What *is* it with you? All of you. You don't have the first civilized sense about genteel behavior, about manners or propriety. Let alone respect for your superiors."

"Yeah," Kylee agreed. "We're real shits. Me in particular. I was learning all those things you said while I was living down at Mundo with only Flash, Diamond, and Leaper for company. Of course,

Leaper blamed me for Rocket's death and would have eaten me to see what I'd learned. But then, like Dek and his girlfriend, I guess we all have our burdens to bear." She looked up. "What are yours, Falise?"

"I have no burdens. I've always done my duty. Proudly."

"Like when Ednund was eaten? Was that proud? You shrieking and fainting in the mud?"

"How *dare* you?" Falise's heart took a skip, the rage beginning to burn at the base of her spine, filling her with . . .

"Because *someone* has to slap the condescension out of you." Kylee seemed unconcerned as she walked, her gaze scanning the trees. "Here's how it lines out, Falise: The old saying is that people come to Donovan to leave, to die, or to find themselves. I think you need to leave."

"Not until I've ensured Taglioni control of Donovanian assets is complete."

"Then you're going to die."

"What if . . . what's the third choice? I 'find myself' isn't that it?"

"You're so fucking lost the only thing you've got is what your family back in Taglioni Tower told you. You're a made-up person. Sort of like a kit that's put together with parts according to a set of directions. And what did they make? A tool. And that's how they use you."

"That's a death sentence, you know. Saying that about a Taglioni."

"Fine, step down here and kill me." Kylee beckoned with her fingers in a "Come on, I dare you" gesture.

Falise blinked, struggled with her rage, then shook her head. The child was serious! "What is *wrong* with you?"

"Maybe I'm not the problem." Kylee glanced up, measuring. "You ever noticed that about yourself? It's always someone else who's got something wrong with them? Who the hell are you, Falise? Sometimes I think you're just a more sophisticated version of fuck-stick Soukup's robot people. The way Dek tells it, like them, you just do what you're told. You say trained? I say programmed."

Falise snorted her derision. Idiocy like that didn't deserve a response. No way this wild forest child could ever comprehend *being* Taglioni.

Kylee made a face. Shrugged. "Okay. Tool then. Assuming that's all you need to have a purpose in life. But, like, wow! You'd sort of expect better from a high-born Taglioni. Like, they have everything. Except, it turns out, a purpose in life."

"Lectured on family, by a child who won't even visit hers? You're no better than an orphan."

"Pretty much," Kylee agreed. "Given that Dya and Mark are dead. And I stood by and watched while Rebecca and Shantaya were eaten by quetzals. For a long time, all I had was rage. Then I got a glimpse of Talina's maturity." She gestured around. "Living out here? It teaches you about life. That everything comes at a price. Grief cost me one of my mothers and a sister. Exile is the price I paid for my rage and hatred. Being part quetzal means people see me as a monster. The only place I belong is with my lineage. That's the price of my life. What's yours?"

"Taglionis don't pay a price for being who we are."

Kylee nodded. "The stupid never do."

"Who," she snapped, "are you calling stupid?"

"Falise, my advice is that when we get back to PA, you step on the first shuttle up to that ship in orbit. Go home."

"That's not an option."

"So, you won't leave. You don't have a chance at finding yourself. And—when it comes to Donovan—that only leaves one other option."

Falise was forming her response when Flute stopped so short that she was scrambling to keep her hold. The quetzal froze and flared his collar. The colors running along his hide went from forest pastels to vivid yellow and black.

"What have you got, Flute?" Kylee asked, unslinging her rifle.

A pattern flashed on Flute's hide and he craned his head around as if searching. As he did, the chime changed, the half-symphony eerily cacophonous.

"Shit!" Kylee spun on her heel, staring off to the east. "Falise! Get off! *Now.*"

"What's happening?" she asked, kicking a leg over and sliding down. As she did, she slipped her rifle around from where it was slung across her back. When she looked back, Flute had vanished. Or seemed to. His hide had changed, mimicking the surroundings, blending so well she could barely make out the quetzal's form where it cowered on the trail.

"Mobbers," Kylee told her. "Coming this way. You might be dead sooner than I thought."

That's when Falise first heard the distant chittering and squealing.

70

When Ensign Schulyer set the A-7 shuttle on the ground, Kalico barely felt the big bird settle on the baked red clay at the Port Authority landing field. After thanking the ensign, she collected her rifle before stepping through the hatch and into the main cabin. The ramp was already dropping; Raya, Talina, and Dek were wheeling the comatose Private Aberash on her gurney down and into the morning light. Raya thought the woman's signs were good enough to justify monitoring her recovery at the hospital instead of shipping her up to *Turalon*.

Two Spot had reported that IG Soukup was already at the hospital. On the flight in, Raya had been in conversation with Vik Lawrence over the IG's condition. Vik had given him a painkiller based on Dya's blue nasty recipe and had last reported that the man was sleeping peacefully. The good news was that Tip Briggs seemed to be out of danger and was recovering, and that Fenn Bogarten's broken leg had been set.

Descending the ramp, Kalico pulled her hat up, using the brim for protection against the sun. She followed the gurney across the fired clay, glancing across at where Pamlico Jones and his crew were stacking shipping containers offloaded from *Turalon*. On the other side of the field, the high stack of clay containers was being dismantled and loaded aboard shuttles to be lifted into orbit.

As she stepped through the gate, giving the marine guard a salute, she could hear Schulyer's shuttle spooling up. The ensign had a ten-minute window to clear the space for another incoming bird.

To her surprise, Fenn Bogarten—perched on crutches—waited in the shade of the warehouse, out of the hot morning sun. He looked all in, eyes swollen, blinking in exhaustion.

"Fenn?" She shifted her rifle, let Raya, Tal, and the rest go on ahead.

"Supervisor." The man seemed to be on the point of reeling. "Gotta talk. I'm just . . ." He blinked harder, seemed to be fighting for coherence. "Shit. Shoulda asked for a stim shot."

"Come on, let me help you." Not that she could really do much to assist a man on crutches.

He gave her a silly grin, hitching around on his crutches, saying, "Moving helps. Listen, shit's coming down. That idiot Soukup. I mean, Kylee and that Falise woman. They got us out. Of the wreck, I mean. And that damned quetzal. I *rode* a quetzal, can you believe? All the way up to the airtruck. And then . . ." He worked his face, as if the action would pump energy into his brain. "Then, I'm getting the airtruck ready to go, and here's Flute. With the fucking IG hanging out of his mouth."

"I don't understand."

"Flute! He *carried* the IG up the hill. Dangling from his teeth, can you believe? Through the forest. And Flute reaches in, tender as can be, and carefully deposits the IG on the deck just inside the door. Then he turns around and vanishes back into the forest."

"Wouldn't surprise me," Kalico said with a chuckle. "Kylee and that quetzal, they're quite a—"

"'Give me that pistol,'" Fenn continued without a break. "That's what the IG says, so I hand my revolver to him. You said to obey his orders. No matter what. I did. And the toilet-sucker points it at me, and says, 'Fly. Now. That's an order.'"

"Wait a minute."

"Yeah. At gunpoint, I'm ordered to fly off. You said to follow his orders, ma'am. But I told him no. He cocked the pistol, aimed it right at my heart." Fenn shook his head, still bobbing doggedly along on his crutches. "I could see it in his eyes, Supervisor. The guy was crazy. I mean, he's got broken collarbones. He can't even hold the gun up, pain sweat's running down his head. But that big revolver . . . braced in his lap like that . . . he's going to shoot me if I don't fly us out of there. And me, with a broken leg!"

"And you did?"

Fenn nodded his head, lips pinched. "For one thing, he's a Board Appointed IG, and you said to follow his orders. For another, he didn't care. He'd have killed me and never batted an eye." He grimaced. "But we left Kylee Simonov and Falise Taglioni out there. Abandoned them. Left them stranded in some really mean bush, ma'am."

Kalico ground her teeth, cursing under her breath. "Have you told anyone?"

"Hell yes!" He spat the words. "Those women? They pulled us out of the wreck. Came to our rescue. And we abandoned them out there. Well . . . the IG did. You give me the word, ma'am. I'm begging for the permission. There's a charged airtruck waiting. Let me ask for volunteers. I . . ."

She steadied him as he almost collapsed. Saw him blinking, reaching up from the crutch to rub his eyes.

"And Supervisor," he said, "there's something else. Granted, I was hurt. But I had to see. On the shuttle, I mean." He glanced sidelong at her with worried and fatigued eyes. "Did you have anything placed in the electronics? Like, maybe to keep the shuttle from flying?"

"No. What are you talking about?"

From his belt pouch, Bogarten extracted an electrical device. Maybe as big around as a tennis ball, it had clips and connectors on the sides. "Found that on the main bus relay, ma'am."

Kalico took it, frowned as she hefted the thing. "I haven't a clue."

"Me, either. But looking back, I'm wondering if the IG, shit on a shoe that he is, didn't have one of his robot-people stick this on the electrics to make it look like you tried to kill him. Like you wanted him to die in that shuttle. I . . ."

Bogarten's eyes rolled back. Kalico barely caught him before he collapsed, struggled to keep him upright on his crutches.

A couple of Hofer's guys were coming down the avenue with a ladder. Looked to be on their way to the landing field to do who knew what.

"Hey!" Kalico called. "Got an emergency here. I need you to get Bogarten to the hospital."

"On the ladder?" one called.

Kalico braced a hand on her pistol, arching an eyebrow.

"You got it!" the second one told her with a worried smile. "But if the boss yells about it . . . ?"

Kalico gave him a deadly grin. "I'll have Kylee Simonov beat the shit out of him again."

She watched as the mumbling Fenn Bogarten was summarily loaded onto the ladder—parts of him slumping between the rungs—and carted off.

For a moment, she stood, considering the device Bogarten had given her. Sabotage? No, it didn't make sense. And when it came to shuttles, Bogarten wasn't even a lowly rated Tech I. The part might be anything, and Bogarten had been badly hurt.

She stuffed the thing into her pouch.

Yvette was hurrying down the avenue toward her, shot a worried look at Fenn as he was carted past, and called, "You heard?"

"Yeah, just now. From Fen."

"Kalico," Yvette told her. "It's going all over town." The woman shook her head. "Damnedest thing. Kylee Simonov might have been the devil's spawn until she smacked the piss out of Hofer and stood by the Briggs boy. But now that this toilet-licker Soukup left her and Dek's sister out there? You'd think she walked on air."

"Anyone told Dek yet?"

"Nope. But I saw him headed into the hospital with Tal, Raya, and that marine. He's going to know any moment now."

Kalico could hear the next shuttle coming in, the roar growing in the east. "Has there ever been a time when a Corporate Inspector General was lynched by a mob?"

"Not to my knowledge."

"Well then, I guess we'll be around for the first."

71

Talina descended the stairs in Inga's. The crowd below, catching sight of her, stilled from a low roar to a speculative rumble. And Inga's was crowded. Word had traveled like wildfire. As Tal took in the crowd, she noted a lot more heavy rifles than was usual; some of the locals had also opted for a brace of pistols on their hips.

The soft meat, who'd come for the novelty of it—or because they weren't sure what it meant—were looking both excited and nervous in their much-too-new, much-too-clean coveralls and shiny shaved heads.

Kalico and Shig were already at the end of the bar and now turned to watch her arrival.

At the bottom of the stairs, it was Hofer who called, "What are we doing, Tal? Kicking Corporate ass? What they did to that kid? After she pulled that shit-sucker out of the wreck? I say we pack his ass up and haul him right back out there where he left 'em."

"No fucking white-assed Corporate patsy's worth a smear of shit on my shoe!" another called.

"Hey! Stow it!" Talina bellowed. "Anyone lays a finger on the IG, they'll deal with me. The scum sucker's under *my* protection, so, back off, and let us handle it."

She felt the quetzal presence in her blood stirring, could feel Demon's hiss.

Grumbles and growls came as a response from the crowd.

Crossing the flagstones, Talina hoisted herself up on her stool. Kalico was nursing two fingers of whiskey and chowing down on a plate of poblanos stuffed with red sauce and diced quetzal meat. A pensive look was on the Supervisor's face. Next to her, Shig—with a similar meal and a half-glass of wine—was staring thoughtfully at the backbar, blunt brown fingers tapping at his chin.

Kalico asked, "Dek and Step got off all right in the airtruck?"

"They did."

"Then, what the hell are you doing here? I figured, given that it was Kylee, you'd be with them."

Talina gave a slight nod of the head to indicate the surly crowd behind her. "You hear them? This town's got a lit fuse. No matter what my heart tells me, I'm still in charge of security."

"What do you want to do?" Kalico asked. "Fen was all for flying back out to that outcrop."

"Won't do any good," Talina replied, as Rocket shifted on her shoulder, clearly worried. "Kylee will have headed for Tyson."

"What about Dek's sister?" Shig asked. "It must be worrisome to know that she's out in the forest despite her being with Kylee and Flute. Bad things happen to even the best of us."

"I don't have a clue what Dek will do if anything happens to her." Talina shrugged "Growing up like they did, it's not like a normal family. God alone knows what it will mean to the Taglionis if she gets eaten. My understanding is that they're not exactly a forgiving bunch."

"And it's even worse," Kalico told her. "Report's back from the med bay on *Turalon*. Bartolome Radcek was poisoned. That's two murders. Both of them from two of the most powerful families in The Corporation. They're going to demand answers and satisfaction. Both of which we're short on."

Shig said, "Most likely it's either Cinque's crowd, or, and I'm sorry, but Falise Taglioni's. She might have been in the bush, but that Clarice is still here. And she was seen with Bartolome the day he was poisoned." A beat. "Could she have done it?"

"Without a doubt, Shig." Talina shot him a knowing look. "I know what you're thinking. Doesn't matter that she's Dek's sister. We'll follow wherever the investigation takes us."

Talina turned to her mug of stout as Inga set a plate of the "special" on the bar before her. "But first things first. People are chewing ions over the fact that Soukup saved his own skin after Kylee, Flute, and Falise got him out of that wreck. That he took the airtruck. Forced Bogarten to fly it at gunpoint. This could turn ugly, real fast."

Kalico looked weary. "Not to mention a dead Grunnel and a dead Radcek."

Shig nodded, lifting his glass of wine. Didn't drink it. Just seemed to enjoy holding it. "I see no way out of this for the IG. I think his *atman* is paralyzed at this point. Stuck in *samsara*. A most tragic figure."

Kalico's expression pinched. "Tragic?"

"Beyond a doubt," Shig said softly. "I have rarely seen a human being so lost in *maya*."

"Whatever." Talina shot a glance Hofer's way where the builder was stomping around and threatening mayhem down at the other end of the bar. He had a couple of his cronies slapping him on the back.

Kalico asked, "What's the news on Soukup? You just came from the hospital."

"Two broken collarbones, three broken ribs. Lots of bruises, sprained joints from the impact. Raya just finished pinning his collarbones and taping his ribs. They were rolling him into good old Room 7 when Dek and I left for the aircar gate. He was feeling *lots* better as the painkillers took effect."

At another slight lull in the conversation, Talina turned to see Cinque almost skipping down the steps. The man was a study in black with his inky garb, his dark gaze taking in the room—no doubt reading the unrest from the tone in the voices, the defiant postures.

He turned in their direction and settled himself on Dek's corner of the bar, resting on an elbow as he took in the room. "You people never seem to have a boring moment. Quetzal raids, murdered nobles, downed shuttles, dramatic rescues gone bad"—he gestured theatrically toward the room—"not to mention talk of grabbing the Board Appointed Inspector General, and . . . excuse me? Tossing him out to die in the bush?"

Talina gave him her most humorless smile. "There are faster ways to piss people off here, but not many. Leaving Kylee and Falise out there to die? The good Inspector General doesn't really understand Donovanian etiquette."

"Indeed." Cinque gestured to Inga, pointing at Talina's half-empty stout and tossing a coin out on the bar. "Nor does he seem to understand Transluna's. When word gets back that he also flew off and abandoned a high-ranking Taglioni to her fate? I wonder what Derek will do when he hears?"

"He's on the way out to find them," Kalico told him as she lifted her whiskey. "Cinque, make light of it as you will, Soukup just did the equivalent of lighting a fuse atop a one-ton block of magtex. Depending on what Dek finds out there, Soukup could find himself locked on the other side of the fence with an armed mob standing at the gate to make sure he doesn't get back in."

"Ah, but Supervisor, you can order them—"

"Not here, she can't." Talina glared to make her point. "And I'm still making up my mind what I'm going to do about that silly Corporate toilet-licker."

"Ah," Shig said in that evenly balanced voice of his, "Talina, your *tamas* is speaking, since both Dek and Kylee have now been put at risk. How do you expect Inspector General Soukup to find his tao unless he has time for reflection?"

"By kicking his ass right back into *samsara*," she growled. "He can start over as a rat's liver."

Shig's expression fell. "I will stand between the Inspector General and the mob. Do we allow vigilante justice to punish a man who acted in fear? Who watched his companions die? Who was terrified and seriously injured? Soukup's decisions were made without any understanding of the bush. He's a Corporate being, a man without a moral compass, operating in an alien environment. And worse, one who has never been held accountable for his actions."

Talina gave Shig a narrow-eyed squint. "Given those are my people abandoned out there in the bush, I'm inclined to say yes."

"Damn it!" Kalico slapped the bar with a frustrated hand. "It goes against every fiber of my being, but he's Corporate. Tal, if anything happens to him in PA? Especially if he's strung up by the crowd? It'll end in a hell of a mess. Maybe not now. But in the future. The kind of mess PA may not survive in the end."

Talina watched as Inga set a mug of thick black stout next to Cinque's elbow, shot him a distrustful look, and took his coin.

Cinque shifted, sipped his drink. "Remarkable how good this stout is given where it's made. But you needn't worry about the mob getting its hands on the IG. Soukup's no longer in the hospital. Seems that when he first got back to PA, he used the hospital frequency to call for Colonel Creamer. That last shuttle that set down? It dropped Creamer off. Taking the guards with him from the gate, he was headed to the hospital. My understanding is that the colonel is moving Soukup to the Admin Dome. He's ordered the marines to assemble there." Cinque smiled. "So, unless these good folks think they can take down eight marines in armor, I'd say Soukup's pretty safe for the time being."

Talina muttered, "Damn it. That's a whole new complication."

Kalico cursed, thumped a fist onto the bar. "I relieved that martinet from duty."

"Soukup reinstated him," Cinque told her with a shrug. "He is, after all, Board Appointed. He can pretty much do what he wants."

Kalico clamped her eyes shut, fingers knotting around her whiskey glass.

"Easy, Kalico," Talina warned. "Don't go off half-cocked."

"This will further inflame the situation," Shig said with resignation. "I do hope that the IG remembers that he is a guest in Port Authority. That he has no jurisdiction here."

Which was when Talina heard the mumblings of the crowd change. Turning, she saw two marines, Ituri and Firiiki, descending the steps. Both were in armor, weapons at port arms.

"Aren't they supposed to be on the gates?" Shig asked, checking his chronometer. Then he accessed com. "Two Spot? Are the marines on the gates?" A pause. "What?" Another pause. "Get Wejee and the others on them. Now!"

Shig shook his head. "What is it with soft meat? They think they can just leave the gates unguarded? Soukup isn't any smarter than Benteen!"

Talina, however, was keeping her eye on the marines. They'd

reached the bottom of the stairs, turned and—walking in step—crossed to Kalico's chair.

Looking nervous, Ituri said, "Board Supervisor Aguila, by order of Board Appointed Inspector General Soukup, you are ordered to accompany us."

"Like pus-sucking hell," Talina snapped, instantly on her feet, taking a stand between the marines and Kalico. Down in her gut, Demon was vibrating, the combat urge rising in her blood. "You're in Port Authority. Corporate has *no* jurisdiction here."

From the nearest tables, a cry went up, people knocking benches back as they scrambled to their feet. Looking past the marines' shoulders, Tal could see pistols, knives, and way too many rifles as they seemed to spring from nowhere.

"Goddam right!" someone cried.

"You'll take Kalico over our dead bodies!" another bellowed. The rest was drowned in a mayhem of shouts.

The marines, taking it all in, looked both stunned and unnerved. Reflexively, they brought their rifles up, safeties snapping off as they faced the crowd. People were closing in on all sides; the soft meat—looking terrified—were wiggling through the press, trying to get as far as they could from the brewing violence.

"*Hold!*" Talina bellowed, stepping between the marines and the closing crowd. She had her pistol out, raised it high, and fired. Heard the impact as the bullet blew a hole in Inga's dome. Well, hell. Deal with that later.

Those in front, obedient as always, pulled up; the yelling dropping to a babble of curses and threats as people crowded around.

Talina turned to the marines. "Ituri? Firiiki? You're new here. But you're on *our* ground. You push this thing? You'll kill a lot of us, but in the end, you're dead, too. And when the fighting's over, so's Kalico, Soukup, and that toilet-licking Colonel Creamer, you get that?"

Ituri was sucking air, looked on the point of hyperventilating. "Got orders, ma'am."

"Fuck your orders!" Marsdome called. "That sorry sack of shit, Soukup, *abandoned* Kylee Simonov and that Taglioni woman! Left them to die in order to save *his* skin after they'd risked theirs to get him out!"

The roar built, Talina turning, raising her pistol again, and thundering, "Shut it! Quiet! Now, goddamn it, or I'll bust heads!"

"Bust those marines first," Hofer cried. A roar went up in agreement.

"Whoa!" Kalico said, stepping forward, her hand raised. She faced the crowd, and Talina saw that old wry grin bend the woman's lips. "No one's dying here tonight. We just busted ass to keep Private Aberash alive, so I'm not too keen to see Privates Ituri and Firiiki shot through the heads and killed for no reason."

Talina—taking in the now-owl-eyed marines—said, "You getting this? We're not the enemy."

Both women, still scared, nodded, looking really miserable.

Kalico stepped out, saying, "I've got this, people. 'Bout time I went and set the IG straight about some things. Now, I want you all to sit your butts back in the seats. This is Corporate business, and me and my people will take care of it." She paused. "Besides, it really pisses Inga off when the furniture gets busted up and she's left having to mop a lot of blood off the floor."

That was greeted by guffaws; even Hofer—who'd pushed his way to the front—was slapping backs as people backed away, most of them calling cheers for Kalico Aguila.

"Inga!" Kalico shouted. "I'm buying a round for the house. Put it on my tab."

That brought another groundswell of shouts and calls of approbation.

Talina vented a breath she'd been holding for too long. "Shit. That was close."

At the end of the bar, Cinque was watching with a most-focused concentration.

"Ma'am?" Ituri asked, a sheen of perspiration now visible on her brow.

"Let's go," Kalico told her. "And if you've got a brain in your heads, you make it look like we're best of friends. Otherwise, that blood Inga's going to be cleaning up will be yours."

olonel Stanley Creamer didn't like it. Not one little bit. Everything about this mission had gone seriously wrong. It began the moment Board Supervisor Aguila humiliated him and relieved him of command. That was followed by news that his patron, Chad Grunnel, had been found murdered. Damn it, of them all, Creamer assumed that Chad would be the one to come out on top. Not that he'd bet all his chips on the guy—he'd made overtures to Bart Radcek, too—but from Creamer's reading of the tea leaves, none of the others were as well-qualified to take over the administration of Port Authority. Then came news of Bartolome's death. Seriously? *Two* of the families had their operatives taken off the board?

Of course, he got still got snippets of information from his marines. But they were just snippets. He'd never been close to them. That wasn't a commanding officer's place. He gave the orders, they followed them. Nor was it fitting for a man of his rank to sit around with them and drink tea. A colonel's role demanded the decorum appropriate to rank, not as a habitué of the gunroom, and he never debased himself to the degree of exchanging the banal banter, sordid jokes, and grab-ass common to the lower ranks.

Most of his information about what had been happening down-planet came from the rotating shuttle crews. Rumors, hints. His people, he'd learned, had acquitted themselves well in the quetzal hunt. Had been receiving exemplary evaluations from the Corporate veterans who'd been giving them "field training." Which was as it should be. They were *his* marines, after all, and their performance—in spite of Aguila—reflected on him. On his training and discipline.

When news of the IG going down in a malfunctioning shuttle broke, it shocked *Turalon*. How could *that* have happened? And the Supervisor hadn't been on board?

Speculation had run rampant, people scurrying around, the *Vixen* crew half-desperate to get their under-repairs ship fixed so they could charge out and survey for the wreckage. Wasn't going to happen with the reactors in pieces.

A second shock wave came from the announcement that the IG had been rescued. Followed within hours by the more shocking news that IG Soukup had stolen Falise Taglioni's airtruck and left her to die somewhere in the wilderness. Say what? Left a *Taglioni* to die?

Unthinkable!

Creamer had been trying to get his head around what that might mean—listening to the scuttlebutt running rife among the *Turalon* crew—when he'd received his order from Soukup to head dirtside and resume his duties. That it had come with an order to reassemble his marines and arrest the Supervisor on grounds of negligence and incompetence had just been sweet frosting on the cake.

Until he'd stepped foot planetside, passed through the shuttle field gate, and ordered the marines on duty there to follow him. Didn't matter that they protested that it was unwise to leave the gate unguarded. He was back in command. And he relished it, marching into the hospital, having Ituri and Firiiki load the IG onto a gurney and cart him to the admin dome.

Problem was, his marines had assembled, all right. But only eight of them. Eight! To his dismay, the rest were still spread out over half the planet. And—expressing reluctance—announced that they were going to be slow to reassemble depending on when they could book transport.

Book transport? They were Corporate marines, goddamn it! Marines gave the orders here.

As he fumed, he paced up and down the long hallway that ran from the front of the admin dome to the rear. God, he *hated* this place. The building had the decrepit look of age. Dingy. Common. It would have barely been adequate for ore storage on one of the Jovian moons, let alone as the center for administration on Port Authority. Calming himself, Creamer kept from reaching out and pounding a fist on the grimy walls just to see if they'd crumble.

He passed the "Corporate" office. Supposedly—along with the barracks—the only place in this benighted collection of hovels where The Corporation had any authority.

Inside the room—the desk pushed back into the corner—and illuminated by the filthy window, Board Inspector General Soukup lay with his back elevated on the gurney. He was staring at something on a palm notebook. His face—drawn despite whatever pain medication the witch doctor over at the hospital had given him—had a pinched look, his brow furrowed.

As Creamer stopped, Soukup slapped the reader down. Rubbed his head. He glanced Creamer's way, saying, "Do you know what it's like? If Turnienko had cut off my legs, I would feel more whole than I am without my Four. Dear God, Colonel. I am cut in half. I am suddenly the equivalent of a legal quadriplegic. Reduced to a head . . . no, half a head, unable to utilize the entirety of my brain. I ask a question, and there is only silence for an answer."

"My marines should appear with Supervisor Aguila, sir." He checked his chronometer. "It's been almost a half hour. And it's not like this shithole is all that big. With respect, sir, what would you like me to do with the woman?"

Soukup grunted, turned his eyes toward the window with its view of the fence and landing field beyond. "Execute her on the spot?" He raised a hand in futility. "No. Tempting as that might be, she must go back and face the Board. I keep imagining her, standing at the foot of that elegant room, The Corporate Board staring down from on high as she struggles to refute the . . ."

The IG seemed to forget what he'd been saying, was staring aimlessly out at the fence just beyond the window.

"Sir?" Creamer asked.

"But there will be no evidence," Soukup said softly. "The Second will not be there to download the files. Third will not provide the analysis and interpretation. It will only be me. My word against hers." He seemed to flinch. "Intolerable! And I am . . . left . . . isolated."

At the sound of feet, Creamer turned, seeing his marines—Ituri and Firiiki—as they clumped toward him. And there was . . . Yes,

Supervisor Aguila, but dressed in local garb. And with her came that security officer, Perez. The one who looked like a character in an animation, given her too-thick black hair, goggling eyes, flaring cheekbones, and pointed chin.

As they walked up, Creamer pulled himself to attention, declaring, "Board Supervisor Kalico Aguila, by order of Board Appointed Inspector General Soukup, you are hereby placed under arrest for—"

"Shut the fuck up, soft meat," Talina told him. "You're without any authority here."

"Arrest this woman," Creamer told the marines. "No one barks at me like some junkyard dog. I want her . . ."

He gaped as the caricature woman seemed to shift, her arm a flash of movement. He'd seen the like with implants, but never in such a blur. The pistol might have appeared like magic, its barrel just shy of his chin.

"I *said*," Perez told him with deadly intent, "that you are without authority here. What you do down at Corporate Mine or Southern Diggings? We could care less. But you are on *our* turf. Now, do you want to deal with this in a civilized manner, or do you want blood on the streets? We're Donovanian, so we're happy to let you have it either way."

Creamer stared into those hard alien-dark eyes. His heart was pounding; he felt suddenly much too hot, could feel sweat beginning to prickle on his skin.

"Colonel," Soukup called from his gurney, "this is mutiny. Civil disobedience. Any action you take will be justified."

To Creamer's horror, Perez just chuckled, humor glinting in those bottomless eyes.

"Sir?" Firiiki asked, voice wavering.

"Don't," Perez told them. "The first shot goes through his skull, the second through yours, and the final one through Ituri's. Nothing you can do, Private. Not against quetzal reflexes."

Creamer wished he could wipe the sweat from his brow, struggled to get his breath. Had a queasy tickle deep down in his gut that urged a rapid voiding of his colon. Thirty years in the Corps, and he'd never been so sure that someone was prepared to kill him.

"Let's . . . Let's do it civilized," he croaked.

And as rapidly, the pistol vanished.

Kalico Aguila, who'd stood back, arms crossed, fingers tapping on the butt of her pistol, said, "Don't look at me, Colonel. When it comes to Tal, I've tried throwing my weight around in the past. It never worked out well."

"We like civilized. Not as much to clean up that way," Perez agreed. "And digging graves up at the cemetery takes too much time out of busy people's schedules."

More steps came from down the hall. Creamer barely tore his gaze from Perez's to see short Shig Mosadek and the tall, hulking, Cinque Suharto as they came strolling forward.

"Ah! Good!" little Shig Mosadek called in a much-too-happy voice. "Talina hasn't killed anyone yet. She has developed a deeper appreciation for *sattva* these days. And that's in spite of her quetzal tendencies. Having been an observer of her evolution, I think her experience on Donovan has significantly accelerated her chances of eventually achieving *moksha*."

Kalico turned. "Shig, what the hell are you doing here?"

"Why, offering Port Authority's assistance in a matter of concern to the Corporation."

Creamer should have stopped Perez, but the woman slipped past him, stalking up to Soukup and thrusting a finger into the IG's startled face. The man swallowed hard, staring up uncertainly as Perez said, "If Kylee and Falise don't make it, you toilet licker, I'll ensure you end up as quetzal shit."

Mosadek sighed. "But even evolution suffers the occasional setback."

"Right," Kalico said, stepping forward. "Now that the dick swinging is finished, let's get this over with. Charge me with whatever you want. According to my rights under the Corporate Code of Justice, I demand an inquest."

"You'll get one," Soukup promised. "Colonel, you will disarm the Supervisor, place her in restraints, and have her escorted up to *Turalon*, where she will be placed in the brig to await charges for—"

"I'm going nowhere," Kalico stated matter-of-factly. "We'll hold it here."

"Absolutely not!" Soukup cried, wincing at the pain it cost him.

"You try and take her off the planet," Shig said mildly, "and we will suffer a most unfortunate reaction from both our people and Supervisor Aguila's. Physically trying to remove her would, I am afraid, lead to substantial bloodshed."

"Yeah," Perez said. "Back to digging graves again." A pause. "Yours."

To Creamer's surprise, it was Cinque Suharto, black, dark, with his eerie eyes, who said, "Board Supervisor Aguila has been informed that she is under arrest for unspecified charges. She submits to the IG's authority in the matter, but under Corporate Charter and Corporate law, demands an immediate inquest, along with the right to call witnesses. That is her right, Inspector General."

Shig Mosadek added, "Port Authority offers to host the inquiry. We have the facilities necessary to—"

"She will go back. Face the Board." Soukup snapped the words, voice brittle.

Cinque turned, fixing those solid black eyes on the IG. "I would have to testify that you denied the Supervisor her rights guaranteed by the Corporate Code to a Corporate—"

"There is no court here," Soukup told him. "She'll have to go back. After the death of my Four, I will need time to prepare my case. This is a *most* irregular situation."

"Ah," Cinque gave the man a knowing smile. "It is indeed. And I understand. Without your Third, you don't have access to her recitation of the regulations, at least, not without reference to *Turalon*'s database. Had you, you would discover that indeed, such an inquest can be held. The required Corporate officers are available to you in the form of Captain Abibi, her First Officer, Tadeo Chin, and Colonel Creamer here. They provide the minimum of three Corporate officials you need for a tribunal."

Soukup studied him, thoughtful. His lips pursed. Then he asked, "What is your point here, Suharto?"

"The same as yours." The smile Cinque gave the man was almost challenging. "I want to see that the guilty get what they deserve."

Creamer watched the sly smile on Aguila's lips bend the unsightly scars on her face.

Soukup snorted. "Very well. But remember, Suharto. At the end of this, I retain authority to make or withhold any appointment."

Creamer saw Perez and Mosadek exchanging knowing glances.

Creamer experienced a sudden lifting of his spirits. So, he, Abibi, and Tadeo Chin would sit in judgment over Kalico Aquila? Why, imagine that. The good Supervisor was already one third of the way on the road to conviction.

He was looking forward to having Aguila locked in the *Turalon* brig for the entire transition back to Transluna.

73

The fire crackled and spat sparks, the flames burning a curious blue color as they consumed aquajade and bits of chabacho wood. The camp was made on one of the basalt outcrops that poked out here and there on the mountainside. Given the bare stone's lack of purchase, the outcrops remained the only safe haven from the eternally questing roots. Overhead, the unfamiliar constellations, the dark shadows of nebulae, and the brighter band of the Milky Way were stunningly clear. Firelight flickered on the leaves where the surrounding vegetation turned its branches toward the licking flames. The night chime, fortunately, sounded rhythmic and partially harmonious.

On the fire, two cat-sized carcasses roasted slowly, sizzling, fat dripping. The smell of the roasting meat sent a quiver through Falise's empty stomach.

She winced, tried to keep from flexing her stinging and pain-filled fingers. Though her rifle lay beside her, she wondered what she'd do if she had to use it. Could she even stand to pick it up? Clutch it? Wrap her traumatized fingers around the wrist and reach for the trigger?

She studied her mutilated hands with disbelief, jaw tightening against the constant dull pain. Each of the deep lacerations criss-crossing her fingers, the backs and palms, looked absolutely hideous. Kylee—nursing her own wounds—had done the best job she could. The clumsy stitches—made with a needle and thread from Kylee's belt pouch—had closed the worst of the gaping and blood-caked cuts.

As part of her training, Falise had been exposed to pain. But nothing like this. Not a constant throbbing anguish. She had never been cut like this, wounded to the point she could barely move her hands. And, damn, if it weren't for the blue nasty that Kylee had found, sliced up, and mashed with rocks, Falise wasn't sure she could have withstood the agony. The clotted blue goo, however, helped—even if it didn't totally deaden the pain.

Across the fire, Kylee kept scowling at the rents in her clothing. She had her own cuts. The girl couldn't help but keep staring out at the darkness. Her head was constantly cocked, listening.

"I'm sure Flute made it," Falise told her.

"It wasn't the entire flock," Kylee repeated once again, as if to reassure herself. "That gave him a chance." Her face worked; she winced where it stretched the cut that ran from just below her eye to the corner of her mouth.

"You're sure he can find us?"

Kylee nodded. "He would have needed to get them strung out, trailing behind him. There were what, maybe ten? Twelve at most?"

Falise shifted, gasped at the hurt it cause the cut in her hip. "Thinking back? I didn't get a good count. I was kind of busy with my own problems. But yes. Certainly no more than a dozen."

Kylee—again turning her gaze to the night—wearily shook her head. "He would have charged headlong through the thickest scrub. Once he had them in a line, he would have turned, tried to snap them, one at a time, as they attacked. Even as fast as mobbers are, quetzals can still take them out. It's only when they get swarmed that the mobbers win."

Falise lifted her hands, caught her breath at the damage. "He didn't have to do that, did he? I mean, Flute could have just let the mobbers kill us. He could have stayed hidden."

Kylee gave a slight shrug. Not enough to open one of the partially clotted wounds. "It's a lineage thing, Falise. I'd have done the same for him if I'd had the chance. But yes. Once that last fucking mobber decided to give you a final look, figured out that you might be food . . ."

"It *bit* me!" Falise closed her eyes, reliving the moment. Seeing those three beady black eyes, staring into hers as the thing landed in front of her. She'd been flat in the trail, following Kylee's orders not to move. Feeling the tendrils of the roots as they started to wind in between the gaps in her clothing.

Heart hammering—terrified like she'd never been—she'd obeyed Kylee's instructions to the letter. Hadn't moved a muscle as the mobber came waddling closer on its four wings, knuckle walking as it stared into her eyes. Then it turned, and, as though in afterthought, bit her thumb.

She'd screamed. Jerked her hand back.

After that . . . everything was chaos. The creature charged. Falise grabbed it by the neck. And while it slashed at her, she throttled the colorful little terror. But that drew another. And another.

"I keep reliving that horror." Falise opened her eyes to study her mangled thumb in the fire's light.

"Be glad the rest of the flock had moved on," Kylee told her. "If the whole mob had heard, they'd have left our picked-clean skeletons for the invertebrates. The remains of what used to be us would be flying over the forest in a hundred mobber bellies. And you know where that's going to end up."

"Before coming here, I could have imagined a hundred different ways to have met my end. Being spread across a thousand hectares of Donovan's forest as manure wouldn't have been one."

Kylee shifted, tossed another chunk of aquajade on the fire. "Guess your father's going to have to rewrite his training program for the Taglioni kids. But you're one up on Dek. He never killed mobbers with his bare hands. He just waited them out while a gotcha vine sent spines into his leg."

"That hurt? As much as this?" Falise extended her ravaged hands.

"Worse by about a thousand times," Kylee told her. "Well, maybe not a thousand, but yeah. If it had been a gotcha bush? You'd be screaming and begging me to shoot you."

"And you people *live* here?" A beat. "On purpose?"

Kylee lifted a slim eyebrow. "You mean to tell me Donovan hasn't been seducing you with its winning ways?"

Falise looked up at the star-encrusted velvet-black sky. "I can't get back to Transluna soon enough."

"What about Dek's half metric ton of rhodium? Won't it piss off your dad and Uncle Miko if you come home without it?"

Falise vented a humorless chuckle. "Kid, I'm soft meat, but I know how close we came to dying today. This place—this whole planet—is hell. I watched a quetzal eat Ednund. Wanted them dead. Extinct. And today one saved my life. May have sacrificed himself to do it. What kind of cucking frazy is that?"

"Welcome to Donovan." Kylee smiled warily as she reached out to pull a sizzling and dripping carcass from the fire. "Never had mobber before. Guess you could say this is an eat or be eaten kind of world."

"I don't think I can hold even a chunk of meat."

"It's got to cool first," Kylee told her, those eyes no longer conveying the alien threat they used to. "I'll help you."

"Then what?" Falise asked, glancing out at the darkness as something screamed out in the trees. "Tomorrow? It won't be any different. Except that I can't hold my rifle. And if those mobbers come back looking for their missing pals . . . ?"

Kylee sniffed the meat, gave a grunt of satisfaction, and propped it to cool while she reached for the second spit. "First we find Flute," she said. "After that, we're most of the way to Tyson Station. Just down the side of the mountain, and we should get there."

"And then what?" Falise asked. "Hope the cannibals don't eat us?"

Kylee turned, listening to the darkness as the chime shifted in key. "They won't. But we use their radio. Got some unfinished business with that Corporate IG."

Falise narrowed her eyes. "He's mine."

"I say we give him to Flute. See if the toilet-sucking slug-licker gives him indigestion."

"I'd rather use my knife. The big one I once thought there was no possible use for. I can cut him apart a piece at a time. No one leaves a Taglioni to die. And after what he did? The Board wouldn't dare to move against me."

Kylee gave her a knowing smile. "See? A couple of weeks on Donovan, and you've already developed several redeeming features to your personality. Who knows what kind of person you'll be after you've been here for a full month."

"Assuming we don't die finding Flute."

Kylee blew on a hot piece of meat. "There's always that."

The voice from the darkness said, "Well, assuming you two itchy trigger fingers won't shoot us, would you mind if Flute and I came in to share your fire?"

Stunned, Falise looked up to see her brother step out of the darkness, his rifle in hand. He was smiling from beneath a wide Donovanian hat, his beard gleaming in the firelight. And behind him, limping, came the big quetzal, patterns of color broken by the wounds on its hide.

"Wow! Family reunion," Kylee chimed.

"Won't this be fun," Falise muttered to her herself, as she met Derek's questioning gaze.

Kylee leaped up to hug Flute and then inspect his wounds. "Piss on a rock! They got you, huh? Are you all right?"

The big quetzal's hide was a riot of color.

Derek's smile went crooked in his face. "So, Little Sister? Looks like you came out second best after a fight with a lion. Having fun on Donovan, are you?"

Deadpan, she told him, "You know, Brother, despite the changes, you're still insufferable."

74

Kalico kept a house down in the residential zone. She'd picked it up in order that she might have a place to stay when she had to lay over in PA. Not that she used it much. Maybe twice a month. She had a contract with Sian Hmong. Once a week Sian would come in, change the sheets, dust, do the dishes, toss any food that had gone bad in the refrigeration, and take out the trash.

The dome wasn't much, just a living room separated from the kitchen by a four-stool breakfast bar; a bathroom was located opposite the storage room with a bedroom in the back. Water, like everywhere in PA, was collected from the roof, run through a mucilage filter, and stored in a cistern.

The deal Kalico had made with Soukup was that she would spend the night here, the dome guarded by four of Creamer's marines to ensure that she didn't flee. As if fleeing—whatever that meant—was really an option. Let alone that she had any intention. Hardly.

As she lay in her bed—the night chime barely audible through the duraplast walls—Kalico continued to line out her defense. Cataloging the actions she'd taken, the compromises necessary, the reasoning behind each decision.

Pulling up the regs from her implants, she carefully added mental notes. Trying to anticipate which ones Soukup would cite. That he no longer had his Four made it so much easier. Nevertheless, she'd played fast and free with the rules. And thank God the inquest would be here. In front of a mob of Donovanians. Better yet that it was Abibi and her first officer, though Kalico didn't know Tadeo Chin. Creamer was a write-off, but she only needed two votes for acquittal. Would there be questions back in Solar System?

Damn straight.

But that reckoning was down the road, and once rendered, a verdict of acquittal would be difficult to overturn.

Abibi and Tadeo Chin would pronounce judgment here, on the planet, where reality wouldn't be the academic abstract it would be back on Transluna. It might even influence Creamer.

No. That was silly. The man wasn't smart enough to recognize when he was face-to-face with disaster. He remained what he was: a Corps martinet.

In the process of running through the various charges Soukup was sure to level against her, Kalico heard the thumping as Privates Firiiki and Asana crossed her living room, marched down the short hall, and into Kalico's bedroom. At their entry, the light sensors triggered, casting dim illumination across the room.

Firiiki looked nervous, Asana, expressionless.

"Ma'am?" Firiiki said. "Orders. You're to dress and come with us."

Kalico sat up in her bed, pulled her thick hair back. "It's the middle of the night. A little past two."

"Yes, ma'am." Firiiki glanced uneasily at Asana, the Nigerian woman's face stiff as a mask. "Will you please comply? If not, you'll have to go as you are."

"Where are we going? Surely you're at liberty to give me that information."

"Our orders are to answer no questions, ma'am," Asana told her in clipped tones. "Now, will you come peacefully? Or do we need to incapacitate you to ensure your cooperation?"

"Bit harsh, don't you think?" Kalico asked as she dressed.

When she reached for her utility belt with its pouches, pistol, and knife, Asana snapped, "No, ma'am. Our orders are to bring you unarmed. The Colonel was quite specific on that."

"Ah," Kalico told her. "Funny thing. I was just having a conversation in my head about the Colonel's mental capabilities. I didn't rank them very high."

Again, the marines shared that uneasy glance.

Kalico wrapped her quetzal-hide cloak around her shoulders,

then donned her hat. "Very well, let's go see what kind of lunacy Creamer has cooked up now."

Firiiki in front, Asana in the rear, Kalico walked out into the night. Two other armed marines stepped in from either side, boxing her.

"Relax, people," Kalico told them. "I'm hardly a dangerous fugitive. Think it through: It's PA. In the middle of the night. Where am I going to go?"

"Order's, ma'am," Firiiki told her in that formal tone that firmly set a prisoner in his or her place.

"So, Private Firiiki, and the rest of you, too. Did nothing that Abu Sassi taught you about Donovan sink in? This place is not about mindlessly following orders. It's about thinking, using your heads. Now, why don't you tell me where we're going in the middle of the night?"

All she got in return was silence.

For the first time, Kalico felt that spear of unease. Whatever this was about, it sure as hell wasn't according to the rules.

They reached the main avenue, turned south. A few more of the streetlights were working, repaired with replacement bulbs taken from the supplies *Turalon* had sent down.

"Assuming," Kalico said evenly, "that this isn't a last-minute offer by the IG to make an apology for a false arrest, you are both aware that you will be witnesses. If what you're doing isn't according to the regulations, you will be held as accomplices under Corporate law."

In the half-light cast by the streetlamps, she could see still more wary glances pass between her captors.

"Ah, I thought so." Kalico crossed her arms, the dead feeling in her gut growing. Looking up, she wished she could see the stars.

To her surprise, however, they turned onto the beaten avenue that led to the shuttle field. Now they were back in darkness, broken only here and there by a pool of light where the streetlamps still worked—and several of them were flickering on their last legs.

"Apparently you are working on a flawed assumption," she told them. "The gates are closed. Locked. And as to what's out there in the dark? Sure that's really smart? Especially when Whitey and at least one of his lineage are prowling around?"

One thing was sure: They kept the lights working at the gate as well as the other side of the fence to ensure that nothing could sneak up on the guards. To Kalico's surprise, Wejee stood to one side, looking very unhappy. In addition, she could see that he'd been disarmed of his rifle. Another marine, Huac Than, rifle at port arms, waited in full armor, helmet clipped to his belt. And there, of course, stood Colonel Creamer.

Kalico strode up to the man, cocked her head, looking him up and down where he stood in his formal dress blues. "You look fit for a parade. Not the appropriate dress for wandering around PA at night, Colonel."

He gave her a pity-laced smile, gestured at his marines in their armor. "I think, ex-Supervisor Aguila, that my people can more than take care of any slugs or night monsters." He pointed out at where the shuttle's silver shape could be made out in the gloom. "We're going to take a ride. You'll enjoy it, Aguila. You'll be out of this fucking shithole and back where civilization reigns."

At the rumble and clatter, Kalico looked back down the avenue, watched as Board Appointed Inspector General Soukup was wheeled into the lights. Another of the marines, Tashi Arakawa, was pushing his gurney. The wheels weren't really meant for gravel. She, like the others, wore armor, helmet clipped at her belt.

"You are out of your scum-sucking minds," Kalico told them. "The pilot and crew for that shuttle should be—"

"On the way." Creamer glanced at his watch. "Don't know why they're not here already."

"So, you're going to fire up and leave in the middle of the night? Extract me to *Turalon*? Hold my inquest up there?"

"I'm not an idiot, Aguila," Soukup told her. "You'll answer for your crimes in Transluna. Standing before the Board. Do you really think I'd let this chaotic rabble you live with be party to your judgment? It would be as much a sham as your tenure here as Supervisor." He smiled, looking weary and pained. "Oh, and by the way, I've already informed Cinque Suharto that, in accord with my authority, he will act as interim Supervisor until a Board Appointed successor arrives."

"Poor Cinque," she replied. "Wonder if he'll last a week?"

"Don't play the loyalty card," Soukup told her in a dismissive voice. "About a third of your people are rotating back to Solar System. The ones who will be staying are new contractees. They'll follow Supervisor Suharto's orders."

"And just like that, you'll whisk me up to *Turalon* and figure that all the loose ends have been tied up?"

"Doesn't matter," Soukup told her. "Your sycophants can wail, rend their garments, and build monuments in your name after you're gone. All that matters is that The Corporation will once again be in control of the mines. Supervisor Suharto will see to that. And I dare say, after your summary replacement, he'll be a great deal more cognizant of the rules."

Kalico gave Soukup a bitter smile. Problem was, the man might be right. Once they had her up in orbit, it wasn't like she could call on allies.

Should have run for the bush. The thought rolled around in her head.

"Ah, here," Colonel Creamer said with relief.

All eyes turned as a shuttle pilot and copilot came trotting down the avenue, a marine behind them, seemingly pushing them along.

"So," Kalico noted dryly, "now what? You think Wejee's going to open that gate?"

Poor Wejee winced as three rifles pointed in his direction. The man said, "Sorry, Supervisor. But the smartest play here is that as soon you're all out, I'm swinging the man gate shut and locking it tight. You know the rules."

"Sure," Kalico said. A sinking in her gut as Wejee stepped forward, used his key on the lock, and opened the gate. Then he stepped back, adding, "They told me earlier, either I opened the gate, or they'd take the keys from my dead body. But either way, they were leaving."

"Yeah, I know," Kalico told him.

"Move it!" Creamer snapped. "I want to be off this forsaken rock in fifteen minutes. Pilot? You first. Marines, keep a fricking close eye on Aguila. Be just like her to make a run for it."

The pilot and copilot, looking uneasy, eyes still sleep-heavy, headed out onto the landing field. A rifle barrel poked Kalico in the back, sent her stumbling out through the gate, half-blinded by the glare of the lights. As she started across the fired clay, she looked back, seeing two of the marines manhandling the IG's gurney through the narrow gate.

True to his word, Wejee had it locked tight as soon as the last of Creamer's marines had the IG out on the field.

The distance to the shuttle wasn't more than fifty meters.

As the crew walked out of the cone of light and into the dim recesses under the shuttle's wing, Creamer was striding purposefully forward, calling, "Lower that ramp. Let's get loaded, people. I've got hot coffee waiting up in. . . ."

The blur might have been a trick of vision. Where the pilot had been, only featureless dark shadow remained.

"Chico?" the copilot asked, turning to where the pilot had started to reach for the ramp control pad.

"What the hell?" Creamer seemed oblivious, back straight as he marched into the shadow, his dress uniform merging with the night.

"Chico?" the copilot continued. "Not funny. I know you're bitching because of the hour, but. . . ."

The woman vanished. One instant she was there, the next, just gone.

"Shit!" Kalico spit the word. "Weapons hot, people. Get your damned helmets on! I need tech, and I need it now! IR and thermal!"

Creamer at least managed to cry, "Where's the . . ."

Kalico saw it. The brief flash of movement. Shimmering color illuminated in the light reflected off one of the marines' armor. The way Colonel Creamer seemingly bent in the middle and flew sideways.

Then Kalico spun, heading for Wejee and the gate. Past the still-clueless Soukup.

The IG yelled, "She's running! Get her! Shoot her!"

Kalico wheeled—blew herself off for a fool—and ripped the hapless IG from atop the gurney. She staggered under his weight, bellowing, "Wejee! Get that gate open! We're under attack!"

Behind her, the marines were fumbling around, reaching for their helmets, calling back and forth in confusion.

Staggering, Kalico struggled under the shrieking Soukup's weight. Wished, not for the first time, that she had quetzal strength. A shot sounded behind her. Another scream.

More shots.

It wasn't more than thirty meters, most of it under the glare of the lights.

Seemed like it was halfway across the planet.

Wejee had the gate open, helped to take Soukup's weight, and once inside, Kalico turned loose of the howling and gasping IG. Let him fall in a heap. As he hit the ground, the man let out another cry of pain. Looked like one of his collarbones had snapped on impact.

"Serves you right, asshole," Kalico muttered, turning back to the shuttle field.

Out in the landing field, two of the marines were down, armor shining in the light. Three were taking random shots, bellowing, frightened. Firiiki had managed to get her helmet on, was taking her time, shooting as if she had targets in her HUD.

Two of the remaining marines dropped by the prone figures, cursing and calling. They grabbed the closest by the shoulder grips in the carapace; then they struggled to bear their burden toward the gate.

And as quickly, it was over.

"Where did they go?" Firiiki was shouting through her helmet speakers. "Three of them. Did you see?"

"Hell, no!" Asara spit the words. "It's fucking dark out here. Where's the crew? Where's the Colonel?"

"Dead!" Kalico called. "Now, get your asses back inside the fence. There's been enough stupidity tonight."

"What the hell?" came the call from behind, Talina emerging from the darkness. "What's the shooting? We heard they were taking you. Came to effect a rescue."

"Appreciate it," Kalico told her. Then she kicked the IG, enjoying the sucking gasp he made as she connected with his broken ribs and reinjured collar bone. "But you're too late. This bit of shit on my shoe has already played hell."

Wejee stepped back as two of the marines wrestled the first body through. The bloody armor belonged to Private Than. His head was missing. Just like Hui Ahn's when Asana and Ituri dragged his bloody and decapitated corpse through the gate a moment later.

"Dear God, what just happened here?" Soukup asked from the ground, his horrified gaze on the headless marines as they were laid on the gravel. Blood began to pool where it drained from the cleanly sliced necks.

Kalico glared down at him. "Welcome to Donovan, you piece of shit," and she kicked him again.

75

The unreality of it continued to haunt Falise. She sat with her butt propped on an oddly shaped basalt rock. The notion of compassionate sensitivity must have gone missing in her long-lost brother; Derek couldn't have cared less. He crouched like a satyr as he ministered to her lacerated hands. Behind him, the fire—snapping and crackling—shot occasional sparks into the star-choked night. Up there, patches of black denoted clouds. Differentiated as they were from the blotchy dark nebulae only by the fact that the latter didn't move.

She gasped, crying, "Damn! That hurts!"

Dek—looking up with feigned surprise—gave her a chiding look. "Don't be a pussy. Think what Father would say."

"He can go screw vacuum." She clamped her teeth shut, tears straining at her lids as Dek used an astringent salve on the most egregious of the cuts on the back of her right hand.

"For once, Little Sister, it seems we agree on something." His smile hinted of amusement.

"*Don't* be such a baby!" Kylee's words carried frustration.

Falise looked past Dek's shoulder to see the girl; she squinted in the firelight as she dabbed at a wound on the big quetzal's shoulder. Flute had sprawled on his belly, head out, jaw resting on the basalt; all three of his eyes rotated around to keep track of Kylee as she ministered to his wounds.

To Falise's amazement, Kylee had walked out into the dark, used her knife to hack off a tooth flower pod, and, one by one, severed the long and deadly thorns from the rims. These she'd used as needles, slipping them through the edges of the long cuts. After that she employed thread torn from her shirt to bind the wounds together with a tight figure eight, sort of like winding a nautical line around a cleat.

In response, Flute expanded his lungs, then blew that flatulent rasping from his tail vents.

"Couldn't have said it better myself," Derek called over his shoulder.

Kylee finished, patting the quetzal and stepping back to survey her work. "For the time being, those cuts are going to play hell with your more conversant side. I guess, given the way that's going to scar, you're going to have the quetzal equivalent of a lisp."

Falise watched the yellow, green, and pink patterns for an interrogative color on Flute's side, the pattern broken by the wounds.

"Yeah," Kylee told him. "My point exactly."

Derek was grinning as he turned back to dab more salve on Falise's hand. "You want me to tighten those sutures? You've only got a nine-hour window before the edges of the laceration die and you'll need surgery to—"

"God, don't tell me that." She stared at her slashed hands. "Just get me back to Port Authority."

"First thing in the morning," he told her. "Step's down at Tyson Station recharging the powerpack for the airtruck." Again, the faint smile. "Probably sleeping inside with the doors locked, his rifle on his lap, one eye open in case the Unreconciled try anything culinary."

"I think he can set down here on the outcrop." Kylee tossed the last of the tooth flower spines into the fire. Then she settled against Flute, back braced by the quetzal's belly, and added, "But I wouldn't linger."

"How'd you find Flute?" Falise asked. "Last we saw, he took off, trying to draw as many mobbers as he could with him."

"He found me," Derek told her, reaching back into the first aid kit he carried and retrieving a bottle of alcohol. "After leaving Step with the airtruck, I plotted a straight line from Tyson to the wrecked A-7. Figured you'd be along that line somewhere. So did Flute. That's where I ran into him. He wouldn't even let me tend his wounds. Insisted we hurry back to the attack site."

Derek's smile accented the twinkle in his oversized yellow eyes.

"Gotta love that quetzal. He's so considerate. Didn't want to leave your picked bones laying around where just anyone might trip over them in the dark. A stumble and fall like that? Someone could get a bloody nose."

"What the hell's happened to you? You never used to be such a—" The rest was a gut-wrenching scream as Derek poured the alcohol on her wounds.

"*Pus in buckets!*" she cried when she got her breath back and could clear the tears from her eyes.

"Sorry," he told her with actual fondness. "Now, tell me. What the hell are you doing out here? You're an urban creature. Even with Kylee and Flute, you're lucky to be alive."

"Back off, Dek," Kylee called where she lay with her arms crossed on her stomach, head back against Flute's belly, eyes closed. "Falise has guts, and she's smart. If she hadn't strangled that mobber when she did, the nasty little fucker would have called in the whole flock. She saved us all."

"Flute saved us," Falise countered, seeing the quetzal rotate one of his eyes in her direction. "Bravest thing I've ever seen."

It was tricky to see in the firelight, but she thought the quetzal turned white-pink.

Derek replaced his alcohol and zipped the first aid kit closed. Then he resettled himself beside her, taking a seat on the basalt, elbows braced on his knees as he gazed at the fire. "Guess you're no longer soft meat. Little Sister, I've never been so proud of you."

As a trio of invertebrates spiraled down into the fire to explode with pops and hisses, she chuckled. "I don't know why."

"People worthy of respect rarely do. That's one of the things that makes them worthy of respect. But, tell me, what are you trying to accomplish here?"

She took a deep breath, feeling weary. "Just what you'd expect: I'm supposed to safeguard the family's interests on Donovan. Ensure that a Taglioni is appointed as interim Supervisor when Soukup replaces Kalico Aguila."

"Good luck with that," Kylee snapped irritably.

"So, that's the Board's plan? Remove Kalico?"

"They're worried, Derek. Too much wealth is pouring out of Donovan. Wealth is power. Kalico Aguila is a known factor. People on the Board fear her. Know she was a shoo-in for a seat on the Board and even had a shot at the Chair. And that was before *Turalon* and *Ashanti* popped back into orbit bursting at the seams with wealth. They want someone they can control."

"Which explains why Chad Grunnel and Bart Radcek had to die. That your work?"

Falise stared woodenly at her hands as she told him emphatically, "Cinque. Not that—given the opportunity—I wouldn't have done the same."

"Anyone ever tell you that you people are fucked up?" Kylee—eyes still closed—asked.

"Falise," Derek said, "you people are fucked up." Over his shoulder, he called, "There, I did it. So, from here on out, the answer is yes."

Kylee was grinning despite her sham at being asleep. "Too late, Dek. Already told her."

Falise watched the subtle change in her brother's alien-looking face. Could tell how much he cared for, cherished, and enjoyed Kylee Simonov. Who *was* this man?

He said, "You mess with Kalico, you'll have a real disaster on your hands. She's Donovanian. One of us."

"There is no 'us.' You're a Taglioni."

"You are not listening. There will be blood on the streets before any of us let Soukup take her." He paused. "Marines, or no, Kalico remains Supervisor on Donovan."

"Soukup's a Board Appointed IG." Falise wished she could rub the back of her neck where the muscles were tight; the sting in her hands was too debilitating.

"And that, along with a siddar, will buy me a glass of IPA at Inga's." Derek squinted at the fire as more invertebrates flitted down on gossamer wings to sizzle and pop. "Falise, I mean it. If Soukup, Suharto, or you move against Kalico, the people here will have her back." A beat. "I will have her back."

"Why?" Falise asked. "Derek, she's a Corporate Supervisor, subject to the laws—"

"I mean it. Something has happened here, among these people, that flies beyond the comprehension of the Corporate mind, let alone the cherry-assed Board. If you and Soukup try and play by Corporate rules, there will be a reckoning, and it won't be pretty."

"So, what do I do?" Falise asked. "I can't stop being a Taglioni."

"Tool," Kylee muttered, actually sounding half asleep.

"Tool?" Derek asked, shuffling his feet where a few wispy threads of roots were working toward his boot.

"Kylee seems to think that's how the family uses me." She paused, hesitated. "Maybe she's right."

"Then stop it." Derek told her. "You want to win on Donovan? You've got play by our rules."

"Like that damned poker game?"

"There's a lesson in that—and not just that you were acting like an arrogant, superior slit who needed the piss slapped out of her."

Falise chuckled, raised her maimed hands in surrender. "All right. I needed that. I just wasn't . . . I couldn't . . ."

"Yeah, I know. You'd never been faced with the likes of Port Authority and its lunatic libertarians. So, sure, that's part of the lesson you needed to learn. Another part you've learned out here with Kylee and Flute."

"So what else was I supposed to learn from that damned card game?"

"You won that night. Let me bluff you. If you'd played that hand out instead of folded, you'd have had me."

"Huh?"

Derek shrugged. "Hey, I screwed up. Dealt you that fourth jack. You'd have won, Little Sister. Taken the whole pot, and I'd have looked like an idiot."

"Wow!" Kylee mumbled and yawned. "A half metric ton of rhodium."

Falise blinked, watched another invertebrate immolate in the fire. "That was a lie, right? Part of the bluff. You really don't have a half metric ton of rhodium, do you?"

"Nope." Derek waved at an invertebrate that flew too close. "When you get it all together, it's more like a ton and a quarter."

76

Inga's, of course, was packed. Not only were the locals there, but so, too, were many of the Corporate Mine crew, some of them preparing to space back home with their plunder. Others, being on rotation, wouldn't have missed Kalico Aguila's inquest for anything. Especially as the story made the rounds that she'd personally saved IG Soukup's life and done so even after the man had tried to abduct her off-planet.

At the same time, a number of folks under Pamlico Jones' supervision were out hunting the quetzals; the sobering realization that five people had died had galvanized a party to search for the raiders. Most upsetting was that the attack had been so successful. Not just that they'd killed a pilot, copilot, Colonel Creamer, and two marines, but Whitey's lineage had learned marines were vulnerable if they were not wearing helmets.

Kalico—dressed in a fresh black security uniform unpacked from one of the *Turalon* shipping containers, her utility belt and pistol again on her hips—had taken what few cares she could to make herself presentable. It had been three years since she'd shredded her last good suit on the Maritime Unit's landing pad. It felt good to look moderately professional, especially since the proceedings would be recorded and played back for the Board.

As Kalico walked through the tavern doors and reached the head of the stairs, she wondered what the candy asses in the Corporate Boardroom were going to make of all of this. One thing was sure, it would be an eye-opener. Especially when they got a gander at the audience.

A cheer greeted her as she started down the long steps to the flagstones. Kalico descended with back straight, head up. From the corner of her eye, she could see the place was brim full, people standing shoulder-to-shoulder in the back.

Board Appointed Inspector General Soukup was propped in a chair just in front of the bar. A sling held his left arm immobile, given the rebroken collar bone.

Behind the bar—in Inga's sacred domain and atop high stools—sat Captain Margo Abibi, First Officer Tadeo Chin, and, most improbably, Cinque Suharto. With Colonel Creamer currently in the process of being digested in some quetzal's gut, Suharto had been seated by virtue of his interim appointment as Supervisor. Technically, the validity of his appointment—while Kalico remained a Board Appointed Supervisor and un-convicted of any crime—was a gray area.

Talina, Shig, and Yvette were waiting at the bottom of the stairs, Tal asking, "You sure you want that soft meat, Cinque, sitting up there?"

Kalico shot the man in black an evaluative look. He seemed to be busy with a notebook, perhaps refreshing himself on the regs.

"Yeah," Kalico said. "It's no different than if Creamer were here. My chances all lie with Abibi and Tadeo Chin. Those are my two votes."

"I say we toss that piece of shit, Soukup, out into the bush!" Hofer called above the hubbub. "He got five people killed!"

"Kalico saved his ass? And now he prosecutes her? Shoot the maggot!" Sheyela Smith cried.

A chorus of "aye" and "hell yes" could be heard over the background of talk.

If any of it upset Soukup, he didn't let it show. Instead, he hunched awkwardly in his chair, fingers on his good hand flicking over a notebook screen.

"Definitely Whitey's lineage," Shig—leaning close—told Kalico. "Pamlico Jones found the tracks this morning. The one that grabbed Creamer? Dragging a right leg."

Talina's large eyes narrowed. "Figures. What's with that pus sucker? Where's he been hiding? In the old days, we'd have hunted his ass down, and we'd be making boots out of his bullet-riddled hide."

"Too much going on." Kalico snorted derisively. "It's depressing to think that if he hadn't killed the crew and Creamer, you might not have been fast enough to rescue me last night. It would have been nip and tuck if you'd been able to stop that shuttle."

Talina gave a friendly punch to Kalico's shoulder. "I'd have stopped it. Even if I had to shoot out one of the turbines."

"That would have put you in good with The Corporation," Yvette noted. "They'd have sent *forty* marines on the next ship, just to take *you* in."

The rapping of a gavel—yes, a real one—carried over the noisy room. Must have belonged to Abibi. The sound brought everyone to attention.

Captain Abibi stood, using the microphone to announce, "Seeing that Supervisor Kalico Aguila is present, I call this court of inquest into session." She looked around the room where people were seating themselves. First Officer Chin, looking nervous, straightened his dress uniform jacket.

"Board Appointed Inspector General Soukup," Abibi began. "you have levied charges against Board Appointed Supervisor Kalico Aguila. Under her right, subject to Corporate Regulations and Legal Code, Title VII, Article XII, Section 4, the Supervisor has requested a hearing to determine the validity of the charges." Abibi looked around the room, as if to communicate the gravity of the situation. "You may now enter your evidence into the record."

Abibi seated herself.

Soukup, winced, rose, and faced the bar. The man looked to be in pain, but had refused additional medication lest it dull his senses.

"Here we go," Shig said softly. "Hope it doesn't turn into a bloodbath."

The booing started the moment Soukup began lining out the legal violations incurred, starting with the sale of Corporate assets, properties, and equipment. Took him almost five minutes to cite each violation by code, section, and paragraph. As he did, the crowd got louder.

Talina turned, rising and pulling her pistol. "Hey! Shut your yaps! Or, by God, I'm coming out there to bust some heads."

"Gonna be a long afternoon," Yvette prophesied.

77

To Kalico's surprise, the list hadn't turned out to be exhaustive. The majority of the charges stemmed from her sale of the Corporate assets and property to the Donovanians. Soukup cited another list of obscure legal code violations relating to her alleged negligence in the Maritime Unit catastrophe. Then came no less than sixteen infractions of law and dereliction of duty when it came to the repair and refitting of *Freelander*, which—according to Soukup—appeared to be a valuable Corporate resource. And all the while, he claimed, Kalico Aguila—in violation of seven different Corporate laws against profiteering and graft—was making herself the richest woman in the universe, and was even now adding Southern Diggings to her amassed fortune.

That brought howls of approbation from the crowd, including calls of "Damn straight" and "Way to go, Kalico!"

He then noted that Aguila had craftily, and with purposeful intent, ordered Colonel Creamer and his marines to be dispersed about the planet, diluting Corporate power, as was demonstrated by her prompt dismissal of Colonel Creamer, thereby taking control of the marines herself.

And, finally, he accused her of purposefully and maliciously sending him out on a malfunctioning shuttle, expecting full well that the A-7 would fall to its destruction, thereby eliminating any chance that Kalico Aguila would be brought to justice for her crimes.

All of the above, Soukup insisted, were but the tip of the iceberg when it came to Supervisor Aguila's malfeasance, neglect, and arrogant abuse, not to mention abrogation of her responsibilities as a Corporate Supervisor.

Through most of it, Kalico remained seated, working on her

nails. She was very much aware of the glances shot her way by Abibi, Chin, and Cinque. Through much of it, rumblings from the audience, outright catcalls, and hisses of disgust and anger came within a whisker of overwhelming the proceedings.

"Board Supervisor Kalico Aguila?" Abibi called, shooting nervous glances out at the crowd. "Do you wish to enter a defense concerning the allegations made by the Inspector General?"

Kalico stood, glancing sidelong at Abibi and her two judges. Then she shot a dismissive look at Soukup, who now sat, back straight, expression wooden. "Captain, would you repeat my title please?"

Abibi warily said, "Board Supervisor Kalico—"

"*Board* Supervisor," Kalico interrupted. "The good Inspector General forgets that I was *appointed by the Board*. Nor was he present when I accepted that appointment. Perhaps I should remind him of why I was chosen for the Donovan mission. It had been years since word of Donovan had been received by the Board. The prevailing wisdom on Transluna was that rogue elements on Donovan had seized seven ships, that this colony was a pirate base being run by Supervisor Clemenceau. I was given the authority—*by the Board*—to come, see, and make a determination about the Colony's fate." She paused, glancing up at Abibi. "Captain, I believe you can corroborate my testimony on this regard?"

Abibi nodded. "I can."

"Given. The. Authority." Kalico emphasized each word. "Carte blanche. Allowed complete discretion. So, I came. I followed my directive and instructions to the letter. Discovered no pirates, no rogue Supervisor. Only a colony of people who'd survived by virtue of their guts, hard work, and surprising innovation."

Whistles, cheers, and wild applause broke out behind her.

Kalico—a twisted smile accenting the scars on her face for the benefit of the cameras—waited until Talina had restored order.

"My call, given my Board-granted authority? Sell Port Authority to the people. In doing so, I estimate that I made something like ten times the return in SDRs above The Corporation's initial

investment. And I offered the people the chance to space home on
Turalon. Not only did only a handful wish to return, but we were
having a hard time keeping crew. Especially in light of *Freelander's*
arrival. A dead ship. One that spent a one-hundred-twenty-nine-
year journey through whatever universe it passed through. Can we
salvage it? You go right ahead, Inspector General. And God help
you."

Again the melee of enthusiasm from the crowd.

Kalico waited for Talina to shout them down.

"Yes, I stayed on Donovan. With my people, *we* built Corporate
Mine. Did we make mistakes? Did people die? Yes. But we shipped
a fortune back to Solar System on *Ashanti*. Can you tell me the value
of that cargo, Inspector General?"

"Several tens of trillions in Corporate SDRs," Soukup said
absently.

"More like forty to fifty trillion," Cinque said, where he continued staring down at his notebook.

Kalico paced warily down the length of the bar, looking up at the
camera recording the proceedings. "It might interest the Board to
know that while I am often called the richest woman in the universe, I'm not. Corporate Mine, Southern Diggings? It's all *Corporate* wealth."

Kalico tossed her belt pouch; it landed with a metallic jingle on
the bar in front of Abibi. "Captain, would you be so kind as to tally
the value of the coins in my purse?"

It took Abibi no longer than fifteen seconds to sort through the
denominations and declare, "I count a total of two hundred
and eighty-seven SDRs worth of the Port Authority coinage,
ma'am."

Kalico chuckled in amusement. "That's all? Could Inspector
General Soukup be right? For a corrupt Corporate Supervisor, I
must indeed be negligent and incompetent. You'd think anyone
with even a little larceny and self-interest would have been able to
skim considerably more than . . . what was it? Two hundred and
eighty-seven? Out of all those trillions?"

The room broke into hard guffaws, feet stomping, people pounding on the tables.

Talina needed a couple of minutes to restore order this time.

As the room began to quiet, Kalico said, "As to the marines, the Inspector General is correct. I ordered them to the planet first thing. Put a third at Southern Diggings under Sergeant Briah Muldare's command. Another third I deployed to Corporate Mine under Lieutenant Dina Michegan, and a third here for training under Captain Abu Sassi. I did that with the intent of having them learn what duty on Donovan entailed. And even with their advantages of on-planet training, armor, and tech, five have died. Five! Would have been worse if Colonel Creamer—ignorant as he was—had been left in charge."

"Then why did you send me out on that malfunctioning A-7?" Soukup snapped.

Kalico walked over, looked down at the man. "We *live with* and *rely on* over-extended equipment. Our aircars, electronics, mining machines, medical technology, all of it is patched together and jury-rigged. I heard the new contractees laughing at our light bulbs, about our crude foundry, and the tire-molding machine. How it's nineteenth-century technology grafted onto the twenty-second. We make our own copper wiring and inefficient batteries instead of n-dimensional qubit matrixes and powerpacks. It's called survival. A word The Corporation may have forgotten.

"Should I immediately have swapped my old A-7 for one of *Turalon*'s new birds? Sure. Didn't think of it. Instead of taking care of business, greeting the new contractees, and processing my people who wanted to transit home on *Turalon,* I had a Board Appointed Inspector General who told me my first priority was to personally attend to him and his Four."

She paused. "Even without your First, you do remember that, don't you?"

Soukup winced, uncomfortable with the mention of his Four.

Kalico pressed on. "But let's put that new A-7 in perspective: Had I commandeered one of *Turalon*'s birds, you'd probably be accusing me of violating some obscure regulation by taking a new A-7 for my own use when it could have been better employed in the transportation of the next fifty trillion worth of SDRs up to orbit."

"Prudence would have dictated—"

"Prudence?" Kalico demanded, bending down, staring into the man's face. "You're alive because Ensign Juri Makarov was talented enough to set you down on the slope of that mountain. He paid with his life. And when Kylee Simonov and Falise Taglioni pulled you out of the wreck, you stole their airtruck and left them to die. And you accuse *me* of malfeasance? You're a shit-sucking coward!"

This time the pandemonium was a riot. Kalico had to stand by Talina's shoulder, waving the crowd down, shouting for order. The banging of Abibi's gavel was drowned in the din.

Kalico reached into her belt pouch again, produced the device Bogarten had recovered from the main busbar on the downed A-7. This she displayed before Soukup's disdainful gaze. "You ever seen this before, Inspector General?"

"I have not."

Kalico turned to the officers behind the bar. "I had a tech check it out. It's a field damper. It's supposed to ground an entire electrical system. Fenn Bogarten found this in my A-7 after the wreck. Now, here's the oddity: I was told by a Shuttle Tech III from *Turalon* that my A-7 couldn't have so much as powered up the thrusters if this had been installed on the busbar in the main control unit. So how did it get there? Bogarten thinks one of the Inspector General's people placed it there *after* my bird went down."

"That's . . . *insane!*" Soukup cried.

When things finally settled down, Kalico turned back to the bar, only to find Soukup standing, good arm outstretched to the judges. "*This* is not a Corporate proceeding," he bellowed. "It's a circus performance. Worse, ex-Supervisor Aguila admits to culpability with regard to most of the charges. I *demand* under Title VII, Article XII, Section 15, that Kalico Aguila be remanded to my custody and returned to Solar System to face charges."

Abibi appeared to be concentrating, obviously checking her implants.

Cinque beat her to it. "According to Section 15, the Board Appointment gives the Inspector General that right." He glanced at the others. "In essence, no matter what we decide here, Section 15 allows him to appeal our decision to a higher authority."

Kalico could see Abibi's lips working, Tadeo Chin was nodding, an expression of resignation on his face.

"Then I can see no reason for us to continue here," Abibi began. "According to the—"

"*Not* all of the evidence is in yet!" The voice carried from above, loud and strident.

Every head in the room craned to see the three people descending the stairs. A low muttering rose, people speculating.

Kalico crossed her arms, waiting as Dek, Kylee Simonov, and Falise Taglioni hit the bottom of the stairs. Dek looked to be as cocky as ever, but Falise was barely recognizable, her three colors of hair tumbling down her back in a mess, face sporting cuts; her lacerated hands—held out before her—were crisscrossed with purple dressing. She limped to boot.

The same with Kylee, though her wounds—but for the one on her cheek—weren't as prominent.

"Who approaches the court?" Captain Abibi asked.

"Falise Taglioni. Daughter to Claudio and Malissa of Taglioni Tower, Transluna." With her wounded hands, she made a gesture toward Soukup. "And that piece of walking shit is Suto Soukup. He's the stinking coward who left Kylee, me, and his own First to die. Abandoned us in the forest at the mercy of mobbers, tooth flowers, and the roots."

Dek stopped short, crossed his arms as he looked up at Abibi. "This bit of shit on my shoe pulled a pistol on poor Fenn Bogarten. Made him fly away when he knew Falise and Kylee were coming. Left Flute, who'd carried his sorry ass up the airtruck, behind as well. Those being the facts, what's the penalty for leaving someone behind when you're not in immediate danger of death?"

"Barring any mitigating circumstances, that could carry a death penalty," Cinque replied after checking his notebook.

"Yeah," Falise said softly. "That's what I thought."

Given how the woman's hands looked, Kalico wasn't sure how she did it, but Falise pulled the long blade from its scabbard on her hip. And though her expression was pain-wracked, she drove the big knife into Soukup's chest. Right up to the hilt.

78

For Port Authority, it had truly been a day of firsts. Shig reflected on that as he leaned back in the old duraplast chair in the Admin Dome conference room. First time a marine colonel had been eaten by a quetzal, first time a Board Appointed IG had been knifed in Inga's—let alone buried up in the cemetery. While it wasn't the first time a wounded quetzal had hobbled its way up PA's main avenue, it was the first time one had done so surrounded by an armed guard. Kylee, Tip, Talina, Dek, and Falise Taglioni, walking on all sides, carrying rifles, had escorted Flute to the hospital where an incredibly nervous Raya Turnienko had rendered medical aid to the mobber-wounded quetzal. When asked why the quetzal was receiving aid before her own cuts were administered to, Falise had replied, "Because Flute's lineage."

In yet another first, Hofer—of all people—had applauded and called out a hurrah as Flute limped past.

Shig glanced down the table to where Kalico Aguila was bent over a notebook, checking figures. Allison Chomko—who would have guessed that she owned *that much* real estate in PA?—had already given her approval for the deal. Allison had conducted the negotiations without so much as a hint of emotion. No wonder the woman was so good at running a casino.

Cinque Suharto—dressed in his light-sucking black suit—arched a questioning brow as Kalico handed the notebook across to Yvette. The silver-haired blonde took it in her long fingers, those hazel eyes going pensive as she checked the numbers.

Cinque's dark features, however, reflected a hint of accomplishment. As though he had prevailed in some way Shig couldn't understand. The man—along with his colleagues, Chad Grunnel and Bartolome Radcek—had come in service of their own ends. What did it mean that Soukup had appointed him Supervisor? How fortunate for Cinque—Shig supposed—that their killers had never been identified.

In the end, Yvette sighed, pushed the notebook to the middle of the table, and said, "Works for me."

"Then we have a deal," Kalico noted, glancing at Suharto. "If you sign off on this, you'll be swimming just as deeply in these waters as the rest of us. And just as culpable if we ever have to face a Board inquest."

Cinque spread his fingers and studied them, a slight smile on his lips. "It's the price of being named Supervisor by that Cretan, Soukup. I'll take the risk. Besides, any reckoning will be a minimum of four, maybe five years down the road. In the meantime, a lot can happen."

"Welcome to Donovan," Kalico agreed as Yvette affixed her signature to the document.

Allison leaned back, her hard blue eyes on the notebook. "So, there it is. A first, for real, hopefully defensible, economic agreement between Port Authority and The Corporation. Our butts are covered. The next IG they send, if they send one, can't use that against us."

"There will be more than enough irregularities to keep such an investigator occupied," Cinque noted. "Donovan doesn't fit into the Corporate mindset."

Kalico ran a finger down the scar on her cheek. "I wonder how my people are going to deal with Corporate life? A little over a third of them are going back. Taking their plunder. It leaves the Board with an ever-increasing conundrum: What do we do with these rich contractees? I'm afraid half of my people will be in jail within weeks, especially when some Corporate officer tries to make them follow the rules."

"Personal wealth is discouraged. I'm surprised Soukup didn't charge you with allowing your people to own plunder." Cinque studied her, interest in his dark gaze. "Was that true? Do you really only have two hundred and eighty-seven siddars in your stash?"

Shig watched Kalico's weary smile as she said, "Had over four thousand once, but I bought a house."

Allison cued on that. "But I thought . . ."

"Yeah," Kalico told her. "Despite all the talk, you *are* the richest woman on the planet. I'm sure when that inquest record gets back to the Board, they'll analyze it for every tell, and in the end, they'll discover that it's the truth. I only 'manage' the greatest wealth on the planet. As long as I'm the Board Supervisor, I will uphold my oath not to personally profit from my position."

"No one actually does that, you know," Cinque told her dismissively. "The only time people are prosecuted for using their offices to get rich is when The Corporation has to find an excuse to get rid of them."

Kalico gave him a grin. "I know. I used to be that way. Then something changed. I had all of my plunder loaded into a crate marked 'Corporate' and shipped back on *Ashanti*."

"You could go back," Cinque told her. "Given everything we know, *Turalon* won't suffer the same fate as *Freelander*. That seat on the Board? It's there, waiting. Played right, with the support of Suharto and Taglioni factions, they couldn't say no."

Kalico shook her head. "I have a mine down at Southern Diggings to develop. Not to mention all these new contractees. Someone has to keep the soft meat alive long enough to learn how to survive on Donovan." The smile grew more wistful. "And I don't think I'd fit back there."

"What about you, Temporary Supervisor Suharto?" Shig asked. "What are your plans?"

"Not sure yet." Cinque studied his thumb before rubbing it against his fingers. "This place isn't anything like we expected. The prospect of four years here?" He shrugged. "Or do I spend another two years cramped up in *Turalon*? And then, there's always the reminder of Dan Wirth. The notion that a piece of gutter scum like him could get so filthy rich? What could a truly talented man accomplish here?"

Allison laughed at that, slapped the table with a flat hand, and stood. "If you'll excuse me, it's getting deep in here. I've got a poker game to run." Still laughing, she stood and left the room.

"What was that about?" Cinque asked.

Shig laced his fingers together. "Merely a question of what true talent is. Given the fates of your competitors, you might have some of the same qualities as Dan. But I'd suggest that you find that berth on *Turalon*. Knowing my fellow Donovanians, Cinque, I think you'd live longer."

79

Flute limped along, his hide mottled with unsightly bandages. The splotches of white pasted on his wounds made a mockery of the big quetzal's rippling patterns of camouflage as they rolled down his side. For Kylee—riding on his back—the effect was eerie, threatening. Something about the look of a blooded warrior, a sort of battle-hardened vet. The kind you'd be an idiot to mess with.

The bush terrain here felt too open and alien. If she looked over her shoulder across the trees, she could just see the top of the high fence that surrounded PA. It shone silver in the distance.

Flute made his way slowly through the scrub aquajade and chabacho, stepping widely around the claw shrub and thorncactus. As he went, he'd extend his triangular head, inhaling for scent; his three eyes carefully scanned the bush around them. Under his taloned feet, the ferngrass twisted and writhed.

This wasn't his or Kylee's country. Nothing about it was familiar or forgiving. It seemed weird to be under a constantly open expanse. Somehow vulnerable from above. She kept scanning the puffy white clouds and turquoise sky for mobbers. That horror remained too close. Too fresh in her and Flute's minds. Like Flute, Kylee didn't dare move too fast for fear of tearing one of the sutures that held her wounds together.

Not that it had bothered Falise when it came to Soukup. After she'd stuck the slug sucker, she'd stared down at the blood where she'd torn the stitches, shrugged, and with two fingers, gingerly pulled the long blade out of the dying IG's chest.

If the stories were true, it must have ruined Inga's mood. Word was she hated mopping up other people's coagulated blood. Nor would the notion of cleaning up her own mess have ever crossed

Falise's mind. Child of privilege that she was, the woman just didn't think in those terms.

Rough place, this Port Authority, but Kylee had to admit, the town was kind of growing on her. The Rocket part of her even felt good about it. Not that she wanted to make a habit of it, but there were certain benefits. Like not having to make one's own clothes. Being able to buy a meal someone else cooked. Things to see and do.

She shifted her slung rifle where it began to rub on one of the mobber cuts on her back.

"What do you think, Flute?" she asked. "We could hitch a ride back to Mundo. Have to deal with some of the local lineage down there. The farm's a mess. Lot of work to put the place back in order. Dome's a write-off. But it's ours. Well, mine and the family's. We'd never need for anything, and we get paid every time a shuttle drops in for a load of produce. Not to mention, I know where Rondo found that deposit up on the mountain. Rubies, Flute. Big red ones where the crust got thrust up by that asteroid that made this place."

She resettled herself in order to keep her leg from rubbing against one of Flute's bandages.

Patterns running down his hide asked her, *Can we go back to see lineage in Sky Fly?*

"Sure." She chewed her lip, thinking it through. "Have to get our own airtruck. No telling what kind of plunder that would take. And then there's maintenance. Keeping the powerpack charged. Might be easier to broker a deal with Kalico. Hire one until we get settled."

Tip come?

"I can ask him, I guess." She resettled on Flute's back, catching the faintest of odors on the breeze blowing in from the Gulf. Just on account of, she unhitched her rifle, swung it around.

Then she added, "Don't know what it means between Tip and me. Last I saw, after we got your hide stitched up, he and that Hmong girl went off to the cafeteria. I thought there was way too much laughing. Really pissed me off, and I was going to do something about it. And damn. There's Talina, in my head, being jealous about Bucky Berkholtz. And I know from her memory to think about it. And I realize, I'm jealous."

Don't know that.

"Emotion, Flute. Very primate. Mad and hurt because someone has what you think should be yours. But then I ask myself why I think Tip should be mine. And I realize I don't want Tip for a mate. He's my friend. That's why the sex didn't work for either of us." She chuckled. "Maturity sucks toilet water, but it's better than being stupid-young. Like when you don't know why you're pissed off."

The sudden patterns of yellow and black alternated with light blue. Flute's collar expanded like a sail around the back of his head.

"Yeah," Kylee told him. "I'm picking it up, too."

She pressed the stud at her throat to access com. "Tal? We're about to . . . Holy shit."

They came out of the scrub chabacho. Three of them. One on each side and one in front. And that quetzal blocking the way? Big. Maybe bigger than Flute. And all three of the quetzals were glowing in crimson, signaling their mood.

"Kylee?" Talina asked in her earbud.

Kylee raised her rifle, got a good look at the big quetzal that stood in the way. Touched the throat stud. "Why, what do you know? Maimed left front leg, bullet scars in his right thigh." Louder, she called, "Hello, Whitey, you piece of shit!"

Kylee swung a leg over, sliding off of Flute's side to the ground. Cradling her rifle, she lifted a hand as Flute's hide began to turn bright red, saying, "Tone it down. Not yet."

She walked out ahead of Flute, rifle at the ready. Whitey and his two cohorts were flashing a series of questions as the crimson attack colors faded to be replaced by interrogatives, out-and-out astonishment, and curiosity.

"Yeah, it's real," Kylee told them. "I'll bet it's a total shock to see a human riding a quetzal. See, it's not always like your fucked-up lineage thinks. And no, Flute's not a rogue. We're here to make a deal." Still holding the rifle, she made a low bow, arms out wide,

squawking in her closest approximation of a juvenile quetzal. And—
like it had that day with the Rorkies—it got a stunned reaction.

"So," Kylee said, not needing to look behind to see that Flute was
translating, "you've got a choice to make. On your behalf, Flute and
I can broker peace with the humans."

She raised a hand as the chaotic colors, edging into violent crimson, began to flash between the three quetzals. Kylee could grasp
most of what they were saying, given her knowledge of quetzal.

"Hey! I know," she cried. "Lineage is a bitch. All that bad blood.
But you can bring this to an end. Yeah, you're good at killing hu-
mans. And you're getting better. But so are they. Flute and me?
We're offering you a way out. Want to make peace?"

She saw the flashing of patterns, the meaning now going way
beyond her ability to read. Then the increase in the crimson, the
anger, and finally the patterns for *Kill rogue*.

"That's the final word?" she asked.

Got a single spot of orange on Whitey's forehead in response.

"Wrong answer."

Kylee almost jumped out of her skin as a high-velocity explosive
round blasted Whitey's head apart. The cracking snap of the bursting bone and spattering tissue made her hunch. The big quetzal's
body spasmed before the limbs jerked out straight and it slammed
hard into the ground.

Kylee was snatched backward as Flute grabbed her by the collar
and pulled her out of the way.

Even as she was being manhandled, she kept hold of her rifle.
Caught the images as the two quetzals on either side stopped short
in their attack. Stared in disbelief at Whitey. Their eyes rotated,
staring upward; colors shifted from crimson to yellow and black. An
instant later, they were blown apart by explosive rounds.

The sound of it would haunt her. Like a meaty bang-splat mixed
together.

And then silence, the chime uninterrupted.

Catching her breath, Kylee turned, seeing Flute's left eye giving
her a thoughtful look. Had to be tough for him, too.

We give chance. The colors and patterns flashed across Flute's extended collar.

"Yeah, we did," she told him, hearing the whir of the airtruck as it made a wide circle above.

From the door, Talina was waving, her rifle in hand.

"*Steaks and leather.*" Talina's voice came through Kylee's earpiece. "*Looks good from up here. You and Flute head back to town. We've got you covered.*"

80

F alise Taglioni snugged her hat brim down tight as the night rain
began to fall on Port Authority. Beside her, Cinque Suharto
paced, wearing a rain suit with the hood pulled up. They walked
down the avenue that led to the shuttle gate, the whole of the route
now illuminated by the newly installed overhead lights that had
been included in *Turalon*'s cargo. The misty rain left silver streaks as
it passed beneath the bulbs.

The night chime could be heard, coming from beyond the fence.

Port Authority had a quiet, almost serene feel to it after the hubbub and carousal they had just left at Inga's. Over the weeks Falise
had been in PA, the tavern had grown on her.

"Thanks for walking with me," Falise told him, amazed at how
Cinque could vanish in the night. Better than a quetzal under a
cloud of mobbers.

She worked her hands, thankful that the last of the scabs had
fallen off.

"I suspect that you want to remind me of our bargain?" he asked
suggestively. "We haven't had to take drastic measures against each
other."

"I hope that remains the case," she told him, fingers lacing
around the pommel of her small knife where it rested in its scabbard
beneath the hem of her shirt. "You have the feel of the place. And,
having served as a second to Kalico Aguila, you are as intimate with
the reality of Donovan as anyone in The Corporation."

He chuckled. "It will take *Turalon* an extra week—just to accelerate the additional mass of the precious metals—before it can reach
position where it can invert symmetry. Doesn't matter that *Turalon*
is smaller, her cargo will be worth more than *Turalon* and *Ashanti*'s
previous cargoes combined."

He glanced sidelong at her from behind the hood. His black eyes might have been holes in shadow. "They will not act to discipline you for Soukup's death. At least, not seriously. Your actions were understandable. Demanded by honor. Not to mention that that fool Soukup left a Taglioni, of all people, to die. My report will ensure Suharto support for your acquittal should any charges be levied against you." A pause. "And, well, perhaps given your known skills, any of the families that might consider pursuing sanctions on Soukup's part will be deterred."

"That's what I wanted to talk to you about." They had reached the gate, the light rain falling, silvering the wires in the chain link. The guard, in full armor, was one of the new marines. The man probably thankful that he'd be shipping up to *Turalon* in the morning.

Falise led Cinque down the narrow gap between the back of the warehouse and the perimeter fence. Out of hearing of the guard, she indicated the silver shuttle gleaming at the edge of the illumination. "I want you to be on that shuttle tomorrow."

Cinque, always the consummate opponent, studied her from behind the dark hood. Falise tightened her grip on the knife's handle, ready to strike.

"I assume you have a reason for making such an absurd demand?"

"I do. The Taglioni family supports Kalico Aguila. And, Cinque, as well as I know you, the day will come when you just won't be able to help yourself. Kalico will be found dead, probably in some back alley, and you'll be forced to remind people that Soukup appointed you interim Supervisor."

"And should such an unfortunate tragedy occur? I give you my word that it would not affect Taglioni interests. I have no problem with your house making as much out of this opportunity as the Suhartos. Neither you, nor the Taglionis, have any obligation or loyalty to Kalico Aguila."

"The rest of us do," a voice said from the darkness.

Falise watched Cinque turn on cat feet, poised, balanced. In a fraction of a second he could strike.

"Don't," she told him. "Kylee's faster than you are. Stronger than you are. And if we kill you here, Flute will ensure that your body will never be found." She asked, "Isn't that right, Flute?"

A melodic tremolo of agreement vented from the camouflaged quetzal's vents.

She saw the shifting, the slight change in posture that meant Cinque understood just how outmatched he was. Remarkable how convincing it could be to have a quetzal for a friend.

"You have everything you need," Falise told him. "With your implants, you've sucked up every bit of information on Port Authority, Corporate Mine, and the promise of Southern Diggings. With what you have in your head, you can prepare a Suharto expedition capable of reoccupying one of the old research bases, or, for all anyone would care, pick your own spot based on the surveys."

"Why don't you let me think about it. I will give you my answer in the—"

"You will be on that last shuttle up. With me. If you are not, you have no more chance than I gave Chad or Bart."

"I would like to know how you managed that."

"Charlotte, of course. To her credit, she has ambitions." She paused, adding, "All the way back to seducing you in that observation blister. And yes, she has told me how much you dread being stuck on Donovan for another four years."

"Charlotte?" He actually sounded stunned.

Falise smiled in the darkness. "So that there are no misunderstandings, Charlotte will be moving into my quarters aboard *Turalon*. She's proven her worth many times over. Enticed Chad into Clarice's reach and helped subdue him that night behind the foundry. Charlotte was good enough to slip a bit of poison into Bart's bottle of fifty-year-old Hennessy while he was out meeting with Clarice in an attempt to capitalize on my humiliation. Dek almost caught her sabotaging Soukup's shuttle. The device was only supposed to keep the thing on the ground so that I could press my case with the man. Charlotte thinks she might have installed it incorrectly and some bump caused it to make contact at the wrong moment."

Falise shrugged. "Damn near got me killed, but it worked out in the end. Like I say, the woman is worth everything that the Taglioni family will pay her."

"You *turned* Charlotte?"

Falise shrugged. "Had to do something after I drained Kramer." A beat. "You will accompany me on that shuttle tomorrow."

He took a deep breath, chuckled. "Charlotte? I never would have guessed. And no. I was not looking forward to being trapped in this forsaken place for the foreseeable future. It would be what? A minimum of two years until the next ship? Then another two years of transition back to Solar System?"

"And if you're not on that shuttle, soft meat," Kylee added from the dark, "Flute and I promise no one will ever know what happened to you."

"It's only two years on *Turalon*," Falise added. "I promise you Taglioni support upon our return. Suharto could do worse when it comes to an alliance regarding Donovan."

Cinque sucked a deep breath. "Well played, Falise. After your arrival here, you seemed so inept, we discounted you. You won't have to stab me with that knife you're holding. I will be on that shuttle." He chuckled. "And I will have you for a companion."

"You don't even like me."

Cinque shrugged, turned to look out at the shuttle. "I don't have to like you. But as tonight proves, you always make things interesting."

EPILOGUE

As the last shuttle vanished into the afternoon sky, Dek, Talina, Kalico, and Shig stood by the fence and listened to the fading roar until it merged with the chime and finally vanished. Around them, the shuttle field was a flurry of action as Pamlico Jones directed his collection of forklifts and loaders in their hurry to get the latest batch of cargo containers stacked before dark. It didn't matter that Flute and Kylee had lured Whitey and two of his lineage into the open; there were always more quetzals.

"Think she'll be all right?" Talina asked, her brown fingers laced into the chain link.

"Falise can handle it." Dek shifted, resettling his hat. "She found something here that she didn't know she was missing. Having put it in place, I think she'll be a stronger asset for the family. Smarter and more competent. Something tells me that old Claudio is due for a rude awakening when his wayward daughter finally makes it home."

"What about Soukup's untimely demise?" Shig asked. "Surely there will be those on the Board who will try and use that against her."

"Of course they will," Kalico told him. "It's the Board. I'd rather be up to my ass in mobbers."

"If my father, Uncle Miko, and Falise can't handle a simple case of retribution after a display of cowardice comparable to Soukup's?" Dek chuckled. "Well, they wouldn't deserve to be called Taglionis."

Talina pushed back from the fence, gave Dek a knowing look. "Meeting your sister? Fascinating insight into your family."

"Now you know why I prefer my lineage," Dek told her, turning. "Speaking of which, by now Kylee's just about made it to Mundo. She and Flute are going to give it a look over. Step flew them down."

"What do Su and the kids think about that?" Shig asked as they started back for the avenue. "It is family property."

Kalico laid a scarred hand on the butt of her pistol, laser-blue eyes thoughtful. "I heard they had a meeting. Not that it was like singing 'Coming Together Under the Bower,' but the family agreed to let Kylee run it for them."

"There's still Leaper and Diamond," Talina reminded.

"My money's on Kylee and Flute," Kalico told them. "Time for beer."

As they turned onto the main avenue, Dek said, "Inga's got quetzal steaks on tonight. She's been keeping them off the menu while Flute was in town. Thought it would be more politic, not that Flute was likely to be a customer."

"I'd hope not," Shig mused, as his dreamy gaze fixed on the high puffs of cloud. "I don't think the stairs would support his weight."

"So," Kalico asked. "Dek? You ever tell Falise about that last hand of cards?"

"Yep."

"How'd she take it?" Talina asked.

"All in stride. Was such a good sport about it that I gave her the plunder. All of it. And threw in a whole ton of the rhodium."

"Thought there was more than a ton," Shig said.

Dek shot Shig a knowing wink. "Gotta keep something so I can pay for steaks and beer."